Christmas with the Surplus Girls

Also by Polly Heron

The Surplus Girls

The Surplus Girls' Orphans

POLLY HERON

Christmas with the Surplus Girls

CORVUS

Published in paperback in Great Britain in 2021 by Corvus,
an imprint of Atlantic Books Ltd.

Copyright © Polly Heron, 2021

The moral right of Polly Heron to be identified as the author of
this work has been asserted by her in accordance with the
Copyright, Designs and Patents Act of 1988.

All rights reserved. No part of this publication may be reproduced,
stored in a retrieval system, or transmitted in any form or by any
means, electronic, mechanical, photocopying, recording, or
otherwise, without the prior permission of both the copyright
owner and the above publisher of this book.

This novel is entirely a work of fiction. The names, characters
and incidents portrayed in it are the work of the author's
imagination. Any resemblance to actual persons, living or dead,
events or localities, is entirely coincidental.

10 9 8 7 6 5 4 3 2 1

A CIP catalogue record for this book is available from
the British Library.

Paperback ISBN: 978 1 83895 235 8
E-book ISBN: 978 1 83895 236 5

Printed in Great Britain

Corvus
An imprint of Atlantic Books Ltd
Ormond House
26–27 Boswell Street
London
WC1N 3JZ

www.corvus-books.co.uk

To the memory of a dear man,
Tom Cook (1918–2010)

And to the Cook ladies,
Carol, Pene and Debbie

Chapter One

September 1922

'Now then, our Nancy,' said Pa after they had all eaten a slice of cake each. 'It's time we had a talk.'

'What about?' Nancy licked a fingertip and dabbed her plate, picking up crumbs of sponge and slipping them onto her tongue, savouring the final burst of sweetness. The Pikes didn't have the wherewithal to splash out on cream, even for a special occasion, but she had baked two thin sponges and smeared a thin layer of jam between them. That was luxury for the Pike family.

Her presents sat on the table, beside them the brown paper in which they had been wrapped, neatly folded now and ready to be used again. A lace-edged hanky embroidered with an N, together with a bar of Cadbury's Dairy Milk, from Lottie and Emily, who had pooled their saved-up Saturday pennies; and, from Mam and Pa, a cardie knitted by Mam in pale-green wool with big green buttons. That was the thing about being a redhead. You ended up wearing lots of green. Not that Nancy was a redhead exactly. Nothing so glamorous. She was more of an orange-head, only darker. According to Mam, her hair was the colour of copper saucepans. Mam had been in service in her youth, working in a big house over Heaton Mersey way. Nancy wasn't sure how she felt about having hair the colour of saucepans, but Mam had meant it kindly or she wouldn't have said it, and at least the saucepans had been in a posh kitchen.

'That sounds interesting, Pa,' said Lottie. 'What's it about?'

'Never you mind,' said Pa. 'You two go and do the washing up, please.'

'It's Nancy's turn,' Lottie objected.

'It's Nancy's birthday.' Emily fetched the tray from the sideboard.

'And don't answer Pa back, our Lottie,' said Mam.

'I never meant to, Pa,' Lottie murmured.

It wasn't unheard of to give Pa backchat without meaning to. He was gentle and mild-mannered, which made him lovely to live with, and was one of the reasons why their flat, for all its drawbacks, had a cosy atmosphere. But it also meant that sometimes, before you knew it, you had overstepped the mark and spoken out of turn. Other girls had fathers who were very much the lord and master, but Pa wasn't a bit like that. Nancy was aware of her responsibility, as the oldest, to set a good example by treating him with the unquestioning respect he deserved, all the more so because, while other men, other fathers, the heads of other households, were tall and forceful, Pa was... Much as she loved him, she couldn't escape from the fact that he was rather – well, weedy. He was thin and pale and inclined to stoop. Although the sight of his face softening with love and concern for Mam made Nancy's heart melt, there were other times when he did that funny thing with his mouth, sucking in his cheek to chew it, that made him look like the world's worst worrier. There was even anxiety in the way he blinked.

While Lottie and Emily loaded the tray with crockery and cutlery, Nancy put the rest of the sponge in the tin and returned the margarine to the marble slab on the shelf in the corner-cupboard that did duty as their larder. The family lived in two rooms – three, if you counted the alcove at the head of the staircase that served as the girls' bedroom, but you'd have to be soft in the head to call that a bedroom and hope to get away with it. For cooking, they had the use of the tiny kitchen in the back of the shop downstairs, where the single gas-ring meant that Mam had become an expert at one-pot cooking. Meals were carried upstairs with great care and at the end of each meal, the tray was loaded with dirty dishes, which were taken downstairs to be washed up in the scullery. It was a fag if you were in the best of health, but for poor Mam, with her anaemia, it was sometimes too much to cope with.

Alongside the permanent smell of tobacco from the shop downstairs, the air in the flat was still sweet with the fruity, bready aroma of the tea-cakes she had brought home from the shop. They were yesterday's tea-cakes that hadn't sold, but the Pikes didn't care about details like that. Tea-cakes didn't have to be fresh from the oven to be a treat.

While Pa gave Mam his arm and helped her from the table to their one and only armchair, Nancy fetched the small brass dustpan and brush, and gave the tablecloth a brisk clean, pretending not to notice as Mam, reaching the chair, dropped into it and then made a fuss of settling herself, smoothing her skirt, as if she had been in perfect control of how she sat down.

Tendrils of late summer sunshine slid through the window, bestowing a golden shimmer on their ancient oak sideboard and almost returning it to its glory days before it was bruised and scuffed and adorned with an unfortunate burn mark. The glowing light lent a silvery edge to the stack of faded piano music and turned the lace doilies to twinkling gossamer; though all it did for the bare floorboards was make them look drab and bland, and never mind the elbow grease that went into scrubbing and polishing them every week, while the corners seemed curtained by inky shadows.

'Come and sit down, Nancy.'

Pa took a ladderback chair from the table and placed it beside Mam's armchair. How many men would do that? Not many, that was for sure, but Pa was a sweetheart. So what if every other man would insist upon sitting on the carver chair at the table, because it was the one chair in their mismatched set that had arms? Pa was happy for Mam to have it, to help her be comfortable, the same as he wanted her to have the armchair. Pa might not be tall and imposing like other men, but he was the most considerate person Nancy had ever met.

She paused in the act of pulling the tablecloth towards her. 'I haven't taken the cloth off yet.'

'Leave it for now,' said Pa.

They never gave up on a task. Living in a small flat, you had to be tidy and organised. It made Mam's life easier an' all. Half smiling, half frowning, she glanced at Mam.

'Don't look at me,' said Mam. 'I don't know what this is about.'

Nancy picked up the oval-backed wooden chair from the table and carried it across.

'It sounds serious.'

She didn't mean it. She only said it to make Pa say no, it wasn't. She smiled at him, giving him a second chance to say it. Pa smiled back, but his smile was tight, not a real smile at all. Nancy's skin prickled.

Pa looked at Mam. 'Our Nancy is nineteen now. We ought to discuss her future.'

'My future?' It came out as a squeak. 'Is this about me not wanting to marry Henry? He's a nice lad and I'm fond of him, but only as a friend. I – I couldn't marry someone I didn't love.'

'You're a lovely girl and you'll meet someone one day, I'm sure,' said Mam.

'Let's hope so,' said Pa. 'Since the war, there are lots of girls who have been left high and dry without husbands. But, just in case, we need to talk about your job, our Nancy.'

'What about it? I love it. I know it's an early start, and I'm on my feet all day, but I love serving the customers and I'm good at it. You – you haven't had a complaint about me, have you?'

'Of course not.'

'We know you work hard, love,' said Mam. 'You're a grafter. What's this about, Percy?'

'Serving in the pie shop doesn't pay that well,' said Pa.

He didn't, he couldn't, want her to leave the pie shop – could he? Nancy leaped in before he could utter the fatal words.

'If it's the money, the twins turn twelve after Christmas. They can go half-time at school and get afternoon jobs. That'll bring in a bit more.'

'Percy.' Mam's gaze darted his way. 'We're managing, aren't we? I know we're hard up, but we always get by.'

Pa patted her hand. 'It's our Nancy I'm thinking of, and her future. She can do more than work in a pie shop.'

'There's nowt wrong with working in the pie shop.' Did that sound defiant? 'I'm sorry, Pa, but there isn't.'

'I never said there was, but you could do more.' He sounded almost jovial, but pretend-jovial, like his smile earlier had been a pretend-smile.

'I don't want to. I'm happy there.'

'You're a good girl,' said Pa. 'Amenable. Helpful. I'm sure you could be happy doing summat else.'

'You mean a different kind of shop?'

Imagine working in one of the posh department stores in town. She might like that. But no, starting there at the grand old age of nineteen would make her stand out like a sore thumb when all the others would have gone there straight from school at thirteen or fourteen. Oh aye, straight from school at thirteen...and straight from the pie shop at nineteen. She would be a laughing-stock.

'Anyroad,' she said, 'I like the pie shop.'

She more than liked it. She loved it. She had never been obstinate in her life before, but now she folded her arms and pressed her lips together. She felt defensive. She felt...no, Pa would never make her feel like that. Not threatened. Not Pa. It wasn't possible.

Yes, it was. Oh, crikey.

Chapter Two

SATURDAY WAS NANCY'S favourite day of the week. She loved every day in the pie shop, surrounded by golden pastry and the enticing aromas of mince-and-onion and cheese-and-onion and the homely scent of meat-and-potato. They sold sweet pastries as well, lardy cakes loaded with sultanas and mixed spice, with sugar twinkling on the top; plump crumpets, good enough to make marge taste like the creamiest butter; and Eccles cakes, packed with the juicy currants that made children call them squashed flies cakes. Plenty of adults called them that an' all, but Nancy wasn't allowed to, because of working in the shop.

It was a grand job. She had started here the morning after she finished school and never once been sorry or wished for summat different. Saturday was the best day of all, because of the mill girls. That was what they were called, mill girls, no matter how old they were. The mill was up the road from the pie shop and it was shut over the weekend, but on Saturdays some of the mill girls topped up their earnings by doing half a day's cleaning. Just after midday, they would burst through the shop door, cheerful at the prospect of being off work until Monday, their tummies rumbling after four hours of solid graft. Nancy didn't kid herself about them. She knew they were bone-tired from the mixture of mill work and domestic responsibilities; but their Saturday visit to the pie shop made the place crackle with energy and good humour and something inside her responded, sometimes with eagerness, other times with a trickle of ice down her spine. Mam would never be in fine fettle like this.

Was that why Pa wanted her to earn more? To provide Mam with a more comfortable life?

Today she was to meet Pa after work and attend an interview for joining a business night-school. Night-school! Her! She had never shone at school and the thought of returning to the classroom made her heart tie itself in a knot, but Pa was determined. She couldn't understand it. He had never suggested anything of the kind before.

The Turners, who owned the shop, started work in the bakehouse at half past four each morning and Nancy arrived in time for the shop to open at half-six. Monday to Friday, the shop stayed open for as long as the stock lasted, though Nancy finished at four. On Saturdays, the shop shut early, at three. Nancy spent the next hour washing the shelves and the counter and mopping the floor before helping to clean the ovens in the bakehouse. Usually she performed these tasks cheerfully, glad of an early finish, but today she felt more like climbing inside one of the cooling ovens and pulling the door to behind her.

'When you catch the bus, ask for Chorlton Office,' Pa had instructed. 'That's the terminus, so you needn't worry about getting off at the wrong place.' He had made it sound as if she wanted to go, as if alighting at the wrong stop would have been a disaster.

Normally she would have taken an interest in the unfamiliar roads, but on today's journey she didn't see anything of what she passed. At last, the bus swung around a wide hairpin bend and entered the open-air terminus, and there was Pa, approaching her window. Too late to duck down and pretend she wasn't here.

'Good. You're on time,' Pa greeted her as she stepped down from the platform. 'It's a five-minute walk to Wilton Close. I've already been to have a look.'

No chance of getting lost, then, and missing the appointment.

From the terminus, they walked along a street with houses on both sides, partway down which a vast tree overhung the pavement and road.

'That's a beech tree,' said Pa, 'and this is Beech Road.'

They passed through the tranquil shade cast by the tree, a golden-tongued breeze shifting through the leaves.

'Round this corner,' said Pa. 'On the other side of that hedge across the road is the recreation ground; and Wilton Close is...here.'

He paused at another corner, but if he had stopped for her to admire Wilton Close, he was wasting his time... No, he wasn't. She might be in turmoil, but she couldn't help admiring the short cul-de-sac. There were two pairs of smart semi-detached houses on either side, and a lone semi at the top, each with a front garden and a side-passage leading, no doubt, to a rear garden, not a back yard. The rich-green leaves and pale-pink blooms of a lace-cap hydrangea nodded over a garden wall on this side of the road and a mass of white roses, as delicate as tissue-paper, tumbled over a wall on the other side.

Pa guided her over the road and opened the gate belonging to the house adjoining the one with the roses. Inside was a neatly edged lawn that could do with a spot of water, and shallow beds of marigolds, their hues ranging from palest lemon to rich gold, the trumpet-blooms of petunias, and scarlet dahlias standing tall above ink-dark leaves.

'...and this must be your daughter.'

'Nancy!' Pa gave her a discreet nudge.

'Oh.' Heat streamed into her cheeks. 'I'm so sorry. I didn't hear the door open. I was too busy admiring your garden. It must be like living in a park.'

Of all the stupid things to say – but the lady didn't look contemptuous. In fact, she didn't look capable of contempt. Older than Mam and Pa, she was thin and pale. At first glance, she was nowt special. Her mid-calf-length dress might be suitable for her years, but it cemented the rather dull impression. But that was before you noticed the kindness in the light-blue eyes, the lines at the sides of her mouth that suggested that smiles came more naturally than frowns, and the gentle way she moved her hands. Nancy warmed to her. Drat! That wasn't meant to happen. She was all geared up for this afternoon to be the last word in unpleasantness. She hadn't anticipated liking anyone or anything.

'This is my daughter, Nancy.' Pa removed his tired old trilby, gripping its brim in both hands.

'I'm pleased to meet you, Miss Pike,' said the lady. 'My name is Patience Hesketh and you should call me Miss Patience. My sister is Miss Hesketh. Won't you come in?'

Nancy had been in houses with hallways, but she had never seen a hall like this. Hallways were meant to be dark and narrow, with a row of coat-pegs on the wall and a poky staircase of bare treads that went straight up. Here, the stairs were carpeted up the centre, and after a dozen treads turned a corner and disappeared. A dark-wood bench, all fancy carving, stood beside the staircase and – was that? Yes, it was – a small cloakroom, with shelves and pegs, sat in an alcove opposite the foot of the stairs. An actual cloakroom – in a house! The last time Nancy had seen a room devoted to coats and hats had been at school.

Miss Patience opened a door and led them into a sitting room. By, it was grand! Fancy having a bay window. Mam would love that. If only Mam could have a bay window where she could look out at a pretty garden, instead of being stuck in grimy Bailiff's Row in a measly flat in which the cloying, fusty whiff of stale tobacco was inescapable.

'Prudence, this is Miss Pike. Miss Pike, allow me to introduce my sister, Miss Hesketh.'

Nancy started to smile, but stopped halfway. Instead of a second gentle, appealing lady, this one was – well, dress her in black, stick a pointy hat on her head and you could call her a witch. Her features were sharp – everything about her was sharp, from the set of her shoulders to the criticism in her glance. Her posture was upright, her manner austere. And yet she had the same grey hair and light-blue eyes as Miss Patience, the same thin build, the same slender hands; but what was soft and gentle in one was severe and unyielding in the other.

'How do you do?' said Miss Hesketh. 'Please sit down. So you hope to be accepted for our business school?'

'Well...' What could she say?

'We usually start an interview by inviting the applicant to tell us about her current position.'

'I work in a pie shop.'

'What do you do there?'

'I sell pies.' Did that sound impertinent? 'And pastries. And I clean up at the end of the day on Saturdays.'

'It doesn't sound very interesting.'

'Oh, but it is.' Nancy sat up straighter. 'I know all the customers by name and who their children are, and which ones are working hard at school and who got the cane for being naughty; and who's engaged and who's expecting. I know everyone's favourite pies and what size pie they need for their family. And I know all the commercial travellers, even the ones who visit our part of the world only once a quarter. I know where they stay and what they travel in.'

'Well, that certainly makes it sound more interesting,' said Miss Patience. Was she being kind?

'It sounds,' said Miss Hesketh, 'like one long round of gossip, which makes you unsuitable for our business school. We train girls in office work. We would never train a known gossip.'

'I'm sure our Nancy isn't a gossip, miss,' said Pa.

'I'm not,' said Nancy. 'It's only chat, not gossip. I would never pass on anything that someone has told me. Having a chat is part of the job. It's called knowing your customer. Folk are pleased if you remember what they had last time.'

'So you know how to be discreet,' said Miss Hesketh.

'Yes.' She said it with conviction. This was her good name in question. 'My customers know they can pass the time of day with me without it being passed on to all and sundry.'

'And you must have a good memory,' said Miss Patience.

'For things like what my customers want, yes; but I didn't have a good memory at school. I can never remember all the capital cities, or which country produces which goods, or any dates apart from 1066.'

'It sounds as if you didn't do well at school,' said Miss Hesketh.

'Not at subjects like that, but I was good at the practical things – sewing, cooking, housework. The school I went to had a nursery attached, so we had proper mothercraft lessons. I enjoyed those.'

Pa cleared his throat. 'She's good at totting up prices in her head and giving change – aren't you, Nancy?' He looked at her almost pleadingly. Why did he want this for her?

'So you're good at shop work and good with people.' Miss Patience looked at her sister. 'That's not a bad start, and she's the right sort of age.'

'The right age to train for office work?' Nancy asked.

'The right age for a surplus girl,' said Miss Patience.

Nancy frowned. 'Surplus girl?'

'The term refers to all the girls who now won't find husbands because so many men were killed in the war.'

'I know about the unmarried girls, of course,' said Nancy. 'Everyone does. But I didn't know there was an official name for them. We call them perpetual spinsters round our way.'

She bit her lip, realising belatedly that she was addressing two maiden ladies who weren't exactly spring chickens. She saw them glance at one another. She hadn't meant to be unkind, but would an apology make it worse, make it even more obvious she had put her foot in it? Then she remembered something.

'When I left school in 1916, mine was the last year of girls to do mothercraft. They weren't going to teach it any more. Was that because they knew they were going to have a generation of – of surplus girls on their hands?' Her fingers curled round palms that suddenly felt clammy. It was a scary thought.

'We believe,' said Miss Hesketh, 'that it is the responsibility of every surplus girl to make the best of herself. Our pupils tend to be girls who became office juniors when they left school. They come to us to broaden their range of skills.'

'But we also want to help girls from other backgrounds, if we can,' said Miss Patience. 'Not just the middle-class girls or the ones who did better at school.'

'You may not know the kings and queens of England,' said Miss Hesketh, 'but you appear to be a willing worker and that's important. Are you proficient in the three Rs?'

'I think so.'

'Come now.' This was said with asperity: her sister would have said it encouragingly. 'Either you are or you aren't.'

Nancy looked Miss Hesketh directly in the eye. 'Yes, I am; and I go to the library. I like novels and poems.'

'Poetry, eh? Do you have a favourite poem?'

Her mind went blank. It was like being at school all over again. 'I used to read *The Owl and the Pussy-Cat* to my sisters when they were little.'

'Really?' Miss Hesketh's politeness was enough to rip your heart out.

At last, too late, she remembered. 'Thomas Hardy. I like his nature poems.'

Miss Hesketh nodded, just once. 'I'm interested in you, Miss Pike.' She looked at Miss Patience and there was a moment of silence as Miss Patience returned her look. 'But I do need to be sure that your written English is of a sufficient standard, so you shall be required to write a letter of application.'

'What do you think you might say in it?' Miss Patience asked encouragingly. 'What makes you a good employee?'

Nancy swallowed. She wasn't used to blowing her own trumpet. 'I'm punctual and polite and I'm honest – I've never tried to short-change anybody. I don't mind what I'm asked to do, because I know it's important to help out. And – and I'm good around the home. My mam isn't well and I've always run errands and done the shopping and the cleaning.'

'Even when you were at school?' asked Miss Patience.

'Oh, yes. I looked after the twins an' all when they were little, but they can see to themselves now. I know it's nowt to do with going out to work, but I try to make my mam's life easier.'

'She's a big help to her mother,' said Pa.

'That's something to be proud of,' said Miss Patience.

Was it? It was only what any loving daughter would do.

'It shows you're capable of organising yourself and your tasks,' said Miss Hesketh. 'Subject to a satisfactory application, we should like to offer you a place with us. I believe we could make something of you.'

'Thank you,' said Pa.

Thank you? These middle-class ladies wanted to make

something of her – and Pa said thank you. What was wrong with her the way she was?

'Say thank you, Nancy,' Pa murmured.

'I think you're wrong, Miss Hesketh.' Nancy died a thousand deaths at the sound of the others' combined intake of breath, but she ploughed on. 'I don't think I'm cut out for office work.' There! She had said it.

Miss Patience sat forward. 'I assure you that our school is a relatively small concern and there is nothing of the classroom about it. Next week my sister will begin a book-keeping course for a group of five experienced office girls, and that is the largest group we've had. When we opened our doors in the spring, all our teaching was on a one-to-one basis. Now each of us has two or sometimes three pupils at a time; but, where appropriate, we should always offer one-to-one tuition, for example if a pupil lacks confidence.'

'That sounds just right, miss,' said Pa.

Tears built up behind Nancy's eyes. They were going to make her do this. Between them, they were going to make her. She turned to Pa.

'What about paying for it?' she whispered. 'We could never afford it.'

'We'll manage,' Pa murmured.

'How?' she hissed. She knew how hard up they were.

Pa spoke without moving his lips. 'Not now, Nancy.' He smiled a shade too brightly at the two ladies. 'There's another thing I'm interested in, if I may make so bold. I understand you sometimes take in a pupil as your lodger—'

'Pa!' The word burst out. Nancy's pulse stopped beating and went to a long skid.

'I'd like to register my Nancy as a pupil-lodger, if you please.'

There was a silence as Miss Hesketh and Miss Patience exchanged glances.

'You are correct, Mr Pike,' said Miss Hesketh. 'We do have a maximum of two places for pupil-lodgers.'

Please say both places are taken, please, please, thought Nancy.

'We have one pupil-lodger at present. The other young lady left us in July.'

'And she got married in August,' Miss Patience added with undisguised happiness. 'She is Mrs Abrams now. Dear Molly.'

'So you have a place free?' Pa said with an eagerness that made Nancy cringe.

'I'm afraid,' said Miss Hesketh, 'that, owing to family circumstances, we are unable to accept another pupil-lodger at present.'

Nancy had recently read a library book in which the heroine felt dizzy with relief and she had thought it rather over-written, but now she knew just what the author meant.

'At present, you say?' Pa edged forwards in his seat. 'Then at a later date, perhaps…?'

'*Pa,*' Nancy whispered. What was going on? It wasn't like Pa to be pushy. He was the politest, most accommodating person you could imagine. Besides, 'family circumstances' could be a polite way of saying no. She willed Pa to stop talking.

'We'll see,' said Miss Hesketh.

'Only I would especially like our Nancy to live in,' said Pa.

'Live in?' Miss Hesketh's thin eyebrows climbed up her forehead. 'Living in is what servants do. Our pupil-lodgers, sir, are our paying guests for the duration of their tuition.'

'Of c-course.' Pa was ruffled. That slight stammer was a dead giveaway. 'I meant no offence. It's just that I see it as an important part of Nancy's professional education that she should live with quality and learn refinement.'

Learn refinement? As if she was a back-street fishwife. Nancy swallowed hard and her throat bobbed.

'Miss Pike has pretty manners, from what I can see,' said Miss Patience.

'But you do work on a girl's social graces, don't you?' Pa sounded almost desperate. 'So I've been told.'

'Certainly we do,' said Miss Hesketh. 'An office girl must conduct herself with due decorum. Tutoring in that area is my sister's speciality.'

'And living with you as your paying guest,' said Pa, 'would help this decorum rub off on our Nancy, wouldn't it?'

Nancy had never felt so small in her life, and for Pa to make her feel that way was horrible. She could hardly hold her head up, and, when it was time to leave, she said her goodbyes in a strangled whisper.

'Well, our Nancy,' Pa said as they walked back to the terminus, 'what do you think?'

'Are you trying to get rid of me? Don't you want me at home any more?'

'Eh, Nancy, eh, lass.' Pa stopped, but she couldn't look at him. 'Of course not.'

'You want to send me away.'

'Just for a time. Just to help prepare you for office work. You heard what the lady said. Due decorum.'

'Oh aye,' Nancy answered bitterly. 'There's none of that in the pie shop, is there, what with me doing the can-can on the counter and showing off next week's washing.'

'Now then, our Nancy.'

'And how am I to be a pupil-lodger? Where's the money coming from? That's board and lodging on top of teaching fees.'

Pa started walking again. 'Aye, well, I've got a bit put by.'

Nancy hurried to catch up. 'Then you should spend it on Mam. Take her to the seaside so she has summat nice to look at out of the window and buy her proper food and lots of it, instead of her looking out at sooty old Bailiff's Row and drinking rusty-nail water every day.'

'It will be spending it on Mam if you go to the business school,' said Pa. 'Think how it'll help her if you bring more money in. That's what this is about, lass, helping Mam.'

Helping Mam. Nancy's resistance crumpled. A better life for Mam – she wanted that more than anything.

Chapter Three

'WELL,' SAID PRUDENCE when Patience returned from seeing Mr and Miss Pike out.

'You said that in your significant voice.' Patience resumed her seat.

'My what? Really, Patience, you do talk twaddle at times.'

Prudence wasn't going to admit it, but she was well aware that, on occasion, she employed a particular tone of voice in her place of work that had her junior colleagues frantically double-checking their spelling before she laid eyes on it. There was something about Mr Pike that had elicited that response from her.

'I'm glad you like Miss Pike,' said Patience. 'It will be good for her to leave the pie shop and move into a better kind of work.'

'Assuming we can lick her into shape.'

'The poor child. She'd undoubtedly much prefer to remain where she is. Mr Pike was most determined that we should accept her as a pupil-lodger, wasn't he? He must have saved very hard to be able to afford it.'

Prudence frowned. 'I wonder what he was saving for originally. It can't have been for this. We only opened our doors earlier this year and we didn't start taking pupil-lodgers immediately. A man from that rank of life couldn't have saved up that quickly.'

'He must be using the family's long-standing rainy-day fund for Nancy's training.'

'Nancy, is it?' Prudence raised her eyebrows. 'I can see that, in your head, you've already got her installed in the old box-room.'

'And why not? I should like to help her. She seemed a sweet girl.'

'You think they're all sweet girls,' said Prudence.

'What if I do? Don't pretend you don't like some of them more than others. You can't deny you've grown fond of Vivienne. You call her by her first name and that's something I never thought you'd do with one of our p.g.s.'

Vivienne.

Prudence's heartbeat picked up speed, sending warmth coursing through her into every corner of her being. Vivienne – her daughter.

'Vivienne is a dear girl.'

It was as much as Prudence could trust herself to say. It hurt more and more to deny the relationship that had changed her life. It hurt to deceive Patience too, but what choice had she? The upright, highly critical Miss Hesketh, spinster of this parish, could never expose her secret disgrace.

'She is a dear girl,' Patience agreed. 'She's been an absolute brick about Lucy.'

'Ah, yes, Lucy.' Prudence shook her head. 'Our "family circumstances" in the flesh.'

'Don't say it like that. It sounds so dismissive.'

'It wasn't intended to, but we do have to be sensible about it.' She especially had to be sensible. It had always fallen to her to be the sensible, practical one.

'Poor Lucy,' sighed Patience.

Poor Lucy indeed. So young, and already she had made a wretched mess of her life. What a shock it had been for Lawrence and Evelyn that their pretty, sociable, sensitive daughter was in the family way. Prudence and Lawrence had been at loggerheads from the moment Prudence had learned to talk, but Lucy's predicament had brought about a truce while Prudence and Patience took care of their niece until it was time for her to be shipped off to Maskell House in the depths of the countryside for the final weeks before the baby was due in December. Lawrence and Evelyn had done everything they could to persuade Lucy to name the father of her child, something she steadfastly refused to do, because she wasn't in love with him. Foolish child! So much for her expensive education and that stint at finishing school. The upper-class marriage her parents had been aiming for was out of the question now. Or perhaps not. By keeping Lucy in Wilton Close, well away from her usual set, followed by sending her away to Maskell House, it should be possible to keep the birth secret, meaning that Lucy could in time return to her old life. Prudence was still getting used to the situation – they all were.

Lucy was blooming. Her skin was radiant, her increased figure for the time being concealed by dresses that were on the large size. Thank goodness for the current fashion for loose-fitting garments. But in a few short weeks she would be sent away…and when she returned, around the end of January, she would be alone. Prudence's heart swelled. Lucy had no notion of how this would haunt her for the rest of her life.

'We're doing the best we can for her,' Prudence said bracingly. 'All we can do is take care of her until she leaves us in October.'

'And Miss Pike can move in afterwards,' said Patience. 'You shall let her be a pupil-lodger, shan't you? Her father seemed desperate for us to take her as a p.g. He was a funny sort, wasn't he? Rather twitchy.'

'He was something of an oddity,' Prudence agreed. 'Anxious to say the right thing, but at the same time somewhat pushy

– a puzzling combination. I think that, since Miss Pike is clearly alarmed at the prospect, we should invite her to start as soon as possible as a night-school pupil.'

'And, after Lucy has left, she can move in as a pupil-lodger for the remainder of her time. It'll be good for her. We can make sure she gets additional typing practice and attends extra lessons, at no charge, of course.'

'I don't think her pride would swallow that.'

'We needn't tell her. We'll say it's part of being a pupil-lodger.' Patience looked around their sitting room. 'I imagine she found this a trifle overwhelming.'

Prudence looked round too. They were so accustomed to the faded gentility of their home that it was odd to imagine others viewing it as the height of graciousness. Belinda Layton, their very first pupil, had all but gasped aloud at the sight of their electric light switch. But the unvarnished truth was that the highly respectable, middle-class Miss Heskeths were as poor as church mice.

Patience bit her lip. 'It feels uncomfortable talking about what will happen after Lucy moves out. I always thought that girls who got into trouble weren't deserving of sympathy. No better than they should be – isn't that the expression? Now here we are with just such a girl under our roof and all I feel for her is anxiety and compassion.'

'It's because she belongs to us.'

'I've always considered myself to be a principled person, but it's easy to have principles when they aren't tested. Before this, I'd have said that, in principle, a girl in trouble was – well – a trollop. That's what I was brought up to believe, but I can't think it of my own niece. It's made me realise that it's all very well having principles, but it's what you do in practice that matters.'

Prudence experienced a sudden urge to pour out her secret. Would Patience understand? It sounded like it. Oh, the relief of sharing her once-shameful but now deeply precious secret with the sister with whom she had lived side by side all their lives, apart from that one brief interval in Scotland. The relief and, once Patience got over the shock, the joy.

But it wasn't as simple as that, because her secret wasn't that simple. Even Vivienne knew only part of it. The secret belonged as much to Patience as it did to either of them. It was just that Patience had no idea – and that was how it must stay.

Chapter Four

ZACHARY ROLLED OFF the mattress, taking care not to whack his skull on the underside of the wooden counter as he came to his feet. He stretched his spine, pulling all the little bones apart and allowing them to re-settle, before eyeing the mattress askance. How could something so thin be so packed with lumps and bumps? Not that it mattered. What was a bit of discomfort compared to the excitement of starting out in business?

'My first day.' The words were all it took to set his heart thumping in his chest. 'Zachary Milner, purveyor and maintainer of fire extinguishers. Full training given.' It was what he had had printed on his business cards.

'My, haven't you made yourself sound grand?' his old landlady had commented, her cheeks pink with pleasure for him.

'You have to when you're in business.'

The memory tugged a smile across his lips. Zachary Milner in business. He had dreamed of this for a long time and had worked hard for it, weighing every decision as he went along. That was why he had woken up under the counter here in the shop in Soapsuds Lane. His modest finances had rendered it necessary to choose between lodgings and business premises and he had deemed the latter to be more important. Essential, in fact. Not that he imagined many customers flocking through the door. For the most part, his work would take him out and about to his clients' buildings. Nevertheless, his own business premises, no matter how humble, were a necessity; so it had been goodbye to his comfortable bedroom, with meals provided and a hot bath once a week, and hello to sleeping under the counter.

But not just any old counter. *His* counter, in *his* shop. So what if the shop was a poky little lock-up, whose tenant ought by rights to leave at six o'clock to head home for a cooked meal, not to mention a hot bath once a week. He didn't mind roughing it, if it helped get his business established. Roughing it? This wasn't roughing it. It was luxury compared to living in the trenches. Something twisted inside Zachary's gut, the way it used to when distant shelling shook the ground. Did you ever get used to it, this sense of loss? The loss of friends... the loss of a brother. He and Nate had joined up in 1915, aged seventeen. Zachary was twenty-four now, but Nate would for ever be nineteen.

Crouching, he rolled up the mattress, with his blanket inside it, securing it with a leather strap, and stood it in the corner under the counter, beside the canvas bag packed with old newspaper and rags that now served as his pillow. Rising once more, he glanced towards the window. He would have to find the money to pay for a blind. It was the beginning of September and although the days were warm and golden, the skies had cooled from the turquoise of summer to periwinkle edged with a suggestion of silver as the shortening days brought crispness to the evenings. Before you knew it, there would be dark evenings and dark mornings and he would need the privacy of a blind, the more so because the counter had to do duty as both desk and dining table.

Behind the counter were two doors. One led to a scullery so narrow he had to turn sideways to ease himself past the stone sink to reach the door that gave onto the yard at the back, where he shared the privy with next door. The other opened onto what the landlord's agent had been pleased to call the storeroom. Zachary was sufficiently proud of his new venture to continue using the word, however cramped the space. It was a good thing that fire extinguishers weren't all that big. In any case, he wouldn't keep more than a handful in the back of the shop, not least because he couldn't afford to. As well as wall-mounted shelves, there were free-standing shelves down the middle of the floor. He would get rid of those, as well as open the boarded-up fireplace and have the chimney swept. Maybe one day he would be in a position to treat himself to an old armchair that could be wedged into that tight corner.

He entered the storeroom now, where one set of wall-shelves served as his wardrobe, with small items and anything that could be folded placed on shelves, and his suit and shirt hanging from the top. He dressed as far as vest and trousers, then went into the scullery for a cold-water wash and shave, taking a glass of water back in the storeroom, where his larder occupied a single shelf – a loaf, a pat of butter, a jar of Marmite and a bottle of fruit cordial. Breakfast was a savoury doorstep and a drink of elderberry. The sooner he got that fireplace sorted out, the better. A sack of coal, a toasting-fork and a hook for a kettle, and he would feel like a king.

He had polished his shoes to a high shine yesterday evening. As he stood up from tying his laces, a flutter of nerves cascaded through his stomach. After all his planning and preparation, today was the day. He had painstakingly constructed a pretend fire extinguisher to use as a model of how a real one worked. He placed this and a real extinguisher inside a carpetbag, which he had lined with a folded blanket to protect the contents, and reached for his new – well, new to him – bowler. Henceforth, his cloth cap was relegated to evenings and weekends.

Last week, he had paid to have some letters typed and had posted them to a selection of small hotels, introducing himself and asking if he might call in to make an appointment to discuss fire safety. He had also sent out postcards to some lodging houses and a number of restaurants. Today he would start visiting them in the hope he had generated interest. He blew out a breath. Maybe, later in the week, he would be hiring the pony and trap belonging to the laundry along the road so he could deliver his first batch of stock. Maybe. Was it foolish to imagine it?

It felt strange going to Wilton Close after a day at the pie shop, and when Nancy thought of it as strange, what she meant was it felt uncomfortable. It wasn't for the likes of her, being in a place like that. She was Nancy Pike from the back streets and Wilton Close was proper middle class. Needing to talk, she told folk about it at the pie shop, anxious to feel the support of her own kind, and the awe in her audience's eyes was a comfort, made her feel they understood; but then some wag called her Fancy Nancy. The name stuck and she came close to dying of shame. She could never tell anyone how much it hurt.

She had vowed to do her best at the Miss Heskeths' school. She already felt at a huge disadvantage and wasn't going to make it worse for herself. It had been arranged that she was to go there two evenings a week, Mondays and Thursdays. On her first evening, she found that the ladies taught in different rooms. Miss Hesketh occupied the dining room, which boasted a long, gleaming table, easily large enough for eight. On each side stood a typewriter on a square of table-felt to protect the table's polished surface. As well as bashing away at the typewriter, Nancy had to deal with stacks of cards like the ones in the library catalogue. They had names on and had to be put in the correct order. Every time Nancy fumbled her way to the end of the task, Miss Hesketh went through her errors with her before spreading out another acre of cards for her to file in with the ones she already had.

What made it harder was that in one of her lessons was a group of three fashionably dressed girls a few years her senior, who clustered at the other end of the table. Miss Hesketh was teaching them about invoices and delivery notices. She would explain something to them, then set them a piece of work while she returned to Nancy's end of the table and corrected her mistakes. The three girls never actually looked her way, but Nancy caught a glance or two passing between them and felt like the world's biggest dunce.

At her other lesson with Miss Hesketh, a dark-haired beauty called Miss Farrow sat at the typewriter on the opposite side of the table, fingers flying as she read the script beside her without needing to look at the typewriter keys. It was like watching someone perform a conjuring trick.

Nancy, struggling to find the letters and hesitating over which finger to use, more than once had her knuckles rapped with a ruler by Miss Hesketh.

Nancy much preferred her lessons with Miss Patience in the front parlour, which she learned to call the sitting room. Remembering what had been said at her interview about social graces, she wondered before the first lesson if she might have to walk around the room with a book balanced on her head. It was a relief to discover that Miss Patience taught social graces of the speaking variety.

Miss Patience introduced her to Miss Thompson, a bespectacled girl who sat with one ankle hooked demurely behind the other. Was this the socially gracious way of sitting?

'In my lessons,' said Miss Patience, 'we practise holding conversations.'

Nancy perked up. She could do that.

'The sort of conversation one might hold in an office environment,' Miss Patience continued, 'such as explaining something or making an enquiry or perhaps an apology if something goes wrong.'

Nancy bit her lip. She rather thought she would be doing a lot of that last one.

'We often use this replica telephone, so that pupils can get used to using the instrument correctly.'

'I work in a warehouse office,' said Miss Thompson, 'and I use the telephone every day.'

'Then perhaps Miss Pike could have the first turn with it this evening,' Miss Patience suggested, causing vivid little pulses to jump about in Nancy's throat and at her wrists. 'The correct way to answer the telephone is to say "Good morning. Brown and Company." Then I'll ask you how to find your office and you can give me directions. Use your journey from home to here and remember to speak clearly. Are you ready? Ring-ring, ring-ring.'

Nancy seized the black telephone, grabbing the small piece that was attached by a flex to the base, and held it to her lips. She put the bit at the other end of the stick from the dial to her ear.

'Good morning,' she began.

'No, dear.' Miss Patience reached for the telephone. 'I'm afraid you haven't got it quite right. You've got the ear-piece and the mouth-piece the wrong way round. Not to worry. It's an easy mistake to make if you aren't accustomed to telephones.'

At the end of Nancy's first week, Miss Hesketh asked, 'Could you possibly attend lessons an hour earlier in future?'

'Yes, miss – I mean, Miss Hesketh.'

Yippee! That would mean arriving home sooner, which, with having to roll out of bed so early to go to work at the pie shop, would suit her perfectly. And was it wrong of her – ungrateful, defeatist – to think that earlier lessons would let her off the hook sooner each time?

Chapter Five

THE CALLS ZACHARY made during his first week in business had been met with polite refusals and it had become increasingly difficult to keep his spirits up, but he pressed on. At the start of the week, he had felt cheery and capable, but by Friday he was dry-mouthed, with a racing pulse, and he spent the weekend trying to ignore a hollow feeling in his chest.

But during the second week, on a rainy day when his arm was aching from lugging his carpetbag around and his stomach had started grumbling with hunger, his luck changed. Mr Kenton, the proprietor of a modest hotel in Seymour Grove, took an interest.

'At a place where I used to work, there was a fire in the kitchen. It soon took control. It caused no end of damage.'

'Fire extinguishers aren't designed to deal with a fire that's already out of control,' said Zachary. 'They're for small fires in emergency situations.' Seeing the fellow's face fall, he added quickly, 'It gives you the chance to deal with the fire before it takes hold. You've seen for yourself what can happen when fire spreads.' He opened his bag. 'Allow me to show you how an extinguisher works. I've got a pretend one here, so you can get a feel for how it operates. And, of course, if you have fire extinguishers from me, even if you take only one, I'll train your staff in its correct use and, for a small fee, I'll come back once a year to ensure your extinguishers are in full working order.'

'Really?' A flicker of interest.

'All part of the service.'

'Show me how it operates,' said Mr Kenton. 'I expected it to be bigger than that.' The look on his face said he wasn't impressed.

Zachary hastened to reassure him, keeping his tone light and informative. 'This is a replica of a pint-sized extinguisher, but they also come in quart-size. You can't have them too big or it wouldn't be possible to lift and aim them. Larger sizes than quart are available, though in your establishment, half a dozen of the quart-size would provide ample protection against emergencies, once your staff have been trained, of course.'

He explained the extinguisher's workings and encouraged Mr Kenton to try out the hand-pump on the replica device.

'That isn't precisely how it feels to use the real thing,' he explained, 'but you get the idea.'

Afterwards they walked round the building and Zachary recommended the most appropriate places to put the extinguishers, explaining his reasons. This seemed to be going well, but he mustn't take anything for granted. When he was in the middle of an explanation, his tummy rumbled at top volume, causing heat to rush into his face.

But Mr Kenton laughed. 'Let me organise lunch for you and we'll sit ourselves in the dining room and talk about cost.'

'That's kind of you, but there's really no need to offer me lunch.'

'Nonsense. It's no trouble. I can't have you fainting on me before we've reached an agreement.'

Later, after a portion of onion soup thickened with a dollop of onion chutney and accompanied by crusty bread, followed by lamb cutlets with mint sauce, Zachary headed for his next call, buoyed up by a mixture of satisfaction and relief at having achieved his first success.

He didn't achieve any further sales that day, but he was given two appointments for next week. A pleasing tiredness accompanied him as he went back to the lock-up, where he wrote a letter to Mr Kenton, confirming details of his order. Although he employed his best writing, it wasn't the same as a typewritten letter. Not as professional. What would a second-hand typewriter cost? And would it be worth the outlay? He mustn't let today's success go to his head.

But it was impossible not to dream.

In her second week at the business school, Nancy travelled to the first of her earlier lessons, giving herself a stern talking-to on the way. She hadn't made the best of starts last week, but she knew what to expect now and she was determined to do better.

She did an' all, in no small part because now she was being taught on her own, which was bliss compared to being in the company of girls who made her realise what a dunderhead she was. She might still be a dunderhead, but at least she was one in private.

'You seem happier this week, Miss Pike dear,' said Miss Patience.

'I am. It's nicer being taught on my own.'

'Good. That's what we thought.'

Nancy went cold. So the Miss Heskeths thought she wasn't good enough to work alongside their other, more capable pupils.

When she arrived on Thursday for her second evening that week, she endured a lesson of typing and filing with Miss

Hesketh before being invited into the sitting room by Miss Patience. A girl was already there. Had they given up on solitary lessons?

'Miss Pike,' said Miss Patience, 'this is Belinda Layton, who was our very first pupil.'

'It's you!' the girl called Belinda exclaimed. 'I didn't know it was going to be you.'

Nancy recognised her at once. 'You used to come into the pie shop sometimes. Though you never bought anything.'

'I worked in the mill up the road and I always took my snap to work with me,' said Belinda, 'but sometimes I walked along to the shop with my friends, though I stopped outside because I wasn't a customer – unless it was parky and then I'd sneak in for a minute.'

'I'll leave you two girls to chat,' Miss Patience murmured and left the room.

A small burst of pleasure brought a smile to Nancy's lips. She had always liked the look of Belinda and had wished that she would come to the counter to buy something, so they could have a chat. Nancy was no good at guessing ages, but she reckoned Belinda was a year or two older than herself. She wore a dark skirt and a cream blouse. That made sense, because Nancy had been told she would be expected to wear a black or navy skirt with a white or cream blouse when she started work in an office. Belinda was fair-skinned with dark-brown hair that wasn't far off black. On her wedding finger, she wore a gold ring set with a row of five little pearls. Not a surplus girl, then. Had she had to leave the business school when she got engaged?

'How are you finding it here?' Belinda asked.

'Fine, thank you.'

'Truly?'

Crikey. Well, why not tell the truth? She couldn't do so at home because of upsetting Mam and she couldn't say owt at the pie shop for fear of looking like a twerp, but all of a sudden she urgently wanted to confide. Besides, it could be a way of making a new friend.

'They've got me coming early so I can have lessons by myself because I'm not good enough to be taught alongside anyone else.'

'That must have been a bit of a blow.'

'Aye, it was.'

'But if you're struggling, it's better to struggle in private, isn't it?'

'I s'pose so. Well, actually, yes, definitely.'

'I'm sure the ladies are doing their best for you. You do know that Miss Hesketh goes out to work, don't you?'

'Does she?' It was hard to believe that a lady who lived in these smart surroundings needed to earn a living. 'I didn't know that.'

Nancy stared at her hands and she must have looked guilty because Belinda said, 'I didn't say that to make you feel bad. I wanted to show you what good sorts the Miss Heskeths are. They're trying to do the right thing by you. They were ever so kind to me.'

'Are you engaged?' Nancy glanced at Belinda's ring.

Belinda looked at it an' all, a smile winding its way across her face. Nancy felt a pang. If the Miss Heskeths were to be believed, Belinda was jolly lucky.

'We can't get married for ages yet. We've got a lot of saving to do. Gabriel – that's my fiancé – wants to have his own bookshop. He inherited the stock from his uncle's shop and the Hesketh ladies let him store it in their cellar. He's a clerk at the moment while we save up to afford the rent on a shop with a flat above. We're both clerks, actually.'

'Miss Patience said you were their first pupil.'

'That's right. She asked me here to meet you.'

'Why?'

'Because you're the lass from the pie shop and I used to be a mill girl. We're the same, you and me.'

'You mean, you weren't clever at school?'

'I'm talking about class. If the other girls at the business school worked in hotels, they'd be receptionists, wouldn't they? You and me, we'd be the chambermaids.' Belinda raised one shoulder in a half-shrug. 'Class.'

Nancy couldn't help laughing, partly from relief. She didn't feel quite so alone now.

'It's true,' said Belinda. 'The point is that, regardless of background, we're all surplus girls who'll probably live out our lives as spinsters – well, I know I'm not a surplus girl any more, but I was one until the spring. Being surplus girls makes us all the same, no matter what sort of background we come from. Try to remember that and, whatever you do, don't give up on having lessons.'

'I won't. I can't. My parents are relying on me. I'm not here just for my future. I'm here so I can earn more money for my family. I'm determined to finish the course.'

'Good for you.'

Aye, and with luck and a prevailing wind, she would finish the course before the Miss Heskeths' 'family circumstances', whatever they might be, could alter. That way, she would never have to come here as a pupil-lodger. She would give anything to avoid that.

Chapter Six

VIVIENNE WALKED HOME to Wilton Close with a definite spring in her step. So what if the afternoon on this mid-September day had turned overcast and drizzly? She had just worked her final Saturday hours at the domestic employment agency, where she had mostly done typewriting and filing to gain office experience. Typewriting and filing were all very well, and obviously it was important to be proficient in such skills, but she would far rather have interviewed the clients looking for domestic help and the women putting themselves forward for the jobs. But working in an office was considered part of the tuition offered at the Miss Heskeths' business school.

The Miss Heskeths – her mother and her aunt. Not that dear Miss Patience had any notion of it. Being reunited with Prudence Hesketh, the mother who had entrusted her illegitimate baby to her good friends, Elspeth and Graham Thornton, to bring up as their own, had been a deeply emotional experience for Vivienne, not to mention a scary one. Suppose Miss Hesketh hadn't wanted to know her, hadn't wished to be reminded? But, to Vivienne's profound joy and relief, Prudence Hesketh had, after years of silent pain, welcomed her long-lost daughter into her heart.

The relationship remained a closely guarded secret. Miss Hesketh's reputation depended upon it. To start with, the secrecy had suited Vivienne too, because she had needed time to adjust to this new phase of her life. Now, however, even while she recognised the need for secrecy, she couldn't help finding it frustrating.

Wouldn't life be simpler if they could tell the truth? It would be wonderful to tell Miss Patience, who, once she had recovered from the shock, would, Vivienne was perfectly sure, adore having another niece. It would be good, also, not to have to keep such an important secret from her dear friend, Molly Abrams.

But respectability mattered more than anything and Vivienne had no intention of jeopardising her natural mother's standing in the community. She might even lose her position in the Corporation, should the truth emerge.

Her natural mother. That was how she thought of her. Not her 'real mother', which was the way most people referred to the woman who had given birth to an adopted child. That description didn't sit right with Vivienne. Her real mother was Elspeth Thornton, the woman who had brought her up, and nothing would ever change that. Vivienne had a strong sense of her identity as the beloved daughter of Graham and Elspeth Thornton.

That her real mother and her natural mother had been friends spoke to something deep inside her. It created a connection between the three of them that endowed Vivienne with a sense of rightness. She still addressed her natural mother as Miss Hesketh. Miss Hesketh wasn't Mother. Mother – Elspeth Thornton – was Mother.

Vivienne had gone down to the south coast for a few days in August after her friend Molly's wedding to Aaron Abrams, to see her father and come clean about her new friendship with Prudence Hesketh, which, once Vivienne had revealed her true identity to Miss Hesketh, had developed quickly.

Vivienne had felt fluttery with nerves all the way down to Brighton, where Dad ran one of the family's hotels. He already knew that she was aware from her birth certificate that her real mother was called Prudence Hesketh; and she had been open with him about finding the article in *Vera's Voice* earlier this year about the business school for surplus girls in Manchester that was run by a Miss Hesketh and her sister, Miss Patience Hesketh. Dad had confirmed that Mother's old friend Prudence did indeed come from Manchester and her sister was called Patience. But that was as much as he knew so far. Vivienne hadn't told him about deliberately moving in with the Heskeths, because there were some things that needed to be said in person, not in a letter. So he didn't know either that she and Miss Hesketh had been reunited.

Or so she had thought.

'I'm glad you finally decided to tell me,' he had said. 'Well, honestly, Vee,' he added when she was too surprised to utter a sound, 'did you think I couldn't put two and two together? You found out about the business school up in Manchester – and then you got yourself a new job up there. I knew you were bound to want to meet Prudence.'

'It's more than just meeting her, Dad. I'm living with her. The address in Wilton Close that you send letters to is the Miss Heskeths' house.'

'Is it now?'

'I'm sorry I didn't tell you before, truly I am, but I thought that if, for some reason, I never told her who I am, there'd have been no point in worrying you with it.'

Dad had taken her hands in his. 'Don't ever think you mustn't worry me. I'm your dad. It's my job to worry. And I'll tell you something else. As an adoptive father, it's my privilege to worry.'

'Oh, Dad, I do love you.'

'I understand why you kept it from me and I appreciate your coming all the way down here to tell in person.'

'How do you feel about me living with Miss Hesketh and being friends with her?'

'It's natural for you to be curious about your real mother, I know that. How do I feel about it? I'm not sure, to tell you the truth. But this I do know: she and your mother were great friends and I'm grateful to her, because I've got you.'

Vivienne smiled at the memory as she hurried home to Wilton Close. She loved living there. It was the first time since she had lost her husband that she had felt truly at home. She still missed Molly, who had been a pupil-lodger until she became engaged, whereupon she had gone back to live under the parental roof until her wedding; but Molly's absence from Wilton Close had its good side, because Molly had slept in the old box-room, which Miss Patience had converted into a darling little bedroom, while Vivienne shared the double bed in the master bedroom with Lucy, the Miss Heskeths' niece and, could she but know it, Vivienne's cousin. After Molly moved out, Lucy had moved into the small bedroom, leaving Vivienne to relish the space and privacy of her large bedroom, the biggest the house had to offer. It had previously belonged to the late Mr Hesketh – her grandfather.

When she arrived home, Vivienne helped Miss Patience make the tea. She enjoyed preparing meals and assisted every Sunday with the roast. She had loved cooking for her husband, but they hadn't had much time together before war was declared. He had volunteered at once and had never come home. Cooking for one, as Vivienne had soon discovered, simply wasn't the same.

Not so long ago, Miss Hesketh would have refused point-blank to permit a p.g. to do anything more arduous in the kitchen than boil a pan of milk for bedtime drinks, but now Vivienne could potter about as if – well, as if she truly belonged here, something she was sure Miss Hesketh appreciated as much as she did.

'How was your final day at the agency, Vivienne dear?' Miss Patience asked as the four of them sat down to curried eggs, which would be followed by cheese pudding.

'I've enjoyed being there,' said Vivienne. 'It's given me plenty of experience with basic office routines, though I don't know whether I'll ever use the knowledge. I'm happy working for the Board of Health and helping the poor and infirm.'

'You never know when these skills might come in useful,' said Miss Hesketh.

'That's why I'm doing the book-keeping course.' And also because it enabled her to remain here as a pupil-lodger. What was going to happen when she ran out of courses? She was nowhere near ready to leave. That made her think of Lucy. 'How have you been today?' she asked the girl.

Lucy sighed dramatically. 'Bored. I'm not allowed to leave the house since my girth increased. I might as well be at Maskell House.'

Miss Hesketh raised her thin eyebrows. 'It can be arranged.'

Lucy retreated at once. 'I don't want to go there until I absolutely have to.'

'You absolutely have to on the second of October,' said Miss Hesketh.

'Daddy and Mummy are going to take you,' Miss Patience added.

'Don't give me that mutinous look,' said Miss Hesketh. 'You'll be between six and seven months and we can't keep you here any longer than that.'

At the end of the meal, as Vivienne was about to help Miss Patience clear away, Miss Hesketh gave Lucy her marching orders.

'Time to make yourself scarce, young lady.'

'It's only Molly who's coming round,' said Lucy, 'and she knows all about my condition. She's going to adopt the baby.'

'It isn't only Molly,' said Miss Hesketh. 'It's Miss Kirby as well. She has no idea of your fall from grace and that's how I wish it to remain, if you'd be so kind.' Her eyes narrowed.

Lucy skedaddled up the stairs.

Soon the visitors arrived. Vivienne was delighted to see Molly, and especially to see how married life and becoming the instant mother of eleven-year-old Danny had brought such happiness to her gorgeous greeny-hazel eyes. She was pleased to see Miss Kirby too. Some ten or more years older than the Hesketh ladies, she was a retired school-teacher, who had been booted out of her job early to make way for a returning soldier and consequently didn't have the financial resources she had hoped to have for her years of retirement.

They settled in the sitting room and Miss Patience started what she called a hospitality fire, just enough to nudge the coolness over the border into an acceptable warmth. She looked round. 'It's just like old times.'

Molly laughed. 'Not so old. It's only a matter of weeks since I moved out.'

'Well, it feels like old times,' said Miss Patience. 'A lot has changed. You're married with a ready-made family and living in a charming house.'

'I'm very lucky,' said Molly.

'How is your new pupil working out?' asked Miss Kirby. 'Miss Pike, isn't it?'

'Not very well, I'm sorry to say,' Miss Hesketh answered. 'I had hoped she'd show more aptitude.'

'It's taking her a while to get into the swing of things, that's all,' said Miss Patience.

'All the other pupils we've had made more promising starts,' said Miss Hesketh.

'Your other pupils aren't like Miss Pike,' said Vivienne. 'She's a simple pie shop girl. The others already work in offices or typing pools or else – I'm sorry if it sounds mean, but they did better at school.'

'Belinda was a mill-girl,' Miss Patience said defensively.

'Who, had she been born into a different family,' said Miss Hesketh, 'would have sat the scholarship for high school, and passed – as you of all people are well aware, Miss Kirby, being her former teacher. I'm sorry, Patience. I'm aware of how fond you are of Miss Pike, but...'

Miss Patience caught her breath. 'You're not going to declare her unfit for office work, are you?'

'When we interviewed her,' said Miss Hesketh, 'I saw something in her. I liked her attitude to her job. She has a spark about her that, correctly harnessed and developed, could lift her out of the pie shop and into more responsible and better-paid work that ultimately will improve her chances of leading a more comfortable life. It will enable her to assist her family too. They're obviously hard up and sending her here must represent a significant sacrifice. I like her. I want to help her, to improve her; and I'd be a pretty poor sort of person if I gave up on her just because she has made a slow start.'

'I hope you'll say some of that to Miss Pike,' said Vivienne. 'It may well be that she needs to hear it.'

'A large part of the problem is that job in the pie shop,' said Miss Hesketh. 'The only clerical experience she receives is when she comes here for her lessons. She badly needs a clerical position in a small environment, where she could be closely supervised. That would bring her along, I'm sure.'

Molly looked up. 'I may have a suggestion.'

They all looked at her.

'One of the girls who left St Anthony's in the summer, a lass called Ginny, was found a post as a maid to an old lady, but unfortunately the old lady has died. It's put Ginny in a tricky position. She didn't just lose her situation. She lost her home as well.'

Vivienne nodded. It was a great shame that the orphans had to be found jobs that included bed and board. It cut down considerably on where they could be placed.

'What a worry,' she commented. 'Where is she now?'

'That's just it,' said Molly. 'Mrs Rostron has taken her back as a temporary measure.'

'Very Christian of her,' said Miss Hesketh, 'but what has that to do with our Miss Pike?'

'I'm coming to that. Mrs Rostron wants Miss Allan to have an office junior. Ginny's a bright girl and might be suitable, but Mrs Rostron is reluctant to give her the position, because she can't single her out for special treatment. It wouldn't be fair to all the other orphans.'

'So you want us to suggest Miss Pike instead?' asked Miss Patience. 'That hardly seems fair on this Ginny girl.'

'Suppose Mrs Rostron offered two temporary posts, say until Christmas,' said Molly. 'Ginny and Miss Pike would each have the chance to learn the clerical routines and prove themselves. Then, come Christmas, one of them would be awarded the permanent position and the other would have some valuable experience under her belt. And no one would be able to say Ginny had benefited from favouritism. What do you think? I know that Mrs Rostron is on duty this weekend if you wish to discuss it with her.'

'I might just do that.' Miss Hesketh frowned thoughtfully.

'What are you thinking?' asked Vivienne.

'It seems to me that if we are to do our best for Miss Pike, we ought to have her here as a pupil-lodger.'

'Her father was very keen on it when she had her interview,' said Miss Patience. 'But of course she can't come until after Lucy leaves.'

'Lucy is leaving?' asked Miss Kirby. 'Which reminds me: I haven't seen her for a while now.' She laughed. 'I wouldn't even know she was staying with you.'

'Lucy will be going to stay with friends for a while,' Vivienne said smoothly, sitting forward and catching Miss Kirby's eye so that Miss Kirby didn't notice the stricken look on Miss Patience's face. 'It's a shame she's been out when you've come round recently. I'll tell her you asked after her.'

'What Patience meant,' Miss Hesketh added, 'is that Miss Pike will have to wait until Lucy leaves so she can have Lucy's room. If the orphanage job could start after that – assuming Mrs Rostron agrees – that would be perfect. Just what Miss Pike needs.'

'I'm afraid it isn't open to negotiation,' said Mrs Rostron.

Prudence bit down on her vexation. She was sitting in the orphanage superintendent's office. She never liked sitting in front of someone else's desk. She would far rather be behind the desk, in the position that said she was in charge. She admired and respected Mrs Rostron without entertaining any particular liking for her and she rather thought Mrs Rostron felt the same way about her.

'I'm prepared to wait one week while Miss Pike works out her notice.' Mrs Rostron consulted the diary which lay open beside her. 'Then both girls can start as office juniors on the twenty-fifth of September. I see no good reason to wait until October.'

And Prudence wasn't going to enlighten her.

Later, at home, she talked it over with Patience, Vivienne and Lucy.

'We shall have to visit Miss Pike at home tomorrow,' Miss Hesketh said to Miss Patience, 'and instruct her to hand in her notice at the pie shop on Monday so that she can leave on Saturday. Then she can start at the orphanage on the following Monday.'

'And I'm going to Maskell House the Monday after that,' said Lucy, 'so she'll have only one week of working at St Anthony's before she moves in here.'

'Miss Pike is a dear girl, but she's going to feel hopelessly out of her depth when she starts in this new job,' said Vivienne. 'We don't want her going home, upset, to her family, especially as I gather her mother is a semi-invalid. If she lived here right from the start, we could support her and gee her along a bit.'

'You're quite right, Vivienne dear,' said Miss Patience, 'but Lucy will still be living here during Miss Pike's first week. There are all sorts of reasons why we can't have that.'

There was a silence. Prudence didn't need to look round to know the others were looking at her, awaiting her judgement. Patience was correct. It would be highly inappropriate to have Miss Pike here at the same time as Lucy. The Hesketh family was entitled to its privacy and needed to keep Lucy's secret hidden. Moreover, an innocent young girl like Miss Pike was entitled to be protected from the shocking truth. But it was also true that Miss Pike would benefit enormously from living here from day one of her orphanage position. Truth be told, living in Wilton Close might be the one thing that prevented her from running back to the pie shop.

Prudence prided herself on doing her very best for all her pupils and, goodness knew, if any pupil was in need of her best, that pupil was Nancy Pike. To do the right thing by her meant bringing her here to live under their roof in time for her to start at St Anthony's. Besides, it was the tidy thing to do. Prudence liked things to be tidy. Regular. Ordered.

Having Lucy here these past three months had felt decidedly messy. Yes, she loved her niece and felt deeply protective towards her in her current situation – but having her in the house had been a tricky business. Just look at Patience's slip of the tongue in front of Miss Kirby. It would be messier still to have Miss Pike here for a week before Lucy departed, but there was no escaping the fact that this was the right place for Miss Pike to be.

'I am firmly of the opinion that we should take Miss Pike as a pupil-lodger in time for her to start at St Anthony's. We can provide additional tuition and discuss any problems she encounters at work. But Mrs Rostron is adamant – and I can see her point – that she won't wait longer than one week.'

'You're not going to send me to Maskell House early, are you?' Lucy pleaded.

'Of course not, dear,' said Patience. 'You're booked in for the beginning of October. That won't change. When the arrangements were made, it was the first available date Mrs Ayrton could offer.'

'What if Miss Pike moves in the afternoon before she starts at the orphanage?' Vivienne suggested. 'That's the latest we can leave it. She'll work out her notice and finish at the pie shop on the Saturday and come here the following afternoon, ready to go to St Anthony's the next morning. It's not as though Lucy is the size of a house, and she's wearing loose clothes. We'll just have to muddle our way through the week.'

'We won't muddle,' Prudence replied. 'We'll plan it and, in particular, we'll think carefully before we speak,' she added with a glance at Patience.

'Where will she sleep?' Lucy asked.

'You'll have to move back in with me, Lucy,' said Vivienne, 'and Miss Pike can go straight into the box-room. Monday to Friday, it shouldn't be too difficult. Miss Pike will be out all day and Lucy always makes herself scarce on teaching evenings.'

'That just leaves the weekend before Lucy goes away,' said Prudence. 'I expect Miss Pike will be eager to spend Saturday with her family.'

'And I can spend Sunday at Molly and Aaron's,' said Lucy. 'They'd like that.'

'Miss Pike strikes me as a naive girl,' said Patience. 'Do you think we can get away with it?'

'We have to,' said Prudence.

Chapter Seven

I N THE PIE shop, Nancy went through the motions in the state of cold disbelief that had descended upon her yesterday when Miss Hesketh and Miss Patience had told her what was going to happen. After six happy years here, she had handed in her notice, smiling as she did it even though she felt stunned on the inside. Everyone was pleased for her. Word got round and all their customers popped in with beaming smiles and words of congratulation. Admiration an' all. They admired her – her, Nancy Pike.

'You're going to mek summat of yourself, lass. You'll be a big help to your mam.'

She latched onto the thought, hugging it close. If she could help her family, in particular if she could make Mam's life easier, then it would be worthwhile. Pa had never earned much, but, if she could contribute more, Mam could have more bottles of blood tonic and more slices of liver and be less reliant on spinach and on water that had had rusty nails boiled in it. Imagine helping Mam to feel stronger. That was worth giving up the pie shop, surely. Wanting to cling on and stay here was short-sighted and selfish.

'Eh, young Nancy's going to be a proper office girl,' said the busy, faded housewives, coming in for a mince-and-onion pie or a suet pudding. They couldn't be more proud of her if she had been their own daughter.

'Careful,' someone laughed. 'You'll make her head swell with all this high esteem.'

But all she felt was shrivelled-up. It was hard to smile and accept good wishes when you wanted to bawl your eyes out.

'A position where you won't be working alone,' Miss Hesketh had informed her, 'but where you'll be supervised.'

'And you won't be the only new employee either,' Miss Patience had added, 'because another girl will start at the same time; and before you ask, no, she doesn't have any relevant experience. In fact, she only left school in the summer.'

So this post was considered suitable for a fourteen-year-old. Would a nineteen-year-old look stupid doing it?

She was going to be taken on at St Anthony's, the local orphanage in Chorlton. Their secretary, Miss Allan, was what Miss Patience delicately called 'an older lady' and if Miss Patience thought that, then she must be ancient. Miss Allan had been poorly in the summer and now that she was back at work, it had been decided that she should be provided with assistance.

Not only had the Miss Heskeths found her this new job to go to, they wanted her to live with them as a pupil-lodger. Nancy's heart had shrivelled into a dry little husk when she heard that. She had hoped so much to finish her course before a living-in place could become available. Presumably those 'family circumstances,' whatever they were, had changed or been sorted out.

Pa's delight was hard to take, but Nancy had to hide her feelings. She couldn't have Mam worrying about her.

'This is just what I wanted for you,' said Pa.

'I'll miss you,' said Mam, 'but I'm that proud. You're going up in the world.'

'You'd better not go all snooty,' said Lottie.

'You know our Nancy better than that,' said Mam.

'I'm concerned about leaving you, Mam.' It was the closest Nancy could get to saying she dreaded going.

'You needn't worry,' said Emily. 'Mam's got us to look after her. We'll all be fine together, won't we, Mam?'

'Of course we will,' said Lottie, 'the three of us.'

'And me,' said Pa. 'Don't forget me.'

Mam and the twins laughed; so did Pa. Nancy tried to, but it wasn't a real laugh. She couldn't bear the thought of leaving them.

The end of September was in sight and Zachary was fairly pleased with how his first month had gone. He hadn't exactly set the world ablaze – which was an unfortunate turn of phrase for a purveyor of fire extinguishers, he thought with a grin – but he hadn't done too badly either. His days were full. A lot of his time was taken up with travelling from one hotel to another, from one restaurant to another. He walked whenever it was possible to save money on fares. Nearly all of his calls were of his own making, because he had written an introductory letter, but one this morning had been through recommendation by Mr Kenton, which felt like a huge feather in his cap. A few more recommendations wouldn't go amiss. It provided a much easier starting point.

This afternoon he had come, thanks to a favourable response to one of his letters, to an old soldiers' home in Seymour Grove, called Oak Lodge. It was owned by Mr Peters, who ran it with his wife. Mr Peters was a genial-looking man, but Zachary had the feeling that nothing got past him. Mrs Peters produced a tray of tea and home-made treats.

'Help yourself,' she told him.

Zachary tried a cinnamon biscuit. 'That's delicious. Thank you.'

'Don't be afraid to take another.'

'You're spoiling me.'

Mrs Peters laughed. 'It makes a change to fuss over a good-looking young man instead of all the old boys we have living here. Not that I'd change any of them for the world.'

Presently, after a discreet signal from Mr Peters that didn't escape Zachary's notice, Mrs Peters gathered up the tea things and Zachary politely got up to open the door for her, receiving a kind smile as she left the room.

'Now then, let's get down to business,' said Mr Peters. 'I'm interested to hear about your fire extinguishers.'

'I can do more than tell you about them. I can show you a replica I made that you can have a try with.'

'You made it, you say?' Mr Peters nodded. 'I like to see initiative.'

Zachary explained all about extinguishers and the services he could offer.

'I'm impressed,' said Mr Peters, 'and I'll definitely order a set of fire extinguishers, complete with staff training and inspections on an annual basis – but not quite yet. We're having some decorating done at present and I'll wait until it's finished before I place my order with you.'

'Thank you, sir,' said Zachary. 'I'll be delighted to hear from you when the time comes.'

'Before you leave, let me introduce you to the residents. They always enjoy seeing a fresh face and some of them don't get visitors of their own. Can you spare a few minutes?'

'With pleasure.'

Mr Peters introduced him to old boys who had fought in the Boer Wars. He even had the honour of meeting a frail old gentleman in his nineties, who had been in the Crimea. Amazing.

'Would you mind if I dropped in occasionally?' he asked Mr Peters. 'I'd like the chance to talk to some of the gentlemen, if you think they'd like it. I'm not saying it so that you'll buy fire extinguishers off me,' he added quickly. 'I'd enjoy it.'

'So would my residents,' replied Mr Peters.

When it was time to leave, saying his farewells took quite some time, as all the old soldiers wanted to shake hands and wish him well, but Zachary didn't mind one bit. He ran down the front steps. Oak Lodge occupied a large plot on the corner of Whalley Road. It was a fair old walk from here to Soapsuds Lane, but he always enjoyed stretching his legs. So many blokes had come home from the battlefields of France minus one leg or both. For Zachary, walking briskly was an act of gratitude, a kind of prayer, if that didn't sound barmy, a thank you for having been spared, a promise to Nate that he would make the best of his life. He would miss his brother until the day he died. Nate's death at such a young age made it all the more important for Zachary to get on with his life. In a way, he was living it for the pair of them.

The day before she started work at St Anthony's, Nancy moved into the Miss Heskeths' house. She had barely slept during her final night at home. The butterflies in her tummy were not so much fluttering as turning somersaults. How was she to cope, not just with this new job but also with living in Wilton Close?

In spite of her fears, there was something rather wonderful about walking up the path and knowing that she was actually going to live in a house that had its very own garden. That was summat she would remember and appreciate until the day she died. Even though it wasn't summer, there were still flowers – golden rod and Michaelmas daisies. If only she could draw, she would create a picture of the garden and one day show it to her children, seeing the marvel in their little faces as she told them 'I lived here once' – except that she might not have children, since she was a surplus girl.

A bolt of fear shot through her. Girls grew up and got wed. Everybody knew that. It was why girls were taught housework and cookery at school. The thought that there was now a generation of girls who would never get married was plain terrifying. All those girls, living alone on low wages and with no family to give their lives meaning. What would happen to them in their old age?

'Welcome, Miss Pike,' said Miss Patience. 'I hope you'll be happy here with us.'

'Here is a door-key for you,' said Miss Hesketh.

'Thank you,' Nancy said politely, but it was another reminder of how living here was going to take her out of her natural place. She would much prefer to walk up the side path and enter the house via the kitchen. Much more in keeping with her station.

'I'll show you around the house and then you can unpack,' said Miss Patience, leading her upstairs. 'We'll start with your room, shall we? It's not very big, I'm afraid. It used to be the box-room, but I've made a sweet little bedroom of it. I hope you like it.'

She opened a door and stood back. Nancy gazed at her bedroom – her very own room!

She turned to Miss Patience. 'Do I really have a bed all to myself?'

She hadn't slept on her own since the twins were removed from the drawer that had been their baby cot. It was a proper bedroom an' all, not a curtained-off space at the top of the stairs, like in the flat. It had a real dressing-table with a big looking-glass, not a speckled old hand-mirror; and that candlewick bedspread hadn't come off a market-stall. There wasn't a hanging cupboard, but only because there wasn't the space. Instead, there were pegs and coat-hangers behind a curtain that was a great deal prettier than any clothing Nancy possessed.

'Molly – that is, Mrs Abrams's brother put up the shelves when this was her room,' said Miss Patience. 'That door is my sister's bedroom and this one is mine. The room over there is Mrs Atwood's. She is sharing it at the moment with my niece, Lucy, who is staying with us; she'll be leaving a week on Monday, so you won't see much of her. Let me show you the bathroom.'

A bathroom! Nancy followed Miss Patience with her eyes on stalks, making sure her mouth wasn't hanging open at the sight of middle-class wonders. It was a relief to escape back to her little room to unpack. She took her time about it, not wanting to make it obvious to her landladies that she had so few clothes and possessions. As if they couldn't work that out for themselves!

She was at the stage of screwing up the courage to walk downstairs as if she had every right to do so, when there was a gentle tap on the door and it opened to reveal Mrs Abrams, whom she knew by sight, having seen her here once or twice after she started coming early to lessons. Mrs Abrams was friends with Mrs Atwood, and the Miss Heskeths seemed fond of her an' all – well, in so far as starchy Miss Hesketh could appear fond of anybody. Mrs Abrams had hazel eyes, though not the usual browny-hazel. Hers were a lovely greeny-hazel. Her hair was a rich blonde, though not golden, as it had a suggestion of red in it. Strawberry-blonde: was that what it was called? Such a pretty colour compared to her own copper saucepans.

'May I come in? This used to be my room, you know.'

'Miss Patience told me.'

'I was very comfortable, living here. I hope you shall be too.'

'Thank you.'

'And I'm sure you'll enjoy working at St Anthony's. It was when Miss Allan was poorly earlier this year that I had the chance to work there.'

'Did you like it?' Nancy asked.

'Well, I got a husband and son out of it, so I can't complain.' Mrs Abrams laughed. 'Miss Allan will retire in a year or two. The plan is that she should have an assistant who will not only help her, but who will also help to ease her replacement into the post in due course. Mrs Rostron – she's the superintendent – calls it planning for the future.'

'You said "an assistant", but aren't there going to be two of us?'

'There are two temporary positions. You'll both be tried out until Christmas, then one of you shall be kept on, and the one doesn't stay at St Anthony's will have gained some useful experience.'

'Who's the other girl?' Nancy asked.

'Ginny Matthews. Children at St Anthony's in their last year at school are called fourteens, because fourteen became the school leaving age after the war. Ginny was a fourteen last year. She was found a live-in job as a maid-of-all-work with an old lady, but, unfortunately, the lady died recently, so Mrs Rostron has allowed Ginny to come back and be one of the two temporary assistants.'

'Well, I don't know why they're bothering to have me,' said Nancy. 'Obviously they'll choose this Ginny.' Annoyance flared. So did fear. Miss Hesketh had made her hand in her notice at the pie shop for this!

Mrs Abrams smiled kindly. 'There's no "obviously" about it, as you'll soon realise when you meet Mrs Rostron. I might bump into you at St Anthony's. I work there a few hours a week, teaching basic office skills to the older girls.'

'I'll be glad to see a friendly face.'

'Trust me, you'll see plenty of friendly faces. Chin up. I know what it's like to leave a job you've been in for yonks and start again. It can be daunting, no matter how keen you are – and I realise you aren't all that keen. A word of advice?'

'Yes, please,' said Nancy.

'I'm not suggesting you forget the past, but don't let it hold you back.' To Nancy's surprise, Mrs Abrams kissed her cheek. 'Best foot forward, eh?'

Chapter Eight

ON MONDAY MORNING, Miss Hesketh and Mrs Atwood set off for work considerably earlier than Nancy needed to, because they had to travel into the middle of town. Lucy Hesketh was still in bed, so that left Nancy with Miss Patience. Nancy had dressed in her Sunday best, namely a white blouse and her good skirt, which had been cut down from an old skirt of Mam's.

'Please don't take offence,' said Miss Patience, 'but I wonder if you'd care to wear this blouse instead of your own. My sister insists upon white or cream blouses, but I thought this ivory cotton might go nicely with your rich colouring.'

Nancy wanted to hug her. Rich colouring? It had never been called that before. It was even more flattering than what Mam said about copper saucepans. Miss Patience was so kind.

'Are you sure?' Nancy breathed. The ivory blouse made her old white look precisely that – old.

'It belongs to my niece and she's happy for you to borrow it while you work at St Anthony's.'

Ah – the niece. Nancy had barely glimpsed her. Fancy lending a high-quality garment to a perfect stranger. Either she was extraordinarily generous or else she had more clothes than she knew what to do with. Was that a catty thing to think?

When Nancy got changed, she found that Miss Patience had starched the ivory blouse for her. It sat beautifully across her shoulders, looking crisp and costly, and so what if the starched collar chafed the back of her neck? It was worth it to wear something so elegant. Elegant – her!

'There,' said Miss Patience. 'You look the part.'

'I feel the part an' all. I mean, I feel it too.' She had to spruce up her English if she was going to be an office girl. 'Thank you.'

Miss Patience smiled. 'There's one final thing before you go. I wondered if you might care to wear this instead of your shawl.'

Nancy's breath caught in delight, trapped by a knot of emotion inside her throat. Miss Patience held a coat-hanger from which hung a light-blue jacket, a proper old-fashioned fitted garment that nipped in at the waist, with broderie anglaise collar and cuffs.

'It's not new by any stretch. Pre-war, in fact.' Miss Patience sounded apologetic. 'I'll quite understand if a young girl like you would prefer not to wear it.'

Nancy found her voice. 'Not want to? Miss Patience, it's lovely. I've never seen anything so smart. Are you sure you want to lend it to me?'

'Positive.' Miss Patience released a soft sigh. 'I thought at the time that the blue would bring out the colour of my eyes – as if that would make a difference to a plain creature like myself.'

'Don't say that. You're not plain.'

'Oh, I am, my dear. I always have been.'

'Not on the inside, you're not. On the inside, you're – you're beautiful.'

'Goodness, what a compliment.' Miss Patience removed the garment from its hanger. 'Try the jacket. Does it fit?'

It did. Miss Patience might be naturally thin, but Nancy was thin an' all after a lifetime of never having quite enough to eat.

'The buttons are for show,' said Miss Patience when Nancy fumbled with them before finding that the garment fastened edge-to-edge, courtesy of concealed hooks and eyes.

'How stylish!' she exclaimed. 'I wish Mam could see me in it. Oh crumbs, did that sound like a gigantic hint? It wasn't meant to, honest.'

'Of course it didn't. Now off you go. Show Mrs Rostron and Miss Allan what a good worker you are.'

Nancy turned at the gate to raise her hand in farewell to Miss Patience, who stood on the step to see her on her way. It felt good to be waved off. Encouraging. As if Miss Patience believed in her – but then, Miss Patience was such a sweetheart. She would give anybody the benefit of the doubt.

'That's enough of that,' Nancy murmured as she walked to the corner. 'Stop doing yourself down.'

Best foot forward. Starting now, that was her motto.

She had never felt so smart in her life as she walked along Beech Road in the blue jacket with the ivory blouse beneath. She rounded the corner onto Church Road, her heart picking up speed as she approached the brick wall surrounding the orphanage. It was a sunny morning, as befitted late September, but there was a definite nip in the air that promised a chilly journey home later on. It would be October this Sunday and she had noticed asters and Chinese lanterns on show in some of the gardens along Beech Road.

Nancy walked through the orphanage's open gates. Thanks to Molly Abrams, she knew this was the girls' playground and that she must turn right, walk past the end of a wing that jutted out from the main building, and cross the boys' playground towards a set of steps leading to a big wooden door with an old-fashioned bell-pull. Before she could reach for it, the door opened to reveal a girl, younger than herself, in a plain white blouse and dark-blue skirt.

'Miss Nancy Pike?' The girl was slender, with mousy-brown hair and a sweet face with a pointed chin and hazel eyes that looked kind but held a layer of...seriousness? Sadness? 'I saw you through the side window.'

Nancy smiled. If this was who she thought it was, she wanted to get off on the right foot. She didn't want any unpleasantness or competition. 'Are you Ginny Matthews?'

The girl uttered a small gasp. 'You mustn't call me that. It's against the rules. You have to call me Virginia.'

She stood back to let Nancy in. Nancy walked past her into a corridor as she closed the door.

'This way,' said Ginny – Virginia. She walked round a corner to where a long staircase stretched upwards into gloom.

Nancy caught her arm, bringing her to a halt. 'Tell me the rules about names. I don't want to make any mistakes.'

Ginny spoke softly. 'The benefactors who set up St Anthony's in the 1870s decreed that the girls must be called by their full names.'

'Mrs Abrams told me you were called Ginny.'

'She shouldn't really have done that, but she's such a kind lady.' Ginny glanced round, as if hordes of listeners might leap out of the woodwork. 'We use one another's shortened names when no one is around who might tell tales. The rule applies to the staff an' all. The benefactors were rich and their children were looked after by nannies helped by nursemaids, so that's what we have here too. The nursemaids are called Nurse So-and-So and it has to be their full name. I know for a fact that Nurse Philomena is called Philly at home, but she's Nurse Philomena when she's here.'

'My sister Lottie would be Charlotte. She'd hate that.'

'Lots of us hate it, but it's the rule. The boys are called by their surnames and if there's a family, the boys are Jones One, Jones Two and so on, in order of age.' Ginny glanced up the staircase. 'Miss Allan's waiting for us.' She waved Nancy ahead. 'After you.'

Trying not to clatter on the bare treads, Nancy went up, pausing at the top. There were no windows. One side was just wall, the other a corridor with closed doors. Ginny guided her round the newel post and along the passage towards an alcove illuminated by oil-lamps, where an elderly lady sat behind a dark-wood desk. Her cheeks had sagged with age, as had her neck, but the glint in her eyes dared you to underestimate her.

'This is Miss Pike,' said Ginny.

'Welcome,' the lady said in a voice that might just as easily have said, 'Put the sack of coal over there,' for all the warmth it contained. 'I am Miss Allan. Mrs Rostron is waiting for you.'

Nancy would rather have followed, but Ginny politely stood back to let her go first, nodding towards a closed door at the end of the passage. Nancy knocked and a low voice bade her 'Come.'

Mrs Rostron sat behind her desk, with her back to the window. She had a serious face and her hair was scooped up into a loose bun that looked like it might give way at any moment. Then Nancy realised there wasn't a single hair out of place. That so-called loose bun must be anchored in place by a host of hidden pins.

Although Mrs Rostron's desk was covered in files and papers, it was meticulously tidy. There were two seats for visitors, but she didn't invite the girls to sit. Ginny stood with her hands folded in front of her, so Nancy did the same.

'Miss Pike? How do you do? I'm Mrs Rostron, the orphanage superintendent. The two of you are here on probation. Depending upon how well you fulfil your duties, one of you will be chosen to remain permanently. The decision will be made at Christmas, so you have until then to make a good impression. Miss Pike, you may be aware that Virginia grew up here. In order that she doesn't have an unfair advantage, I'll ask Miss Allan to release you from your clerical duties regularly to start with, to allow you to spend time with the nursemaids and the children and familiarise yourself with our routines.'

Spend time with the children? Nancy perked up. 'Thank you. I'd like that.'

Mrs Rostron's eyebrows slid up her forehead. 'You'd like to be released from your clerical duties?'

Drat. 'I mean, I'd like to get to know the routines.'

'Hm. There is the question of what you are to be called. Ordinarily, you'd be Miss Pike and Miss Matthews, but Virginia is in rather an odd position, because she lives here. Should she fail to be chosen at Christmas, how could she cease to be Miss Matthews and return to being plain Virginia while we sought another post for her elsewhere? That wouldn't do at all. Therefore I've decided you'll be known as Miss Virginia and Miss – is Nancy short for Anne?'

'No, Mrs Rostron.' And may God forgive her for lying, but she had never been called Anne in her life and she wasn't going to start now.

'Miss Virginia and Miss Nancy,' said the superintendent. 'Remember, even though only one of you will be kept on after Christmas, the other will require a reference, so it is in your interests to acquit yourselves to the best of your ability. I know that I can rely upon Miss Virginia to do this. Can I rely on you also, Miss Nancy?'

It was the last week of September and Zachary had secured five orders so far that month. It didn't sound much, put like that, but each was for at least six extinguishers and all but one customer had signed up for an annual inspection. One had even requested annual training so that the staff didn't forget what to do, and Zachary decided to add this to the list of services he could provide.

He had an appointment to look forward to in early October, which had sprung from Mr Kenton's recommending him to a colleague in the hotel trade. This was the second time Mr Kenton had recommended him and that had sparked another idea.

'Would you kindly write a testimonial I could show to prospective clients?' he asked Mr Kenton. He felt embarrassed asking, but what the heck. He couldn't afford to be bashful where his business was concerned.

'Certainly,' said Mr Kenton. 'I'll recommend your sound advice and prompt service, as well as the quality of the training you provide.'

'Thank you.' Zachary was relieved as much as grateful that his request hadn't been considered inappropriate.

Mr Kenton smiled. 'I hope it's of assistance to you. It can't be easy setting up on your own.'

He was right about that, but the one person with whom Zachary would gladly have gone into business had copped it at Passchendaele. Zachary felt a pang of old sorrow. He would never stop missing Nate.

Might he secure another order before the end of September? On Tuesday he visited a potential client, whose interest made him look very promising. Zachary spent half a day talking about fire safety and going round his premises, explaining the best positions to site extinguishers, only for the fellow to say no at the end, leaving Zachary annoyed at having his time wasted but also worrying about what he had done wrong.

That evening, he did his paperwork, then went for a walk, as had become his habit. Sometimes he popped into the Bowling Green pub for a pint. He had done this enough times now to have struck up a few acquaintances and maybe a friendship or two would grow. It wasn't easy settling into a new place, but he hadn't wanted to live in his native Cheshire without Nate. Since returning from the war, Zachary had moved around a bit, doing various jobs and saving hard against the day he could start his own business. When he came here to Chorlton-cum-Hardy, he had known this was where he wanted to be.

It was a fine evening for a walk. Thank goodness for the dry spell. Imagine being stuck in his lock-up shop evening after evening with the rain drumming on the roof and streaming in curtains down the windows. He had soon found that the lock-up was a grim place to bunk down in. September had proved to be a glorious month of golden sunshine, but it was becoming chilly at night. Zachary knew that as the days shortened throughout October, he was going to feel less inclined to take an evening constitutional. There was nothing for it. The armchair he had dreamed of as a luxury to look forward to had become a necessity.

A shop on Beech Road sold second-hand furniture. It would be shut now, but he could look in the window. As he set off along Soapsuds Lane, a young woman left a house up ahead and went in the same direction, walking alongside Chorlton Green and turning the corner into Beech Road. A minute later, she stopped outside the second-hand shop, the same as he intended to. Zachary hung back, feeling self-conscious. If she had been aware of him behind her, she might get the wrong idea if he stopped at the shop. She stood close to the window and peered inside, then went on her way. Good.

Zachary went to the shop. The window display offered a chest of drawers with a matching china bowl and ewer on the top, a rocking horse, a selection of pots and pans, and a glass-fronted cabinet containing shelves of small items of jewellery and cutlery. A grandmother clock...a dining table... Was there an armchair anywhere? Then he saw a typewriter and a filing cabinet.

Forget the armchair. That office furniture was what he needed.

Talk about how the other half lived. In Wilton Close, they had a separate room just for dining – or it would have been just for that, if it hadn't been used for lessons in the evenings. And – Nancy hadn't known such things existed – they had a small breakfast room. Different rooms for breakfast and dinner! All the chairs matched and you couldn't call their plates crockery. Nay, they were real china. Nancy might never have seen china before, but she knew instinctively that that was what it was.

As for the indoor plumbing – well, it seemed like a magic trick to turn on taps and have water pour into the bath. Hot water an' all, and without having to boil the kettle over and over again. The privy was indoors as well, though, working class or not, she was too much of a lady to think about that in any detail.

She would have felt more at home if she had been their maid. Then at least she would have known what was expected. No one was unkind to her, or impatient, or anything other than civil and pleasant, but that was the nobs for you. Manners were everything. You didn't know what they were thinking about you, though, did you? She had already made a twit of herself by not knowing an egg-spoon from a teaspoon.

'Take your time and watch what the rest of us do,' Miss Patience quietly suggested afterwards when it was just the two of them; and that was jolly decent of her when you thought about it. Kind. Even respectful, in a way. Helping her out without showing her up.

If only Miss Allan were that sort of person, Nancy was sure she would gradually become more adept at clerical work. As it was, she soon despaired of making a good impression on the orphanage secretary. Far and away the best thing about St Anthony's was the children. She might be there to assist with the filing and the typing, but it was the children's company she liked best. Liked? Loved. It reminded her of school, where mothercraft had been her favourite lesson. There was something about children that brought her confidence to the fore.

She was meant to eat her dinner in the staff dining room, but she didn't. On her first day, when she had walked across the children's dining room, she had felt horribly self-conscious even though the room was largely empty, most of the children being at school. Just then, a small child began wailing. There were six children at the table, in the charge of a nursemaid who was occupied with mopping up a spillage, so Nancy grabbed a chair, plonked it beside the sobbing child and said in a cheery voice, 'Goodness me, what a racket. What's all this about?'

She had ended up remaining at the table and the grateful nursemaid, Nurse Carmel, asked for her meal to be brought to her, which suited Nancy far better than braving the staffroom.

After that, she sat with the smalls, as they were called, each day. She didn't ask anyone's permission, in case the answer was no. She just told Nurse Carmel it was important for her to get to know the children and left it to her to spread the word among the other nursemaids.

When Nanny Duffy stopped beside her at the table to say, 'I'm pleased to see you helping, Miss Nancy. It's important for the clerical staff to be familiar with the children,' she knew she could get away with not eating in the staff dining room – for now at least.

She adored eating with the smalls. Her heart leaped with delight the first time one of them called, 'Sit next to me, Miss Nancy.'

'No, next to me,' piped up another. 'It's my turn. Tell her it's my turn, Nurse Eva.'

If only Miss Allan could be that easy to win over! But she was a dour lady. If you performed a task correctly, that was simply what was required so she never spoke a word of praise, though woe betide you if you made a mistake. Had she been a teacher, she would have been one of those that was quick to reach for the ruler to rap you over the knuckles.

'It's just her way,' said Ginny as she and Nancy boxed up the information files on the children who had left over the summer. 'Wait.' She picked up a file Nancy had just added to a pile.

'That's the right pile.' Nancy's heart beat faster. 'L to Z.'

'You've put it on L to Z boys instead of L to Z girls.'

Heat crept into Nancy's cheeks. What a nincompoop she was. Ginny was a natural at clerical work.

'What was your other job like?' she asked.

'The old lady was dotty, but nice with it. I liked her, but it's not easy being a maid-of-all-work. You never stop. I was up early to open the shutters and get the fireplace ready and I couldn't go to bed until I'd cleared up after my mistress retired. She was a real night-owl.'

'It sounds tiring.'

'One of the good things about this job is not being tired all the time.'

'Was it hard coming back here to live?'

Ginny shrugged. 'I didn't have anywhere else to go. When the orphans leave here, we have to go to live-in jobs. Otherwise we'd have nowhere to sleep. I was lucky Mrs Rostron took me back. There, that's done.'

Ginny put the lids on the boxes and stood up, smoothing the blue skirt that was made from the same fabric as the nursemaids' uniform dresses. What would become of her if she didn't get this job? Would another position in service be found for her? That would be a shame, with her being so good at clerical work. Nancy would be happy for Ginny to be given the St Anthony's job...except that she herself would be then obliged to start all over again elsewhere. What was the likelihood of her getting another position that gave her the chance to be with children?

She thought of all the years she had spent at the pie shop, where she had been so happy. But now, she knew she had found her true place. How could she never have realised it before?

Chapter Nine

A FEW EARLY SHOPPERS were about as Prudence and Patience walked along Beech Road to the second-hand furniture shop on Saturday morning. One evening earlier in the week, Vivienne had spotted a typewriter and a filing cabinet through the shop window.

'Another typewriter would be most useful,' Prudence had declared at once, but it was frustrating to think that she wouldn't be able to go and try it out until the weekend. It was no use asking Patience to do it as she wasn't trained in typewriting.

But Patience came up with a good idea. 'I'll pop into the shop and reserve it. No, wait, I won't be able to get along there tomorrow morning and it's half-day closing.'

'Put a note through the door in the afternoon,' said Vivienne.

'I'm sure Mr Marchant will be happy to keep the typewriter for us until Saturday morning,' said Patience. 'He's very obliging.'

As the two of them walked along, children were out playing in the streets that led off Beech Road. What was it about playing in the street that was so enticing? These children were a stone's throw from the recreation ground. Why not play there? The scent of the privet hedge surrounding the rec was almost fruity at this time of year.

'It won't be long before the leaves start to fall,' Prudence observed.

'Don't wish the year away,' said Patience. 'Especially don't wish this fine weather away.'

Not so long ago, Prudence might have told Patience not to be daft, but now she had good cause not to wish the time away. Every moment spent with Vivienne was precious. That was why she had asked Patience to accompany her this morning – to make sure she didn't give too much attention to Vivienne. She mustn't single her out, much as she wanted to.

What was going to happen when Vivienne no longer needed to be a pupil-lodger? She was now part-way through the book-keeping course that was the most advanced skill Prudence taught and one to which only a handful of pupils aspired, but what would happen at the end of the course? Patience would, of course, expect Vivienne to look for alternative accommodation to make way for a new pupil-lodger. Prudence didn't know how she would bear it.

Crossing the road, she and Patience caught the delectable scent of freshly baked bread wafting out of the bakery on the corner and a uniformed constable emerged from the police station, touching his helmet to them. As they approached the second-hand shop, the laundry cart came along the road from the opposite direction, driven by a young man. He reined in the pony outside the second-hand shop and jumped down, though he didn't reach into the cart for a parcel. He was probably stopping to buy a barm cake for later from the bakery. He wasn't the usual delivery man. In fact, standards must be slipping at the laundry if they considered this to be suitable apparel for an employee to wear when out in public. Under his tweed jacket he wore a knitted pullover, and the lie of his collar suggested his top shirt-button was unfastened beneath the knot of his tie.

Prudence steered Patience towards the shop, surprised to find the young man heading the same way. He got there first, but, seeing them behind him, held the door open for them, the little brass bell jingling above their heads.

'Thank you.' Patience smiled as she passed him.

'Thank you.' Prudence didn't smile at strangers. She saved her smiles for special occasions. She nodded to him, doing one of her quick assessments. Not overly tall. Hazel eyes and sandy hair beneath the cap he touched to acknowledge her. A pleasant face. Not handsome, but open and frank. Good-natured. She followed Patience inside. 'Vivienne said they were on the right-hand side. Over there, look.'

The shop smelled of old wood, dusty upholstery and pipe-tobacco. In spite of its vast window, it was gloomy inside. Not even the reflection in a large mirror in its ornate gilded frame lent a gleam of brightness. Mr Marchant wasn't interested in such niceties as display. If he had it for sale, he stuck it in the shop, simple as that, and Prudence took care not to stub her toes while walking zigzag fashion across the floor, avoiding a piano-stool, a music canterbury, a heap of leather-bound suitcases, a variety of chairs, a tray of thimbles and a stuffed badger.

She looked across the shop to where Mr Marchant was standing. 'Good morning, Mr Marchant.'

'Morning, ladies. You've come about the office pieces, haven't you?'

'May I try the typewriter?' asked Prudence. 'I've brought a sheet of paper with me. We're interested in the filing cabinet as well.'

She slid the paper into the space at the back of the roller and turned the knob at the side without waiting for a reply. A figure appeared beside her – Mr Marchant, of course. She rattled out the standard sentence about the quick brown fox. Good. All the letters worked.

'Excuse me, but I'm interested in those items as well.'

Prudence looked round. It wasn't Mr Marchant beside her. It was the young man. She dealt him a hard look. His build was slim and wiry, but not weedy, and that pleasant face had taken on a determined look. She felt a stirring of interest. She couldn't be doing with the wishy-washy, the indecisive, the irresolute. After taking charge very effectively at a young age when Mother died, she had no time for ditherers.

'We aren't here by chance,' said Prudence. 'We reserved these items earlier in the week and have come today specifically to view them – and purchase them, if they are of sound quality – which the typewriter appears to be, Mr Marchant. Excuse me,' she added to the young man. 'I need to inspect the filing cabinet.'

He didn't budge. 'I've reserved them as well. That's why I've brought the pony and cart.'

'You must be mistaken,' said Prudence. 'Had you attempted to reserve them, Mr Marchant would undoubtedly have informed you that such a thing wasn't possible as the items were already spoken for.'

'I didn't talk to Mr Marchant in person. I put a note through the door on Wednesday afternoon.'

'As did I,' put in Patience.

Prudence turned to Mr Marchant. 'Which did you receive first?'

'I couldn't rightly say,' answered Mr Marchant. 'They were side by side on the mat. Perhaps if one of you took one piece and t'other t'other...'

'The typewriter is of more use to me,' said the young man.

'To us also,' said Prudence. 'Why do you require these things?'

'I've not long since set up in business, selling and maintaining fire extinguishers.' The young man brightened as he spoke. 'I've got a lock-up shop, but no furniture except for a counter and some shelves, and I've only got those because they're built in.'

'That must be inconvenient,' said Patience.

'It doesn't affect me most of the time, because I'm out drumming up custom. It's when I get back at the end of the day that I notice it. It would look more professional if I could send out typed letters and invoices instead of handwritten.'

'Undoubtedly,' Prudence agreed. 'Tell me, Mr...?'

'Milner. Zachary Milner.' He removed his cap.

'Do you know how to use a typewriter, Mr Milner?'

'I've never touched one in my life, but I can learn. I've had to learn all about fire extinguishers, so I'm sure I can get to grips with a typewriter...though it looks like I'll have to wait longer for the chance.'

'It can't be easy, being responsible for every single thing,' said Patience.

'That's the way of it when you start up.'

'Mr Milner,' said Prudence, 'I have a proposal to put to you. My sister and I run a business school, where we teach office skills. We will retire from the fray and leave these items for you to purchase.'

'That's jolly decent of you.'

'Kindly permit me to finish, young man. In return, we ask you to accept, at no cost to yourself, an hour's clerical assistance on two evenings a week from one of our pupils, who would benefit from clerical experience. What do you say?'

Nancy was certain that the only thing that enabled her to get through that first week of living in Wilton Close and working in the orphanage was the prospect of going home to see her family on Saturday. She had lain awake each night, imagining pouring out how hard it was to have been removed from her proper station in life and her parents turning to one another in shock.

'What were we thinking, sending our Nancy there? She were never fetched up to such things.'

'Nancy, love, we're that sorry. You must come home at once.'

But, when she went home on Saturday morning, it didn't happen like that at all.

'Imagine our Nancy having the chance to live in such a lovely home,' said Emily, with stars in her eyes.

Lottie tossed her head. 'As long as she doesn't get above herself.'

'Nay, lass, she'll never do that,' said Pa. 'She's a good girl, is our Nancy.'

'Lemon saws and pickle forks and sardine tongs.' Mam sighed. 'Eh, that takes me back, that does. We had all them things when I were in service. Do they have sandwich tongs an' all?'

'I don't know.'

'Fancy my lass living above stairs.'

'I'm not above stairs, Mam.' Nancy fought to keep the frustration out of her voice. 'They don't have above and below, not like you mean. Miss Patience does the light housework and she lets me help a little, and there's a daily called Mrs Whitney, who does the rough.'

When her descriptions of middle-class splendour failed to provoke the desired response, Nancy waited until the twins had been despatched downstairs to make a pot of tea and then played her trump card.

'The worst bit about living in Wilton Close is that they want me to call Mrs Atwood and Miss Lucy by their first names.' Nancy paused, waiting for a response.

Mam and Pa glanced at one another and Pa said, 'That's... unusual.'

'It's worse than unusual,' said Nancy. 'It's unnatural. It's not respectful.'

'But it must be respectable,' said Pa. 'The Miss Heskeths are real ladies. They wouldn't do owt that wasn't respectable.'

'What do they say about it?' asked Mam.

'Miss Patience told me when I moved in. She said that I was to call her Miss Patience and her sister Miss Hesketh at all times, but that they like to create a family atmosphere, so I should call Mrs Atwood and Miss Lucy by their first names, though never in front of other pupils.'

'And do you use their names?' asked Mam.

Nancy was shocked. 'No, I do not. I...I don't call them anything.'

Mam and Pa looked at one another again.

'I suppose it's like this Miss Patience says,' said Mam. 'It makes a cosier atmosphere. But don't mention it to the twins. We don't want them getting ideas. You know what they're like.'

Nancy trailed back to Wilton Close. She had set such store by her parents rescuing her and it had come to nowt. Ah well, she would just have to make the best of it.

But she had barely arrived before things became a lot worse. Miss Hesketh called her into the dining room, where Miss Patience was seated at the table. Nancy waited for Miss Hesketh to sit down before taking her place. Miss Patience smiled at her.

'You are aware, Nancy,' said Miss Hesketh, 'that we find places of work for our pupils, where they can gain relevant experience. The work is unpaid, but is nonetheless an important part of the training we offer.'

'But I'm already working at the orphanage to gain experience,' said Nancy.

'And now we've arranged for you to gain more,' was the implacable reply.

'You'll be working for a Mr Milner,' Miss Patience said in her kind voice. 'He is a pleasant young man, just starting out in life. He rents premises down Soapsuds Lane. I always think that's such a pretty name. It isn't its real name, but there has been a laundry there for donkey's years, so that is how it is known. Isn't that charming?'

Nancy thought of Bailiff's Row and said nothing.

'You're not to be anxious,' said Miss Patience. 'The work will be typewriting, nothing more.'

'Mr Milner has a letter he sends to prospective clients in the hope of piquing their interest,' said Miss Hesketh. 'Typewriting those will be straightforward because they are all the same, apart from names and addresses. Then there are letters confirming details of orders and training, followed in due course by invoices. The work will build your confidence.'

Build her confidence? Give her a fit of the vapours, more like.

'Normally, when we set up these positions for our pupils,' said Miss Hesketh, 'they are undertaken on Saturday afternoons when our girls generally are not at work; but because we know how important it will be for you to visit your family on Saturdays, you shall work for Mr Milner for an hour in the evening on Tuesdays and Fridays, after you finish at the orphanage, starting this coming Tuesday.'

Nancy's determination to make the best of things wobbled violently and nearly shattered. She wanted to do her best, she really did, but the thought of taking on a second job made tears rise behind her eyes and she had to blink them back. She would look a proper twit if she showed how churned-up she felt.

She nodded and tried to smile, then, with a mumbled 'Excuse me,' she rose and left the room. She felt as if she ought to be stumbling, but somehow she stayed upright. She needed to go to her bedroom and hide away for a while.

Miss Lucy was on her way upstairs. Nancy automatically glanced up – then looked again.

So *that* was why Miss Lucy was leaving here on Monday.

Chapter Ten

VIVIENNE LOVED SUNDAYS in Wilton Close. The Thorntons were in the hotel business and Vivienne had grown up knowing that there was no such thing as a day of rest. Now she relished her Sunday lie-in. It was only an extra hour, but, goodness, what a treat! She read for a while before getting up, creeping about the bedroom so as not to disturb Lucy, who was still asleep.

The girl stirred as Vivienne returned from the bathroom.

'Stay put,' Vivienne said softly. 'You're having breakfast in bed today, remember.'

Lucy smiled. 'Hiding from Nancy.'

'You can get up when she goes to church.'

Breakfast was a leisurely affair on a Sunday and they pushed the boat out by having boiled eggs and soldiers. Miss Patience had a knack for soft-boiling eggs to perfection, so that the white was firm while the yolk was gorgeously runny.

Before they started, Nancy looked at Lucy's empty place. 'Oughtn't we to wait?'

Vivienne smothered a smile. Nancy might think she was being discreet, but it was blindingly obvious that she had spent all week avoiding calling both her and Lucy by their names.

'Lucy is going to have breakfast in bed,' said Miss Patience.

Afterwards, Miss Hesketh invited Nancy to attend church with them.

'No, thank you.' Nancy's face went pink. 'I thought I'd go with my family.'

'Of course, Nancy dear,' said Miss Patience. 'I hope that seeing them yesterday hasn't made you homesick.'

'If it has,' said Miss Hesketh, 'you'd do better to spend the day here.'

'I'm fine, honestly.' Nancy got up. 'Excuse me. I'll get ready.'

She left the room hurriedly, as if the three of them might leap on her and not let her go. A minute later, she stuck her head around the door to say goodbye and off she went.

Vivienne laughed. 'Lucy and I needn't have arranged to go to Molly's for the day after all.'

'You'll still go, won't you?' said Miss Hesketh. 'Nancy won't be out all day.'

'Of course we shall. We aren't going just to keep Lucy out of sight. I'm going because Molly's my chum and you know how she likes to spend time with Lucy.'

The doorbell rang and they looked at one another.

'Who can that be at this time on a Sunday?' Miss Hesketh said disapprovingly.

'Perhaps Nancy forgot something.' Miss Patience was about to rise to her feet.

'Stay where you are,' said Vivienne, getting up. 'I'll answer it.'

She opened the door to find the telegram boy in his smartly buttoned uniform and peaked cap. Her heart gave an almighty thud and then seemed to sink all the way down through her body to the floor. It had been exactly like this when she had received word that her darling husband had been killed in action.

'Miss Hesketh?' asked the boy.

'I'll take it for her.' Vivienne started to hold out her hand, then had to clench it to stop it shaking before she tried again. 'Thank you.'

Shock and memories swirled inside her head as she took the telegram to Miss Hesketh, who quickly opened it.

'It's from Mrs Ayrton at Maskell House. I'm to telephone her urgently.'

'Good heavens,' breathed Miss Patience. 'I hope all is well. What a silly thing to say. They can't be well or there wouldn't be a telegram.'

'I'd better go straight to the newsagent's and make the call,' said Miss Hesketh.

'They won't like it,' said Miss Patience. 'They don't like calls being made on a Sunday.'

'Unfortunately, emergencies aren't confined to other days of the week,' Miss Hesketh said crisply.

'I'll come with you,' said Vivienne. Whatever had happened, she wanted to provide support. 'Miss Patience, why don't you stay here and look after Lucy? We shan't be long.'

They set off for the newsagent's, where the chilly expression on Miss Hesketh's face was all it took to make any objection to the telephone call crumble to dust. Miss Hesketh sat inside the little booth and placed the call. Vivienne would have dearly liked to squeeze in with her, but there wasn't room, let alone the fact that it would have looked highly singular for the lodger to take such a liberty. Sometimes it was extra hard having to keep their mother and daughter relationship secret.

Miss Hesketh emerged from the booth looking pale but not distressed. Vivienne waited to speak until they were outside.

'I'd rather not discuss it out here,' said Miss Hesketh, glancing at a couple of people who were coming towards the shop.

When they got home, Lucy was up and dressed.

'What's happened?' she asked.

'Let us get our coats off first and then we can talk about it,' said Miss Hesketh, handing her coat and hat to Miss Patience to put away.

'Please tell us,' said Lucy when they were all sitting down, 'or I'll burst.'

Miss Hesketh looked round at them. 'There has been an outbreak of sickness at Maskell House.'

'No,' whispered Miss Patience, lifting her fingers to her throat.

'Now you're not to imagine all the mothers and babies going down with the measles,' said Miss Hesketh. 'It's a sickness bug, vomiting and so forth. Very unpleasant and, of course, they have to take great care of the babies, but there's no reason to suppose anyone is in danger. The problem from our point of view is that we can't send Lucy tomorrow. Mrs Ayrton won't accept any new girls until the bug is gone and there has been no sign of its returning for a fortnight, just to make sure.'

'So Lucy can't go for a whole fortnight,' said Miss Patience.

'Longer,' replied Miss Hesketh. 'The bug has to run its course before the fortnight starts. Mrs Ayrton says we should expect Lucy to be able to go in three weeks.'

They all looked at one another.

'What are we to do with her until then?' asked Vivienne.

'For a start, she'll have to keep to the house even more than she is already, so that the neighbours don't get wind of what's going on,' said Miss Hesketh, 'though, frankly, that seems the least of our problems.'

'You mean Nancy,' said Miss Patience.

'I'd never have brought her here if I'd known Lucy would have to stay so much longer.'

'I could go to Molly's,' Lucy suggested. 'After all, she is going to adopt the baby.'

'You know how your father feels about that,' said Miss Hesketh. 'He's not at all happy about the child not being adopted by a middle-class family. He still intends to talk you out of it. He'd never agree to your staying with Molly and Aaron. That reminds me. He doesn't know about this. Mrs Ayrton should have sent the telegram to him, but mine was the first address that came to hand and she didn't realise her mistake until afterwards.'

'We have to tell Lawrence at once,' said Miss Patience, 'or he'll turn up tomorrow expecting to spirit Lucy away.'

'Another telephone call?' suggested Vivienne.

'If only it were that simple,' said Miss Hesketh, 'but if he gets a bee in his bonnet, he's likely to turn up here later, ranting about the plan going to pot. Besides,' she added darkly, 'you never know whether the operator is listening in. No, I'll have to go round to his house and tell him face to face. He goes to an early service, so we'll have plenty of time to talk it over and I can still be back in time for dinner.'

'That just leaves Nancy,' said Lucy.

'You'll have to carry on hiding away,' said Vivienne. 'I know it's a frightful bore, but there's no choice.'

'It is going to be a very long three weeks,' said Miss Hesketh.

Hurrying along the grimy cobbled streets of two-up two-downs with peeling paint and the occasional shattered window, Nancy turned the corner into Bailey's Row, known locally as Bailiff's Row because of its reputation for moonlight flits and hiding from the money-lenders. Other streets had corner shops that occupied a reasonable amount of ground, but the shop in Bailiff's Row's was crammed into the middle of the terrace, its narrowness echoed in the size of the flat above, where Nancy had grown up. Poor as the Pikes were, it said something for Pa that he had never inflicted a moonlight flit on them. They managed to keep their heads above water – just.

The tobacconist's shop was shuttered. Nancy pulled out her key and opened the door beside its entrance, stepping straight onto a staircase composed of bare treads that you had to be wary of, as several were loose and likely to tip up, sending your foot crashing through the resulting hole. How Mam had managed the stairs when Emily and Lottie were little was anyone's guess.

The boxed-in staircase stank of tobacco; and at the top, the flat reeked of it too. Aye, reeked. What had seemed like a background aroma when she had lived here now assaulted Nancy's nostrils as an outright pong. It couldn't be more different from number 4 Wilton Close, where the air had smelled of freshly laundered linen on Monday, and the rich aroma of beeswax every other day. Beeswax was used in the flat too, of course, and one of the twins' jobs was the weekly trip to the wash-house, but the Pikes' home, as Nancy now realised to her shame, smelled primarily of tobacco.

Was she ashamed of her home? She had been in Wilton Close barely five minutes. Had it spoiled her for her true station in life? Already? Panic streaked through her. She had to get herself back here as soon as possible.

'It's only me.'

Passing the curtained-off area where she used to sleep, she entered the parlour.

'Nancy, love, what are you doing here? Shouldn't you be at church?'

'I'll go later. How are you today?' As she bent to kiss Mam's cheek, she had all the answer she needed. There were grey smudges under Mam's eyes and that tell-tale paleness at her lower eyelids. 'Didn't you feel up to going out today?'

84

'You know, I don't feel so bad today; but, as Pa said, if I walk to church, it might knock me up, so I'm stopping indoors for a rest this morning and that'll help get me through the day.' Mam's eyes clouded. 'The reverend understands. He comes and has a prayer-time with me now and then. He's very kind.'

'Good old Rev Nev.'

'You shouldn't call him that. It's isn't respectful.'

'Mam, everybody calls him that except you. It just goes to show: if your name's Neville, you shouldn't go into the church.'

'Oh, our Nancy.' Mam was perking up. It got her down summat chronic, being stuck indoors so much; and it wasn't as though she had green lawns and flowerbeds to enjoy when she ventured out. 'It's better than a blood tonic to see you. What brings you here?'

'I've come to see you, of course. I thought if I came now, while the others are out, we could have a bit of time on us own.'

'Aye, I'll enjoy that. Run downstairs and pop the kettle on, there's a good girl.'

Nancy started for the door, then came back. She pulled the footstool closer.

'Are you sure you don't need to put your feet up?'

Mam sat forwards, her pale flesh suddenly ashen. 'What's wrong, love? And don't say it's nowt, because I can tell. You haven't come just for a chinwag, have you? Summat's wrong.'

Nancy sank onto the stool. She wanted to lean against her mother for comfort, but that might make Mam have to support her and even if the effort was only small, it would still take it out of her.

'I want to tell you about summat at Wilton Close and I could never say it in front of Pa. I'd die of embarrassment. And you wouldn't want it said in front of the girls either. They're too young.'

'Tell me.'

'I told you yesterday about the Miss Heskeths' niece that's stopping with them. She's called Lucy. She's nicely fetched up and has her clothes made specially for her and you can tell her hair has been cut by an expert.'

'She's not lording it over you, is she?'

'No. In fact, she wouldn't be in a position to, even if she felt like it. She's...' Heat scorched Nancy's face. 'She's in the family way.'

'And she's not wed?'

'No.'

Bright spots of colour touched Mam's cheeks. She pressed her lips together, nodding slowly. 'You've come home from the pie shop more than once with news that Mrs So-and-So's daughter has had to get married in a hurry.'

'I know; but I didn't think it happened to posh girls.'

'Oh, sweetheart, it can happen to anyone. It's not a class thing.'

'I s'pose not.'

'That sounds half-hearted.'

'Well, the Heskeths are meant to be our betters, aren't they?'

'And that means they should be above ordinary frailty?' Mam smiled. 'Life doesn't work that way, love. We all have the same problems and temptations. It's just that some folk have the money and the know-how to smooth things over for themselves.'

'Pa wouldn't like it, would he, if he knew there was an unmarried mother-to-be in Wilton Close?'

'I'm sure he wouldn't.'

'He'd take me away from there immediately.'

'Is that what this is about? You never wanted to go to that business school and now you've found a reason for Pa to take you away from lodging there.'

Nancy's head jerked back in surprise. Was she so transparent? 'I wouldn't say that.'

'I would. Listen, my girl. This is a chance for you to better yourself. I know it's shocked you that the Miss Heskeths are looking after their niece who's got herself into trouble, and it's come as a shock to me an' all, but you mustn't use it as a reason to turn your back on this opportunity. You mustn't.'

'But I don't belong there.'

'I know, chick, but it's only for now. Me and Pa would be so proud if you could find a better job. Imagine it, my lass an office girl.'

'I can't believe you're sweeping Miss Lucy's condition under the carpet. I thought you'd be outraged.'

'Do I want my daughter living under the same roof as a fallen girl? No, I don't. Do I want my daughter to have a chance to set herself up for life? Yes, I jolly well do. But I can't have it both ways. Are you going to let another's girl's mistake rob you of this chance? Or rather, are you going to let this Miss Lucy's mistake give you the excuse to run away? And there's summat else...' Mam's gaze ping-ponged about, landing everywhere but on Nancy's face – then suddenly focused on her with an intensity that made Nancy sit up straight. 'Why d'you imagine me and Pa got married so young? Way too young. No money, no nothing, and it's been a struggle ever since.'

Nancy's breath caught in her chest. 'You fell in love.'

'Aye, we did that, all right, fell good and proper.' Mam rubbed her forehead. 'Eh, I never thought I'd be telling you this.' Her hand dropped to her chest. 'My heart's fluttering like a trapped bird. Nay, leave me be. It has to be said. I were in the family way with you, that's why we got wed so young and that's why we don't acknowledge us wedding anniversary – in case folk look at that date, and look at your birthday, and do the sums.'

'You got married because of me?'

'Don't say it like it's your fault. If there's any fault, it's ours, because we couldn't keep us hands off one another. And I know you won't ask, but I don't regret it. I don't regret getting married and I don't regret having you so young. You're the light of my life.'

'Oh, Mam.'

'You have to understand, our Nancy, your own mam is in no position to judge the young lady at the Miss Heskeths'. And if you make a judgement against her, you'll be making a judgement against me an' all. You aren't going to do that, are you, love? You're not going to think badly of your poor mam?'

Nancy returned to Wilton Close, still reeling from Mam's revelation. She had never thought of it before, but now she realised she couldn't remember her parents mentioning their anniversary, still less celebrating it. Not that the Pikes had the wherewithal for an actual celebration, but even poor folk like them could raise a cup of tea to one another in acknowledgement of a special occasion. Nancy pressed a hand to her heart as gratitude surged up inside her. Bless Mam for calling her the light of her life. There must be plenty of oldest children in her position who were regarded by their parents as the start of everything going wrong. Things had always been tough for the Pike family. Marrying so young, and with Mam's uncertain health, they had never had sixpence to scratch themselves with.

When Nancy walked into the house, the Miss Heskeths and Mrs Atwood were in the sitting room and there was a definite atmosphere. There was no sign of Lucy and Nancy knew why.

'I'd better get on with dinner,' said Miss Patience. 'The chicken's in the oven, but I haven't touched the vegetables yet.'

Mrs Atwood stood up. 'Nancy and I will do the dinner.'

Nancy followed her out of the room. When she helped set the table, Mrs Atwood scooped up the cutlery Nancy had put in front of Miss Lucy's place.

'Not needed,' was all she said. She smiled, but her smile was brittle and that wasn't like her.

Suddenly Nancy knew. She just knew.

'It's the baby, isn't it?'

'What baby?'

'Miss Lucy's baby.'

'Oh, cripes. Wait here.' Mrs Atwood disappeared into the sitting room. A minute later, she called, 'Come through.'

Feeling like the naughtiest child in the school, taking the doom-laden walk to the headmaster's office, Nancy obeyed.

'Please sit down, Nancy dear,' said Miss Patience.

'What do you know?' demanded Miss Hesketh.

'Nothing.'

'You mentioned a baby.'

Nancy wasn't defiant exactly, but she felt the need to speak up for herself. 'If there's one thing a back-street lass can do, it's recognise a girl that's in the family way when she sees one. You shouldn't have let me move in if you didn't want me to know.' How stroppy she sounded! Just like their Lottie in a frap.

Miss Hesketh's narrow eyebrows lifted. 'Indeed?' She looked at her sister. 'I believe we've just been put in our place.'

'I'm sorry.' Nancy was mortified.

'We didn't want you to move in until after Lucy had left,' said Miss Patience, 'but when the orphanage post came up, this was the best place for you.'

'And you and Lucy were only supposed to overlap until tomorrow morning,' said Mrs Atwood.

Nancy experienced a twinge of alarm. 'Summat's happened, hasn't it? Is Miss Lucy all right?'

Silence fell as the other three looked at one another.

'She's never lost the baby?' Nancy whispered.

All at once, that was the only thing that mattered. Her discomfort at living here evaporated, as did her distaste at the posh folk trying to hide their mucky secret. All she cared about was poor Lucy and her baby. Her heart filled with compassion.

'I'm not being nosy and I'm not…' She remembered Mam's words. 'I'm not judging her.' Or you, she might have added, but didn't.

Another silence. More looks were exchanged between the other three.

'Thank you for taking such a generous attitude towards our family's shame,' said Miss Hesketh. 'Lucy has let a lot of people down, not least herself, but we couldn't turn our backs on her.'

'Of course you couldn't,' said Nancy. 'No one would on their own lass. Leastways, some folk do and the poor girl has a terrible time.'

'Lucy was meant to go to a mother and baby home tomorrow,' Miss Patience explained, 'but there is illness there at present, so she must remain with us a little longer.'

'Which will be a great deal easier now that you are aware of the situation,' said Mrs Atwood.

'Assuming that you wish to stay,' said Miss Hesketh. 'We fully intended to pull the wool over your eyes when we brought you here and we shall, of course, understand if you would prefer to move back home.'

And here it was – the perfect reason to leave. An invitation to leave, no less. She could go home to Mam and say the Miss Heskeths were happy for her to return home, that they recognised that Wilton Close wasn't the right place for her under the circumstances. It had nowt to do with what had happened in Mam's past, nowt to do with Nancy passing judgement on anybody. It was the Miss Heskeths judging themselves.

But somehow it didn't sit right with her.

'No,' she heard herself say. 'You don't turn your back on someone that needs help. It might not matter to you whether I'm here or not, but it matters to me. Miss Lucy has done a wrong thing, but so have plenty of other girls and the last thing any of them needs is someone walking out on them. It would be unkind, so I'll stop here, if it's all the same to you.'

Chapter Eleven

B Y THE TIME Tuesday came round, Nancy had talked herself into feeling better about this new job. It was only a couple of hours a week and it might be good for her to do some typewriting without the fear of Miss Allan breathing down her neck. Besides, if this Mr Milner was just starting out in business, then presumably he wouldn't exactly be snowed under with orders, so there wouldn't be vast amounts of typewriting to do and she would be able to take her time over it.

That evening, when she left St Anthony's, she headed for Soapsuds Lane. Miss Patience had told her how to get there and she had taken the precaution of popping round there on Sunday afternoon. Now it was twilight and the lamplighter was on his rounds, stopping beneath each lamp-post and using the hook on the end of his pole to open the hinged pane of glass and tweak the chain that started the gas supply. Nancy walked down the side of Chorlton Green, her heart picking up speed as the end of Soapsuds Lane came into view across the road from the brick wall that surrounded the old graveyard, with the tower over its lych-gate.

Along Soapsuds Lane stood a cart, its pony waiting patiently while a young man unloaded something. This must be Mr Milner and the things must be fire extinguishers. He carried them through the open door of his shop two at a time.

When she arrived outside, the cart was empty and Mr Milner had his back to her as he put his key in the lock. Should she wait for him to turn round? No, that might make her look like a helpless girl who stood around waiting for things to happen. It was important to look capable, even though she felt a bit quivery with nerves.

'Excuse me,' she said. 'Mr Milner?'

He turned to her – and her heart did a little tap-dance. Mr Milner had hazel eyes and, beneath his bowler hat, she could make out sandy hair. He looked old enough to have done his duty for King and country and lucky enough not to have been gassed or badly injured. He had an energy about him that said he was a grafter. Nancy's internal quivers changed to a different sort of fluttering. It was the first time she had ever responded like this to a man.

'Miss Pike? You're earlier than I was expecting.'

Was that a bad thing? 'Only a few minutes.'

'You can wait here or you can come with me to take Jerry back to the laundry.'

'I'll come with you.'

Mr Milner went to the pony's head, patting its neck and rubbing its muzzle in a way that made Jerry toss his head and whicker. 'C'mon then, boy. Let's go home.' He slid a finger under the bridle and Jerry was happy to be led in this casual fashion along the lane.

They came to a long, low building that must be the laundry. At any rate, the pony didn't need any prompting to walk down the side and into a large yard at the rear, with a tatty-looking stable in one corner, next to an open-sided wooden shelter, which was presumably where the cart was housed. A whiff of straw made Nancy's eyes prickle. A boy appeared, greeting Mr Milner or Jerry or possibly both of them with a grin.

Mr Milner dug in his pocket and produced, of all things, a white paper bag, like you got in sweet shops. He took out something small and white and held it on the flat of his hand for Jerry to help himself. Honestly, he was paying more attention to that dratted pony than he was to her.

'He likes his mints, does our Jerry,' said the stable-lad.

Turning his back to her, Mr Milner murmured something to the boy. Then, in a normal voice, he said, 'He deserves a good rub down. He's been all the way to Fallowfield today. I need a word with Mr Rutledge to see about hiring him again.' He glanced at Nancy. 'Excuse me.'

'You his girl?' asked the lad.

'No!' Was the boy a mind-reader? 'I'm the clerical help.'

'He must be doing well, if he can afford help already.'

'I don't discuss the boss's business.'

Instead of being crushed, the boy grinned. 'D'you like horses? Come and say how do to Jerry. He's not a horse, mind. He ain't big enough. He's a pony. Don't worry. He's friendly – especially if you've got a treat for him.'

He vanished inside the rickety stable, reappearing with a piece of carrot. Jerry shifted, stamping a hoof on the cobbles, tossing his head in a show of interest.

'Here.' The boy held out the carrot to Nancy. 'Not you, cheeky.' He batted away Jerry's muzzle. 'Hold your hand out flat – like this – and let him take it.'

It hardly seemed appropriate when she was meant to be at work. But Mr Milner wasn't here, besides which hadn't he given Jerry a mint? Hooking her handbag over her arm, Nancy drew off her glove and stretched her hand so flat she almost bent her fingers backwards as she offered the carrot. Jerry's head made an arc in her direction and she stepped back.

'Don't pull away,' warned the lad.

She held her hand out properly. How safe were her fingers from Jerry's teeth? The pony's muzzle closed in on her palm. His breath was warm and snuffly and damp, his lips unexpectedly gentle and tickly as he took the carrot and chomped it down.

Nancy laughed, suddenly comfortable. 'May I stroke him?'

'He'll like that.'

'Right-o, I'm off back to the shop.'

There was Mr Milner, looking ever so smart and business-like in his suit and bowler; and here she was, snuggling up to the blessed pony. What must he think? His next words answered that question.

'I'll see you there later, Miss Pike, when you've finished playing at stable-lads.'

Her mouth dropped open. She had never been spoken to like that in the pie shop. But now, in Mr Milner's eyes—

He grinned and cocked an eyebrow in the boy's direction. 'Well, Oswald?'

'Passed with flying colours, Mr Milner.' Oswald gave a chirpy nod. 'Jerry likes her an' all.'

'Shall we go, Miss Pike?'

Mr Milner headed out of the yard. Nancy put on a little spurt to catch up. Mr Milner wasn't a longshanks with a ground-eating stride, but he set a brisk pace.

He unlocked the shop door and waved her inside.

'Oh.' The sound was surprised out of her.

'What is it?' He closed the door behind them.

'I were expecting shelves full of fire extinguishers, but all there is, is those that you brought indoors a few minutes back.'

'Aye, and they shouldn't be here.'

'Why not?'

He shut his eyes for a moment. Was it a stupid question? Her spine stiffened. She couldn't be expected to know about the fire extinguisher business. It wasn't in her nature to give cheek, but it was time to stand up for herself.

'Mr Milner, I don't know if you're aware of it, but I used to work behind the counter in the pie shop. I didn't fire up the oven and I didn't do the baking, but I did know how those things were done, and knowing made me a better shop worker. I don't know why it did, but it did. So if you want me to do the best I can here, it'd help if you told me a bit about the business. I shan't blab it to all and sundry, if that's what you're worried about.'

To her surprise, he smiled, reducing her heart to mush. 'I'm sure you won't. You've already passed that test.'

'You what?' The mush solidified.

'Before I went to see Mr Rutledge, I had a quiet word with young Oswald in the yard and asked him to pump you for information.'

'So that's why...'

'Aye. It was too good an opportunity to miss. I wanted to see if you'd tell him you're working for me for nowt. It wouldn't do my business reputation much good if that got round. You look offended.'

Was it wrong to take offence at being tested? Nancy smoothed her expression. 'You could simply have had a conversation about confidentiality.' Miss Hesketh had hammered it into her how important this was.

'But I couldn't, could I? I never had the chance. You aren't here because you applied for a paid position. You aren't here because I interviewed you and selected you as the best candidate.'

A sheen of heat settled over her face. 'I know I'm here to get experience, but it's to your advantage an' all.'

'Let's hope so. The real reason you're here, Miss Pike, is because it's the only way I could get my hands on a typewriter and filing cabinet.'

What an oaf. How could he have spoken so bluntly to poor Miss Pike? It wasn't her fault she had been foisted onto him and it certainly wasn't her fault he had had such a pig of a day. Zachary lay awake under the counter. He would make his peace with Miss Pike on Friday when he saw her next. Poor girl, he couldn't have her dreading coming here. He, of all people, understood what it was to be starting out and if she was trying to better herself by learning to be an office girl, she deserved encouragement.

By, he could do with a spot of encouragement himself. He had known it wouldn't be plain sailing when he set up in business, but it was turning out to be harder than he had anticipated. Take the matter of training people to use extinguishers. He had arrived to train the staff at one hotel, only to be told that half the staff were available today and he must make a separate appointment to train the other half.

'It's not my fault if you were daft enough to think all the staff could stop work and be trained at the same time,' said the proprietor. 'And no, I'm not paying you to come back a second time. You quoted me a fee to train my staff and I'm keeping you to it.'

Lesson learned. He wouldn't make that mistake again.

Then there had been the occasion when he trained the workers in a small factory.

'Yes, you can train 'em all in one go,' said the manager, 'as long as it doesn't take too long.'

But when the training took place, one worker was absent because he had gone to a funeral.

'He still needs training, though,' said the manager. 'You'll have to come back another time. What? Pay just to have one bloke trained? Come off it!'

'But...'

'Be reasonable, lad. You can see I'm not trying to pull a fast one, can't you?'

Well, yes, he supposed he could; but that didn't make it any easier to give unpaid training to the bereaved worker.

Thereafter, both of these possibilities had to be included when Zachary explained to customers about training. Did it make him look like a nit-picker? But he couldn't afford to be caught out again.

After that, there was the hotel proprietor who ordered brass extinguishers, which Zachary had duly purchased, but when he went to install them, Mr Savage wanted to change to chrome. Panic had streaked through Zachary, but he held his voice steady.

'I'm sorry, Mr Savage, but it's too late to change your mind. You ordered brass extinguishers and I've provided them in good faith.'

He held his breath. Would Mr Savage cut up rough?

But Savage shrugged. 'Oh well, it was worth a try.'

Worth a try? Mr Savage didn't seem bothered either way and certainly gave no indication of realising how he had almost caused Zachary's hair to turn white. Zachary had felt rattled for the rest of the day. That was something else he was going to have to make clear to customers, that once their order was placed, it couldn't be altered.

'You're full of ifs and buts, aren't you?' commented a customer.

'I have to be.' He tried to laugh it off.

'And you seemed such a cheerful bloke when you arrived.'

Why was nothing straightforward? Why weren't people straightforward? Well, many were, of course, but he seemed to get more than his fair share of the other sort buying fire extinguishers off him.

And then there was what had happened today. It had put him sufficiently out of sorts that he had ended up being disagreeable to Miss Pike. And he wasn't a disagreeable person. He knew he wasn't. Was that the problem? Did his frank manner and transparent honesty make sharper, more artful people feel it was worth their while trying to take advantage? But if he wasn't pleasant and obliging, no potential customer would give him the time of day.

On Friday, he made sure he was back at the lock-up in good time before Miss Pike was due. It was going to be deuced inconvenient if he had to come hurrying back each time to let her in. He would have to lend her his spare key. Or maybe, after the way he had spoken to her on Tuesday, she wouldn't return. Then again, she probably had no option. He couldn't imagine the formidable Miss Hesketh letting either of them off the hook.

The door opened – he must attach a little bell above it – and in she came. She was a slender girl, undersized in the way poor folk were, which stopped her looking well-to-do, no matter how beautifully cut that jacket was. She approached the counter with her head held high. Good for her. Her hair was a rich auburn, her skin fair. She would be a nice-looking lass if she had a bit more flesh on her bones. Not that he had any time to be thinking about lasses while he had a business to set up.

'Good afternoon, Mr Milner. What would you like me to do today?' As if she had acquired a thousand skills and he could take his pick.

'I'd like you to sit down while I say something.'

He indicated for her to come behind the counter. When he had purchased the typewriter and filing cabinet, he had also bought a tall stool to sit on to type. Miss Pike perched on it, hands folded in her lap, her handbag dangling from her wrist, her expression attentive as she awaited instructions. He had shifted his rolled-up mattress and makeshift pillow from under the counter, to hide the fact that he slept there.

'Yes, Mr Milner?'

How to start? Oh heck, just get on with it.

'Real men don't apologise,' he said.

'Don't they?'

'Not according to my father. He often said that to my brother and me when we were growing up. Apparently, an apology makes you look weak.'

'Oh.'

'But I disagree. An arrogant man, my father. I don't want to be like him. I don't know why I'm going all round the houses like this. What I want to tell you is that I apologise wholeheartedly for my manner on Tuesday. I was blunt, to say the least, and I'm afraid I was downright rude. I'd had a rotter of a day and, to cap it all, it made me late getting back here instead of being in the shop before you arrived. I know that's no excuse for my manner, but it's all I can offer, other than the assurance that I'm not usually like that.'

She smiled and her shoulders relaxed. Zachary realised her smile changed her whole face.

'Thank you,' she said simply. 'What made it such a horrid day?'

'I had an order from a hotel near the station and I bought the necessary extinguishers, but then it turned out the hotel was owned by two brothers. The brother I dealt was over-ruled by the other one, who'd been away when the order was placed.' He glanced at the extinguishers he had been obliged to bring back here on Tuesday. 'That left me with those extinguishers and nobody to sell them to.'

'But if the first brother agreed to buy them, then...?'

'Then what?' asked Zachary. 'I can't force someone to buy my services, even if they start off by saying they will. According to the second brother, the first one had no business making such an important decision when he wasn't there. When you were here before, you talked about wanting to understand the business. Well, this is how it works. I get orders from my customers and I buy the fire extinguishers from the supplies warehouse in town. If and when my business gets established, I'll be able to purchase on account and pay at the end of the month; but that's a long way off. For the foreseeable future, I have to pay on the spot, out of my own pocket.'

'So you have to pay up well before your customer pays you.'

'It makes money very tight for me, but I have to look confident and well-to-do or my customers won't believe in me.' Zachary glanced at the extinguishers on the shelf. 'What I need now is to find another customer as quickly as I can, and not only that but one who wants chrome extinguishers. Most want brass. I did have a customer who ordered brass, a Mr Savage, but then he wanted chrome instead when it was too late for me to change. I wondered about offering him a straight swap, but if I did, the extinguishers I took back from him, even unused, would technically be second-hand, and if word got round that I was dealing in second-hand extinguishers...' He huffed a breath. He felt he had acquitted himself well in his apology and explanation. That was another thing real men didn't do: explain. Giving Miss Pike a smile, he held out his right hand. 'Shall we start again? I'm pleased to meet you, Miss Pike. Welcome to Milner's Fire Safety Services.'

Chapter Twelve

I T WAS SURPRISING how things could turn around. Instead of leaving her shocked and disapproving, finding out about Lucy's pregnancy had made Nancy feel more at home in Wilton Close. She and Lucy had become – well, if it hadn't been that they came from different social classes, Nancy might have said they had become friends, but things being the way they were, she wouldn't dream of taking that liberty.

Nancy tried not to let it show, but she was fascinated by the idea of the proposed adoption.

'It's completely different to what would happen in the back-streets,' she told Lucy. 'Where I come from, either the young couple would be marched up the aisle quick smart or else the girl would bear the shame for the rest of her life and the best she could hope for would be a big-hearted chap to come along, who would take on her and her brat and never hold it against either of them – I'm sorry. I don't mean to call your child a brat.'

'My family is in the fortunate position of being able to make my problem disappear.'

'Money solves a lot of problems,' said Nancy. 'It doesn't seem fair, does it?'

'It's the way things are,' said Lucy. She might say her family was fortunate, but Nancy didn't think she truly understood it and what it meant. It was the have-nots who best understood that kind of thing, not the haves.

Something else that fascinated Nancy, but which she couldn't bring herself to talk about, was Lucy's refusal to name the father, which was the maddest thing Nancy had ever heard of. Apparently, it was because Lucy wasn't in love with him. Well, if that was the case, what on earth had she been up to, getting herself into *that* situation? You heard of lads and lasses getting carried away. Was that what had happened to Lucy? Nancy recalled how her own skin had tingled in Zachary's presence. Was that how it started? Was that the first step to getting carried away?

Zachary! She knew his name because she had to type *Z Milner Esq* on his letters and she had asked, 'Excuse me, but is this really a Z?' because she didn't want to make a mistake – yes, all right, and she had seized the chance to find out his first name an' all – and he had told her it stood for Zachary.

'That's unusual,' she had commented, but he hadn't asked her for her first name.

Even the thought of him made her heart beat faster. Each night she tumbled into bed and indulged in daydreams in which his feelings matched hers. She had a key to his shop now, so she could let herself in if he wasn't there. She had felt glad at first because it meant he trusted her, but then she realised it meant she couldn't rely on seeing so much of him – and an hour twice a week hadn't been much to start with. But she refused to be downhearted. These new feelings were wonderful and exciting and she wanted to enjoy every moment – yes, even the painful little tug she felt each time Zachary looked at her, making her wish with all her heart that he felt the same.

She might not have wanted to join the business school and become an office worker, but it had brought Zachary into her life, which just showed that you never knew when something good was going to happen. Her favourite daydream was that Zachary's business did really well and he offered her a job with him after Christmas.

But that was just a dream and for now it was important to do as well as she could at St Anthony's. She knew she must work harder if she were to impress Miss Allan. As a start, instead of just lapping up the time she spent with the children, she would do summat constructive with the time. That should make Miss Allan look more favourably on her.

One afternoon, when Miss Allan, with a sigh and a roll of her eyes, gave her permission to go downstairs to spend time getting to know the orphanage, Nancy set herself up in a corner of one of the common rooms and helped some of the younger children with their reading, giving ten minutes to each child. Years ago, when the twins started school, she had listened to them reading. It had helped them, and helped Mum an' all, because it gave her the chance of an uninterrupted sit-down. Rests had been few and far between after Lottie and Emily came along.

Miss Allan pounced on her the moment she reappeared upstairs, demanding to know where she had been and what she had done.

'I've been helping some of the youngsters with their reading,' said Nancy, trying not to sound pleased with herself.

'Is that all?' said Miss Allan. 'When Mrs Rostron gave permission for you to have time away from your clerical duties, it was for you to familiarise yourself with our rules and routines, not to play at being a teacher. That isn't what you're here for.'

A chill ran through Nancy at the thought of being deprived of her time with the children. Later, she trailed home feeling tearful.

Miss Patience took one look at her and settled her in the sitting room, her gentle face filled with concern. 'My dear child, what's wrong?'

'It's nowt, honestly.' She tugged at her collar. Miss Patience had far more important things to worry about.

'Have you made another clerical error? A little more concentration would work wonders, you know.'

A little more concentration? If only it were that simple. Why did everybody treat her as if she wasn't trying hard enough? As if it was her own fault she wasn't doing better?

Nettled, she explained. 'I thought I was doing a good thing by helping with the reading, but now Miss Allan thinks I'm a slacker.'

'You can't really blame her, can you?' said Miss Patience, causing Nancy's eyes to pop open in astonishment. Was Miss Patience taking Miss Allan's side? 'I don't mean to be unfeeling, but reading is done with one child at a time, so you can see how this might make you appear to be taking advantage – even though you aren't, of course. We should put our heads together and think of an idea for you to use with a group of children. What about sewing?'

'The girls are taught dressmaking and mending.'

'And you mustn't tread on anyone's toes. I see that, but what if you led a sewing project? Something simple that wouldn't take too much time and that they could get on with on their own. All you'd have to do is start them off.'

'I like the idea, but what about the fabric?' She wasn't going to have to pay for it herself, was she?

'Not to worry.' Miss Patience smiled as she rose. 'I have my off-cuts box. In fact, I have two boxes. Let's plunder those.'

Nancy started to say, 'I couldn't.'

'You know how it is with off-cuts. You keep them, thinking they'll come in handy, but they seldom do.'

Miss Patience led the way into the hall, where she opened the cupboard under the stairs and drew out a large cardboard box and plonked it in Nancy's arms before taking another from the shelf. They opened them on the dining table, revealing a selection of pieces in a variety of materials, some patterned, some plain.

'This is pretty.' Nancy picked out a piece of pink cotton festooned with daisies.

Miss Patience sighed. 'That's my trouble. I love pretty things, but they don't love me. I made myself a blouse from this three or four years ago, but my sister didn't approve. Mutton dressed as lamb, you see. In the end, I gave it to our charwoman for her daughter. She got married in it, actually, so it was put to good use.' Another sigh, then she roused herself. 'What could the girls make from off-cuts? It has to be something small.'

And, just like that, the idea popped into Nancy's head. 'Christmas stockings. It's the middle of October now, so that gives plenty of time for everyone to make one who wanted to. Not full-sized ones, but little ones, about six inches long. Decoration-sized, with a loop for hanging. A keepsake to remind them of St Anthony's when they're grown-up and have Christmas trees of their own to hang the stocking-decorations from.' Anxiety tingled through her. 'Does that sound silly?'

'It's a charming idea.'

'I'll make a template out of card and I'll make a stocking so the children can see what the finished thing will look like.' She felt a flutter of hope. 'Thank you for helping me.' Not allowing herself time to think, she leaned across and kissed Miss Patience, then wondered how she had dared; but Miss Patience touched her cheek and flushed a little, looking pleased.

Christmas stocking decorations. The thought delighted Nancy and it inspired her to think again about the children's reading. She wanted to make a success of it – but how? Then she remembered her mothercraft lessons and how much the tinies had loved being read to. What if she encouraged the older children to read to the little ones? But some of the older girls did that anyway and it might look like she was interfering. Besides, she needed to think of summat new, that hadn't been done at the orphanage before; and summat that would impress Miss Allan and Mrs Rostron, which meant that it had to be linked to learning – but it also must be enjoyable or the children wouldn't be interested.

What if she expanded the idea of older girls listening to younger children reading? What if each young child was paired with an older one and they shared a story just for ten minutes a day? They could take turns to read a page each or the older one might read the story all the way through before the young one had a go. As well as helping the little ones learn to read, it would build relationships between the age groups.

Some of the older girls were happy to join in, but when Nancy tried to recruit the older boys, she didn't get far.

'Nah, that's sissy,' said Layton Two and he wasn't the only one.

Then Layton One who went to school in the mornings and worked half-time in the afternoons said he wouldn't mind having a go. To Nancy's delight, this led to a scramble among the other lads all offering to help out.

Layton Two came to Nancy. He stood in front of her, bouncing the toe of one shoe on the floor. 'You know this reading malarkey? I might as well have a go.'

Nancy swallowed a smile. Ginny had told her how Layton Two had made a bad start at St Anthony's but had now turned over a new leaf and looked up to Layton One, who was a good example to follow.

What with the shared reading and the Christmas stock-ings, Nancy felt she was a part of the orphanage in a way she hadn't been before. It was impossible not to feel pleased with herself, though she was careful not to let it show. She didn't want to appear big-headed. Besides, what did she have to be big-headed about? When Christmas came and Mrs Rostron had to choose between her and Ginny, it would be Ginny's skills that were rewarded, not Nancy's imagination.

Nancy opened her handbag and took out her key to unlock Zachary's shop, almost as if the place was hers and she had her own typewriting business. How daft! She picked up the letters from the mat and popped them on the counter. Zachary had left some work for her. As well as polite letters of introduction about Milner's Fire Safety Services, there was an invoice to produce, which he had written out in clear handwriting that was easy to read.

She reached under the counter for a fresh sheet of paper. She had bought a dozen sheets, which she had added to Zachary's small pile. It was a way of hiding her mistakes, a sort of insur-ance policy. If she made a real pig's whisker of a letter, she could now re-do it without worrying about using up Zachary's precious paper. It was funny in a way. She was meant to be working here for nothing, but this meant she was paying for the privilege. It was yet more proof of how unsuited she seemed to be to this kind of work, no matter how hard she tried.

She looked over her shoulder to check the clock on the wall. Ten to seven. What was she supposed to do if Zachary didn't return? Stay late? Lock up? But the door opened and he walked in, bringing in a waft of freshness that was more than just the keen evening air. It was partly a sense of the cordiality that was so much a part of his make-up.

Zachary picked up the letters from the counter.

'Excellent!' he exclaimed. 'Not one but two postcards in response to my letters, asking me to call, which will be much easier than calling on people who haven't invited me. This one says "at your earliest convenience". I can't tell you how good that makes me feel. It isn't easy turning up uninvited on someone's doorstep, even if you have written in advance.'

'But you have the right sort of manner for it.' She had barely got the words out before she drew a breath of horror. 'I don't mean to be cheeky. It's not my place to say things like that.'

'Don't apologise for paying a compliment.'

That gave her courage. 'It's not a compliment. It's true. You're naturally friendly, but without overdoing it. I can picture you behind the counter in the pie shop, getting along with all the customers.'

'Behind the counter in the pie shop? Now I know it's a genuine compliment.'

Was he laughing at her? No, he wasn't. He was being good-natured. He must be ever so good at his job. He had such a pleasant way about him.

'Your family must be proud of you for doing this.' She waved a hand to indicate the shop.

Zachary looked down at his mail again. Had she said the wrong thing? But then he looked up.

'Possibly.'

Nancy thought of the father who had told his sons it was weak to say sorry. 'I didn't mean to pry.'

Now his smile was genuine. 'You're not prying. It's a natural assumption to make. I don't have much in the way of family, to tell you the truth. My late mother was an only child and both of my father's brothers emigrated to Canada years ago. During the war, Dad married a woman I'd never met.'

'While you were away fighting, you mean? That must have felt strange when you came home.'

'A lot of things felt strange. I – I left my brother behind in Flanders, if you know what I mean.'

The breath caught in Nancy's throat as she instinctively reached out a hand towards him. Fortunately, he didn't notice or he would have thought her forward and she drew it down by her side.

'Were you older or younger?' she asked softly.

'Older – by ten whole minutes.'

'You're a twin? My younger sisters are twins.'

'Being a twin is the best thing in the world – until suddenly you're on your own. Those ten minutes were all-important when we were lads. I was the big brother trying to make him toe the line, but he wouldn't have it, of course.' Zachary laughed, though there was sadness in his eyes. 'I never quite grew out of feeling that I was older and it was my job to protect him.' He swallowed hard, then he lifted his chin and looked her straight in the eye. 'Losing Nate was the worst thing that ever happened to me.' He looked around at the shop. 'He should have been here with me, doing this.'

The words 'You mustn't feel guilty about it' were on the tip of Nancy's tongue, but she changed them to, 'Does it make you feel guilty?'

When he looked at her, the bleakness in his eyes was replaced by warmth. 'Thank you for that.'

'For what?'

'Usually I get told not to feel guilty. I did feel that way for a long time. I had to learn that I mustn't let losing Nate hold me back. That was tough to accept, because it was a kind of letting go.'

'It must have hurt.'

'It did.'

Nancy's heart yearned towards him. 'What about your father and stepmother?'

'Nate and I never really got on that well with Dad, to tell you the truth. Mum was the one who held us all together.'

'And you lost her and then you lost Nate...'

'My stepmother's all right, but she and my dad are happy enough on their own. Don't get me wrong. You aren't to imagine me being chucked out of the house. When I came home, I lived with them for a while, but it didn't really suit any of us, so I left.'

'I can't imagine not being close to my family. They mean everything to me.'

'Then you're a very lucky person, Miss Pike. Tell me. How are you getting on at the orphanage?'

Nancy's face broke into a smile. 'I love it. I love being with the children.'

Zachary frowned. 'I thought – that is, I assumed your post there was clerical.'

'It is, but I'm finding it a bit of a struggle, to be honest.'

'Whoever appointed you must have thought you capable.'

A flush of discomfort warmed Nancy's cheeks. 'It wasn't quite like that. There are two of us on probation. One of us will be made permanent at Christmas.'

'I see. And the other one?'

'She will have gained valuable experience.' The words trotted out automatically.

Zachary nodded. 'And does your couple of hours a week here count as valuable experience too?'

'Definitely.'

'Valuable – but not fun, like when you're with the children.'

'I don't want to be with the children so I can skive off work,' Nancy said with a touch of indignation, 'though it is fun. I always knew I liked children, but this has shown me how much. I always enjoyed helping Mam with the twins when they were little and I loved doing mothercraft at school.' That didn't sound very professional, did it? She sat up straight. 'It's very important I do my best as a clerk. That's what I need to get good at.'

'There's a lot of learning to do when you start off in some-thing,' said Zachary, 'but it's surprising how quickly you can pick things up.'

He was talking about himself, of course, starting out in the world of fire safety, which was his chosen path. How lucky he was. Nancy's future as an office girl had been chosen for her and, much as she would like to help make her family's lives easier, especially Mam's, it wasn't easy knowing that she faced a life of struggling to do her job properly.

Chapter Thirteen

T HE TIME HAD come at last. Vivienne was aware of a change in the atmosphere in the house and of how torn Miss Patience felt.

'It's only right and proper that Lucy must leave us, of course,' that dear lady declared, 'but I'll still be sorry to see her go. I've got used to her being here. It's been a pleasure, in spite of everything.'

'That's because you're such a wonderful looker-after,' said Vivienne.

Today was Sunday and tomorrow, Lucy's parents would take her to Maskell House, where her baby would be born in December. After she recovered from the birth, she would be taken home – to her real home, not this temporary one – to resume her life as Miss Lucy Hesketh, privileged daughter of Mr and Mrs Lawrence Hesketh, and nobody in their social circle would ever know of her disgrace...including the baby's father.

Whether Molly and Aaron would receive the new addition to their family before or after Lucy quitted Maskell House had not been discussed. Indeed, neither had it been settled exactly how the Abramses were to receive the baby; whether they would go and collect him or her or if the baby would be brought to them and, if so, by whom. Mr Lawrence Hesketh wasn't in the slightest bit pleased by Lucy's wish to have her child adopted by the orphanage caretaker and his wife. That they were a decent, contented couple, who were already the devoted parents of an adopted son, mattered not one jot to him. Were he and Lucy's mother intending to bring pressure to bear once Lucy was ensconced in Maskell House? Did they intend that the baby should go to a more affluent family?

'It worries me, too,' Molly had confided, 'that if Lucy wants the adoption to go ahead, that Mr Hesketh will come storming along afterwards and overturn everything.'

'He couldn't do that – could he?'

Molly had shaken her head. 'I really don't know. When we said we wanted to adopt Danny, his Uncle William raised no objection and it was all perfectly straightforward. But nothing seems straightforward with Lucy's baby. I wish they'd hurry up and bring in this new law that's being talked about that's going to turn adoption into a proper legal process. That would stop Mr Hesketh storming along afterwards.'

When it was time to go to church, Vivienne and the Hesketh ladies took a detour to Soapsuds Lane to drop off Lucy at Soapsuds House, formerly a pair of two-up two-downs, which Molly's father and brother, who ran a building company, had converted into a single substantial property.

Vivienne attended the service at St Clement's before returning to Soapsuds House, where Molly showed her into the parlour. Originally, this had been two rooms. Now there was ample space for a sofa, a pair of armchairs, a piano, shelves for ornaments and books and the model boat that Aaron and Danny had built together, and two or three useful little tables that Aaron had constructed. He was a carpenter and joiner by trade and he had built the impressive spiral staircase in the corner.

'Where are the boys?' Vivienne asked.

'Aaron has taken Danny for a long tramp across the meadows,' said Molly, her face softening with love as it always did when she spoke of the two chaps in her life. 'I made them sandwiches and a flask and they won't be back for ages, so we've got plenty of time to have a good talk. Before you came, Lucy was about to tell me how she's feeling on her last day here.'

Lucy pulled a face. 'You know how I've been dreading going to Maskell House, but now that it's about to happen, I – well, I wouldn't say I'm looking forward to it, but I feel better about it. Since I got past six months, Aunt Prudence and Auntie Patience have barely let me out of the house. It's a strange thing to say, considering that I'm being shunted off to a home for disgraced girls, but I'll have more freedom. I'm going mad, stuck in my aunts' house. I can't wait for it all to be over.'

'There's a while to go yet,' said Molly. 'I'll think about you every day.'

Lucy sat up straight, pressing a hand to her back.

'Are you all right?' asked Vivienne.

'Just a twinge.' Lucy stretched her spine. 'I had a couple in the night. I thought I was lying awkwardly.' She picked up her cup and saucer, then clattered them down again almost at once. '*Oh.*'

'Another twinge?' Molly flung a look of concern in Vivienne's direction before going to crouch beside Lucy's armchair. 'And you had some in the night as well?'

Lucy's eyes widened. The colour fled from her face, then flooded back, deepening to crimson. She stared down at herself, lifting her hands away from her body.

'Another one?' Molly asked.

'No, no, it isn't.'

'What, then?'

'It's nothing. I – I can't say it.'

'Sweetheart, we're here to help you.'

'I think I may have...had an accident.'

'Lucy, have your waters broken?'

'Have my what...?'

Molly huffed out a breath. 'Don't you know anything about giving birth?'

'I don't need to know for yonks yet.'

'I wouldn't be so sure about that,' said Molly.

When Lucy had been helped to bed, Vivienne went for the doctor. As she stepped outdoors, heart fluttering like mad, she spied Mr Milner along the road, about to enter his shop. He wasn't working on a Sunday, was he? She ran down the lane, hanging onto her over-sized beret.

'Mr Milner! Excuse me, but it is Mr Milner, isn't it?'

He turned round. He had a frank, open face, though a frown clouded it at the sight of her. 'Can I help you?'

'Could I impose on you?' Vivienne came to a standstill, breathless not from the short dash but from the outburst of nerves occasioned by what was happening in Molly's house. 'Could you possibly run and fetch the doctor? Then I can get back and help, you see.'

The frown vanished, replaced by a look in which concern mingled with alertness. 'What's wrong and where?'

'A baby. Tell him it's early, not due until December. Soapsuds House.'

'I'll be as quick as I can.'

He took off at a lick before she could thank him. She hurried back to the house and ran upstairs. Molly looked round as she entered the bedroom.

'I've sent a neighbour,' Vivienne explained. 'What can I do?'

Soon she was boiling the kettle and sorting out towels. She knew next to nothing about this birthing lark. She knew where babies came from and knew it was a jolly painful process, but that was about it. She had never had a baby herself and had never attended a birth.

When she carried the hot water upstairs, Molly met her on the landing.

'Thank heavens you know what to do,' she murmured to Molly outside the bedroom door.

'Because I've had one, you mean?' Molly laughed, a brief, harsh sound. 'Believe me, I didn't pay attention to the fine details.' Her eyes went bleak. 'And my baby was full term. Goodness knows what's going on with Lucy. Not that we say any of that to her,' she added before opening the door.

Vivienne followed her in, going to Lucy's side and holding her hand. 'The doctor's on his way. You just need to hang on a little longer.'

Lucy, who was propped up by several pillows, lurched forwards, doubling over her stomach, eyes wide, mouth agape. She gasped for air and her lily-white hand that had never done a day's work squeezed Vivienne's hand astonishingly hard. Vivienne's knuckles crunched under the pressure.

'It hurts,' Lucy groaned.

Molly scuttled around the other side of the bed. 'I know, love. I think the baby's coming. Vivienne will fetch a bowl of cool water and a flannel and bathe your forehead for you. How about that?'

With some difficulty, Vivienne disentangled her hand from Lucy's and went to do Molly's bidding. When she returned, Lucy was sitting bolt upright, resisting Molly's attempts to ease her back onto the pillows.

'Stop saying it's going to be all right,' Lucy exclaimed, tears running down her face. 'You don't know that.'

Depositing the bowl on top of the chest of drawers, Vivienne hurried to assist. Going to the opposite side of the bed from Molly, she sat on the edge as close to Lucy as she could and, putting her arms around the girl, held her firmly, cradling Lucy's dark head against her shoulder.

'I know how scared you are, Lucy. Frankly, we all are, but the doctor's coming and we'll do our best for you until he gets here.'

'Please try to be calm,' Molly added.

Lucy's head swung away from Vivienne's shoulder. 'What if this is happening because I never wanted the baby?'

Molly threw an anguished look at Vivienne, but her voice was steady as she said, 'Why don't we let Vivienne go downstairs to wait for the doctor, so she can let him in the moment he appears. Meanwhile I'll tell you everything I can about giving birth. You'll feel better if you know what to expect.'

Gently Vivienne prised herself free and went downstairs. She opened the front door and positioned herself in the doorway, like the village gossip on the look-out. The instant she saw Mr Milner and another man with a doctor's bag jogging up the lane, she started towards them, then realised what a pointless thing this was to do.

'Doctor Keen,' the doctor introduced himself. Vivienne recognised the name: this was the doctor who had been summoned when young Danny had come close to drowning some weeks back.

'Is there anything else I can do?' Mr Milner asked.

'I don't think so,' said Vivienne. 'Thanks awfully.'

'I'll be in my shop if you need me.'

'Mother upstairs?' asked Doctor Keen as Mr Milner went on his way and Vivienne shut the door.

'Yes.' She reached out a hand as he turned away. 'She's only young.' Well, maybe not as young as all that. Eighteen, nineteen? Plenty of working-class girls had a toddler in tow and another on the way at that age, as Vivienne knew all too well from her job. 'I mean to say, she's frightened this is happening because she doesn't want the baby.'

'Doesn't want it? That's unnatural. Why not?'

'She's not married.'

'I see. Well, she's not the first.' Doctor Keen gave Vivienne a sharp look. 'You haven't been giving her gin to drink, have you?'

She bridled. 'Certainly not!'

'I'll know if you have. I'll smell her breath.'

'Feel free.'

'Is someone with her?'

'Yes – Mrs Abrams. I think you know her.'

'A sensible creature. I'll go up.'

'Should I inform Lucy's aunts? They're responsible for her at present.'

'Nothing to inform them of at present. Let's wait and see if there's a worthwhile baby first, shall we?'

Zachary got up from his armchair and blew out a breath. He felt too edgy to sit down. He half-laughed. Running for the doctor had got him all fired up. Was that daft? He didn't even know who it was who was having the baby. Certainly not the lady who lived in Soapsuds House, because he knew her by sight and had exchanged good mornings with her and she definitely wasn't in the family way. It must be a visitor. He hoped everything would go well. Sending the neighbour for the doctor suggested an emergency. For a moment, that empty place deep inside him that was the loss of Nate swelled and filled him with the darkest chill. Was it like this for other bereaved twins? Did they all carry the other one's death inside them for evermore?

With an effort, he pulled himself together. Today's situation wasn't about him. It was about an unknown mother-to-be. And if summoning the doctor made it an emergency, it also represented hope. It represented the best possible treatment and support for the mother. That was what mattered. Zachary had long since stopped praying, but somehow or other he had started to believe in hope. He hoped with all his heart that mother and baby would do well. Hope mattered. He had lost it for a long time after Nate died, but gradually it had crept back into his life and he knew all too well how precious it was. It was the difference between carrying on willingly in spite of everything and carrying on because you had to.

Would the Soapsuds baby be a boy or a girl? He would like to have a family of his own one day. He had always assumed he would. Everybody grew up making all kinds of assumptions, didn't they? That had been one of his. Then Nate had died and he hadn't wanted anything at all. But now – now he had a future. He had survived his darkest days and emerged with the ability to accept that his life would go on and it could be a good life. That was what he wanted. He wanted to work hard in his own business – well, he was already doing that – and ultimately he would like a wife and children. For some reason, Miss Pike popped into his head – presumably because she had talked about how much she enjoyed being with children. She would be a good mother one day. She was kind and reliable and when she had talked about the children at St Anthony's, Zachary had seen something in her eyes that had suggested that quiet little Miss Pike had a fun-loving streak. He smiled at the memory.

Good grief, what was he thinking? Rushing off to fetch the doctor, plus a natural concern for the mother-to-be in Soapsuds House, had got him thinking daft things. Dismissing Miss Pike from his mind, he put the kettle on.

Had there ever been a more emotionally gruelling day? But Prudence knew it was more important than ever to focus on what lay ahead. Lucy, looking amazingly young, was now the mother of a tiny baby boy. Tiny but perfect, or so it appeared.

'He seems fine,' said Doctor Keen, 'but he'd be better off in a clinic, just as a precaution.'

'Presumably that would be best for Lucy too,' said Patience.

'She's well,' said Doctor Keen, 'just tired. She'd have had a harder time if she'd gone to full term. Narrow hips.'

Narrow hips. Prudence knew all about narrow hips.

'Should I make arrangements?' asked the doctor.

'We ought to wait for Lucy's parents to arrive,' said Prudence.

'You know where I am if you need me.'

Later, Lawrence and Evelyn burst into Soapsuds House, all decked out in their Sunday best. As difficult as it was to imagine them in better clothes than they wore the rest of the week, here they were in something smarter and more costly, though Lawrence's crisp lapels and gold tie-pin and Evelyn's flowing silk and two-tone shoes were distinctly at odds with the hectic speed of their arrival and the wild concern in their faces.

'Is she all right?' Lawrence demanded. 'What went wrong? Did something happen?' Alarm turned to anger as he glared at his surroundings, as if lower-class contamination had brought on the premature birth.

'Don't be absurd,' said Prudence. 'It has nothing to do with where she is. In fact, we should all be grateful she was here. In other circumstances, she'd have been all alone at home while the three of us went to St Clement's and Nancy attended church with her family.'

'You can huff and puff and blow the house down if you want to, Lawrence,' said Evelyn, 'but I'm going up to see my daughter. If you wish to come too, kindly leave your temper behind.'

Prudence exchanged a look with Patience. They had never seen Evelyn put Lawrence in his place before. The lioness protecting her cub?

When Lawrence came downstairs once more, leaving Evelyn with Lucy, he threw himself into an armchair and covered his lean face with his hands as a huge breath shuddered out of him.

'I never thought I'd become a grandfather in these circumstances.'

Prudence's heart went out to him, but then he surged to his feet and stood, tall and decisive, in front of the fireplace, back to being his real self, the half-brother she had fought with all her life.

'They're not staying here.'

'That's what the doctor recommended,' said Prudence. 'He suggested a clinic.'

'Just to be on the safe side,' Patience added. 'He offered to make arrangements.'

'I can do that myself,' said Lawrence. 'Lucy can go into a private clinic, though I'll have to ensure first that nobody of our acquaintance is currently a patient. After keeping the secret all this time, we can't have the truth trickling out now.'

'If you can find a clinic that is happy to divulge the names of its patients to you,' Prudence said drily, 'I shouldn't think it was the kind of place to which you should entrust your daughter.'

Lawrence made a harrumphing sound. 'Well – maybe so. Then she'll have to be taken further afield. It's the only way.'

'You can't expect her to undertake a long journey,' Patience protested. 'She's just had a baby. She needs bed-rest for at least ten days.'

'What would you know about it?' Lawrence demanded, his tone dismissive. He didn't utter the words *dried-up old spinster*, but he might as well have.

A fierce temptation flared inside Prudence. Oh, to say, 'Patience might not know, but I do,' but she couldn't, she mustn't. She must never be goaded into speaking the truth.

'I'll choose a suitable clinic tomorrow,' said Lawrence, 'and Lucy can go there on Tuesday by private ambulance.'

Evelyn appeared, almost on tiptoe, as if the smallest sound might disturb the baby. Her face had lost its customary snooty expression, her pudgy features positively glowing.

'He's so tiny,' she whispered.

'Like a doll,' breathed Patience. 'Lucy and Felicity were both small babies, weren't they?'

'Not as small as this.' Clearly, the new grandmother wasn't about to permit a mere great-aunt to think herself an authority.

'Lucy must have got her dates wrong,' said Prudence.

'Certainly not,' said Lawrence. 'She swore that she and the father, whoever he is…she swore it was just the once and the baby was due in December. I hope you aren't suggesting,' and he turned a furious look on Prudence, 'that she – that she – more than once.'

'I'm suggesting nothing of the kind.'

'She was born early,' said Evelyn and everyone looked at her. 'Lucy came early and so did Felicity. Nothing like as early as this, of course. Less than a month, in fact, but they were both early. Don't you remember?'

Prudence had to look away. It didn't ring any bells. She had virtually ignored her nieces when they were babes in arms, which had caused no end of ill-feeling, but what choice had she had? She had been mad with jealousy. And suppose she had plucked the infant from her lace-bedecked cradle and run away with her? What then?

'She wants to call him Charlie,' said Evelyn.

'What?' thundered Lawrence.

'Short for Charles.'

'I know what Charlie is short for, thank you,' Lawrence retorted. 'She can't name him. It isn't up to her.' He stopped, his eyes narrowing as his mouth tightened.

Patience made an anxious movement. 'What is it?'

'I'm trying to recall if we know anyone with a son called Charles.'

'We don't.' Evelyn met her husband's gaze. 'Do you imagine I didn't think the same thing?'

'Good gad, what a mess this has turned out to be,' said Lawrence. 'If this could have happened just a day or two later, she'd have been installed in Maskell House and everything would have been straightforward. Well, the baby will still have to go to Maskell House for adoption.'

'Lucy wants Mr and Mrs Abrams to have him,' said Patience.

'Lucy has shown no common sense whatsoever throughout this sorry business,' said Lawrence. 'The boy will be given to a couple with education, money and prospects, who reside elsewhere in the country. I won't have it brought up—'

'Him,' Evelyn put in.

'Him, then. I won't have him brought up by the orphanage caretaker, a ten-minute walk away from where my sisters live. The baby must be—'

'Got rid of,' said Prudence.

Lawrence took a couple of steps and loomed over her where she sat. 'Got rid of? Yes, if you choose to call it that. Kindly don't speak as if I am the hard-hearted Victorian papa in a ridiculous story-paper serial, throwing my wronged daughter out into a whirling blizzard. You know as well as I do that this is the only way. The only way,' he repeated heavily.

And he was right. It was. Prudence's mind was awash with memories of long conversations with Elspeth. Their plans for the birth. How to keep everything secret. How they would never see one another again. There had to be complete separation. That was how the adoption of an illegitimate child worked.

Prudence looked up at her brother and, for the first time in her life, said, 'You're quite right, Lawrence. I apologise.'

Chapter Fourteen

NANCY CAME HOME from going to church with her family to the news that the baby had arrived during Lucy's visit to Soapsuds House.

'Mother and baby are doing well,' said Miss Hesketh. 'The child is early, but seems to be in good health.'

'May I go and see her?' Nancy asked. 'I'd like to give her my best wishes and tell her I hope she can come back here soon.'

'She shan't be returning here,' said Miss Hesketh. 'She and the baby have to go away now. Lucy's father is arranging for her to recuperate in a private clinic. Afterwards, she will return to her family home.'

'I'm sure she'd like to see you before she goes,' said Miss Patience.

'It would do Lucy good,' said Vivienne.

'I'll take you on Monday evening,' said Miss Hesketh, 'just for a short visit. We shall be cancelling lessons for a day or two.'

'Oh.' The word popped out, almost as if the sudden bump of Nancy's heart had given it a shove. 'If I haven't got a lesson, perhaps I could do an extra hour at Mr Milner's shop tomorrow. Would there be time?'

'I don't see why not,' said Miss Hesketh. 'It is gratifying to see you showing such application to your duties.'

If only she knew!

'I dislike letting our pupils down,' said Miss Hesketh, 'but until Lucy has moved on, we need to hold ourselves ready. Her parents need to be able to come here without worrying about whether they're interrupting lessons.'

Nancy averted her gaze, hoping no one could see the guilt in her eyes. They were thinking of Lucy – and she was an' all, of course – but she was also thinking about Zachary and nothing could prevent her skin from tingling in anticipation.

She was brought down to earth with a bump the next day.

'Miss Nancy, what is the matter with you?' Miss Allan demanded. 'The standard of your work always leaves something to be desired, but this morning you've made silly mistakes. If you don't pull your socks up, I'll inform Mrs Rostron that there's no need to wait until Christmas to decide who is to remain here on a permanent basis.'

Nancy gulped and pulled herself together. There was nothing she could say to excuse her scattered thoughts, because no one could be allowed to know about Lucy's baby. She did her best for the remainder of the day and tried not to be distracted by the prospect of seeing Zachary this evening.

As she approached his shop, she swung her handbag up so she could open it and take out the key. Her hand felt about. Drat these gloves. You could never feel as well as you could with bare hands, especially when you were after something small. She pinned her bag under her arm, pulled off her glove and delved inside the bag again – and again. Where was it? Oh no, no, no. She couldn't have lost it. She mustn't have lost it. Please let it be here, please, please.

'Evening, Miss Pike.' Zachary had come up behind her. 'Allow me.'

He already had his key in his hand. He opened the door with a cheerful flourish and she stumbled inside. Her key, her key... She wanted to have another look. She wanted to turn her handbag upside down and give it a good shake. But she couldn't, she mustn't, because that would make it look like she had lost her key. Well, she had lost it, hadn't she? But she couldn't say so. What would Zachary think?

'I wasn't expecting you this evening,' said Zachary. 'I say, are you quite all right, Miss Pike?'

Forcing a laugh, she turned to him. 'Yes, thank you. Why wouldn't I be?'

Because you've gone and lost your shop key, that's why. Idiot. Nincompoop. Worrying about your typewriting, when the real problem was keeping the key safe. One measly little key. All you had to do was look after it and you couldn't even manage that. Oh glory. What now?

She forced herself to take her place on the stool, putting her bag on the shelf under the counter to buy herself a moment before she had to look Zachary in the eye.

'I wrote this up last night,' he said. 'It's a list of instructions for using a fire extinguisher. If you'd be kind enough to type some copies, I could leave them with my customers and perhaps keep a few on the counter as well, just in case anyone ever actually comes into the shop.'

'Yes, Mr Milner.'

The piece of paper rustled in her trembling hand as she took it. She put it down quickly, almost slapping it onto the counter beside the typewriter.

'If we splash out and use a fresh piece of carbon paper, the copies will be good enough to use too, don't you think?' asked Zachary.

Heart thudding, Nancy removed the dust-cover from the typewriter and reached underneath the counter for clean sheets of paper. Paper, carbon paper, paper. She fed the paper-sandwich into the machine, turned the drum and settled the top copy in position. With her hands poised on the edge of the counter, ready to lift above the keys and commence typing, she rolled her shoulders and looked at the instructions on the sheet of paper beside her, but her mind was too full for her eyes to absorb what was written. What had happened to the door-key? She had definitely had it last time, because she had let herself in, but that was the last time she had seen it, because Zachary had done the locking up.

'Is there a problem?' asked Zachary. 'You look as if you're struggling to read my writing.'

'No, it's fine, honest.'

She dragged her eyes into focus and began work. It was hard to concentrate and her hands were shaky. She had to tap down extra hard on the keys. It felt like the longest hour of her life, but at last it was time to go. She didn't know where Zachary lived. On previous evenings, she had ached for them to walk up Soapsuds Lane together, but the situation hadn't arisen because Zachary had stayed behind in the shop; and today, she was grateful for it.

With a farewell smile brittle enough to put her face in danger of shattering, she closed the door behind her and raced along Soapsuds Lane to Chorlton Green, where she threw herself onto a bench and, tearing off her gloves, scrabbled through her handbag.

It wasn't there.

Where was it? It could be anywhere. Had she dropped it outside the shop the last time she unlocked the door? Had someone picked it up and walked off with it? Someone who might come back in the dead of night and slide silently inside...? No – no – don't be daft. If it had fallen, she would have heard it land – wouldn't she? She trudged along Beech Road, her gaze glued to the ground. Which pavement had she walked along the last time she had gone home from the shop? Or maybe it had dropped out of her handbag somewhere near the orphanage – but how could that have happened? Perhaps it was in the Miss Heskeths' house. Perhaps, when she got home, Miss Patience would ask, 'Have you lost a key, by any chance?' Oh please let that happen.

But it didn't.

The key wasn't on the floor in the cloakroom or anywhere in her little bedroom. Oh, where could it be? She even looked down the back of the sideboard in the dining room, where it couldn't possibly be, but it seemed worth checking.

At the tea-table, she had to wrench her thoughts back to Lucy.

'I take it you still want to visit her,' said Miss Hesketh.

They set off after tea, Nancy walking beside Miss Hesketh's rigidly upright figure in her old-fashioned coat and hat. Should she own up about the key? She knew she should, but at the same time she wanted to give herself more time to find it. With luck, no one would ever need to know what had happened.

The door of Soapsuds House was opened by a skinny lad with freckles on his oval face and a little dent in his chin.

'Hello, Miss Hesketh. Have you come to see the baby? He's a bit pongy at the minute. Mum's changing him.'

He stood back to let them in.

'Good evening, Danny.' Miss Hesketh swept inside, Nancy in her wake. 'This is Miss Pike. We'll go straight up and see Lucy. Kindly inform your mother we'll see her shortly.'

Nancy had heard about Soapsuds House being two houses knocked into one. There was a spiral staircase in the parlour, apparently, but she didn't get to see that, because Miss Hesketh headed up what was presumably the staircase belonging to what had once been the other house.

Lucy was lying up in bed in a plain but clean room with pretty curtains and blue-and-white splashback tiles on the wash-stand. The moment they walked in, she sat up straight.

'Aunt Prudence, get my baby back off Molly.'

'Don't be silly, child. She's taking care of him.'

Tears welled in Lucy's eyes. 'I don't want her taking care of him. I want him back. I want to keep him.'

When she arrived outside Zachary's shop on Tuesday, Nancy's ears were buzzing with pent-up worry. The situation hadn't magically resolved itself. And how had she thought she was going to gain entrance to the shop without it?

Why hadn't she confessed to Zachary immediately?

Unable to get into the shop, she walked along to the laundry. Perhaps one of the laundresses had found the key outside the shop and taken it for safe keeping. As if. But she checked all the same, only to end up back outside the shop, stuck for what to do next. She didn't possess a timepiece, so she had no idea how long she waited. She tried cupping her hands round her eyes and pressing her nose to the window in an attempt to see the shop clock, but couldn't make out the time.

At last Zachary appeared.

'What's the matter? Can't you get in?'

He unlocked the door and they went inside. Nancy hung back near the door and Zachary swung round to face her.

She said quickly, 'I've lost my key. I'm so sorry.'

'We'll have to retrace your steps.' He made a move, as if to hurry outside.

'I've already done that. I – I didn't lose it today.'

Zachary froze. He seemed to look not simply at her, but right inside her. 'When?'

'Yesterday.'

He frowned. 'But you had it yesterday. You let yourself in – no, wait, I unlocked the door for you yesterday, didn't I? Where did you lose it?'

'If I knew that, I'd know where to look for it.' She pressed her fingertips to her mouth. 'I'm sorry. I shouldn't snap. I don't know where I lost it. I didn't realise I had until I wanted to unlock the door yesterday.'

'So you didn't necessarily lose it yesterday. You might have lost it before – last week, even.' Zachary tried to push his fingers through his hair and nearly sent his bowler flying. 'And you said nothing.' He shook his head, huffing out a breath of sheer disbelief. 'If you'd lost the key to the pie shop, would you have kept it quiet?'

'I never had a key to the pie shop.'

'But if you had?'

'No.'

'Exactly. You'd have owned up. But it's all right to keep me in the dark, is it? I know I don't employ you as such, Miss Pike, but it seems to me that you ought to conduct yourself as if I do – or is that me being fanciful?'

'Of course not.'

But he had already moved on. 'Will you stay here while I cut along to the locksmith's? Well, what did you expect?' he asked, forestalling her. 'Somewhere out there is a key to my premises. It might have fallen out of your bag right outside the door. It might have been picked up by someone who knows which door it opens. I can't take the chance. I've got to have the locks changed. Wait here until I get back. I'll be as quick as I can.'

Jamming his bowler securely on his head, he dashed off. Ought she to get some work done? It would be impossible to concentrate, but if she didn't try, it might look as if she didn't care. Tears filled her eyes, but she wouldn't let them spill over. Taking the dust-cover off the typewriter, she settled herself to produce more sets of instructions for using fire extinguishers. There was an invoice to produce as well, for a Mr Grant. It was the least she could do. Yes, indeed, the very least. What she really ought to do was reimburse Zachary for the new lock – but how? She gave nearly all her wages, such as they were, to Mam.

She and Zachary had seemed to be getting along so well, but had she now lost his good opinion? If she had, it was her own fault.

Prudence had hardly arrived home from work and sat down than the doorbell rang three times in quick succession. Patience went to answer it and, a moment later, Lawrence surged into the sitting room, still in his homburg and his overcoat with the astrakhan collar.

'I hope you're pleased with yourself,' he said accusingly.

Prudence wasn't going to let him get away with that. 'Ecstatic,' she retorted. 'And if you must barge into our house, kindly have the manners to remove your hat.'

Lawrence wrenched it from his head. 'On the subject of manners, how about you having the good taste to remember that this is my house?'

Patience showed Evelyn into the room. There were bags the size of soup-plates under her eyes and the line of her costly wool dress wasn't as smooth as it might have been, as if even her corset was tired out from all the upset.

'Sit down, dear,' said Patience and Evelyn sank onto the sofa.

Prudence relented. Lawrence and Evelyn had taken an emotional battering since the baby's birth the day before yesterday. She tried to be conciliatory.

'Is Lucy safely in the clinic?' She addressed the question to Evelyn.

Evelyn nodded. 'Yes, thank heaven, all comfortably settled.'

Instead of taking a seat, Patience was still hovering. 'May I take your coat, Lawrence?'

'What? Oh – yes.'

He shrugged out of it and thrust it at her. Prudence wanted to tell him to hang it up himself, but that would be asking for more vexation. Patience, living up to her name as she was so often called upon to do, quietly took his coat, together with his hat with his gloves inside it, and disappeared for a few moments. When she returned, she sat beside Evelyn.

'What is it I'm supposed to be pleased about?' Prudence asked.

'She told you before she told us,' exclaimed Evelyn. 'She told you she wanted to keep the baby.'

'I hoped she might change her mind once she'd slept on it,' Prudence said wearily. 'I take it she hasn't?'

'She's determined to keep him.' Evelyn looked drained, but her eyes started to shine. 'So determined, in fact, that she's ready to name the father.'

There was a loud gasp from Patience. 'That's wonderful news.'

'It certainly is,' Prudence agreed. 'If the father is...' Goodness, what word would fit the bill? 'Available. Suitable.'

'He's both.' Evelyn scrabbled inside her handbag and produced an embroidered hanky.

'That's a relief,' said Patience.

'A relief?' Lawrence exclaimed. 'Why couldn't she have named him in the first place? Think of everything she's put us through: that nonsense about not being in love, then wanting to hand the child over to that lower-class couple. It's been one crackpot idea after another. I know some women go deranged when there's a baby on the way. Lucy is a case in point.'

'But if she's put it all behind her,' Patience ventured.

'She certainly has,' said Evelyn.

'At this stage,' said Lawrence, 'frankly it would have been

better if she hadn't. A few months ago, we could have organised a hasty wedding and nobody would have dared comment when the baby came along. Now...' He shook his head. 'Now everyone will know. It could affect my chances of becoming an alderman.'

'It has no bearing on that,' said Prudence.

'Everything has a bearing on that,' said Lawrence.

'You haven't said who the father is,' said Prudence.

'No one of your acquaintance.'

'I didn't imagine he was, but I'd like to know something about him.'

'Dickie Bambrook,' said Evelyn. 'The Bambrooks are friends of ours. We've always been so fond of Dickie. He was most awfully cut up when Lucy vanished off the scene earlier in the year.'

'That's a good start,' said Patience.

'I think so,' Evelyn agreed.

'I'll kill him,' said Lawrence.

'But not until after he's made an honest woman of Lucy,' said Prudence.

'This is no laughing matter,' growled Lawrence.

'What happens next?' Prudence asked.

'I'm going to see Dickie and his father and tell them what's what.'

'Might I make a suggestion?' asked Patience. 'If you don't mind.'

'If you insist,' said Lawrence.

'Rather than you tackling Mr Bambrook and his son, might it perhaps be better to let Evelyn break it to Mrs Bambrook?'

'Don't be ridiculous,' snorted Lawrence. 'It's the duty of the heads of the households to deal with this.'

'Quite, quite,' murmured Patience. 'I just thought it might be a gentler way of going about it. After all, these are dear

Lucy's future in-laws. And it would be a shame to spoil your long friendship.'

Lawrence looked ready to explode, but Evelyn nodded.

'Do you know, Lawrence, I rather think Patience might have the right idea.'

Prudence smothered a smile. 'After all, the more smoothly this is handled, the less chance there is of its spoiling your opportunity to be an alderman.'

'There is that,' Lawrence murmured thoughtfully.

'Might I ask,' said Patience, 'how was dear Molly when Lucy and the baby left?'

'What? "Dear Molly"?' Lawrence repeated. 'Who's dear Molly?'

'Mrs Abrams, of course,' snapped Prudence. As if he didn't know. 'The lady whom Lucy all along wanted to adopt her baby. *That* dear Molly.'

'I was never in favour of that scheme,' said Lawrence. 'Most undesirable.'

'So you've said at every possible opportunity,' said Prudence. 'I believe Patience wished to enquire after Mrs Abrams's well-being.'

'She was offered handsome recompense for Lucy's bed and board and the general inconvenience,' said Lawrence, 'which she saw fit to decline. End of story.'

Patience winced. Prudence longed to call their brother a brute, but discretion prevailed.

'Why are we discussing Mrs Abrams?' Evelyn asked. 'We should concentrate on Lucy and her forthcoming nuptials. Mrs Richard Bambrook. Oh, Lawrence, we're going to see our grandchild grow up.'

And she burst into tears.

Chapter Fifteen

BEING ADMITTED INTO the Hesketh family secret had made Nancy feel not only a true member of the Wilton Close household, but also rather grown-up, which was an agreeable feeling. She might have carried a lot of responsibility all her life, what with helping Mam in any way she could, but it had never made her feel grown-up. Helping their mams was what all working-class girls did, especially when there were younger children to be taken care of; and if Nancy's mam needed more support than others, so what? That was just the way it was.

She shared the delight at Lucy's decision to get wed instead of giving her baby away.

'But what a terrible blow for poor Molly Abrams and her husband,' she said, 'having the baby practically wrenched out of their arms, and after they'd had a chance to start getting to know him an' all.' She stopped. Had she sounded too dramatic? She hadn't intended to. She meant every word of what she said.

'Unfortunately,' said Miss Hesketh, 'there are times when one simply has to grit one's teeth and make the best of things.'

'That's rather harsh,' Miss Patience protested.

'It's rather true,' Miss Hesketh replied. 'If you go and see Molly, Patience, for pity's sake don't fling your arms round her and burst into tears. You know what you're like.' She turned to Nancy and firmly changed the subject. 'May I ask you a favour? My brother has offered to take my sister and me to visit Lucy in the clinic on Saturday afternoon. I know you usually go to see your parents on Saturdays, but might you be available to be in the house at that time to admit someone? It would be a big help.'

'It's nothing to worry about,' said Miss Patience. 'Belinda Layton will be coming with her fiancé, Mr Gabriel Linkworth. They store books in our cellar.'

'Yes,' said Nancy. 'Belinda told me.'

'Mr Linkworth comes here now and again to fetch some. He sells books by post until such time as he can set himself up in a shop. If you could be here, it would save putting him off until another day.'

'Of course I will. I'll see my folks on Sunday.'

How lovely to be trusted. It meant the Miss Heskeths regarded her as a proper member of the household and that was a good feeling, a mixture of pleasure and, yes, a touch of pride. She would enjoy seeing Belinda again an' all. As well as liking her, Nancy had appreciated feeling she was one of a pair – two working-class lasses out to better themselves. She hoped they could be friends.

'I'd better show you where I keep the key to the inner cellar,' Miss Hesketh added.

'The inner cellar?'

'As well as keeping boxes of books in the main cellar, Mr Linkworth also stores some items – ornaments and so forth – that used to belong to his late uncle and aunt. The cellar has a separate section that is behind a locked door and this is where these personal items are kept. I felt that it wouldn't do any harm to give them some additional security. The key to the inner cellar is kept in my dressing table drawer, in case you need it, though I don't imagine you will. I've only ever known Mr Linkworth to collect books.'

Warmth rose in Nancy's cheeks. Another key. It sounded as if she wouldn't need to use it, but if she did, she vowed she wouldn't do owt stupid this time. But the main thing was that Belinda was going to come round to the house. That was something to look forward to.

Before that, though, she had to face Zachary in his shop on Friday evening. What an idiot she had been about that blessed key. She would work extra hard on Friday to make up for it.

Zachary filled in some details in his order book and blotted the ink before closing it. This week, he had done some fire extinguisher training with a shopkeeper, who, if Zachary was lucky, might suggest to some of the neighbouring shopkeepers that they would do well to install extinguishers of their own. He had also trained up half the staff in a hotel in West Didsbury and he was going to train the other half next week. On top of that, he had secured a fresh order for extinguishers for a small factory in Stretford. You couldn't exactly call it a full week's work, but the amount he was doing was increasing each week and that was what mattered. In fact, he would have counted this as a pretty good week, all told, if it hadn't been for that fiasco with the key, which had ended up costing him a pretty penny.

He was disappointed in Miss Pike. He had trusted her and she had let him down. Was he over-reacting? He didn't think so. It had been an honest mistake on her part and everyone made an error at some point, of course; but this wasn't the sort of mistake where you could say, 'It's all right. It doesn't matter,' because it did. Losing someone else's key mattered a lot, especially when it was the key to their business premises.

In this case, it was also the key to Zachary's home, though Miss Pike had no idea of that.

The door opened and she came in, looking apprehensive.

'Good evening, Mr Milner.'

He nodded. 'Miss Pike.'

'I'm glad you're here. I wondering on my way what I'd do if you weren't.'

'I had to be here, didn't I? I couldn't leave you standing outside waiting in the cold.' Was that unkind? He wished he hadn't said it – no, he didn't. It needed saying. But even so... 'I'm sorry. I didn't say it to make you feel guilty.'

She tilted her head slightly, the equivalent of a shrug. 'You're in the right. I did a bad thing. I made a mistake and then made it worse by trying to hide it. I'm the one that should be apologising.'

A smile tugged at his lips. 'You did enough of that on Tuesday. Come and sit down. There's some typewriting for you to do.'

There was a suggestion of relaxation in her shoulders. Relief? That was good. Zachary hated to be on bad terms with anyone, but he had quickly learned in the course of his business dealings that running a business had nothing to do with making friends. The matter of the lost key had made him realise he was going to have to think about how a relationship between employer and employee should be conducted. He had been cheerful and pleasant towards Miss Pike before, but should he have held himself aloof? Would that have made her more careful? But he didn't want to turn into his father. He never wanted any employee of his to be in fear of him because he held rigid views.

Miss Pike settled down to work on producing copies of the instructions for using a fire extinguisher. Zachary put his order book away in the back room, keeping the door pulled shut so that she couldn't make out the evidence of his living in there. It wasn't that he was ashamed of his basic mode of living, but it didn't exactly give the impression of a thrusting young businessman.

Coming back into the shop, he shut the door behind him. The truth was there was nothing more for him to do today regarding his work and, left to his own devices, he could get his evening started. Should he tell Miss Pike she could clear off early? Or would that give the wrong impression of him as a boss?

He realised the tapping of the typewriter keys had stopped. Miss Pike's fingers were poised over them, but she had lifted her head.

Zachary smiled. 'I'm sorry. I wasn't checking over your shoulder. I know how off-putting that sort of thing is.'

'Oh, it is,' she agreed. 'Miss Allan at the orphanage... Anyroad, if I was better at typewriting, she wouldn't need to stand over me, would she?'

'Ah, but how much better will you get if you're worried about being watched?' Oh, crikey, that was the very last thing a boss should say. It sounded as if he was undermining this Miss Allan.

Miss Pike smiled. It was a small smile at first, then it built, and her eyes softened. He hadn't realised she was so pretty. 'You understand. Thank you. I feel such a dud a lot of the time.'

'You're learning. We all have to start somewhere.'

'I just want to do well and make my parents proud of me and I want to set a good example to my younger sisters an' all.'

'Then I suggest you don't mention the lost key,' said Zachary. It was meant to be a joke, but Miss Pike bridled.

'Of course I'll tell them. I'm an honest person, whatever you think of me.'

She was obviously a good daughter. But it was more than that. Her words and the feeling they contained showed her love for her family. Zachary felt drawn to that. Mum had been lovely, but he and Nate had always had a difficult relationship with Dad.

'It sounds as if you're from a happy family,' he said.

'I am,' she answered at once.

'I know there's you, your parents and your twin sisters. Are there more of you?'

'No, it's just the five of us. It's lucky there aren't more, really, because – well, we're not exactly rolling in money. And Mam has anaemia badly. I don't mean she suffers from pernicious anaemia, but...' Her words trailed away.

'But it doesn't have to be pernicious to be bad.'

Miss Pike nodded. Was that a sheen of tears in her eyes? Zachary felt the most ridiculous urge to wipe them away. Grasping for something to say, he asked, 'What are your sisters called?'

'Emily and Lottie – Charlotte. Mam loves books by the Brontës. And we all have middle names from Jane Austen, because she's Pa's favourite author.'

'Then your name must be Anne.'

'Nancy for short.'

Nancy. He approved. Nancy suited her. She wasn't an Anne. He was about to say so when he caught himself up sharply. What had got into him? First wanting to wipe away a tear and now on the verge of making a personal remark – what was he thinking? If he'd had a sister, and her boss had treated her like that, Zachary would have stepped in quick smart and told the fellow where to get off.

'Mr Milner,' said Miss Pike – Nancy. 'I just want to say that I'll pay you back for the work the locksmith did. It'll take a while – well, quite a long time, actually – but I will do it.'

'There's no need, honestly.'

All of a sudden, the tension was back in her body. 'You mean because my family's poor? That isn't why I told you about them. I won't have you feeling sorry for us. We get by and we always pay what's owed.'

It wasn't the first time he had seen a flash of spirit in her. He admired it and also the way she didn't want to duck off paying, but he knew that, however unwelcome the locksmith's bill had been to him, it would be infinitely harder for Nancy to pay it.

'We'll talk about it another time,' he said.

'I don't want you to think badly of me.'

'If I didn't think well of you, I wouldn't bother telling you about my new idea, would I?'

'What new idea?'

'This one: fire blankets.'

Nancy frowned. 'What are they?'

'Exactly what they sound like. You use them to smother a fire. Some of them contain asbestos, but mostly they're made from leather, felt or wool. It's important for a fire blanket to be flexible.'

'And you just throw it over a fire?'

'More or less.'

'Surely the blanket would catch fire. A wool one would – and a felt one.'

'Obviously they have to be a certain thickness and you have to take care to cover the fire completely. That means oxygen can't get to it, you see, so it goes out. You have to leave the blanket in place for at least a quarter of an hour, to make sure. They're especially useful in kitchens.'

'Maybe the hotels that already have your fire extinguishers will take one of these fire blankets an' all for the kitchen.'

'There's no harm in asking,' he agreed. 'You approve of my idea, then?'

'Definitely. I like the way you've looked round for something new to add to your business instead of just having extinguishers.' Nancy bit her lip. 'I'm not saying that to try to get round you because I lost your key. I mean it.'

She did too. He could see it in her eyes. There was no guile in this girl. She was honest through and through...though she hadn't been honest when she had tried to hide that she had lost his key, had she? But wasn't that what most folk would have done? Panicked and spent ages searching in the hope of finding it, so that the loss need never come to light? Her response, if not laudable, had certainly been natural and had nothing to do with whether or not she was honest at heart.

'Look, shall we forget about the key?' said Zachary. 'I don't pay you for your time here. Let's say that the cost of the locksmith is instead of paying you a wage. No arguments,' he added when she started to protest.

After a moment, Nancy said, 'Thank you,' although he could see it was hard for her to accept what some might call charity. She didn't really have a choice, though, because she didn't have the wherewithal to repay him.

In any case, it wasn't charity. It was a good deed, that's all. Good deeds were important. They made the world go round, providing odd moments of warmth and light relief. Such moments made a world without Nate that little bit more bearable.

Chapter Sixteen

LEFT ALONE IN the house on Saturday afternoon, Nancy looked forward to seeing Belinda again and she was curious to meet Gabriel Linkworth. Such a romantic name – like a poet. A picture of him with dark, brooding eyes and a ruffled shirt-front popped into her head and she almost laughed.

Of course he wasn't like that at all. When she opened the front door to them and Belinda performed the introductions, Nancy found herself looking into a pair of hazel eyes that were serious but kind. He had a narrow face that fitted his slim build – and was it disloyal to Pa to realise that a man could be slim without being weedy?

'Are the Miss Heskeths in?' Belinda asked. 'We ought to say how do before we disappear into the cellar.'

'It's just me,' said Nancy, standing aside to let them in. 'They asked me to stop in.'

'For our benefit? That's good of you.'

'It's no trouble,' said Nancy. 'I saw my mam this morning and did her shopping.'

'Belinda's mum lives over the road.' Gabriel nodded at the houses opposite.

About to shut the door, Nancy paused, staring across the road, unable to square the thought of working-class Belinda having a mother who rented in Wilton Close.

Belinda smiled. 'She's the maid at number one.'

Nancy shut the door, not wanting to seem nosy, though it was probably a bit late for that.

'Should we fetch the books right away?' Belinda suggested. 'Then we shan't take up too much of your time.'

'Don't rush on my account,' said Nancy. 'I've been looking forward to seeing you again.'

'In that case,' said Gabriel, 'I'll find the books and leave you two to chat.'

'Would you like to nip downstairs and see our book-cavern first?' Belinda offered.

The cellar door was in a corner of the kitchen.

'There's no electricity down there,' said Gabriel, taking an oil-lamp from a shelf and lighting the way.

As Nancy negotiated the steps, she trailed her hand along the wall rather than hold the wooden rail on the other side, feeling more secure that way. The cellar was cold and dark, stretching all the way under the house.

'It's dry down here,' said Gabriel, 'which makes it a suitable place to store books.'

In the glow of the oil-lamp, Nancy gazed at piles of boxes, each one carefully labelled and numbered.

'It took ages to do the inventory and box everything up,' said Belinda.

'I bet it did. Miss Hesketh says there are other things as well as books.'

'That's right. There are all sorts of bits and bobs – ornaments, things like that – that used to belong to Gabriel's uncle and aunt. To be honest, we aren't sure what's in those boxes, other than in the most general terms. We never made an inventory of them. Gabriel took out a few things he liked and wanted to keep and they're in his lodgings now. As for all the rest, we hope we'll be able to sell them one day. They're lovely, but there are far too many for us to keep. Gabriel, hold up the lamp so Nancy can see better – do you mind if I call you Nancy?'

'Not at all. I'd like it.' Like it? She'd love it. It showed Belinda wanted to be friends.

'Good. And we're Belinda and Gabriel.'

Nancy nodded shyly at Gabriel, not liking to use his name. She and Belinda went back up the steps to the kitchen, where Nancy put the kettle on. She had a nice little warm feeling inside. Moving onto first-name terms meant a lot to her. Soon they were sitting in the front room with a tray of tea and Miss Patience's home-made petticoat tails.

'I hear I have you to thank for getting my little brother reading,' said Belinda, then laughed at Nancy's confusion. 'Jacob Layton, or should I say Layton Two? And Layton One is Mikey.'

'They're your brothers? I didn't know. But – but your mother lives over the road.'

'Not every child at St Anthony's is an orphan. A few have families who can't look after them. That's what happened to us.'

'How sad.'

'My dad abandoned us, leaving Mum with my sister Sarah and the boys. I helped them do a moonlight flit, but the cottage I took them to got burned down – not by us, I hasten to add. We don't know who did it. Gabriel saved all our lives. He's a hero.'

'No wonder you fell in love with him.'

'I'd already done that,' said Belinda, her skin taking on a radiant glow. 'Afterwards the family had nowhere to go. Sarah came to live with me and my late fiancé's family. How did we get talking about this? Oh aye – you've got our Jacob reading with one of the little boys every day. That's little short of a miracle, that is. Mum couldn't believe it when I told her. How are you getting along with your studies here?'

'So-so.'

'Are you a scholarship candidate?'

'A what?'

'It's a special scheme the Miss Heskeths have, so that girls from poor backgrounds like us can have places in their school at reduced fees. You need a letter from your old school to say you would have passed the scholarship to go to grammar school if you'd taken it.'

'Well, that counts me out,' said Nancy. 'I was nowhere near bright enough for that. You must have done well at school.'

Belinda wrinkled her nose. 'My dad would never have let me stop on at school once I was old enough to go out to work. I hope you aren't offended that I mentioned scholarship candidates.'

'Of course not.'

Belinda sighed. 'It's a bit of a sore point at home. I got the school's very first scholarship place because Miss Kirby – have you met her yet? – wrote me a letter of support. When I did well here, Mum, Sarah and I all got it into our heads that perhaps Sarah could be the next scholarship pupil. I'm afraid we were too busy thinking about the reduced fees and what it could mean for Sarah's future and we clean forgot she'd have to have the letter about having been clever enough for grammar school even though she never went there.'

'Wasn't she clever enough?' asked Nancy, wincing on Sarah's behalf.

Belinda shook her head. 'No, so she wasn't eligible.'

'What a shame.'

'She got into a bit of a snit about it, I'm afraid, as if I'd led her up the garden path on purpose. She has a stroppy side, does our Sarah.'

Gabriel came in, carrying a pile of books. Nancy poured tea for him, noting the smile that passed between him and Belinda as he sat beside her. How lucky they were to have one another. If only Zachary would look at her like that. Frankly, she was lucky she still had a job after what she had done.

Then she had an idea. There weren't any fire extinguishers in the orphanage, but maybe there should be. Just imagine if a fire took hold of St Anthony's. If she suggested getting fire extinguishers and Mrs Rostron agreed, might that go some way towards paying Zachary back for swallowing the cost of the locksmith?

Making the Christmas stocking decorations was proving to be a popular idea, though one or two of the girls grouched about it.

'I bet us girls end up being told to make them for the boys as well.'

But Nancy was ready for this. 'That's the way of the world, I'm afraid. I suggest that if the boys want you to make stockings for them, they have to pay for it by polishing your shoes.'

That made the girls laugh and the air buzzed with excitement.

Nancy wanted another idea that would catch the children's interest, especially the boys'. One evening, when she was holding a skein of yarn looped around her hands for Miss Patience to wind it into a ball, an idea popped into her head. Tying knots! She knew plenty of knots and their purposes, because Pa's job as a warehouseman meant he had to be an expert at knots and he had started teaching her when she was knee-high to a grasshopper. When other children were getting to grips with cat's cradle, she was busy learning reef knots, slip knots and figure of eights.

'It won't just be fun,' she informed the lads the next day when they came home from school. 'It'll be useful. Knots are used for different purposes, not just for tying things together, but to make pieces of rope shorter in a way that's safe and secure. Once you've learned these knots, you'll use them all your life, I promise. Who's interested?'

They all were – and so were the girls. Nancy was delighted, but if she expected Miss Allan to be impressed, she was doomed to disappointment.

'I'm perfectly well aware of what goes on under this roof, thank you,' Miss Allan declared, cutting her short when she wanted to describe the success of the knot sessions.

To Nancy's surprise, the nursemaids weren't best pleased, either, which was upsetting because they had liked her so far.

'The stocking decorations, the reading – and now this,' Nurse Carmel said tartly. 'If I didn't know better, I'd say you were in line for a nursemaid's job, not a clerical position.'

'I can't do right for doing wrong,' Nancy told Vivienne later at home. She liked and respected Vivienne, who treated her as if she was worth listening to. Was this what it felt like to look up to an older sister?

'I think you're doing the right thing,' said Vivienne. 'By coming up with ideas to occupy the children, you're showing an interest in the orphanage as well as an understanding of what might be of benefit.'

'But if the nursemaids don't like it...'

'Then they can lump it. They'll soon realise you aren't there to usurp them. The next time you get a wigging from Miss Allan, they'll be on your side again, believe me.'

'I don't intend to get into any more trouble with Miss Allan,' said Nancy.

She put more effort into her clerical duties. Pride as much as anything made her want to do well. She might not have been clever at school, but six years of being highly thought of in the pie shop made it hard now to be seen to struggle. The trouble was that Ginny was a quicker learner, but when Nancy tried to keep up, she made foolish mistakes, which Miss Allan pounced on, leaving her feeling two inches tall.

Well, she wasn't able to keep up with Ginny and she shouldn't try. It would be more sensible to slow down and check her work as she went along.

'Slow but sure,' she murmured to herself, frowning in concentration over her typing and filing.

She thought she was doing rather well, but then she overheard Miss Allan talking about her to Nanny Duffy.

'She needs to pull her socks up. She's happy enough to muck about with the children, but she's regrettably slow to knuckle down to what she's actually here for. I swear the only job I can trust her to do adequately is take letters to the pillar-box. What a dunce.'

Nancy was busy with her typewriting in Zachary's shop on Friday evening when there was the sound of an engine and a black motor car came to a halt outside the shop. In the glow of the street-lamp, she saw a gentleman emerge. He was dressed in an old-fashioned tailcoat and he clapped a gleaming top hat onto his head as he stopped to read the sign above the shop before throwing the door open and marching over the threshold. His tailcoat was unfastened, revealing a waistcoat of brilliant white. A black bow tie sat beneath the sharp wings of his collar.

'You there – Milner.'

'Mr Grant, isn't it?' Zachary stepped forward, smiling a welcome. 'From The Laurels Hotel. What can I do for you, sir?'

'You can desist from your charlatan practices, that's what you can do, sir.'

'I – I don't know what you mean,' Zachary began.

'I bought a dozen fire extinguishers from you and paid for my staff to be trained. The price was agreed.'

'And I have supplied the extinguishers and trained your staff. Is there a problem, sir?'

Mr Grant scooped a piece of paper from his pocket and waved it in the air. 'This is the problem. This bill is the problem. It practically gave my lady wife a fit of the vapours. Not that she should have opened it, of course. All correspondence is addressed to me. Screamed, she did, sir, when she saw it – screamed.'

'The cost was agreed between us—'

'It was indeed and then you had the nerve to send me this, adding a further twenty pounds.'

'Nothing was added,' said Zachary.

'Twenty pounds! Outrageous!'

'If I may see that.' Zachary held out his hand, which obliged the irate Mr Grant to stop waving the paper around and hand it over. Zachary looked at the paper. He dropped his chin to his chest for a long moment, then lifted it again.

Nancy leaned forward. What was he going to say?

'I can only apologise, Mr Grant. This is a terrible error.'

'Error? Error, he calls it. Sharp practice is what I call it, sir. Sharp practice.'

'No, I assure you it is a genuine mistake, a slip of the finger when the invoice was typewritten.'

When the – oh no. Oh no no no no no.

'I'll have a new invoice typed up at once, Mr Grant,' said Zachary.

'You'll do better than that, Milner. You'll knock a consideration off the price.'

'Mr Grant, I really—'

'Do you know why I'm togged up like this? I'm on my

way to the Grand Annual Dinner of the Medium-Sized Hotels. D'you want me to tell my colleagues how you tried to fleece me? Eh? Do you? Because you're going the right way about it.' Mr Grant's waistcoat had ridden up in his agitation. He yanked it down. 'I won't be treated like this, Milner. You've caused distress to my lady wife, and deep vexation to me, not to mention putting me to the trouble of coming here to sort it out. I want redress. I want money knocked off. I'm entitled to that. Get your girl over there to draw up a fresh invoice and make it for ten guineas less than the original price.'

'Ten guineas?' Zachary exclaimed. 'But that's—'

'What? Daylight robbery? Or adequate compensation for a client who has the power to ruin you by the time the soup has been served? Ten guineas, I say.'

Zachary spread his hands in a helpless gesture. 'Ten guineas, Mr Grant.'

'Good. I knew you'd see sense.' Mr Grant headed for the door, turning round again before he passed through. 'And I expect to be reimbursed for the cost of this taxi-cab as well.' Throwing out his chest, he marched back to the waiting motor-car.

Nancy slid off her stool. It was all she could do to stay upright and not slide straight onto the floor. Her mouth was so dry that she had to peel her tongue off the roof of her mouth before she could utter a word.

'Mr Milner, I – I don't know what to say.'

She had been so careful to check her spelling on every letter, every invoice, every set of instructions. Her spelling, yes, but she hadn't checked her numbers, had she? A prickling sensation ran up and down her arms as all the hairs lifted. 'I know when it happened. It was Tuesday, the day when—'

`Of all the times for you to make a mistake. I normally check your letters and invoices before they're sent out, but that day...' Zachary rubbed the back of his neck. 'Good grief, it's cost me a small fortune. Ten whole guineas! I can't afford to lose that. My God – this might have ruined me.' His face had drained of colour. 'I'm sorry, Miss Pike. After the trouble you've caused this week, I've come to the conclusion that I'm better off as a one-man band. I think you'd better go – and don't come back.'

Chapter Seventeen

'J UST WHEN WE have all breathed a sigh of relief over Lucy,'
Vivienne murmured, 'now we have Nancy to worry about.'

It was Saturday morning and Miss Hesketh had sent Nancy
home to see her family, with strict instructions not to breathe
a word of the trouble she had caused. 'Think of your mother's
health,' she had said darkly and poor Nancy had paled, as if
last night's disaster might cause the collapse of Mrs Pike's
health. And it wasn't just yesterday evening when something
had gone wrong, as it turned out. Nancy had confessed to
having mislaid the key to Mr Milner's shop earlier in the
week, though she had found this yesterday evening, tucked
inside a tear in the lining in her handbag. She had wanted
to rush back to the shop to return it, but Miss Hesketh had
twitched it out of her fingers.

'I'll return it,' she said in her crispest, most no-nonsense
voice. 'It is imperative that I speak to Mr Milner immediately.'

She had gone out, looking strained but determined. When
she returned, she declined to discuss what had been said.

'I need to sleep on it,' was all she would say, with a quick
glance in Nancy's direction, and Vivienne had understood that
she didn't want to speak in front of the girl, or not yet at least.

Now it was Saturday and a subdued Nancy had set off to
see her mother. Miss Patience had gone to the front door to

see her off. Then came the sound of the door clicking shut and Miss Patience came into the sitting room.

'She never intended to cause trouble,' she said, always the peacemaker.

'That's beside the point,' said Miss Hesketh, forthright as ever. 'She did cause trouble and what are we to do about it? We recommended her for the position at Milner's shop – I recommended her, I personally. In fact, I dreamed up the position in the first place – and now see where it has led. None of our other girls would ever have done something like this.'

'What did Mr Milner say yesterday?' Vivienne asked.

'He won't have her back, and who can blame him? He has poured all his savings into his business and this has set him back considerably. It has wiped out the small profit he has so far made and has also severely compromised his ability to buy the equipment that he then sells on to his customers.'

'That's serious.' A chilly feeling rippled down Vivienne's spine.

'Poor Nancy was in floods of tears yesterday,' Miss Patience reminded them, 'despairing over how to pay him back.'

'She can't and her family can't,' said Miss Hesketh. 'They're on their uppers. We shall refund Mr Milner ourselves. We sent her there – I sent her there. It's up to us to pay for the damage.'

Miss Patience gasped. 'How? I'm not questioning the rightness of it, but – how?'

'We haven't spent any of the money we've earned in fees from our pupils.' Miss Hesketh sighed and that in itself spoke volumes. Miss Hesketh wasn't given to sighing. She was far too practical, far too busy making decisions and sorting out problems. 'I've been setting it aside for a rainy day. A couple of window-sashes could do with replacing, and that won't come cheap. Neither would a lick of paint go amiss. But now...'

She shook her head and Vivienne's heart went out to her.

One thing she had learned through living here, not from anything that had been said, but rather through things that had gone unspoken, was that the Miss Heskeths of Wilton Close belonged to the ranks of the genteel poor. Miss Hesketh would be appalled if she thought anybody realised – humiliated, too. There was nothing more pathetic than being genteel poor. Miss Kirby was the same, only more so. At least the Miss Heskeths were lucky enough to reside in a decent house. Miss Kirby rented a couple of rooms.

'I'll go and see Mr Milner this morning,' said Miss Hesketh.

'I'll come with you,' said Miss Patience.

'There's no need.'

'There's every need,' Miss Patience said stoutly. 'The business school belongs to both of us and Mr Milner is entitled to see that, as joint proprietors, we take this matter seriously. Besides, this is such an upsetting matter and I don't want you facing it on your own.'

A small smile touched Miss Hesketh's narrow lips and she raised no further objection. 'There's one more thing. Nancy mustn't know about this.'

'She has to be told that Mr Milner is being reimbursed,' Vivienne pointed out. 'She's worried sick about what she's done.'

'I'll tell her that we have – or rather that the business school has reimbursed him,' said Miss Hesketh. 'I'll say that we have special insurance against this sort of thing. And I suppose I'd better find out whether such insurance exists, so that we can pay for it in future.'

It took Zachary a few days to shake off the shock of what had happened with Mr Grant. The end of October was approaching. The trees were shedding their greens and taking on a mantle of red and bronze. The days were shorter, the nights colder. By, but the nights were colder. Zachary thought longingly of the plan he had hatched when he first moved in here to have the chimney swept in the storeroom that doubled as his living quarters, so that he could use the fireplace and be comfortable – and have hot water and toast, to boot. Heaven help him, he had even promised himself a second-hand armchair. He hadn't done either of those things, as it had turned out. He had invested in a large blind to pull down inside the shop-window to ensure privacy on dark evenings, but even that had stretched his finances almost to snapping point.

Miss Hesketh had reimbursed him for the payment he had been obliged to make to the odious Mr Grant. It had been humiliating to accept the money from her. It shouldn't have been – it was after all a matter of business, but all the same he had felt belittled by it; belittled by the knowledge that he couldn't afford to say 'There's no need.' Moreover, he was pretty certain that two middle-class ladies wouldn't be running a school unless they were in need of the income. He had tried to save face, and also let Miss Hesketh off the hook a little, by carrying the cost of the locksmith himself, even though he could barely afford to do so. Had that been foolish of him? Maybe. But starchy Miss Hesketh was trying to do right by him and he wanted to reciprocate.

But Miss Hesketh hadn't finished doing the decent thing.

'If you'd like me to arrange for another girl to work for you, I can organise it – an experienced girl, you understand, who has already worked in an office for some time and who would be able to assist you on Saturday afternoon.'

'As recompense for Miss Pike, you mean?'

'Frankly, yes. You're a young man starting out in the world and my business school has unfortunately caused you a serious set-back.'

'Thank you for the offer, but I'd rather not. I managed alone quite well before and that suits me for the time being. To be honest, I only agreed to take Miss Pike because I wanted the typewriter.'

The moment the words had left his mouth, he wanted to bite off his tongue. What a cruel thing to say, and being true didn't make it any less cruel. Cruel and flippant. Nancy didn't deserve that. She might have caused him no end of trouble, but none of it had happened through laziness or any lack of willingness on her part. She was a hard worker, he knew that. Moreover, she was a good-natured lass with a pleasant manner. If she hadn't brought trouble crashing down on his head, he would have liked her – admired her, even, for trying to better herself, which was very much to her credit.

It was a shame she had selected a form of work for which she was so ill-suited. Poor girl, she was probably stuck with it now, having signed herself up to the course at the business school. She wasn't the sort to have the option of chopping and changing. You only had to glance at her shoes to see how hard-up her folks were. Footwear was a dead giveaway. You could tell how new or old the shoes were and whether they were all-purpose shoes for every single occasion or if the wearer possibly owned a second pair. You could tell – literally – if a fellow was on his uppers.

That was why Zachary had bought himself a brand-new pair of leather lace-ups before he started his business. Like his bowler, they were an investment. Nancy's shoes had been polished on a daily basis, but the polish probably acted as the glue that held them together. She could never have repaid him for her blunders in a month of Sundays.

The shop door opened and the postman came in, popping a letter onto the counter. It was all Zachary could do to restrain himself from snatching it up and tearing it open as the two of them exchanged a few words before the postie went on his way.

Zachary eagerly openly the envelope. Had another of his letters of introduction borne fruit? No, it was from the superintendent at St Anthony's, the local orphanage, where Nancy worked. Mrs Rostron wanted him to make an appointment to visit the orphanage to discuss the installation of fire extinguishers. He hadn't been in touch with her, so his reputation must be growing. Zachary nodded crisply. It was time to forget Nancy Pike and the trouble she had caused him and concentrate on the future.

It was Nancy's final week of being granted time to spend with the children. The prospect of seeing less of them made her feel sore inside. She didn't want them to end up thinking she had lost interest in them, so she made a point of going out with the groups Molly's husband took out in the evenings to collect pennies for the guy. It kept her from dwelling too much on what had happened at Zachary's shop an' all.

Using a holey sheet, Mr Abrams had helped the children make a straw-stuffed guy. A face was painted on and the children made a tatty wig of black wool. Then the guy was dressed in old clothes, complete with a floppy hat. Mr Abrams helped the bigger boys make a cart to push it around in and Nancy oversaw the painting of a PENNY FOR THE GUY notice that was nailed to the front.

The bonfire was going to be on the playground and groups of children were taken to the meadows to look for bits of wood.
Build a bonfire,
Build a bonfire, sang the children.
Put the teachers on the top.
Put the prefects round the middle,

And burn the blinkin' lot.

As well as the bonfire, there were going to be Catherine wheels pinned to some of the trees that edged the playground and Mrs Wilkes, the cook, had promised a feast of spicy parsnip soup, baked potatoes, toffee apples and gingerbread.

'I think you're more excited about it than the children,' said Vivienne with a smile when Nancy described the forthcoming delights.

'I've never had more than a sparkler on Bonfire Night before,' said Nancy. There was another reason for her excitement, one she shouldn't share in case she made a twit of herself, but somehow the words came tumbling out all the same. 'Did you know that Mr Milner has an appointment at St Anthony's in the morning?'

'Is Mrs Rostron thinking of having fire extinguishers?'

'Yes. As a matter of fact, I suggested it.' She winced. That sounded big-headed.

'And I expect you mentioned Mr Milner's name,' Miss Patience said kindly.

'I'd actually thought of speaking to Mrs Rostron before I caused such trouble for him,' said Nancy. 'It was talking to Belinda about the fire her family was caught in that made me think of it.'

'Good for you,' said Vivienne.

Nancy would dearly have loved to ask Vivienne exactly what she meant by that, but she couldn't for fear of making her feelings for Zachary obvious. She and Ginny would be in the alcove with Miss Allan when he came for his meeting with Mrs Rostron. Nancy's heartbeat picked up speed. Would Mrs Rostron mention to him that the idea for fire extinguishers had come from Nancy? Would he be pleased? Or might he think that it was the very least she owed him? What if even the sight of her annoyed him all over again? She didn't think she could bear it.

The next morning, Zachary came up the stairs, shown the way by Nurse Eva. Nancy heard their footsteps on the bare treads and heat rushed into her face, obliging her to bend her head over her work. She was folding letters and placing them inside envelopes. Ever since she had put the carbon paper in the typewriter the wrong way round, Miss Allan had declared that folding letters was all she was good for.

'This is Mr Milner, to see Mrs Rostron,' said Nurse Eva, stopping in front of Miss Allan's desk.

Nancy looked up, her gaze drawn inexorably to Zachary. He looked smart in his suit with a blue tie. He was carrying a carpetbag containing something bulky and he had his bowler underneath his other arm. Taking it off had mussed his sandy hair a little. He didn't wear hair-cream the way most men did. Nancy longed to say something welcoming, something encouraging, but Miss Allan would have her guts for garters.

'Miss Virginia, will you please show Mr Milner to Mrs Rostron's office?' said Miss Allan.

Ginny got up from behind the typewriter. 'This way, Mr Milner.'

A couple of minutes later, a beautifully dressed plump lady with a fox fur around her shoulders and cherries dangling from her hat was shown upstairs.

'Good morning,' she said in a plummy voice. 'I hear from Mrs Lowe that her husband is coming here today to take part in a discussion concerning the possible installation of fire extinguishers.'

'That is correct, Mrs Wardle.' Miss Allan made a show of consulting the diary on her desk. 'Mr Lowe is indeed due any minute now, but we weren't expecting you this morning.'

'No matter. As the official visitor, I make it my business to be involved in all important decisions.'

So saying, Mrs Wardle swanned down the passage and knocked at the office door, leaving Miss Allan to show her disapproval by drawing in her chin with a sniff. Mrs Wardle's arrival was soon followed by that of a gentleman with a pencil-moustache, wearing a dark overcoat, whom Miss Allan greeted as Mr Lowe.

'It is good to have you back with us, Miss Allan,' he said. 'I trust you are in good health now?'

'Yes, thank you,' Miss Allan replied. 'Mrs Rostron is expecting you. Miss Virginia will show you the way and announce you.'

Ginny got up from the typewriter to lead Mr Lowe to the office door, which she knocked on and opened before returning to the alcove. Nancy felt a flicker of vexation. So what if Miss Allan thought she wasn't up to snuff with the dratted typewriter? She was perfectly capable of opening a door for a visitor. It was a good job she was fond of Ginny. If she wasn't, she would probably hate her for being Miss Allan's pet.

'Miss Nancy,' said Miss Allan, 'the lady and gentleman whom Miss Virginia showed into Mrs Rostron's office were Mrs Wardle and Mr Lowe. They are both on the committee in charge of St Anthony's.'

Nancy nodded. A few minutes later, when Miss Allan was busy with a telephone call and Ginny had finished her typing, Ginny whispered to Nancy.

'I don't know anything about Mr Lowe, but Mrs Wardle is what's called the official visitor. That means she comes and goes as she pleases. I don't think the official visitor is really meant to do that, but it's how Mrs Wardle behaves. She's meant to make an appointment if she wants to come here, but she's always turning up unannounced. It's just like her to barge in on this meeting with Mr Milner. Honestly, she treats St Anthony's as if it's her personal property.'

Mrs Wardle seemed like a formidable lady. What would her opinion be of having fire extinguishers? Did it matter what her opinion was? Mrs Rostron was pretty formidable an' all.

Things must have gone well, though, because Zachary was all smiles when he emerged from the office. Nancy felt breathless with relief on his behalf.

'If you have those envelopes ready for the post, Miss Nancy,' said Miss Allan, 'kindly take them to the pillar-box.' She made it sound as if Nancy should have done this without being told, even though neither Nancy nor Ginny was permitted to leave the premises without direct permission.

'Yes, Miss Allan.'

Miss Allan left the alcove and went downstairs. Nancy stood up. Mr Abrams had attached a hook to the wall beside one of the cupboards for her coat and hat. She reached for her hat as Zachary came along the passage towards the alcove. Her skin tingled with awareness. She picked up the pile of envelopes. If she got downstairs first, she could linger at the bottom while he caught up. Asking about his interview with Mrs Rostron and the others would provide the perfect excuse to speak to him.

'Miss Nancy,' said Ginny.

Nancy pretended not to hear. All she could think about was getting downstairs.

'Miss Nancy.'

This time Ginny's voice was louder. Not only that, but the sound of footsteps on the bare floorboards showed she intended coming after her. Drat. Nancy turned round and found Ginny looking alarmed.

'What is it?' Nancy asked.

'Stamps,' said Ginny. 'Have you stamped the letters?'

Nancy could have curled up and died. What a stupid mistake to make – and in front of Zachary an' all.

'It's a good thing you have a colleague to watch over you,' he remarked.

For one moment, Nancy wished she could sink to the floor and trickle through the cracks in the wooden boards, but then something changed inside her. She was sick to death of being constantly ashamed and embarrassed about her clerical work. She had never had a problem when she was at the pie shop and it wasn't right that she had been made to leave. She had felt inadequate ever since. On top of that, she had felt sick with shame ever since Mr Grant had demanded that ten guinea refund from Zachary – money that the Miss Heskeths had had to pay back to him, though admittedly that had come out of that special insurance rather than out of their own pockets. Even so, it was humiliating to know that she, Nancy Pike, was the only pupil who had ever caused that policy to be activated. And now, here she was, having made yet another mistake – and it wasn't because she was stupid, it wasn't because she was lazy...but try telling everyone else that! No one else seemed to see that she was doing her very best.

She lifted her chin and glared at Zachary.

'Well, I'm sorry if I'm not perfect, Mr Milner, only it were never my idea to work in an office. I was perfectly happy where I was in the pie shop. And before you tell me I should get myself back there, let me tell you summat. You should be thanking me for getting you this appointment here today. I was the one who mentioned fire extinguishers to Mrs Rostron and I recommended your service in particular – but I shan't bother recommending you again, not if you can't keep a civil tongue in your head.'

Chapter Eighteen

ZACHARY WAS ASTONISHED at being spoken to like that – at being torn off a strip by Miss Nancy Pike of all people. But before anything else could be said, the office door along the passage opened and, glancing over his shoulder, he saw Mr Lowe appear. Not wanting to be caught dragging his heels, he hurried for the stairs and ran down them. His heart should be racing with excitement after the success of the meeting in the superintendent's office, but instead he felt all in a flurry because – because of the effect Nancy Pike had had on him.

When she had berated him, her fair skin had been invaded by a rosy flush that had made her light-brown eyes take on a richer nut-brown hue. Her face, which he had thought of as pinched and thin, was actually finely shaped and delicately boned, while her small, spare body had a daintiness about it. She was – dash it, she was lovely. Not only that, but she wasn't stupid or careless, just out of her depth and doing her best in a form of work she hadn't wanted in the first place.

At the foot of the staircase, he stopped and looked back up, but he couldn't hang about waiting for her to stamp her letters and come down. What if someone saw him? Besides, Mr Lowe would be coming downstairs at any moment.

Zachary hurried from the building, holding the carpetbag

containing his pretend extinguisher and his diary by his side. He ran down the front steps, crossed the playground and walked around the single-storey wing that protruded into the grounds and turned what would have been one massive playground into two smaller ones. It had presumably been built that way on purpose so as to keep the boys and the girls separate from one another.

In the playground where the gates were, the caretaker was ferrying a heap of sticks in a wheelbarrow. They knew one another by sight because of both living in Soapsuds Lane. It was to his house that Zachary had sent the doctor that time. He didn't know the Abramses to speak to and hadn't liked to knock and ask after the health of the lady who had had the baby.

Now, though, he had a good reason to speak to Mr Abrams – two good reasons.

'Good morning,' Zachary said.

The caretaker glanced round and stopped, setting down the handles of the wheelbarrow and letting its back legs touch the ground. Without being thick-set, he looked strong; he held himself with the confidence of a man accustomed to physical work. Beneath his cap, his hair was dark, as were his eyes.

'Mr Abrams, isn't it?' said Zachary, switching his carpet-bag to his other side so he could offer his hand to shake. 'Zachary Milner. We're near neighbours in Soapsuds Lane.'

'Aaron Abrams. You have the fire extinguisher shop.'

'That's right.'

'Business going well?'

'So-so. That's why I'm here today. Mrs Rostron is inter-ested in having extinguishers put in.'

'It's a good idea. We've got a couple of lads who might easily have died in a fire – not a fire here, I hasten to add – back in the spring.'

'That's what Mrs Rostron said. I gather you're having a bonfire this weekend.'

'That's right. Fireworks, toffee apples, the lot.' Abrams grinned. 'The kids are going to love it.'

Zachary nodded at the wheelbarrow. 'Is that wood for the bonfire? I suggested to Mrs Rostron and her colleagues that I could attend and help with safety.'

'Fire extinguishers?'

'No, I couldn't afford to offer extinguishers. I was thinking of buckets of sand and water, strategically placed.'

'Good idea. Thanks for offering.'

Zachary wetted his lips. 'I assume the staff will be at the bonfire.'

Abrams nodded. 'Every single one of them. Those who aren't on duty strictly speaking don't have to come, but—'

'But it would be frowned on if they didn't.'

Good. That meant Nancy was bound to be here and he was certain to see her again. If that mistake with the stamps was anything to go by, she couldn't afford to blot her copy-book by staying away. Besides, why would she want to? Bonfire Night was fun.

The week couldn't pass quickly enough for Zachary. He had a couple of appointments with prospective clients and he conducted a training session for the staff of a hotel. He returned to the orphanage to look round to choose the most appropriate places to site the extinguishers. Before he arrived, he couldn't help hoping that Nancy might be given the job of showing him round, which might be considered a suitable task for a girl who struggled with clerical duties; but it was Aaron Abrams who accompanied him around the rambling building.

'I'd no idea it was like this inside,' Zachary commented, as they yet again went down a couple of steps into a room.

Abrams laughed. 'The whole building is like this. Up a few steps here, down a few there, and no such thing as a straight corridor. It's all corners and hidey-holes.'

'Good for hide and seek.'

'Don't let Mrs Rostron hear you say that. The children aren't allowed to mess around upstairs.'

Thank goodness for the order from St Anthony's. It allowed him to have the chimney swept in the storeroom and immediately his living arrangements improved considerably. As well as the coal fire, he had hot water and toast, which made him realise how miserable his domestic life had been before, something he had refused to let himself see. He also treated himself to a second-hand folding camp-bed and enjoyed the best night's sleep he'd had in ages. Things were looking up. Work was, if not booming, then bobbing along well enough to keep his head above water; he had a few of the comforts of home life; and, come the weekend, he would get to see Nancy again.

He spent part of Sunday painting one of the walls in the shop, keeping the blinds down on the window and the pane of glass in the door so that no one could peer in and be offended at his working on the day of rest. A day of rest was the last thing he could afford to have. Besides, painting the wall provided a distraction from obsessively watching the hands on the clock.

At last, darkness fell and he set off for the orphanage. He had promised Aaron Abrams he would get there in good time to sort out the buckets. He arrived to find that the bonfire had been built and children were milling about, chattering excitedly.

'Evening,' said Abrams. 'This lad here is Layton One. He'll show you where the buckets are and help you fill them.'

Layton One? What sort of a name was that? Zachary and the boy filled the buckets with sand or water.

'Where do you want them put?' asked Layton One.

'If you take these four and line them up against that wall, I'll see to the rest,' said Zachary. He reckoned the best place for the remaining buckets was over by the gates at the front of the playground, where they would be out of the way but close enough in any emergency. He decided to stay beside them, just in case.

More children appeared, all of them wrapped up inside coats, the smaller children in the company of young women whom he had learned from Abrams were called nursemaids. They were the ones who took care of the children, under the supervision of experienced woman called nannies. It sounded posh, but there was nothing posh about growing up in an orphanage. Where was Nancy? Zachary's eyes were practically out on stalks. Then he saw her. She had a group of little ones around her and she was bending down to listen to them. She looked a lot more comfortable surrounded by children than she ever had sitting at his typewriter.

Layton One appeared at his side. 'I've put the buckets in position, sir.'

'Good lad. Tell me – that young lady over there – she's not one of the nursemaids, is she?' He couldn't resist the opportunity to talk about her.

The boy looked round. 'No. That's Miss Nancy. She's working for Miss Allan until Christmas. There's her and Miss Virginia. One of them will be kept on after that.'

'What about the other one?'

Layton One shrugged. 'Dunno, sir, but it'd be a rotten shame if Miss Nancy had to leave. All the kids love her. She's good fun and she really cares about us. Mind you, we don't want Miss Virginia to leave either. We all know her because she was one of us up until the summer.'

'So you all like Miss Nancy, then?'

'Oh aye, sir. She's a good egg. She even got my younger brother reading and no one has ever managed that before.' For all his cheerful politeness, the boy was obviously trying not to bounce on his toes in impatience.

Zachary dismissed him with a jerk of his chin. 'Off you go. Enjoy the bonfire.'

It was a splendid evening. Abrams lit the bonfire and there were crackles and sparks before the fire took hold and began to lick its way up through the heap of wood. The toffee apples Abrams had mentioned turned out to be part of a feast that started with soup and potatoes, the smell of which made Zachary's mouth water. The oldest girls had the job of bringing round trays of food and Zachary helped himself to a mug of soup, which was creamy-smooth and pleasantly spicy, followed a few minutes later by a potato in a deliciously crisp jacket.

After that, it was time for the fireworks. After some fussing by the nursemaids, the children sat on the tarmac, automatically putting themselves in height order as if they were at school, so that they were all able to watch the Catherine wheels whizzing and sparkling on the trees beside where Zachary was standing. Afterwards, he helped Abrams set up a line of Roman candles in front of the wall, the children swivelling round to see the coloured lights bursting out amidst showers of flickering sparkles. The children's chorus of oohs and aahs touched Zachary's heart. These poor little blighters had a tough time of it, being orphans, and they deserved a treat.

Then he helped Abrams set out a line of milk bottles, popping a rocket on a stick inside each one. Abrams stepped forward and lit each blue touchpaper one at a time, sending the rockets shooting up into the sky, each one accompanied by a cry of delight from the audience, all except for one tot who burst into tears and had to be lifted out of the sitting crowd and taken away. One by one, the rockets burst into a shower of glittering colours high above.

When the fireworks were over, a woman appeared followed by some of the older girls, each with a large plate, and the children lined up to be offered a piece of gingerbread. A girl brought Zachary a slice, the bold smell of ginger making his mouth water even though he had already enjoyed his soup and baked potato.

The children were milling about now, the bright light of the bonfire illuminating the happy scene. Zachary was glad to be here, a feeling that was nothing to do with his desire to see Nancy Pike again – though her presence made this evening all the more special. He could see her clearly in the light from the bonfire. She was in the middle of a group of children and she was laughing. She looked relaxed and bubbly both at the same time. Bubbly? He wanted to join her – his feet actually started to move – but he forced himself to stay put. His job was to be at hand with the buckets, should the need arise. It would destroy his professional reputation should a piece of burning wood come tumbling out of the bonfire and he had gone wandering off.

The breath caught in his throat as she disentangled herself from her little group and started to – was she really coming towards him? Seeking him out? Yes, yes, she was. It was all he could do not to grin all over his silly face. He felt ten feet tall.

'Good evening, Miss Pike. Isn't it all splendid?'

'Yes, it is. The children are having a wonderful time.' She bit her lip and glanced away for a moment. Then she looked back at him, turning her face up to his. 'I wanted to say I'm sorry.'

'What for?'

'For snapping at you the other day when you said what you did about me needing someone to watch what I'm doing at work. I shouldn't have done it.'

'I'm sorry I hurt your feelings. It just popped out.' He didn't want to talk about that. 'I saw you with the children. They like you.'

'I'd like to think so.' She hesitated before suggesting, 'Would you like to meet them?'

'I'm sorry, but I'm busy.'

She stared at him in astonishment. Then her eyes narrowed. 'Too busy to give a few orphans some attention?'

Zachary wanted to groan out loud. 'I didn't mean—' But before he could explain that he couldn't leave his post beside the buckets, another voice chimed in.

'Milner!' It was Mr Lowe, smiling affably. 'I gather you're here to help out with safety. Good show.'

'It's a pleasure, sir,' said Zachary, forcing a smile.

Mr Lowe moved on, but when Zachary turned back to speak to Nancy, eager to explain himself to her and possibly even show his interest in her, she had already marched off.

Chapter Nineteen

NANCY COULD BARELY believe it. Zachary Milner – too 'busy' to come and meet some children? Talk about being given the brush-off! Well, that had showed her good and proper, hadn't it? He didn't want anything to do with her – and frankly, who could blame him after that disastrous mistake she had made with Mr Grant's invoice? Even so, it still hurt. But it was time to accept that all those hours she had spent daydreaming about Zachary Milner had been a complete waste of time. To him, she was the person who had caused havoc in his shop, and that was all she would ever be. She would have to get used to it and cast him from her thoughts for ever. All those hopes and wishes, all those little stories she had lived inside her head, were just so much twaddle and that was all there was to it. Starting now, she had to get a hold of herself and stop thinking about him.

Oh, but it would be hard. If only he wasn't coming back to the orphanage to install the fire extinguishers – no, she didn't wish that. She wanted the children to be safe, of course she did. She just wished she wouldn't have to see him. Could she possibly wriggle out of the training?

'Certainly not,' said Miss Allan the next day. 'What sort of a slacker are you?'

'I'm not a slacker – begging your pardon,' Nancy added hastily as she found herself on the receiving end of one of Miss

Allan's icy glares. 'I just thought that with me possibly being temporary—'

'I'm glad you realise you're *possibly* temporary,' Miss Allan replied, her tone laced with sarcasm. 'Every member of staff is to be trained and that's all there is to it, though heaven help us if we have to rely on you in an emergency, Miss Nancy, if you're as inept with one of these fire extinguisher contraptions as you are with everything else.'

Well, at least the training was to take place in the next day or two, so that would get it over and done with. After that, she would never have to think about Mr Zachary Milner again.

There were two lists on the noticeboard in the staff dining room. Zachary would be taking two training sessions and each list included notes about who would be covering whose duties while they were being trained. Nancy and Ginny were on different lists because of covering for one another and Nancy was going to be in the first batch of trainees. She would rather have gone second, so she could have found out what was involved. Since she had left the pie shop, she seemed to have lost some of her confidence – and no wonder, when she thought what a pig's ear she had made of everything since then. No, not quite everything. She might be a dunderhead when it came to office work, but she was good with the children.

The training began in the big dining room as soon as it had been cleaned after the children had departed for school. Zachary stood at the front and held up a cylinder with a rubber hose coming out of it.

'This is what a fire extinguisher looks like. The most important thing to remember is that it isn't meant to be used on a fire that's already out of control. You use it on a fire that has yet to take hold. This is a replica that I have made. I'll explain how to hold it and how it works and then I'll pass it round so everyone can try it and get a feel for its size and weight and also have a go at unfastening the top. Then I'll show you the fire blanket and talk about how that works. After that I'll answer any questions and then we'll go outside and one of you can have a go with a real extinguisher. I thought it was important today that you have the chance to see one working.'

Nurse Carmel raised her hand. 'Excuse me, but why is it important today? Don't you always use a real extinguisher when you are training people?'

Was that a suggestion of a blush in Zachary's cheeks? 'Not normally, no. But normally I train either groups of men or else mixed groups of men and ladies. I, er, I just thought that, with a group of ladies, such as yourselves, it would be a good idea for you to see an extinguisher in action, so that you can see there's nothing to be scared – nothing to worry about,' he finished hastily.

Nancy bristled. Did he imagine he was facing a group of silly females who would go to pieces in an emergency? Her hand shot up before she knew what she was doing.

'Please can I volunteer to try out the real extinguisher?'

She paid close attention as Zachary talked about the fire extinguisher and when the replica was handed round, she scrutinised it closely, testing its weight and making sure she could hold it in one hand while directing the hose with the other. She would have liked to stand up to do this, but everyone else had remained sitting down, so she felt she had to an' all.

Presently it was time to go out onto the boys' playground. It was a cold, overcast morning. In the middle of the playground was a small heap of twigs.

Zachary got them all to stand in a semi-circle while he once again went through the routine for using an extinguisher. Then he removed a different one, presumably the real one, from his carpetbag and beckoned Nancy forward. Quelling a quiver of anxiety, she went to take the cylinder from him, but he stepped away from her.

'Not yet,' he said. 'In a real situation, you wouldn't have it already in your hands. I'll put it over here beside this tree, like so, and then I'll set light to these twigs and once the fire is going, you can deal with your emergency, Miss Pike. There's nothing to worry about. I'll be just over here, so that I can step in if necessary.'

It was tempting to declare that it wouldn't be necessary, thank you very much, but she kept it to herself. She was aware of everyone watching closely as Zachary got a small fire going. He made sure it had taken well, then he nodded at her.

'Fire!' he called. 'Fire!'

Nancy made a dash for the extinguisher, seized it and rushed to the rescue, but when she set it working, the pressure inside the hose took her by surprise and it almost slipped from her grasp – and, to her horror, she found herself extinguishing not the fire, but Zachary.

Nancy stood outside Mrs Rostron's office, like a naughty child sent for by the headmaster to receive the cane. Miss Allan was inside the office with Mrs Rostron, no doubt pouring out the story of Nancy's shocking behaviour and how she had let down St Anthony's through her foolishness. She was probably recommending that Nancy should be sacked without a reference.

Tears welled behind Nancy's eyes. It had been an accident, though you'd never have thought so from the look of thunder on Miss Allan's face. What must everyone think of her? She would be a laughing stock. She would never be able to hold up her head again. As for Zachary – well, he had had a low opinion of her before this, so his opinion now must be dragging along the floor in the dirt. Nancy blinked away her tears. She wouldn't cry. She wouldn't be an even bigger twerp than she was already.

The sound of footsteps coming along the passage towards Mrs Rostron's office made her look round. Zachary! His suit was covered in dark patches where the liquid had soaked him and his hair was wet an' all. She experienced a most inconvenient desire to dry it for him. Then she remembered how he had snubbed her and hardened her heart.

'Excuse me.' Zachary moved past her and knocked on the door.

'Come,' called the superintendent's calm voice.

He went in, pulling the door to behind him, but not clicking it shut. Nancy stretched out her hand to close it, then let her hand fall away. Eavesdropping was wrong, but she couldn't help it.

'Mr Milner,' said Mrs Rostron, 'I apologise most sincerely for what happened. Miss Allan has told me all about it. This isn't the first time Miss Pike has shown herself to be less than satisfactory and I can assure you she will be dealt with.'

What did that mean? Was she going to be sacked? She would never get another job if that happened, not even in a shop. Nancy's mouth went dry.

'Please,' said Zachary, 'I wouldn't like to think of there being any repercussions. Miss Pike is – well, she's a good sort of girl.'

'She is an awkward and inept sort of girl,' said Miss Allan. 'She has bungled more or less every task I have set her. What happened this morning was yet another example of her inability to do the simplest thing.'

'Mrs Rostron,' said Zachary, 'please don't be hard on her. It was an accident. The pressure of the release of the foam through the tube caught her unawares. It's understandable.

It's harder for a girl to handle a fire extinguisher than it is for a man.'

'It is generous of you to take such a view, Mr Milner,' said Mrs Rostron.

'A generosity that Miss Pike does not entirely deserve, if I may say so,' said Miss Allan. 'The girl is probably incapable of being trained to do even the most basic office work.'

Nancy went cold right to the centre of her being. She knew she was no good at clerical work, but hearing the words spoken so frankly came as a shock even so.

'Miss Allan,' said Zachary, 'I understand your disappointment in Miss Pike's clerical work. She did some work for me in my shop and I know she did her best, but…well, her best wasn't good enough. As I understand it, she has a temporary post here until Christmas. Won't you please let her keep it, Mrs Rostron? Forgive me for speaking bluntly, but if I don't hold today's mishap against her, then why should you? Let her see out her time here and, who knows, maybe she'll find her feet.'

That was it. Nancy had heard enough. Turning, she marched away down the passage and ran downstairs. Let them send for her if they wanted her. She wasn't going to hang about outside Mrs Rostron's office while her fate was decided and while Zachary poured out how sorry he felt for her. He thought her a sap. Simple as that. He wasn't standing up for her because he liked her; he wasn't even doing it because he believed in her. He was doing it because he felt sorry for her.

Well, if she kept her job here, all well and good. But she never wanted to see Zachary Milner again. She didn't want to be the object of anyone's pity.

Chapter Twenty

W HAT WAS SHE going to do when the book-keeping course came to a conclusion? The point of being a pupil-lodger was that you lived in for the duration of your learning and then you left. Vivienne didn't want to leave Wilton Close. She wasn't ready. She felt comfortable here – and not just because of the opportunity to build a relationship with her natural mother. She valued Miss Patience's companionship as well. The house in Wilton Close had become dear to her heart. Its faded smartness said so much about the Hesketh sisters, about standards and respectability and putting on a brave face.

Someone else who was putting on a brave face was Molly.

'Lucy was always something of a loose cannon, wasn't she?' said Molly. 'That business about refusing to name the father because she wasn't in love with him was downright daft. And her father made it clear from the start that he didn't want Aaron and me to have the baby. It was never a settled thing. I always knew I mustn't depend upon it.'

Truth or bravado? Even if Molly had schooled herself to be sensible about it beforehand, surely she should still be more upset than this by losing the baby. But Molly clearly didn't wish to be pressed and so Vivienne, troubled and not knowing quite how to respond for the best, decided to leave well alone.

Lucy, meanwhile, would be getting married. Imagine that. Vivienne remembered her turning up on the doorstep in the spring. It seemed like an age ago now. It was obviously on Miss Patience's mind as well.

'It feels strange not to be close to Lucy and her situation any more,' she said. 'It seems we are excluded now.'

Mr Hesketh turned up the next evening before lessons started. He sat down, stood up again, then resumed his seat, giving the appearance of being edgy and satisfied at the same time.

'The wedding has been arranged. The Bambrooks were shocked, of course – stunned, more like – but they've taken it on the chin.'

'And Dickie Bambrook?' Miss Hesketh asked.

'Couldn't be happier. He has missed Lucy ever since she vanished off the scene when she came here.' Mr Hesketh clenched his jaw.

'You seem vexed, Lawrence,' said Miss Patience, 'but if Dickie is happy, that's a good thing, surely?'

Vivienne said quietly, 'Perhaps Mr Hesketh would prefer the man who deflowered his daughter to suffer, which is understandable, but I'm sure what he wants most is for Lucy and Dickie to have the best possible start to married life.'

Mr Hesketh looked as if he was about to explode. 'Kindly don't tell me what to think about this damnable situation.'

'Language, Lawrence,' Miss Patience murmured.

'I apologise,' Mr Hesketh replied stiffly, 'but, great Scott, after everything I've had to put up with—'

'Tell us about the wedding,' said Miss Hesketh. 'When will it be? I thought it might already have taken place by special licence.'

'It would have, if I'd had anything to do with it, but Evelyn and Cissie Bambrook put their heads together and decided that, with Lucy needing bed-rest for a fortnight, a three-week licence would do. The earliest she and Dickie could marry is this coming Saturday, but it's Armistice Day, so that's out. It'll be the Saturday of next week instead. Evelyn and Cissie decided on a proper wedding, not some hole-and-corner arrangement. Cissie's brother lives near Southport and we've sent packed suitcases on behalf of Lucy and Dickie to his house, so they can claim that as their address. The wedding will be celebrated in his village church. A small affair – just immediate family on both sides and no one there who doesn't need to be, but enough of a turn-out to produce some decent photographs. Dickie's grandmother lives in Italy and he and Lucy will go there for a year.'

'And when they return,' said Miss Hesketh, 'it's remarkable how fuzzy people can be about dates.'

'Quite.' Mr Hesketh rose to leave. 'You'll receive your invitations by tomorrow's post.'

'We're invited?' cried Miss Patience. 'Oh, how lovely. Thank you.'

'Evelyn and I appreciate the assistance you've given us in this matter.'

The next morning, as the four of them sat at the breakfast table, it didn't escape Vivienne's notice that Miss Patience had left the door open. When the letter-box flap clicked in the hall, she jumped up.

'I'm sorry, Prudence. I know I shouldn't, but I can't wait.'

She hastened out, returning a moment later with two creamy envelopes of the highest quality and a third of good quality but of a more everyday variety.

'Two with Evelyn's handwriting and one from Lucy.' Miss Patience gave one of the posh envelopes to her sisters. 'This must be our invitation – and there's one for you as well, Vivienne dear.'

To Vivienne's surprise, Miss Patience handed her an envelope. She opened it to find a scallop-edged invitation to the wedding of Lucy Emilia Hesketh and Mr Richard Angus Bambrook. She had never expected this. Then she unfolded the accompanying letter.

'Have you been sent a wedding invitation?' Miss Patience asked.

Vivienne was stumped for a reply. 'Yes – but Mrs Hesketh has enclosed a note to say that – let me read it out. *My husband and I are aware of the kindness you have shown our daughter.*'

'That's nice,' said Nancy.

'She goes on to say that I mustn't feel obliged to accept the invitation if it is at all inconvenient to attend. In other words: don't come.'

Miss Hesketh huffed out a breath of annoyance. 'That's despicable.'

'Wait.' Miss Patience had opened the remaining envelope. 'This is from Lucy. Thank you for everything we've done for her... et cetera et cetera... *I insisted that Mummy must invite Vivienne, but I think she might have penned a note to try to put her off. Please tell V she simply has to be there* ("has" underlined three times) *or I shan't get married.*'

'That's that, then,' said Miss Hesketh. 'You're coming.'

'You shan't mind?' Vivienne addressed her question to Miss Patience. 'I wouldn't want to push in.'

'Whyever should I mind?' asked Miss Patience. 'You were endlessly patient with Lucy, especially when she was first here. I'm pleased with her for inviting you and, if you don't mind my saying so, I'll be glad to be in your company on the day. I've grown fond of you in the time you've lived here.'

'Thank you.' Warmth poured through Vivienne. 'I'm fond of you too.'

'In fact, I'm really rather dreading the approaching end of your book-keeping course,' said Miss Patience, 'because you shan't need to be a pupil-lodger any more, and that will be such a shame. In fact...' She looked at her sister. 'I apologise, Prudence. I know I should have discussed this in private with you first, but this feels like the right time to say it. Vivienne dear, after you no longer require to be a pupil-lodger, would you like to stay on as an ordinary paying guest?'

November the eleventh. Armistice Day. Poppy Day, the orphans were calling it, according to Nancy, which was rather sweet. Vivienne drew in a breath, then realised she was about to sigh – and didn't, wouldn't let herself. Sighing didn't make any difference; neither did tears. As a war widow, she knew that all too well. She refused to feel sorry for herself. She was better off than many, if not most. The soldier's pension on which lower-class women struggled to pay the rent and bring up their children was, to her, a welcome addition to her salary, enabling her to live quite comfortably. That was something to be grateful for.

The Miss Heskeths had gone to St Clement's, but Vivienne, having a strong link with St Anthony's through her work at the Board of Health, had chosen to attend the Remembrance Day assembly at the orphanage, where some of the children had lost their fathers in the war. It felt important to be with children on this special day.

'Because children represent the future?' asked Miss Patience.

'It's not that,' said Vivienne. 'It's because it's so important that they grow up remembering; and those that aren't old enough to remember must be encouraged to honour the fallen and recognise the sacrifice that was made. No one must ever forget.'

Her heart filled. For the sake of all those soldiers, including her own dear husband, no one must ever forget.

Mrs Rostron required all her members of staff to attend her Remembrance Assembly and Nancy had set off early to help get the children ready. Vivienne followed later. It was a crisp, dry morning. She passed a few pedestrians on her way, all of them wearing their red paper poppies. They bade one another a sombre good morning.

Vivienne turned the corner into Church Road. All the way to the far end of the road was a long line of terraced houses with tiny front gardens. At the end stood the orphanage. Vivienne entered the grounds through the gates that were standing open this morning to admit the expected visitors. Grounds! That made it sound far more grand than it was. In reality, it looked more like a school, with its ground-floor windows set too high in the walls for an adult to see out of, let alone a child.

Vivienne walked past the single-storey wing that jutted out. She crossed the boys' playground, stooping to pick up a lost poppy before she went to the stone steps leading up to the front door. Drayshaw One and Ellen, the head boy and head girl, stood just inside, ready to greet visitors.

'Good morning.' Vivienne smiled at them, allowing a moment for the bow and curtsey Mrs Rostron insisted upon. She held up the poppy. 'One of the children has dropped this.'

Drayshaw One took it from her and turned it over. 'Amelia Jones.' He grinned at her. 'We've written the names of the children on the back of all the poppies this year.'

'That's a good idea.'

'Miss Nancy thought of it,' said Ellen. 'She's ever so thoughtful where us children are concerned.'

Drayshaw One politely showed Vivienne into the dining room, where the tables and benches had been pushed aside to leave a big space, like a school hall. Nurse Eva sat at the upright piano, playing softly. There were chairs for adults at the back and a few chairs along the sides, where orphanage staff would sit to keep an eye on their charges. At the front was a lectern.

Vivienne took a seat, nodding to those already present. Some must be relatives of the orphans, including a few parents. Mrs Layton, mother of Michael and Jacob, sat further along the row. Aaron, Molly and their lad, Danny, came down the couple of steps into the room and headed for the seats, exchanging small smiles with Vivienne. Not long ago, Danny had been one of the orphans, though not a real orphan, because his dad had been desperately ill in a sanatorium. A special bond had grown between Danny and Aaron and, after poor Mr Cropper had passed away, the newly engaged Aaron and Molly had arranged to adopt him.

Nurse Eva, having apparently received a signal, brought her music to a tinkling conclusion. There was a pause, then Mrs Rostron appeared in the doorway. She came down the steps and swept along the room to stand behind the lectern. She was followed by her staff and her charges in silent single file, little children first. The children all sat cross-legged on the floor, a poppy on the front of each grey pullover and grey pinafore. They wore black armbands as well. The nannies, nursemaids and office staff sat in the wooden seats dotted along both sides of the room; the kitchen staff sat at the back.

The service began with the children singing 'The Lord is My Shepherd', then Drayshaw One and Ellen each gave a short Bible reading. After that came 'Abide With Me', during which more than one of the adults' voices cracked and stopped singing.

Mrs Rostron looked round the room. 'Forty-four of our children live here because they lost their fathers in the Great

War. I will now read out the names and ranks of those brave men, who gave their lives for King and country.'

She read the names, pausing after each one. Some of the children, hearing their dads' names, sat up straight and looked round proudly. Others almost curled up in distress. One of the fourteens sobbed so loudly that Nurse Philomena had to escort her from the room.

'Now we come to the St Anthony's Roll of Honour,' said Mrs Rostron. 'When children leave here, we have to find them situations that include somewhere to live. For many of our boys, that means going into the army. Three hundred and seventy-six of our former boys are known to have given their lives in the Great War and we may never know the true number.' Her gaze swept over the children whom it was her duty to protect and bring up. 'Three hundred and seventy-six is a very big number. We have about a hundred and twenty children at any given time, so if you all look round at one another and then try to imagine two more dining rooms with the same number of children, that is roughly how many of our boys we know lost their lives in the war – though you mustn't imagine them as boys. Most of them were grown-up men; and even the very youngest were older than the oldest children here. They all gave their lives so that we can live in peace. Our Roll of Honour is, sadly, too long for me to read out this morning, so I will read out the same number of names as we have children under our roof.'

As she did so, Vivienne marvelled that she could do it without so much as a waver in her voice. Such self-control! Nanny Duffy and Nanny Mitchell mopped their faces. They must have brought up some of those lads. As for Miss Allan, how could she bear it? She had been here longer than anyone.

'At eleven o'clock exactly,' said Mrs Rostron, 'we shall have a two-minute silence to honour the fallen. The children should remain seated and bow their heads, but will the adults please stand?'

There was a little shuffling as the adults complied, then stillness descended. Mrs Rostron rang the bell – a single bright *ding* – and everyone bowed their heads. Vivienne curled her hands into fists, cursing the gloves that prevented her from digging her nails into her palms to cause a sharp sting that might hold back the tears. What a dear man she had lost. What a waste. Oh, the life she should have had – the children, the family home. All those lost sweethearts, husbands, fathers. All those lost breadwinners. The war might be over, but its effects would last for ever.

Another *ding* brought the silence to a close. Mrs Rostron nodded to Nurse Eva, who struck up the introduction to 'The Day Thou Gavest, Lord, is Ended'. With some clearing of throats among the adults, the singing began. A couple of rows in front of Vivienne, Molly leaned across Danny and spoke briefly to Aaron, then hurried out via the door at the back of the room that led to a passageway beside the kitchen and a door that opened onto the back of the girls' playground. Vivienne stooped to grab her handbag and followed, catching up with Molly as she fumbled with the outer door.

'Molly, wait. Why are you so upset?'

Molly turned round. Her face was white, her greeny-hazel eyes filled with tears.

'I'm sorry. I meant to sneak away. I hope I haven't made a spectacle of myself.'

'Everyone feels overwhelmed today.'

'Folk will wonder what makes me so special that I have to leave early, as if my grief is worse than theirs.'

Vivienne stepped closer to her friend. 'Tell me to mind my own business, but I'd like to help, if I can, if you'll permit me.'

Molly wrenched open the door. 'Let's get some fresh air.'

She marched across the playground to the gates and started up Church Road, heels tapping.

'Are we going to Soapsuds House?' asked Vivienne.

Molly stopped. 'I don't know. I don't know why I took off at such a lick. It's not as though I can outpace my thoughts.'

Vivienne linked her arm. 'Let's walk round to the Green and sit on a bench.'

Without speaking they made their way to the corner, then onto Beech Road and from there onto Chorlton Green. The trees that edged it all the way round were almost bare, the last of their leaves scattered across the expanse of grass. The old lamp-post in the centre stood tall and black beneath winter-white clouds in a grey sky. Vivienne steered Molly towards a bench and sat close beside her.

'Tell me,' she said simply.

Molly pressed her lips together hard. She turned and looked straight at Vivienne.

'My family is so lucky. Our Tom came home safe. His hair had turned silver, but he was safe and all in one piece. We're unbelievably lucky when you compare us to other families. The people over the road from my mum and dad lost all four of their sons. Imagine what today is like for them.'

'We're not here to talk about them,' Vivienne said gently. 'We're meant to be talking about you.'

'What today means to me – and I know how wrong it is; I know I ought to be thinking of all those fallen soldiers – but today what I can't stop thinking about, what fills me to the brim, is the baby I had to give up.'

'Oh, Molly.'

Molly had fallen in love during the war. She and her Toby had anticipated their wedding vows, leaving Molly pregnant and alone when Toby was killed. Although it had broken her heart to do it, she had had no choice other than to give up their son for adoption.

'And now I've lost a second child as well.' The words burst from Molly's lips.

'Lucy's baby.'

'Aaron and I told ourselves all along it wasn't definite, but what you tell yourself, what you know in your head, isn't the same as what's in here.' Molly splayed her hand across her chest. 'I hoped for that baby so much. I kept telling myself not to, but I couldn't help it. Then, when Lucy went into labour in our house and Charlie was born upstairs, it felt like an omen.' Her glance was rueful. 'I know how ridiculous that sounds.'

'It's not ridiculous at all,' said Vivienne.

'It felt so *right*. And then Lucy changed her mind – which she was perfectly entitled to do, of course. I, of all people, know what it is to give up a baby. If I'd had a choice, like Lucy did...'

'I know, love. I know. Forgive me if this is insensitive, but there are plenty of little ones needing families at St Anthony's.'

'That's what Aaron said. And Danny, though he said he wanted to do the choosing.' Molly gave a watery smile before her eyes clouded again. 'But I can't think about that yet.'

'Your heart was set on Lucy's baby.'

'I wish Lucy well, I honestly do, but I was ready to be that child's mother. I was *ready*.'

Chapter Twenty-One

AFTER THE REMEMBRANCE Day assembly, Nancy felt the tug of home. Today of all days, it was important to be with your family and appreciate them, even pesky younger sisters. After the Sunday roast in Wilton Close, she set off for Bailiff's Row.

Beneath the layer of tobacco that lay for ever in the air in the Pikes' cramped flat was the smell of – oh, she recognised it, but she couldn't put her finger on it. She sniffed.

'Corned beef fritters,' Emily told her.

Corned beef fritters – for Sunday dinner. It showed how she had gone up in the world. She thought nowt these days of having chicken on a Sunday or pork with crackling and apple sauce. She experienced a moment of shame.

'Eh, we do miss the day-old pies you used to fetch home from the pie shop, our Nancy,' said Lottie, 'but that was before you got above yourself and went piking off to live in yon posh place.'

'That'll do, Lottie,' Mam chided. 'Don't begrudge your sister her chance to better herself. We'll all benefit from it in the long run, when she's earning a decent wage.'

Oh aye, if she ever managed to cope with clerical work!

'Did you go to church this morning, Mam?' Nancy asked.

'Aye, love.'

'Your mother was determined.' Pa smiled fondly at Mam. 'Weren't you, Marjorie?'

'It's the least I could do for Eddie and Les.'

There was a sorrowful silence. Nancy thought of her uncles. Twins ran in the family.

'Let's talk about summat cheerful,' said Mam. 'What have you been up to this week at that orphanage, my lass?'

Nancy glanced away as guilt tugged at her. It didn't feel right to talk about her job. Mam and Pa would worry if they knew how unsuited she was. If she made out she was coming along nicely, would that be sparing their feelings or would it be outright lies?

'If you want to hear summat cheerful, the Miss Heskeths and the other pupil-lodger, Mrs Atwood, are going to a wedding next Saturday. The ladies' niece is getting wed somewhere near Southport.'

'Oh, a wedding.' Mam sounded sentimental, but then her eyes narrowed. 'Is this the niece you mentioned to me once before?'

Nancy nodded.

Mam's face cleared. 'I'm pleased to hear she's getting married and I wish her well. Do you know what the Miss Heskeths and the other lady are going to wear?'

'Mrs Atwood always dresses well.' A smile caught at Nancy's lips as she went on, 'Miss Hesketh will look smart, but she won't have any frills or fuss.' If it had been just her and Mam, she would have shared Miss Patience's fears about mutton dressed as lamb. As it was, she said, 'Miss Patience is such a sweet, gentle lady. I hope she has summat nice to wear.'

When it was time to leave, Pa put on his threadbare coat to walk Nancy to the bus stop.

'So it'll be you on your own in Wilton Close next Saturday?'

he remarked as they walked along Bailiff's Row. The afternoon was drawing in. He pulled his scarf more snugly round
his neck. 'Would you ask if I can call round to see you?'

'You and Mam?'

'If she's up to it, but you know what her health is like. But
if she can't come, I'd still like to.'

They stood at the bus stop, stamping their feet to ward off
the chill. As the bus rumbled into view, Pa touched Nancy's
arm and she looked at him. He wasn't much taller than she
was. His face was pinched with cold. He and Mam were in
their thirties, but years of a meagre larder and a poor coal
scuttle had made them years older.

'You won't forget to ask the ladies, will you, our Nancy?'
said Pa. 'About me coming next Saturday?'

'You and Mam,' she corrected him.

'Me and Mam, aye.'

Would the Miss Heskeths mind? Would they think she was
taking a liberty, asking to have visitors in their absence?

'That will be quite in order,' said Miss Hesketh when
Nancy made her request. 'I'm sure your mother will like to
see where you are living.'

'If she's well enough to come,' said Nancy.

'Let's hope she is,' said Miss Patience. 'Would you like to
take her upstairs and show her your bedroom?'

'Thank you. She'd appreciate that.'

Nancy spent the week looking forward to Saturday, the
more so because she was now stuck with doing clerical work
all day. Oh, but she missed being with the children!

'Aren't you interested in our Christmas stocking decorations now?' asked the children.

'Of course I am, but I have jobs to do.'

'Don't you want to read with us any more?'

'I'd love to, but I'm not allowed to leave my duties.'

This reply was greeted with disappointed faces and some groans. Nancy couldn't bear to let the children down. She plucked up the courage to tap on Mrs Rostron's door.

'Please may I come here in the evenings to spend time with the children?'

Permission was granted and, on the evenings when she wasn't having lessons, Nancy returned to the orphanage after tea. She imagined she would simply continue with the sewing and reading as before, but Vivienne pointed out that she was doing this in her own time and therefore she could now pick and choose. Something unfurled inside her, like flower-petals opening in the sunshine. She no longer had to restrict herself to worthy and useful pursuits. She could play with the children. Jigsaws, cards, snakes and ladders. Tiddlywinks, ludo, pick-up-sticks. And it didn't have to be just games played at a table or on the floor. As long as the dining tables were put back afterwards, she was allowed to organise circle games, like oranges and lemons and the farmer's in his den. Would hide and seek be permitted, if she found out exactly where the children were and were not allowed to hide?

Her heart lifted. If her parents asked her on Saturday what she had been doing at St Anthony's, she would have plenty to tell them.

On Saturday, Nancy stood waiting in the bay window, gazing eagerly at the corner, but it was only Pa who walked into Wilton Close. Her heart dipped, but she didn't let her disappointment show when she opened the front door as Pa came up the garden path.

He kissed her cheek, his skin chilly as it brushed hers. She took his outdoor things.

'Isn't Mam well enough?'

'It's only to be expected.'

Nancy hugged him. 'I'm glad you're here, anyroad. Come and sit down. We'll have a natter before I put the kettle on. Miss Patience made a sponge cake. Wasn't that kind of her?'

They spent a while in the sitting room, but when Nancy got up to make the tea, Pa stood up an' all.

'Before you put the kettle on, would you mind if I have a little look round?'

Nancy froze. It was one thing to have permission for Mam to go upstairs to see her room, but what would the Miss Heskeths think of a man walking round their house?

'The – the cellar,' said Pa.

'The what?'

'All those books that are stored down there.'

'How do you know about them?'

Pa laughed. 'You told me. How else would I know? Can I take a look?'

'There's nowt to see. They're all boxed up.'

'Even so. I expect the boxes are labelled, aren't they? It'd be interesting to read the labels and get an idea of the range of the stock. I – I went to that bookshop once.'

Mam must have told Pa. That was it. Nancy had told Mam about Gabriel Linkworth's bookshop stock and Mam must have mentioned it to Pa. Only – Pa had said, 'You told me.' A slip of the tongue.

She took Pa down into the cellar, lighting their way with an oil-lamp. Pa took the lamp from her and examined the labels on the boxes. Nancy soon got fed up. Honestly, what was so interesting?

'I'll make the tea.'

But Pa didn't take this as his cue to leave. He just nodded. 'Give me a shout when you're ready.'

He lit her way to the foot of the steps. Feeling miffed, Nancy returned to the kitchen to prepare the tea. Then she went back into the cellar, taking the steps carefully. They were dark because Pa had the lamp on the far side.

'Pa, it's time.'

He jumped in shock. As he looked round, Nancy saw past him – to a couple of open boxes.

'What are you doing?' she whispered, horrified.

Was Pa a thief?

Flanked by Patience and Vivienne, Prudence walked along the curve of the church path towards the arched entrance to the deep porch of the Saxon church. She was dressed in her Sunday best, with Mother's cameo brooch in the front of her collar. Vivienne had suggested placing it on the lapel of her coat, where it would be on show in the photographs, but Prudence had pooh-poohed the idea.

'I don't know where girls wear cameo brooches these days, or even if they still do, but in my day, and in my mother's day, they were worn at the blouse collar.'

Dear Vivienne was wearing her calf-length olive-green dress with its sash of bottle-green that buckled at her hip, beneath her wool coat. Her light-brown chin-length bob was topped by her stylish oversized beret. To complete her ensemble, she wore dark-green suede shoes with wide bar-straps, with a matching handbag in two tones of green suede. Prudence felt a glow of pride. With her heart-shaped face and clear hazel eyes, Vivienne was such a good-looking girl and always so well turned-out. Prudence had never particularly noticed what other women wore, except in the most general way, but since being reunited with her daughter, she had taken pleasure in seeing what Vivienne wore each day.

Inside the porch, along one side of which was a long seat

built into the stonework, stood a pair of double doors, one of which was open. The sound of organ music floated out. A young man in a grey suit with a yellow rose in his button-hole smiled at them.

'We're the bride's family,' said Patience.

The young man's smile widened. 'I'm Rodney Bambrook, Dickie's brother. Allow me to escort you up the aisle.'

He offered an arm at the same time as Vivienne linked with Prudence.

'I'm sure Mr Bambrook would rather escort you, Vivienne dear,' said Patience, but Vivienne didn't let go and so, with a little flutter, Patience took Rodney Bambrook's arm and was led up the aisle.

Following, Prudence experienced an unexpected pang. Perhaps it made her link more tightly, because Vivienne tilted her head towards her.

'Are you all right?' she murmured.

'Poor Patience. If ever a woman was born to get married and have a family and a home of her own—'

'Life doesn't always work out the way we'd like,' said Vivienne, 'as you and I both know.'

They side-stepped along the old wooden pew, avoiding the tapestried hassocks and trying not to knock hymn books off the shelf attached to the pew in front.

'How pretty it all looks,' Patience whispered when they had settled themselves.

Indeed it did. At this dark time of year, the church was brightened by large arrangements involving rich red berries and leaves of deepest green, emerald and gold. There was even an arrangement on the lid of the ancient font.

'Perhaps they'll hold the christening after the wedding,' Prudence whispered to Vivienne, causing her to smother a snort of laughter.

A middle-aged couple sat on the opposite side. The uncle who lived in the village, and his wife? Another couple arrived and sat in the pew behind the front pew on the groom's side.

'Mr and Mrs Bambrook,' Patience whispered.

'Must be,' Prudence agreed.

'It's definitely them. We were introduced to them at that party we attended at Lawrence and Evelyn's in the spring.'

'I don't recall.'

'No, you wouldn't,' murmured Patience.

'What's that supposed to mean?'

'You were so furious at being there, I don't suppose you noticed anything.'

Prudence's conscience smote her. Had her rudeness been that obvious? There could be no excuse for bad manners. But even now, the memory of being forced to go to Lawrence's party and sing his praises caused her jaw to tighten.

A young man – and he really did look horribly young – walked up the aisle and slid into the front pew. A couple of minutes later, Rodney Bambrook escorted Evelyn and Felicity to their places in front of Prudence's pew. So Lawrence and Evelyn had decided to let Felicity in on the secret. Presumably there had come a point where they'd had to. The mother of the bride was resplendent in an ankle-length coat of gold crushed velvet with fur at the collar, cuffs and hem. Her wide-brimmed hat sported a band of the same gold velvet around the crown. To look at her, one would never guess that her daughter's reputation was today being salvaged from the mud.

A frightful grinding sound clashed with the gentle strains of the organ music. Glancing round, Prudence saw that both halves of the double doors were now open. Rodney Bambrook hurried up the aisle to join his brother. A moment later, the vicar took his place on the altar.

The music ceased and, at a signal from the vicar, the small

congregation rose. The organist started to play 'Jesu, Joy of Man's Desiring' and Lawrence brought his daughter up the aisle. Lucy's dress – a mid-calf-length ivory affair with a square neckline, worn with a headdress of flowers and a long, fluttering veil – was a testament to what could be achieved at short notice by money and maternal determination when there was a crisis to be averted.

What a cat she was. Just because she and Lawrence didn't get on. Why not believe that the lovely dress was a reflection of how precious Lucy was to her parents? That was undoubtedly what Patience was thinking.

The young couple turned to one another and the vicar opened the ceremony that would join them in holy matrimony, thereby securing their baby son's place in the respectable world.

Beside Prudence, Patience sniffed discreetly and dabbed with a hanky, but there was no room for such sentimentality in Prudence's heart. What she felt was a fierce awareness of Lucy's good fortune. How different her own life would have been if... But that had never been a possibility.

At the end of the ceremony, the newlyweds and their parents disappeared through the door into the vestry to sign the register, after which they walked down the aisle of the almost-empty church – a stark reminder of the disgrace underpinning the happy occasion.

The photographer was waiting outside with his tripod and camera all set up. He organised the group, then he held up the flashbulb and took the first picture. While he took a picture or two of Lucy and Dickie, Prudence edged closer to Felicity.

'Did you really not know about Lucy's being in the family way?'

Felicity glanced at her, all dark-eyed innocence, but her lips twitched mischievously. 'Don't tell Mummy and Daddy.'

Girls today. Honestly.

Dickie's father appeared beside Prudence. 'We're going to my brother's house now.'

As Prudence looked round for Vivienne and Patience, Lucy approached.

'Congratulations, my dear,' said Prudence.

'Thank you. I can't wait to get back to Charlie.' Lucy held up her bouquet of yellow roses and trailing greenery. 'When you go home, Aunt Prudence, would you and Auntie Patience like to take my bouquet with you? You've both been so good to me through all this.'

'What a kind thought. I appreciate it, Lucy, but would you mind giving your flowers just to Auntie Patience? It would mean a lot to her.'

Lucy smiled. 'She's such a love.'

'Yes, she is.'

Prudence followed Lucy to where Patience was standing.

'Auntie Patience, I'd like you to have my bridal bouquet.'

There was an audible gasp from Patience. 'Lucy, dear, are you sure?'

'Completely. You've been an angel these past few months and no one has been kinder.' Lucy held out the bouquet. 'You deserve it and I want you to have it. Please.'

'Darling girl,' Patience murmured, a becoming blush invading her cheeks as she accepted the roses. 'Look what Lucy has given me, Prudence.'

'Lovely,' said Prudence.

As Patience went to show Vivienne, Prudence hung back, intending to say a word of approval to Lucy, but Evelyn inserted herself between them.

'Are you and your new husband ready to go to the wedding breakfast, Lucy? Get your flowers back off Auntie Patience.'

'I've given them to her.'

'You've what?' Evelyn's smile froze.

'I want her to have them, Mummy.'

'Don't be silly, darling. You can't present your wedding flowers to an old spinster like that – no matter how sweet and kind she is,' Evelyn added swiftly when Prudence gave her the evil eye. 'It simply isn't the done thing. The bridal bouquet is traditionally given to a young girl and then she is the next one to get married.'

'I don't want it,' put in Felicity.

Lawrence approached, his lean face looking relieved. 'Everyone ready to go to the wedding breakfast, Evelyn?'

Evelyn turned to him. 'Lawrence, you won't believe what Lucy has done. She's only given her bridal bouquet to Patience.'

'To Patience?' Lawrence repeated. 'Lucy, it might have been appropriate, more grateful, to have presented it to your mother.'

Evelyn cast her gaze up to the skies. 'No, Lawrence, you don't understand. Whoever receives the bridal bouquet will be the next one to get married.'

'The next to…? Patience?' Lawrence threw back his head and laughed, his topper clinging on. 'Patience getting married? That's the best joke I've heard in years.'

Chapter Twenty-Two

'I CAN EXPLAIN,' SAID Pa. 'It's not what it looks like.'

Not what it looked like? There was Pa with his hands inside an open box belonging to Gabriel Linkworth, his thin face not glowing in the lamplight but reduced to a sickly grey, and his chin wobbling as if he might burst into tears. Nancy's heart beat hard as if she had run all round the rec and back again. Summat nasty invaded her mouth, a sour taste – the taste of shame. Shock an' all. She swallowed and her face twisted as it burned its way down her throat.

'Nay, Nancy, don't look at me like that,' begged Pa. He gazed down at his hands, as if only just realising where they were, and jerked them out of the box. His Adam's apple bobbed up and down above his frayed collar.

Nancy couldn't bear it a moment longer. Turning sharply on her heel, she stumbled up the steps into the kitchen. Pa burst out of the door behind her.

'Don't run away from me, lass. I – I—'

'You what, Pa? I saw you. I *saw* you.'

She dashed tears aside. Her heart was pounding with shock, but beneath the shock was a flare of anger that Pa would do such a thing. Pa! He might not be big and strong like other dads. He would never command a room simply by walking into it. He was meek and nervy, but Nancy had always been proud of his honesty. What would Mam say? Oh, Mam must never know.

'I know what you saw, love, but it's not what you think. Eh, I'm sorry you had to see. I never meant you to.'

'Were you...were you going to steal a book from Mr Linkworth? I know we're hard up, Pa, but honest to God—'

'It's not like that. It's...'

With a groan, Pa covered his face with his hands. His thin shoulders shuddered. Was he crying? Nancy didn't know what to do. She didn't want to comfort him, but somehow she found herself going to him and putting her arms round him. He clung to her for a moment, hiding his face in her neck, then he gently put her from him.

'I only came down to tell you the tea's ready,' Nancy whispered.

'I told you just to give me a shout.'

'Oh aye, and now I know why.'

'No,' Pa said with sudden vigour. 'You don't. You don't know nowt. You don't know what I've had to live with.'

Pulses jumped inside Nancy's wrists and at her throat, sending little spikes of fear through her skin. What was going on?

'Let's sit down,' said Pa, 'and I'll tell you everything – anything to stop you looking at me like that.'

'I'd better go down the cellar first and make sure everything is as it should be.'

'Don't worry. It is.'

'I'd best check, all the same.'

It was just as well she did. In his haste, Pa had left the lamp down there, though that was the only sign of his presence. Nancy scrutinised the stacks of boxes and couldn't see owt untoward. She brought the lamp back to the kitchen, extinguished it and returned it to its shelf.

'Are we still going to have tea?' Pa asked humbly.

'We better had. It'll look odd if we haven't eaten any cake.'

She picked up the tray. China clinked. She grasped the tray harder, trying to overcome the tremor in her hands. They were supposed to have tea in the sitting room, but that wouldn't be right after what had happened. She dumped the tray on the breakfast room table instead, catching the look on Pa's face as he realised, though he said nowt.

They sat down. Nancy poured and cut the cake, releasing its sweet, sugary scent. Goodness knew how she was going to manage her slice, but she would have to.

'Go on, then,' she said. 'Tell me what this is about.'

The silence stretched out for so long, she thought Pa had changed his mind, but at last he replaced his cup on its saucer with a clatter and began to speak.

'You have to understand, our Nancy, me and your mam were very young when we got wed.'

'I know.' Lord, he wasn't going to tell her about Mam being in the family way, was he? She would die of embarrassment if he did.

'It's not a good idea for a man to marry too young. You need time to save up and get on a bit at work. Not that I'm sorry I married your mam, mind. That's all I wanted from the moment I set eyes on her. But it were hard. Money-wise, it were hard. My Marjorie has never enjoyed the best of health and the doctor doesn't come cheap. Anyroad, things went from bad to worse and I got desperate. In the end, I...' Pa made a small choking sound before forcing himself to carry on. 'I stole money from my employer.'

Nancy sucked in a gasp of horror. Pa – a thief. The thought had assaulted her down in the cellar, but hearing the words fall from Pa's lips made it worse – made it real.

'It was only ever meant to be a loan. I promised myself I'd

pay it back and I honestly meant to, I swear.' Pa laughed bitterly. 'I wish I had done. I wish it had been as simple as that.'

'What happened?' Nancy whispered.

'Mr Arthur Rathbone happened.'

'Mr Rathbone? The gentleman who sometimes gives you bits of work to do?'

'Aye, he's a fine fellow these days, but he weren't back then. Back then, he was the same as me, a warehouseman, only he ended up marrying the boss's daughter of another firm and eventually he inherited that place.'

'I didn't know that,' said Nancy. She didn't see what it had to do with this either.

'Him and me were colleagues, and he found out what I'd done. I were that scared of what he was going to do – tell the boss, go to the police – but he offered to help me. "Percy," he says – we called one another Percy and Arthur in them days. "Percy," he says, "I'll put back the money you stole. I'll repay it from my own pocket and you can pay me back as and when." I were that grateful, it were all I could do not to break down and skrike like a babby. Only, he said we had to keep things above board and he got me to write a letter, see, to say I'd pinched the boss's money and he'd repaid it for me. I never thought owt of it when I wrote it. With him repaying the money for me, it seemed only right. Only...'

'Only what, Pa?'

'He never intended it to be a way of keeping things right and fair between us. He wanted it for blackmail – my confession, written in my own hand. He's had me over a barrel ever since. I prayed for it to stop when he married well, but it didn't – not even when he inherited from his father-in-law.'

'Oh, Pa.'

'It's never stopped, never. The first few years, he just took money from me. When he went up in the world, I thought it'd stop because he had no need of the odd few bob from me. But then he started getting me to do jobs for him and it's been that way ever since – oh, nowt illegal, just fetching and carrying. "My man will see to that for me," he tells folk and I have to do his bidding. I have to take time off from my job to do it and that costs me more than I ever handed over in cash in the old days. I say at work that Marjorie has took bad ways and I have to fetch medicine for her, so they have to give me the time off, only then, of course, they dock my wages; and all the while there I am dashing around fetching Mr Rathbone's latest purchase and delivering it to his house and bowing and scraping, and all because of that damn letter, pardon my French.'

'Pa, that's dreadful. All because of a mistake you made when you were young and desperate.'

Pa leaned across the table, his eyes suddenly bright. 'But he's given me a chance to break free from it. Back in the spring, he sent me here to Chorlton to pick up a box of bric-a-brac from the bookshop on Beech Road. It's closed now.'

'That would be the bookshop Gabriel Linkworth used to have.'

'Linkworth? Nay, this place were called Tyrell's Books. Anyroad, I picked up the box and fetched it back to Mr Rathbone's house. He opened it and looked inside and then he went spare. Grabbed me by the lapels, he did, and accused me of stealing.'

Resentment stiffened Nancy's spine. How dare the dastardly Mr Rathbone accuse Pa of such a thing? Never mind that she had herself recoiled in horror down in the cellar. That was swept away now as understanding crept up on her.

'He ended up storming back to the bookshop to complain about the missing item and it turned out it wasn't missing at all,' said Pa. 'It had been put into another box of bric-a-brac.'

'Did he buy it?'

'He wasn't allowed to. There were some legal shenanigans going on and the bookseller was supposed to get back all the things he had sold since the old bookseller popped his clogs.'

'So Mr Rathbone had to take back the box you had collected for him.'

'Aye, though he hung onto a piece from it.'

'That proves what a rogue he is,' said Nancy. 'What was so important he wouldn't hand it back?'

'A letter-opener.'

'Is that all? That doesn't sound very special.'

'Well, it is – and it'd be even more special if it was married up with the companion piece, a page-cutter. Mr Rathbone says that each piece is worth a modest amount on its own, but if you put the pair together, the value shoots sky-high.'

'So this page-cutter is what was missing from the box you collected?'

'Aye,' said Pa, 'and it's in one of them boxes in the cellar right now.'

'That's what you were searching for.'

Pa slumped back in his seat, looking drained. 'That's why you're here, lass. It were in the *Manchester Evening News* that the Miss Heskeths had took pity on a local hero what had saved a family from a fire and they had stored all his boxes of books and what-not in their cellar. So Mr Rathbone told me I had to get you took on here as a pupil-lodger, so that I'd have access to the house.'

A sharp intake of breath filled Nancy's lungs with the chill of shock. 'So all that about me bettering myself – and being a surplus girl – and helping Mam—'

'It was all to get you accepted here.' Pa hung his head.

'I thought – at one point I thought you wanted rid of me.'

Pa reared up, throwing his hands across the table to clasp

hers. 'Not that, never that. Eh, lass, you know I'd never want rid of you.' Flopping back again, he heaved a sigh that made his puny chest rise and sink. 'I'm sorry. I've made a mess of everything.'

A fresh idea made Nancy's skin crawl. 'Is Mr Rathbone paying my fees?'

Red blotches stained Pa's scrawny cheeks. He nodded.

'Oh, Pa.' She looked away, not sure whether what she was feeling was disbelief or disgust. 'How could you?'

'It weren't my doing. It's Mr Rathbone's.' Pa leaned forwards, his eyes suddenly keen. 'Don't you see? If I find this page-cutter, Mr Rathbone will give me back my letter and then all our troubles will be over. That's what he said. No more fetching and carrying, no more taking time off work to run errands.'

'I don't see why he still bothers pushing you around, if he's gone up in the world.'

'He does it because he can.' Pa's lips twisted bitterly. 'He does it to keep me in my place. He does it so I can never forget the hold he has over me. I'm always scared that they'll get fed up of me at work and give me the sack for being unreliable. They've always been understanding about your mam's condition, but they're not obliged to be. I hate using Marjorie's anaemia as an excuse, but how else am I to manage? If I could just get my hands on that page-cutter...'

'So you didn't come here to see me,' said Nancy. 'You came to steal the page-cutter. And you never intended to bring Mam. You just let me hope she'd be well enough to come. She doesn't know you're here.'

'I'd pinned all my hopes on finding the page-cutter today, but all the labels on them boxes looked like books. I opened up a couple of boxes, but that was sheer desperation.'

'You won't find it in those boxes.'

Pa fixed his gaze on her. 'Do you know where it is?'

'It could be in Gabriel Linkworth's jacket pocket, for all I know. But it won't be in any of those boxes in the main part of the cellar. There's another bit, with a door that's kept locked. Apparently, Miss Hesketh insisted that the boxes of ornaments and personal things had to go in there, so you can tell Mr Rathbone he can't have the page-cutter.'

'He'll be furious.'

'Then he'll have to be furious, won't he?'

'Aye,' said Pa, 'and I'll be stuck with doing his bidding for ever.'

Chapter Twenty-Three

'IT FEELS QUIET here now,' said Patience, gazing fondly at Lucy's wedding flowers, which enjoyed pride of place on the mantelpiece. 'After all those weeks of taking care of Lucy, and then the worry over Charlie's early birth, and the wedding last Saturday, it feels very quiet.'

After a tea of kidneys and mushrooms followed by apple fritters, Prudence, Patience and Vivienne were in the sitting room, relaxing before tonight's pupils arrived. Nancy had had tea at St Anthony's and was staying there for a while to play with the children and was to return in time to attend her lesson about delivery notes.

Prudence would also be teaching book-keeping this evening. There were only four more lessons to go, but that no longer mattered because, thanks to Patience's kind heart, Vivienne would be staying on as an ordinary p.g. Prudence's gaze darted towards her sister. It was wrong to deceive Patience, but what choice was there?

The doorbell rang and Patience got up to answer it, returning a moment later with Lawrence. Vivienne half-rose, offering to leave, but Prudence stopped her, only just managing to refrain from saying, 'You're family.'

'I thought you'd like to know that Lucy, Dickie and the baby have arrived safely at old Mrs Bambrook's villa in Tuscany. They sent a telegram to let us know.'

'Oh, good,' said Patience. 'I wonder if the library has a book about Tuscany. I'd like to be able to picture where they are.'

Lawrence snorted. 'I must say I'm surprised by the manner in which you and Prudence have accepted Lucy's situation – especially you, Prudence. I thought you, of all people, would have slung her out on her ear the moment you knew she was in trouble.'

Prudence spoke in a consciously light voice. 'Really? I know I'm viewed as strict, and rightly so, but I like to think there's more to me than that.'

'Of course there is,' said Lawrence. 'You're judgemental – unsympathetic – critical. Oh yes, there's a lot more to you than merely being strict.'

'Lawrence, don't be unkind,' Patience protested.

'Who's being unkind? It's the simple truth. You're the only one hurt by it, Patience. It doesn't hurt Prudence. She's not the sort to crumble under a few home-truths.'

But it did hurt. That her brother could speak of her in such a way – of course it hurt. Did he think that because she had stood up to him all her life, because she was capable and independent, this meant she lacked the finer feelings?

'Frankly,' Lawrence ploughed on, 'I wish I'd had the opportunity to deliver a few home-truths to Lucy, but Evelyn wouldn't let me say a word, not even to Dickie, to tell him what a rotter he was for taking advantage of my daughter.'

'It's better not to say such things,' ventured Patience. 'They're married now and that's what matters. Lucy deserves her happy ending.'

'Deserves?' Lawrence demanded. 'Deserves? When I think of the anguish she caused Evelyn and me – and the shame! Things might have turned out well for her in the end, but you can't claim she deserved it. How could she let us down like that? How could she let herself down? I put her on a pedestal

211

and she's well and truly fallen off it – jumped off it, no less. Whatever happened to my sweet little girl? She cast aside her morals and her upbringing and behaved like a – like a—'

'That's enough.' Prudence stepped in before he could utter words unfit for mixed company. 'Lucy made a mistake, that's all.'

'Is that what you call it? A mistake? One that's had her mother sobbing night after night into her pillow. I'm shocked at you, Prudence, for dismissing it so lightly.'

Prudence went deathly still. Then she drew back her shoulders. It was only the fact that she would never do anything so slovenly that stopped her from pushing up her sleeves. Resolution bloomed inside her. She knew exactly what had to be said.

'I'm not dismissing anything, lightly or otherwise. Lucy has been in a shocking situation and, whether she deserved it or not, things have turned out for the best. You should be grateful, Lawrence, but it appears you're still angry because you never had the chance to punch Dickie on the nose – something which, if you had done it, would only have upset Lucy and what would have been the good in that? Yes, the child made a mistake, but – but it's easily done and then it's devilishly difficult to resolve.'

'What are you blathering on about?'

'I'm blathering on, as you so elegantly put it, about what happened to me years ago.' Prudence rose to her feet and went to stand beside Vivienne's chair. 'You say you're shocked that I could accept Lucy's predicament. Well, I did so because – because I once faced the same dilemma myself, but in my case it didn't end with a veil and flowers and a prolonged honeymoon in Italy. It ended – I thought it had ended when I was obliged to give up my baby for adoption.'

'When you *what*?' Lawrence blustered.

A warm confidence settled on Prudence. 'I thought that was

the end, but I was wrong.' She reached for Vivienne's hand. 'My happy ending came looking for me all these years later.'

Lawrence made a gurgling sound. 'D'you mean to say—'

'Vivienne is my daughter, the child I was forced to give away. And that,' she added fiercely, 'is why I've been so scared for Lucy all these weeks. You might have been jumping up and down with rage, Lawrence, but I've been frightened for her – frightened – because I know what it cost me to give up my child and I couldn't bear her to have to live with the pain, the regret and the guilt. And the silence.'

Lawrence was opening and closing his mouth like a landed fish. 'Your – your daughter?' he kept saying. 'Your daughter?'

Prudence ignored him. She went to Patience. 'My dear, I'm truly sorry it has come out in this way. I know how shocked you must feel.'

'How long have you known?' Patience whispered.

'Since the day I took Lucy to Maskell House and brought her home again, because I couldn't bear to leave her there; since that evening. I'll tell you my story later, I promise.' She looked at Vivienne. 'We both shall.' She turned to Lawrence. 'I've told you this so that you understand what Lucy has been saved from and it's got nothing to do with being respectable and having a ring on her finger. It's to do with a mother needing to be with her child. It would have been a lot tidier if Lucy had got married before she had Charlie, or if she had named Dickie back in the spring, but that isn't how it happened. Accept it for what it is, Lawrence, and set your anger aside. Be grateful your daughter has been spared the anguish of being separated from her baby.'

Lawrence at her in slack-mouthed shock.

'One more thing,' said Prudence. 'What I've said stays between the four of us. You mustn't tell anyone else, Lawrence, not even Evelyn.'

A sound that was composed of disgust and disbelief exploded from Lawrence in a brief burst of laughter. 'I think we can safely say I'll never breathe a word. To think that you – you – with your disapproval of everyone who falls below your high standards – and your holier-than-thou criticisms – to think that you—'

'That's quite enough.' Vivienne spoke firmly. 'Please don't talk about my mother like that. It doesn't become you.'

Lawrence stared at Prudence. 'When?' he demanded. 'How?'

'In Scotland,' said Prudence, 'and that's all you need to know.'

'So that's why you came home with your tail between your legs.'

'Quite so,' she said stiffly.

'Good gad.' All manner of thoughts flashed across Lawrence's lean face. 'Good gad.'

Vivienne went to sit beside Patience. 'I apologise for deceiving you. I'm here, not exactly under false pretences, because I truly did want to learn office skills, but I did come with the ulterior motive of getting to know Miss Hesketh. I hope you can forgive me.' She glanced at Lucy's wedding roses. 'You were so generous to Lucy. I hope you'll be generous to me too.'

'Good gad.' Lawrence's eyes had glazed over.

'I don't know what to say.' Patience's voice was quiet and a touch breathless. 'It's such a shock.' She blinked at Vivienne. 'Prudence is your mother?'

Vivienne smiled. 'Yes. Miss Hesketh is my mother.'

Patience shut her eyes, then opened them again. 'Prudence is your mother.'

'Good gad,' said Lawrence.

Worry about Pa was eating away at Nancy, day and night. It made it all the more important for her to do well at the business school and the orphanage. Could she possibly pull her socks up to the point where she was considered good enough to remain working at St Anthony's? But in that case, what about Ginny? Nancy wondered if she could at least do well enough under Miss Allan's merciless eyes to get a good job elsewhere. Ginny was definitely better at every clerical task, but surely Nancy had strengths of her own? Well, she was good with the children – but what use was that?

Wait a minute. What if she organised a Christmas party? She would have to find out what the usual arrangements were and think hard about what she could add to make the party even better. She had to show herself to be a capable organiser. That would go in her favour, surely. It would show initiative an' all. Miss Hesketh was a great believer in initiative, as long as you didn't get above yourself.

Nancy thought about it. She would need permission, of course, and, preferably, the support of the nursemaids. As well as needing their help, it would show she was capable of working alongside others. That was important in an office, according to Miss Patience. And of course, organising a party for the children she had come to care for so much would in itself be a great pleasure.

'What happens here each Christmas?' she asked Ginny. 'To celebrate, I mean.'

'On Christmas Day, brothers and sisters are allowed to sit next to one another in the dining room instead of sitting with boys or girls of their own age. We have a carol concert and a party with games and paper hats, then there's a tea afterwards with jelly and cake; and we have a tree. The nursemaids light the candles.'

'Is there owt else?' Nancy asked.

Ginny looked at her. 'Isn't that enough? It's more than a lot of children get.'

Nancy didn't say why she was asking. She wanted to keep it to herself until she had got it sorted out in her mind. She needed to come up with some ideas before approaching Mrs Rostron, but Ginny's description had covered all the obvious Christmassy things. Well, what had she expected? That the orphanage staff had never previously bothered to make Christmas a special time for the children? She would have to put her thinking cap on if she intended to come up with something worthwhile.

What about cards for the children? If each child made one, then every child could receive one out of a sack. But where would the card come from to make them? They could be made out of paper, which would be cheaper, but it would still have to be paid for. Nancy thought of the orphanage's special bedroom, which was set aside for a visiting family member. That had been paid for by Mr Lawrence Hesketh. It was called being a sponsor. Might a sponsor be found to pay for the card or paper for the children to make Christmas cards? It was the sort of question Mrs Rostron would be able to answer.

But she couldn't go to the superintendent just with ideas that needed paying for – especially if the money turned out not to be forthcoming. She had to have ideas that wouldn't cost anything. What about paper-chains? Or were they made every year and Ginny just hadn't mentioned them? Even if they did usually have them, Nancy envisioned having longer chains, and more of them, than ever before, if Mrs Rostron would permit the children to go door to door to ask for old newspapers. Cutting, painting and pasting together could be organised into various competitions – the longest chain, the prettiest, the most carefully made and so on.

She could think of ways to alter well-known games an' all. Her heartbeat sped up. She was getting into the swing of this. Hunt the thimble could become hunt the star. Who stole the watch and chain? could be Who stole the cake and pud?

There could be a treasure hunt – ah, but that would require prizes. She chewed her lip thoughtfully. What about being allowed to light a candle on the tree, as a prize? That would feel special, because lighting the candles was a grown-up thing to do.

These were all good ideas, but she needed summat more, summat – well, bigger, that would link everything together, that would link the children and staff together, and make the festive season extra special.

'The best Christmas ever.' That was what she dreamed of everyone saying afterwards. 'The best Christmas ever.'

Patience kept having to stop and sit down while she did the housework and the cooking. Not because she was tired or in any way incapacitated, but just because...well, she couldn't have said why. It was as if the shock made it necessary for her to step outside her life for a few minutes every so often while her heartbeat dulled and her thoughts struggled to form. Prudence had a daughter. *Prudence.*

She had always been so upright, so quick to judge, so critical and often unforgiving. And all the while, she had harboured this secret. This disgraceful secret – yes, disgraceful. Whichever way one looked at it, it was a profound disgrace. Having a child out of wedlock was an appalling thing to do. It tainted a family for ever. Just look at the nightmare Lawrence and Evelyn had endured this year as they all struggled to conceal Lucy's shame.

Prudence.

It was hard to take in. *Prudence.*

And yet, now that Patience knew, certain things slid into place. Prudence calling Vivienne by her first name. Prudence seeming at times kinder, more tolerant. Had Prudence become a better person through being reunited with her long-lost daughter? Had this other Prudence been inside her sister all this time?

Prudence – a mother.

Patience felt as if her own identity had been stripped away. She and Prudence had always been the Miss Heskeths, spinsters of this parish. Maiden ladies, liked and respected, of course, but also looked down on and undoubtedly felt sorry for. Now she had to look at Prudence through new eyes.

Prudence – a mother.

It was what Patience had always wanted – always. She had grown up wanting to get married and have a family of her own. A daughter of her own would have been... She had to close her eyes as all the old yearning poured through her. A daughter of her own. She had once thought, oh, years ago now, that she had met her future husband and her dream of a happy family life was going to come true. But he had left her and there had never been anyone else.

And Prudence, who had never once expressed any interest in having children, had borne a child. Was it wrong? Was it unfair? Or was it just...life?

Had Prudence deliberately never talked in terms of having a family specifically because of the dreadful pain she had suffered in being forced to give up her child? Oh, how it must have hurt. Patience's heart swelled, as if reaching out towards Prudence. Patience knew all about the absence of children from one's life. She had felt that absence as an ache inside herself – an ache that had returned in full force since Prudence had made her announcement. Being childless was part of being a spinster. Some spinsters minded more than others – at least, Patience had always assumed so. It wasn't something that was ever discussed. But now Prudence wasn't childless after all.

Prudence.

Except that she was childless, in a way. She had been child-less all these years until Vivienne came into her life. Patience had been childless because the chance to marry had been torn from her and Prudence had been childless because her baby had been torn from her by the demands of respectability. Poor, dear Prudence. How she must have suffered.

Now Prudence's child had come back to her and, beneath the shock and the struggle to believe what had happened, Patience knew she was the last person to begrudge her sister this chance of happiness. Vivienne was a dear girl and Patience had grown enormously fond of her these past months.

Vivienne was her niece. Family. Joined by blood.

Unbelievable – and yet, so very welcome.

On Saturday afternoon, Vivienne walked along to St Anthony's. After Molly left the orphanage to get married, she had started teaching some of the cleverer fourteen-girls basic office skills for a few hours a week. It had been Miss Hesketh's idea and it was she who provided Molly with the lesson plans. Mrs Rostron took a keen interest in the girls' progress, as this scheme might lead to some of them being able to be found jobs as office juniors – as long as accommodation could be secured for them. Vivienne was interested too. If this worked well at St Anthony's, she might be able to promote it within the Board of Health, so that the idea could be extended to other orphanages.

It had become part of the routine that, on the weekends when Mrs Rostron was on duty, after Molly finished her teaching session on Saturdays, she, Vivienne and the super-intendent would have a cup of tea together and – not chat, exactly, because Mrs Rostron wasn't the sort to encourage familiarity, but they would talk about various things, usually starting with the fourteens' progress.

The orphanage had a special sitting room, heavily over-furnished, that was used for teaching the girls how to clean properly and the three of them sat together in here. The tea tray was brought in and Mrs Rostron poured. Mrs Wilkes had sent a plate of buttery-smelling shortbread as well.

'How are the girls coming along?' asked Mrs Rostron and Molly supplied a quick overview of their progress.

'Abigail Hunter is especially quick at filing cards in alpha-betical order and spotting errors in pretend invoices.'

Mrs Rostron nodded. 'Just make sure she isn't too quick. I know her of old. She's a bright girl but very competitive and sometimes she lets herself down. She's determined to finish first and that can lead to mistakes.'

Molly nodded. 'That's happened once or twice. I'll watch out for it.'

'In general, everything is going well, wouldn't you say?' Vivienne asked Molly, who agreed. 'One day, it might be pos-sible for girls to learn office skills at school too, which would be a big improvement.'

'It would indeed,' said Mrs Rostron. 'Even though we have a generation of surplus girls who will never get married, many people are still old-fashioned in their views and are opposed to the idea of girls being trained for the workplace, except in the most menial jobs.'

'That's why it's so important that you are letting these girls receive office training,' said Molly. 'It could make all the dif-ference to their future prospects.'

'How are Miss Allan's two assistants getting along?' Vivienne asked.

Mrs Rostron eyed her. 'I am aware that you lodge in the

same house as Miss Nancy. I'm sure I don't need to remind you that anything said here is confidential.'

'I understand,' said Vivienne. 'I don't think it's any secret that Nancy is struggling, but I know she is doing her best.'

'She has certainly settled in very well, I'll give her that,' said Mrs Rostron, 'and she has initiative. She has all sorts of plans for making Christmas special for the children.'

'Good for her,' said Molly.

'Pictures of apples and oranges keep appearing, pinned to the picture rail in the dining room. At first Nanny Duffy insisted the nursemaids must take them down, but they appeared again and the children asked why, which was when Miss Nancy suggested it must be Christmas magic. Since then, more pictures have been appearing. There was a stampede every morning to see if there's a new one.'

'Oh dear,' Vivienne murmured.

Mrs Rostron smiled. She didn't often smile. 'Miss Nancy told the children that Christmas magic is fragile so it's important to creep up on it. That ended the stampedes.'

'I'm impressed,' said Molly. 'She's thought it through, hasn't she?' She laughed. 'Whatever "it" is. What is the purpose of these pictures?'

'She won't say,' replied Mrs Rostron.

'Not even to you?' asked Vivienne. That had taken some bravery.

'Not even to me. Maybe you could ask her at home and share the secret with me.'

'If she won't tell you, she certainly won't tell me.'

'Pictures of apples and oranges appearing "by magic" in the dining room,' said Vivienne. 'How intriguing. Do you know, I think there might be more to Nancy Pike than meets the eye.'

Chapter Twenty-Four

NANCY WAS DELIGHTED by the way her pictures of apples and oranges had generated such excitement. Even Nanny Duffy had stopped being annoyed. She was surprised an' all that Mrs Rostron hadn't demanded to know what it was all about.

'I have agreed in principle to your Christmas ideas,' she had said. 'I don't need to know all the ins and outs. Besides, it will be interesting to see how well you cope – whether you sink or swim.'

That had been a scary moment, but when Nancy thought about it afterwards, it made her feel all the more determined.

'I could do without all this excitement,' said Nurse Carmel. 'It's not December yet.' Then she smiled. 'But it's lovely to see, isn't it?'

Ginny expressed her admiration of Nancy's plans. 'But I'm afraid it makes me look bad.'

'What do you mean?' Nancy asked in surprise.

'You're organising all these things, having all these ideas. It makes me look a right lump.'

Nancy stared, eyes wide with incredulity. 'I never thought of it that way. You could help me.'

'I can't hang onto your coat-tails.'

'Why not? I've hung onto yours enough times. You're always saving me from getting into trouble with Miss Allan.'

That conversation with Ginny left Nancy feeling better about herself. Since she had left the pie shop, she had become accustomed to thinking of herself as a hopeless dunderhead and Ginny's admiration meant a lot. She set off for home that evening with a lighter heart, not caring about the cold or the darkness. The gas-lamps along Beech Road cast golden pools of light at regular intervals. Some of the folk she passed were warmly wrapped up against the chill, but others, not so lucky, didn't possess a scarf or a coat or stout shoes. Suddenly the golden light seemed more of a dingy yellow.

Nancy spied Zachary further along the road. He was coming towards her, but on the opposite side – heading back to Chorlton Green and then Soapsuds Lane, maybe? Her heart gave a little bump and she couldn't pretend it hadn't. The last time she had seen him had been the day she had 'extinguished' him during the fire safety training. He had spoken up for her and in all probability saved her job, but he had done so purely out of pity. She was in no doubt about that. Was it foolish to want to speak to him now? She had sworn to herself that she didn't want anyone's pity – and she didn't. But she couldn't help wanting to run across the road to him. Oh, she should have more pride.

'Mr Milner,' she called. She could thank him for saving her job. That wouldn't make her look stupid, would it? It wouldn't make her look needy.

'Nancy!'

For one unbearably sweet moment, her stupid ears heard Zachary's voice and elation coursed through her before she had a chance to think of putting the brakes on. Not that she could have stopped it.

'Nancy!'

It was Pa. Nancy's stomach clenched with disappointment before shame burned her face. Fancy being disappointed to meet Pa.

'Eh, our Nancy.' Pa had stepped out from the corner by the rec and was right beside her. 'Was that you calling to a young man? In public? That's not the way a young lady behaves.' He folded his arms, but that could have been because he was trying to keep warm rather than because he wanted to appear stern. Anyroad, when had Pa ever managed to look stern? 'Do you know him?'

Nancy glanced round. Zachary had stopped, but Pa pulled her arm and took her in the direction of Wilton Close.

'Who is he, anyroad?' Pa wanted to know.

'Mr Milner. I used to work in his shop some evenings.'

'Well, I'm sure he doesn't want you calling after him in the street – not if he's a respectable fellow, anyroad. I'm sure the Miss Heskeths wouldn't want you behaving like a – a strumpet.'

'Pa!' Nancy exclaimed. Now it was her turn to drag him along the road, as if hauling him away from an audience all agog to hear what else he was about to call her.

But Pa dug in his heels and brought her to a standstill. 'Hold on, lass. I need a word.'

'What about?'

Pa's face was always thin and pinched. Now it looked meagre and wasted, as if the cold had eaten away at his flesh. But it wasn't just the bite in the air that made him look like that. The way his eyes shifted away from hers made her realise that part of what had shrivelled him was shame.

'It's Mr Rathbone, Nancy,' Pa said. 'He's got a job for you.'

Vivienne arrived home from work to an empty house. Nancy wasn't here yet; maybe she had decided to stay on at St Anthony's for a while because of her Christmas plans and would dash home just in time for tea. There was no Miss Patience either, because Miss Kirby had had to go to the dentist this afternoon for an extraction and Miss Patience had accompanied her and was seeing her home afterwards to provide home-made soup and blancmange.

So unless Nancy turned up, it would be just her and Miss Prudence – that was what Vivienne called her now. It had been Miss Patience's idea and it showed how Miss Patience had accepted the relationship between them.

'We're feeding ourselves,' Vivienne reminded Miss Prudence when she arrived home from work and the two of them were in the sitting room together. 'Miss Patience left me my instructions. I'm to do vegetable rissoles and poached pears. Actually, I'm glad we've got a while to ourselves. It doesn't often happen.'

'I'm glad too. I have an important matter to discuss with you.'

Was that a blush on Miss Prudence's pale cheek? Vivienne sat forwards, ready to pay attention. The last time they had talked intimately, it had been when the truth had come out about their relationship. That had been on the night of that dreadful storm when Molly and Aaron's Danny had come close to losing his life.

'I never told you about your father,' said Miss Prudence and it was all Vivienne could do to hold back an exclamation. She hadn't expected anything of this nature. 'His name was Jonty Henderson – short for Jonathan.'

Jonty! Vivienne absorbed her father's name. Vivienne, daughter of Jonathan.

'We met when he came to stay in the hotel where I was working in Loch Lomond,' continued Miss Prudence. 'He was tall and handsome with dark hair, though his eyes were hazel – like yours.'

That sent a frisson through Vivienne.

'He worked in his family's law firm and he had come to the area on business. It's a very simple story to tell, though it felt unbearably complicated at the time. I fell madly in love and he loved me too – or so I thought. I would never have...if I'd thought for one moment he didn't love me every bit as much as I loved him—'

'He seduced you.' Something inside Vivienne hardened. It wasn't what she wanted to hear about her father.

'I'm not sure about that. It wasn't as though I had any doubts at the time. It wasn't until – until I discovered I was pregnant that I found out the truth. While I was wrapped up in believing that I'd met my husband, he was...' Miss Prudence's voice trailed away. Then she sat up straighter. 'All he wanted was a romantic dalliance to spice up his free time.'

'What happened?' asked Vivienne. 'I'm sorry. That's a stupid question. I know what must have happened. He abandoned you. You told him I was on the way and he...'

'He ran for his life. I'm sorry to tell you this about your father. I never intended you to know, but you'll see why I've changed my mind when I get to the end of the story.' Miss Prudence reached for her hand and pressed it. 'You had a far better father in Graham Thornton, believe me. That was what happened next – I made the arrangement with Elspeth and Graham that you would be born in secret and they would adopt you. Then I had to carry on with my work and my everyday life as if nothing had changed, while I waited for the time to come when I would have to go away and prepare for the birth.'

'You've told me about that, about how you fell ill and ended up having me in the cottage hospital, which meant I had to be registered as yours instead of as Elspeth's.'

'There's more to it than that, things that I didn't tell you before – things that happened way before the birth. Patience came up to Loch Lomond for a holiday. It had all been arranged ages previously and was intended to be a long stay. She came on her own, but then Pa discovered that he didn't like looking after himself and he followed her up. In other circumstances, it would have been enjoyable to have the pair of them there,' Miss Prudence added wryly. 'Quite the family reunion.'

Vivienne sat quietly, sensing that more was coming.

'Then I had a visitor.'

The breath caught in Vivienne's throat. 'Not Jonty Henderson?'

'No. His brother, Niall. He didn't stay in our hotel – he stayed elsewhere – but he came to see me. Evidently, he was shocked by what Jonty had done and he was prepared to render financial assistance. He offered me a monthly allowance with the possibility of school fees later on. This money wouldn't be from Jonty or from the Henderson family. It would be from Niall himself, to right the wrong done to me by his brother.'

'That was generous.'

'Very.'

'He sounds like a much better person than Jonty.'

'I don't think there's any doubt about that, but then it wouldn't take much to be better than Jonty Henderson,' Miss Prudence said in her crispest voice. 'Anyway, I had already made my arrangements with Elspeth and Graham, so I didn't need to consider Niall's offer. Besides, nothing would have induced me to have anything to do with Jonty's family after what he'd done to me. I'm sorry to make your real father sound like a complete cad, but it's what he was.'

'I don't know quite what to think,' Vivienne admitted. 'When I first knew I was adopted, I wondered mainly about my real mother rather than about my father. I don't know if that's natural for adopted children, but it's the way it happened to me. Since I met you, I haven't thought much about my real father. Maybe that's because I knew there couldn't be a happy story behind what happened. You've never spoke about him, so, deep down, I knew there couldn't be anything very good to say.'

'I'm sorry if you feel let down.'

'I'll just have to be sensible about it and tell myself that out of my four parents, three of them are the best sort of people, and three out of four makes me jolly lucky.'

'I would never have told you if I didn't have a very good reason,' said Miss Prudence. 'Listen to what happened next and then you'll understand. During his spell in Scotland, Niall met Patience and they fell in love.'

'No! As if things weren't complicated enough.'

'I was appalled, I don't mind telling you. My sister – in love with the brother of the man who had treated me so shamefully. It felt unbearable to me. So I sent him packing. I threatened to tell Patience what his brother had done and what sort of a family he came from – and Niall left. I did it for Patience's sake. I wanted to protect her.'

Vivienne was almost light-headed with distress. 'Poor Miss Patience – and poor you too, being left in trouble like that.'

'Don't waste your sympathy on me. Needless to say, Patience knows nothing of this. I don't know what Niall said to let her down, but he certainly didn't tell her the truth.'

'So Miss Patience did have a sweetheart once upon a time. I just assumed love had never touched her life.'

'I imagine everybody makes that assumption,' Miss Prudence said drily. 'They assume it of me as well.'

Poor, dear Miss Patience. She was a born looker-after. She adored taking care of her p.g.s, lavishing every kind attention upon them. She took a warm interest in the other pupils too. Was she making up for the lack of a family of her own? What a sad thought.

'Is there more to your story?' Vivienne asked.

'Not in the way you mean. But I would like there to be more to it. I should dearly like to give it a happy ending.'

Vivienne frowned. 'I don't follow.'

'I have got my happy ending – you. And I'd like my sister to have her happy ending as well. I'm the one who sent Niall Henderson away. I'm the one who destroyed my sister's chance of happiness. Will you help me to find Niall Henderson? If he's single, I want to reunite him with Patience. I want them to have the chance I couldn't bear to let them have thirty years ago.'

Nancy and Pa walked up the road, past the end of Wilton Close and kept going. They ended up on High Lane, walking in the direction of Church Road, where St Anthony's stood on the corner.

'I'm that sorry, lass,' Pa said – again. He had apologised several times already, each time with a gulp in his voice. 'I should never have involved you in this wretched business, but I had no choice. When Mr Rathbone tells me to do summat, I have to do it. I didn't like it when he wanted me to send you to the Miss Heskeths' school, but I never imagined there'd be owt more to it. You being there was just a way of getting me into the house. At least, that's all I thought it would be.'

'What's this job he wants me to do?' Little pulses were throbbing indignantly at her wrists and the base of her throat. How dare Mr Rotten Rathbone try to shove her around? He could, though, couldn't he? Just like he'd shoved Pa around all these years.

'I told him the page-cutter wasn't gettable on account of being in an inner part of the cellar and I thought that'd be the end of it. I thought he'd be forced to give up and forget it – but I were reet daft, Nancy. I wanted him to know how hard I'd tried, so I told him about how you'd caught me in the act and – and that gave him this idea.'

'What idea?'

'He says he'll give me back my letter and leave me alone if – if you fetch him the page-cutter.'

'Oh aye?' Nancy exclaimed. 'Not content with sending you to do his thieving for him, now he wants me to do it.'

'Keep your voice down.' Pa's glance flicked from side to side in a way that made him look guilty as sin.

Nancy steered him round the corner into Church Road. She didn't bother pointing out the orphanage on the opposite corner.

'I won't do it. I won't steal off Gabriel Linkworth. He's my friend. That is, I've only met him once, but I know his fiancée and I'm friends with her. I can't steal off them and I can't steal from under the Miss Heskeths' roof neither. Even if I didn't know any of them, even if they were all strangers to me, I still wouldn't do it. I'm not a thief.'

'I know, love.' Pa hung his head. 'I'm sorry. I shouldn't have asked.'

He sounded so downcast that Nancy felt wretched. What an unholy mess this was. But she wasn't going to steal the dratted page-cutter for Mr Rathbone, she wasn't, she wasn't. Only...

'I don't blame you,' said Pa. 'It's a terrible thing to have hanging over you. Not a day goes by when I don't regret helping myself to that money. I've paid for my crime over and over, believe you me.'

'I know, Pa.' Nancy's heart swelled with emotion. 'It must have been so hard for you.'

No wonder the Pikes had always been so hard up, with Pa having money docked from his wages every time he had had to run an errand for Mr Rathbone. Poor darling Pa. He was a good man who had made one stupid mistake out of pure desperation.

'You must be exhausted, Pa. All these years of being in Mr Rathbone's power, all the worry and struggling to make ends meet.'

'That's been the worst part, seeing my family suffer,' said Pa. 'Never being able to afford a better home, never putting sufficient food on the table…being grateful when you brought home day-old goods from the pie shop. I've been a poor excuse for a husband and father and that's the truth.'

'No you haven't!' cried Nancy. 'You're good and kind and you've fetched up me and the twins to be decent girls.'

'Aye, and look at me now, asking my own daughter to steal summat.'

'You did a wrong thing all those years ago, but you did it for the right reasons. You intended to pay back what you took. It wasn't your fault your so-called friend turned out to be a bad lot. You're a good man, Pa. I believe that with all my heart.'

With all my heart. Uttering those words made things shift into a new position in Nancy's mind. All at once she knew what she had to do.

She stopped walking. Pa stopped an' all and turned to face her. His thin face, which had been taut with anxiety, had crumpled at her words and the glow from the street-lamp showed the gleam of tears in his eyes.

'You went against your principles when you took that money, Pa,' Nancy declared. 'You've suffered for it ever since and so has your family. Now it's time for me to go against my principles.'

'Oh, Nancy, are you sure? I don't want…' Pa's voice faded away.

'Don't ask me if I'm sure. I'm not sure at all about doing summat wrong. But I'm very sure about rescuing my family from Mr Rathbone's clutches.'

Chapter Twenty-Five

W HEN ZACHARY ARRIVED at St Anthony's to install the fire extinguishers, Miss Allan was downstairs.

'I'm busy at present,' she told him. 'If you go upstairs to my office area, my assistant will show you around the building.'

Zachary knew exactly where the extinguishers were going to be placed, but he didn't object. Anticipation fluttered inside him. Would Nancy be upstairs? He took the stairs two at a time, only to find the other girl, Miss Virginia, in the alcove.

Her smile was shy, but she was obviously expecting him. She picked up a piece of paper. 'This says where the extinguishers are to go.'

She went with him to each designated place, in each of which there was a new wooden shelf and, attached to the wall, a pair of straps to hold the extinguisher in position.

'Very impressive,' said Zachary. No other institution had made such preparations.

'Mr Abrams did it,' Miss Virginia replied.

As they went round, Zachary spied evidence of various preparations for Christmas – boxes of paper chains, simple crackers and strings of glittery beads that on closer inspection turned out to be balls of tin foil. Everything was home-made. His own Christmas would be spent by himself. He experienced the usual pang as he remembered Nate. He wasn't alone in having lost family. All the children under this roof had gone through the same thing, but at least it looked like they were going to have a good time.

He said as much to Miss Virginia.

'A lot of it is down to Miss Nancy,' she told him. 'The strings of tin foil beads – they were her idea. We always make paper-chains, but she's got the children churning them out like never before. Come and look at this.'

They were in the front hallway. Miss Virginia opened a door at the back of the area and leaned inside, looking both ways before she signalled to him to follow her. He went down the two steps into the dining room, where Miss Virginia could barely hide her smiles as she waited for him to notice whatever it was she had brought him here to see. Zachary glanced round. It took him a moment, but then the pictures caught his eye. Simple pictures on pieces of paper pinned to the picture rail. Each picture was either an apple or an orange.

He turned to his guide with a puzzled frown.

She laughed. 'No one knows. According to Miss Nancy, it's Christmas magic. Every time a new picture appears, it drives the children mad with curiosity.'

'I don't suppose they're the only ones,' said Zachary. Could all this really be down to the same lass who had made such a pig's ear of Mr Grant's invoice while working at Milner's Fire Safety Services?

When Zachary had fixed all the extinguishers in position, Mr Abrams walked round the building with him, ostensibly to double-check that the straps were secure, but Zachary didn't kid himself. He knew Abrams had been handed the task of giving his work the once-over. That was fine. He never did anything less than his best.

At the end of the tour, Abrams shook hands with him.

'Are you heading back to your shop now? If so, I'll walk with you. Come for a cup of tea in Soapsuds House and I'll introduce you to my wife.'

'I'd love to, but I've brought my invoice with me,' said Zachary. 'I always present it the day I do the installing. I'll pop upstairs with it now. But perhaps another day?'

Abrams nodded and smiled goodbye, while Zachary headed up the stairs.

And who should be behind the desk in the alcove but Nancy herself? Zachary felt like whooping for joy. He had seen her the other evening and was sure she had called his name, only she had then walked off with another chap. Zachary's spirits had slumped so deeply they had all but landed splat on the pavement, until he had realised that the chap was somewhat older. Much too old for a girl like Nancy. A family friend, perhaps? A neighbour? At any rate, not a young man with the same sort of interest in her that Zachary felt.

He almost bounded along the passage to the alcove in his eagerness, only to become ridiculously tongue-tied when he was standing in front of her. In the end, he thrust the invoice at her across the desk, saying, 'Here.' Really? 'Here'? Was that the best he could do?

'I'm glad to see you, Mr Milner,' she said, looking up at him, her light-brown eyes appearing soft in the gloom of the alcove. 'I wanted to thank you for speaking up for me that time after the fire safety training. I could easily have lost my job but for you.'

His heart filled. She was grateful to him. She appreciated what he had done for her. But before he could say anything, a new voice intervened.

'Is that your invoice, Mr Milner?' said Miss Allan. 'Good. Now, Miss Nancy, if you've quite finished flirting, perhaps you would oblige me by getting on with your work.'

Vivienne and Miss Prudence were alone in the sitting room. Miss Prudence had a tray on her lap, which she was leaning on to write the all-important letter to Niall Henderson.

'I remember the address of the law firm, so let's hope they are still at the same premises. My letter asks if I might consult Mr Niall Henderson on an important family matter.'

'Well, that's true,' Vivienne murmured.

'I've been turning it over in my mind all day and I wonder if you'd mind if the letter was sent in your name. It might not be a good idea at this stage to use mine.'

'You mean you don't want him to run for the hills.'

'Something like that.'

The letter was duly sent and the two of them awaited a reply with suppressed eagerness.

When it arrived, they sat on Miss Prudence's bed with the door shut.

Vivienne leaned closer. 'What did it say? Was it from...him?'

'No, he's no longer there. He has passed on – I don't mean that kind of passed on,' Miss Prudence added swiftly. 'He passed on his part of the business to two of his sons-in-law. The firm is now Carter, Rodwell and Minford. Rodwell and Minford must be the sons-in-law, because it used to be Carter, Henderson and Sons.'

'Oh.' Vivienne experienced a thud of disappointment. 'If he has sons-in-law...'

Miss Prudence, who never sighed, let go a small sigh. 'I know. Poor Patience. Poor dear Patience. What a blow. I was so hoping...'

'What does the letter say?' Vivienne asked.

'*We would be happy to assist you, should you wish to instruct us.* How frustrating.'

'It's immaterial...isn't it?' said Vivienne. 'If he's married, that's the end of it.'

'Not necessarily.' Miss Prudence looked at her. 'There's still you to consider. If there is no Henderson listed in the firm's name, that means that Jonty doesn't work there any more either. Might you wish to meet Niall? Of course, for all I know, you might wish to meet Jonty.'

'No, I don't think so,' Vivienne said at once. 'At least, not at this stage. But meeting Niall and having the chance to talk things over... I'd quite like to know what happened to Jonty even if I don't choose to meet him. Goodness! I feel all fluttery just thinking of it.'

'Well, think about it now. According to this letter, Niall has left the firm in order to enjoy other pursuits. I'm sure plenty of us would like the opportunity to give up work and do that, if we had the means. Would you like to meet him, if we can manage it? Do you need time to think about it?'

'No.' Suddenly she knew exactly what she wanted. 'I'd like to see him, even if it's just the once, as long as it can be done without causing any difficulties in his family.'

'I'd like to see him too,' said Miss Prudence. 'That time in Scotland changed the whole of the rest of my life. It sent me back here to an old life that I'd sworn to leave behind. It gave me a huge secret and a regret that I could never speak of. And now it has given me you. Patience lost the chance of marriage because of what happened. Niall clearly met someone else – well, that's fair enough, but I'd like him to see you, his niece. He tried to do the decent thing by you and me and I'd like him to know that those events that turned our lives inside out and upside down resulted in something wonderful...you. I just want him to *know*.'

'Then we must go and find him.'

Miss Prudence glanced at the letter. 'I can't write back,

asking his whereabouts. Would that I could.' She lifted her chin. 'We have to go to Annerby ourselves and see what we can find out. I shall have to take a day off work, though it will be difficult at present because of illness among the staff. Vivienne, if you find out when you could have time off from the Board of Health, we'll take it from there.'

Vivienne duly produced a choice of three dates, which Miss Prudence took to work with her to see what she could organise.

'The one date I can manage to take off from the office,' Miss Prudence told her a day or two later, 'is Friday the first of December. Is that still all right for you? If we don't go then, I don't know when we'll be able to, because Miss Langley is leaving to get married mid-month and they haven't done anything yet about replacing her.'

Vivienne drew in a breath and smiled. 'Friday the first it is.'

'There's a holly picture as well now,' cried a young voice, immediately followed by other exclamations of delight. 'It's more Christmas magic!'

Nancy hid her smiles. It wasn't easy finding the right moment to pin up a new picture, but somehow she had managed so far not to get caught by any of the children.

Nurse Carmel sidled up to her and murmured, 'Go on. Tell us what it's about.'

Nancy widened her eyes innocently. 'I can't think what you mean.'

She just hoped that when the 'real' piece of Christmas magic happened, no one would be disappointed. In the meantime, it would be the start of December this Friday – and on Saturday Mr Rathbone wanted to see her. She fingered her collar, which suddenly felt too tight. She knew what he wanted her to do, and she had told Pa she would do it, but she wasn't sure now where that determination had come from.

Instead she tried to concentrate on Stir-Up Sunday, the first Sunday in December, when traditionally the Christmas puddings were made. She had found out that Stir-Up Sunday had never been observed at St Anthony's. She found herself concentrating on it as if it was the most important date on the calendar. Was that because, on Sunday, she would have lived through Saturday and her meeting with Mr Rathbone? The thought of meeting him, and what she had promised to do, turned her insides to mush, and a very sickly mush at that.

She wanted to suggest that all the children at St Anthony's should have the chance to help stir the puddings on Stir-Up Sunday, but if she asked Mrs Rostron, would Mrs Wilkes think she had gone behind her back? She was scared of Mrs Wilkes, who, as Mam would have put it, wasn't backwards at coming forwards, meaning she wasn't frightened of speaking her mind. That made Nancy realise she had lost her initial wariness of Mrs Rostron. Yes, she was in awe of her, but she was no longer scared of going to her with a new idea.

She had to ask Mrs Wilkes, she knew she did. Taking a deep breath and finding that it failed to fill her with confidence, she walked up the dining room to the end where the large serving-hatch was and went through the door next to it, which led into a big lobby with walk-in cupboards on the left, a door to the rear of the girls' playground straight ahead and the door to the kitchen on the right.

Nancy knocked. When there was no response, she tried again, feeling foolish. At last, she summoned up the courage to open the door and peer into the kitchen with its banks of tall cupboards and long shelves of jars and canisters. A couple of doors led off into other rooms and there was a vast old-fashioned range to one side. The combined smells of onions, meat and something fruity filled the steamy air.

'Yes?' Mrs Wilkes, wearing her big white apron and mob-cap, glared in her direction. 'What do you want?'

The kitchen girls glanced in Nancy's direction, but didn't stop chopping, peeling or patting pastry into dishes.

'Please, Mrs Wilkes,' said Nancy, reverting to the language of the classroom, 'may I ask you something, if you have the time?'

The cook pushed her fists into the back of her waist and pulled back her shoulders. 'Very well, if you must. Come right in. Let's see if there's a body attached to that face.'

Nancy slid inside and closed the door behind her. Evidently standing just inside the door was as much as was permitted if you weren't kitchen staff, because Mrs Wilkes marched across and loomed over her.

'Well? What is it?'

'It's about Stir-Up Sunday, if you please. There's a tradition that everyone is supposed to stir the pudding.'

'I'm well aware of that, thank you. This is your good deed for the day, is it? Passing on Christmas customs?'

Nancy's face burned. 'What I mean is…' Inspiration struck. 'I have Mrs Rostron's permission to do special things for Christmas for the children and I wondered if you would kindly let them all stir the puddings this Sunday.'

'What, all of them? Have you any idea how many children there are?'

'A hundred and twenty, Mrs Wilkes.'

'I didn't mean you to tell me, you stupid girl. I know full well how many there are. Don't I have to feed them every day?'

'Yes, Mrs Wilkes. I'm sorry to have bothered you.'

'Hang on a minute. Good heavens, you creep in here like a mouse and now you're about to vanish again. Let's think about this. I've got all my dried fruit ordered and it's coming tomorrow, and…' She moved towards one of the shelves, where there was a jumbled line of glass jars, filled with jewel-coloured preserves. 'Yes, there's the marmalade to mix in. There's always plenty of flour. Florence! Check the demerara sugar. Mildred, do we need more suet?' Mrs Wilkes rounded on Nancy. 'I wasn't going to make my puddings until next week, but we can just as easily do 'em this weekend, can't we, girls?'

There was a chorus of 'Yes, Mrs Wilkes.'

'There you are, then,' Mrs Wilkes said to Nancy. 'Stir-up Sunday. They can do the stirring in the hour before teatime. That do you?'

'Yes, Mrs Wilkes. Thank you, Mrs Wilkes.'

Hardly able to believe she had survived the encounter, and not only that but she had got what she wanted, Nancy was backing out of the kitchen, picturing the children's excitement, when there was a scream. Flames were leaping upwards from a pan on the range, getting higher every second.

'Chuck water on it!' someone yelled.

'No!' The word burst from Nancy's lips before she had time to think.

She looked round for the – yes, there it was – the fire blanket. Seizing it, she shook it out. She was trembling madly on the inside but on the outside, her body was oddly controlled. Darting forwards, she held up the blanket, took aim and threw it over the flames. The fire's brightness vanished in a flash and she had to blink her eyes back to normality.

'She's put the fire out,' said one of the girls. 'Mrs Wilkes, she's put the fire out.'

'I can see that, thank you, Mildred,' said Mrs Wilkes. 'I've got eyes in my head. Well done, lass. That was quick thinking on your part. I'd forgotten all about that fire blanket thing.' She raised her voice, addressing one of her staff.

'Daisy, get that blanket took off that pan and let's see the damage to the onions.'

'No,' said Nancy, stepping forward. 'I mean, beg pardon, Mrs Wilkes, but you're supposed to leave the fire blanket where it is for fifteen minutes to make sure the fire has gone out.'

'Fifteen minutes? That's a long time.'

'It's what you have to do,' was Nancy's determined reply. 'I – I used to work for Mr Milner, who put in the fire extinguishers and the fire blankets, so I know these things.' And what would Zachary say if he could hear that grand claim?

'We'd best follow the rules, then,' said Mrs Wilkes. She nodded at Nancy. 'It's a good job you were here and I'll make sure I tell Mrs Rostron so.'

Word flew round the building and all the nursemaids made a fuss of Nancy. When the children came back from school, they listened open-mouthed to what the smalls told them and then they all wanted to crowd round Nancy and get her to tell them the story of her bravery. Mrs Rostron congratulated her and even Miss Allan had a good word for her.

'You saved the kitchen from a nasty incident, Miss Nancy,' said the secretary. 'That was a clever thing to do. You remembered your fire-safety training…which seems to have been more than anyone else did.'

Nancy felt overwhelmed by all the attention, but she was delighted too. A little of the confidence she had always felt when working behind the counter at the pie shop came creeping back.

But it wasn't long before her thoughts returned to Mr Rathbone. She had never met him, but he was never far from her mind these days. She had felt brave and determined when she had vowed to rescue her family from his clutches, but her courage had soon vanished, worn away by fear and worry.

Had she made a big mistake by declaring to Pa that she would go against her principles? Never mind what she had done to put out the fire in the kitchen. That would soon be forgotten if the truth came out about other things. What sort of an example did setting aside her principles make her for someone who longed to work with children?

Chapter Twenty-Six

As the train headed north through the countryside, Vivienne was struck by the view of a landscape of light mist swirling around winter-bare trees beneath overcast skies streaked with pearl-grey. As the journey continued, the skies lifted, changing to a brilliant blue that drew sparkles from the dusting of snow on the fields and hills below.

Miss Prudence, who had also been gazing out of the train window, now looked at Vivienne as she remarked, 'The last time I travelled by train, it was when Molly and I took Lucy to Maskell House, intending to leave her there until her child made its appearance. We got as far as saying goodbye and setting off in the taxi to return to the station. Climbing into that taxi was one of the hardest things I've ever had to do.'

'But you didn't leave her,' said Vivienne. 'You made the taxi driver turn round so you could go back and fetch her. I'm so glad you did. Had you left her there, I might never have found the courage to tell you the truth about being your daughter.'

'I'm grateful you did that. It has made all the difference to my life.'

'And to mine.'

Now here they were on another journey. Vivienne felt a stirring of excitement at the thought of meeting Niall Henderson. Her uncle! She liked what she had heard about him, which was more than could be said for the way she felt about her father. It wasn't easy knowing that Jonty Henderson had been a rotter. But hadn't she known it, deep down, ever since the summer? Back in July, on that evening of torrential rain, when Miss Prudence had told the story of what had happened in Scotland, the only mention of Vivienne's father had been, 'I met someone. A man,' followed a few moments later by, 'You were born the following September.' So it shouldn't have come as a surprise to Vivienne – should it? – when she had learned the truth about Jonty Henderson. And it hadn't, not really, though it had still come as a shock. Did that sound daft? Half-knowing, half-expecting something, and then being shocked by it? But that was how she had felt.

It had made her wonder about herself too. That man's blood flowed in her veins. Did that mean she too had the capacity to be selfish and ruthless? But she knew she didn't – and, oddly, it wasn't the thought of Elspeth and Graham Thornton and Prudence Hesketh that gave her this confidence. It was the cherished, bittersweet memory of her darling husband. She knew the happy, utterly unselfish person she had been during her marriage. That was who she was. That was the real Vivienne. Whatever she might or might not have inherited from Jonathan Henderson, she didn't have his nasty streak.

At last the train approached the market-town of Annerby in the north of Lancashire. The familiar cadence of the wheels on the tracks changed as the train coasted alongside the platform. There was a sharp hissing sound followed by the shriek of brakes, then a clunk as the train halted. Up and down the line of carriages, doors banged open as passengers descended, bags in one hand, tickets in the other, some of them in a tearing hurry to get where they were going.

Vivienne and Miss Prudence climbed down and walked along the platform, handing in their tickets at the barrier and walking through the small booking-hall and out of the building, emerging onto a road with a public house and shops.

Miss Prudence looked round. 'There it is.'

She had booked them rooms in the Station Hotel. They just had to cross over a small side-road to get to it. Inside was a pleasant foyer with a chintz sofa beneath an oil painting, and a large parlour palm beside the foot of the staircase. Having announced themselves at the desk and signed the register, they were shown upstairs to adjoining rooms on the first floor, overlooking the street. It didn't take long to unpack. Vivienne knocked on Miss Prudence's door and they went downstairs together.

'Do you have a telephone directory, please?' asked Miss Prudence.

The clerk produced one from under the counter and they took it to a table in the residents' lounge. Vivienne's heart beat hard as she watched Miss Prudence flick through the pages, murmuring as she did so.

'H...H...Harrison...Harrop...Henderson. Here we are.' She looked up. 'Good heavens.' She pressed a hand to her chest. 'I hadn't appreciated quite how nerve-racking this would be. Here he is. He's the only Henderson, N, and here's his address, so at least we know he's still in the vicinity.' She paused before adding, without looking at Vivienne, 'There's no Henderson, J, listed, though, of course, that might simply mean he doesn't have a telephone.' She closed the book, saying briskly, 'Now we need to find the Old Market Square, which is where the law firm is, and see if we can get Niall to meet us here in the hotel.'

The clerk provided directions and they made their way to a large cobbled square with a horse trough at one end and a stone cross in the middle. The day was drawing in and around the edges of the square, lamps were glowing in windows and some curtains were already drawn. There was a public house, a small hotel, some shops, a smart house or two and some office buildings. Beside the front door of one, a brass plate, looking golden in the light cast by a street-lamp, announced *Carter, Rodwell & Minford.*

Miss Prudence turned to Vivienne. 'I've written a short letter to Niall, saying that I'm staying at the Station Hotel and I wish to see him on an important matter. I haven't mentioned your presence. Shall we go in?'

The door was unlocked and gave onto a hall which could have done with having the light switched on. On the right was an open door to an office, where a man in his thirties sat behind the main desk while an older lady with salt-and-pepper hair sat behind a typewriter placed on a smaller desk.

'Good afternoon,' said Miss Prudence. 'I wonder if you can help me. I wish to contact Mr Niall Henderson. May I give you a letter for him?'

The clerks looked at them in open curiosity.

'Perhaps you are unaware that Mr Henderson no longer works here,' said the man.

'I am aware of that, thank you. He retired, I believe, and his sons-in-law have taken over his share of the business. This is a personal letter.'

The lady-clerk held out her hand for it. 'I'll send our messenger-boy directly.'

'I'm obliged to you,' said Miss Prudence. She flashed a look of triumph at Vivienne, though she waited until they were outside to say, 'That means his home must be nearby. With luck, we might hear back from him this evening and I hope...'

Miss Prudence didn't articulate what she hoped. She didn't need to. Would Niall Henderson wish to meet her or had they come all this way for nothing?

With her arm linked through Vivienne's, Prudence walked around the middle of Annerby. She didn't say so, but she was allowing Niall time to send a reply to the hotel. Annerby was a pleasant, bustling little town, though when the two of them stood on an old stone bridge above a river with a steady current, the waters beneath were maroon-coloured.

'There must be a dye-works,' said Vivienne.

Anticipation rose within Prudence as they returned to the Station Hotel. Would there be a note for her from Niall? Her heart delivered a thud as the clerk turned to check the pigeon-holes behind the desk.

'I'm sorry. There's no message.'

Prudence was surprised by what a let-down it was, but she didn't let it show. They went upstairs to wash and change. Prudence had brought her Sunday best to wear on the two evenings they were to spend in the hotel. She never much minded what she wore, as long as she looked tidy and appropriately dressed, but her heart swelled with pride at the sight of Vivienne in a simple ankle-length evening dress of honey-gold that brought out a new richness in her light-brown hair. Around her head, she wore a matching honey-gold band with a couple of feathers. The dress had a pale chiffon over-dress that created a pretty, floaty effect and she wore a long bead necklace.

Prudence laughed. 'We look like a glamorous heiress and her dowdy old chaperone.'

Vivienne linked arms with her and kissed her cheek. 'We look like what we are: two women with very different taste in clothes but exactly the same taste in friends.'

In the dining room, the curtains were closed and a fire crackled in the grate beneath a handsome mantelpiece. The maître d' showed them to a table laid with crisp Irish linen and set with bone-handled cutlery, and presented them with menus.

When he withdrew, Vivienne leaned forward and said, 'I'm always interested in hotels, because of the family business.'

'I can understand that. I find myself remembering what I was taught in Loch Lomond.'

Looking round the dining room, Prudence was thrown back to that time when she had believed that her future lay in the world of hotels and hospitality. Her friend Elspeth had married into a well-to-do family with a string of hotels, which was how Prudence had ended up working on the shores of Loch Lomond, secretly imagining herself becoming the first female hotel manager in the company. But then Jonty Henderson had appeared and her ambition, together with her common sense, had flown out of the window. For years, she had looked back and boggled at the young fool she had once been; but now she was reunited with her precious daughter and the old foolishness had slipped into a new perspective.

Prudence scanned the menu, choosing mushroom soup followed by chicken. A young waiter took their order and departed. Moments later, the man from the reception desk entered the dining room and looked round. Spotting them, he threaded his way between the tables.

Anticipation caused an uncharacteristic flutter inside Prudence even before she caught sight of the envelope in his hand.

Chapter Twenty-Seven

Prudence lay awake for much of the night, her mind teeming with memories. Even so, she wasn't tired when morning came. On the contrary, she felt sharp and alert. In the note that had been delivered yesterday evening, Niall had offered to come to the hotel to meet with her. Did he intend to protect Mrs Niall Henderson from this aspect of his past?

Vivienne had agreed to wait in her room. A few minutes before the appointed time, Prudence headed downstairs, feeling foolishly self-conscious, to choose where to sit in the lounge. She got as far as the half-landing, turned the corner on the stairs – and stopped dead.

There he was.

This was how she had seen Jonty that very first time in the hotel on the banks of Loch Lomond. She had been descending the staircase and he was in the lobby below. He had just walked through the front doors for the first time and had stopped for a moment to get his bearings. He had removed his hat and looked round. From above, Prudence had seen his dark hair, his broad forehead and straight nose. There had been a glimpse of a generous mouth and a confident jawline.

Her heart took the next few beats at top speed. Her legs wouldn't move. She forced life back into them and made them carry her the rest of the way down the stairs. Before Niall could approach the reception desk, she spoke to him.

'Mr Henderson?'

He turned and a thrill of shock rippled through her. The same face, the same dark eyes. He was older, of course, and subtly different, with greying hair and lines, but at the same time he was exactly the same and instantly recognisable. It made her realise how old she must appear. She hadn't enjoyed much in the way of looks to start with, and now she was faded. But it didn't matter. She wasn't here on her own account.

'I never expected to see you again,' he said.

'Nor I you.'

Niall glanced about. 'We should go somewhere private.' He glanced towards the front door.

'There might be a quiet corner in the lounge.'

She led the way. Dark curtains hung either side of diamond-paned windows. Bookcases and paintings filled the walls and a good fire drew the eye to the far wall, where the fireplace boasted a gigantic mahogany surround comprising three over-mantel shelves and various niches as well as attached candelabra, around which holly had been twined. A generous alcove contained a pair of armchairs with a table between and this was where Prudence took a seat, waiting for him to follow suit.

'I was most surprised to receive your letter yesterday. May I ask: are you still Prudence Hesketh? Or did you sign your letter in that way simply so I would recognise you?'

'I am still Prudence Hesketh.'

All those years ago, she had had a leather suitcase – she still had it, actually, gathering dust on top of the wardrobe in Wilton Close – stamped with the initials PWH. On the banks of Loch Lomond, when she was young and in love and toying with the possibility of Prudence Henderson, it had delighted her to think that her suitcase was already stamped with the correct initials.

'I apologise for appearing out of the blue,' she said, 'but there has been some upheaval, you might call it, in my life in recent months.'

'Have you come to me for help?'

She hadn't expected that reaction. 'Heavens, no. I'm perfectly capable of taking care of myself.' She felt flustered, an unusual experience for her.

'Then what brings you here?' Niall's face clouded. 'Is it – has something happened to Patience? Although why you would come all this way to inform me – after all these years—'

'I'm not here about Patience, who, incidentally, is fit and well.'

'Did she – did she ever marry? Silly question. She must have done, a lovely lady like that.'

This wasn't the script Prudence had prepared in her head. She had to get the conversation back on track.

'I'm here to talk about what happened in Loch Lomond.'

'I repeat: after all these years?'

'Yes. When we parted, you never knew what happened afterwards – what happened to me, I mean, and – and to the child.'

A wave of colour passed across Niall's features, then vanished, taking his natural colour with it.

'I'd be lying if I said I never wondered.'

Good: that was a start. Prudence nodded. 'I – Jonty – had a daughter.'

'A daughter?' Niall's eyes softened. 'A daughter.'

Prudence was taken aback by the tenderness in his expression, but it was there for only a moment before the shutters came down and he hid whatever he was thinking.

'I don't suppose you recall the couple who were in charge of the hotel,' said Prudence, 'a Mr and Mrs Thornton. Elspeth Thornton was my friend. We were at school together. When I confided in her about my condition, she and her husband offered to adopt the baby as their own.'

Niall's eyes widened. He had crow's feet now and his lids were hooded, but as his eyes widened, they turned back into the eyes of the handsome young man who had tried to do the right thing by her and her unborn child.

'You mean that if I had ever returned to Loch Lomond, I might have – I might have seen Jonty's daughter – my niece?'

'No,' Prudence said quickly. 'Elspeth and Graham moved to the south of England to another of the family's hotels. That was part of the plan. They wanted to bring up the child as their own – their very own, I mean. They didn't want the adoption to be known.'

'And you? Did you stay in touch with them?'

'No. That was part of the plan too.'

'I see.' Niall looked pensive. Prudence let him think. Finally he said, 'Why are you telling me this now?'

She drew a breath and summoned the steadiest voice she could manage.

'Because, earlier this year, my daughter tracked me down. She's upstairs in this hotel right now.'

Saturday. Nancy had spent all week dreading today. Was she really going to be forced to steal from Gabriel and Belinda, from under the Miss Heskeths' roof? But everything depended upon it. Her family's future depended on it.

But – but maybe she had a way out of this situation. A tiny hope wriggled inside her, though it was an uncomfortable feeling that didn't seem at all positive. When she explained to Mr Rathbone that she couldn't possibly get her hands on the key to the inner cellar, he would have to let her off the hook – wouldn't he?

Mr Rathbone lived in Whalley Road in Seymour Grove in a large red-brick house, the sort that was called a villa. Shrubs grew taller than the garden wall, giving privacy to the bay-windowed house. Nancy experienced a little spurt of what might have been anger as she walked through the gate and saw the house and compared it to the cramped flat over the tobacconist's in Bailiff's Row. Was she supposed to knock on the front door or go round the back? It wasn't as though she was a proper visitor. As she dithered, the front door opened and a woman wearing a white apron let her in.

'Are you Pike's lass? Mr Rathbone is expecting you.'

Nancy walked into a hall that seemed as big as a room. There were doors on both sides. In the doorway of the back room on the left, a tall, thin gentleman appeared. Nancy had never realised before that you could be thin without looking underfed.

'I'm off to do the shopping now, sir,' said the servant. She started to remove her apron as she walked away.

'This way,' said Mr Rathbone, standing with his back to the open door to wave her into the room.

It must be a study, Nancy supposed. She had never seen one before. There was a desk with shelves behind it, and there was a cabinet in the corner nearest the door. There were bookcases with glass doors and even a pair of armchairs.

Mr Rathbone left her standing while he took his seat at the desk. On the wall behind the desk were two paintings of galleons in full sail. Was that how Mr Rathbone saw himself? A prosperous gentleman in full sail?

'So,' he said, not looking at her, but fingering a solid glass paperweight as if it was of far more interest than she was,

'Pike has shared our little secret with you. What do you think of him now, eh?'

Nancy lifted her chin. 'I think you took advantage of him all those years ago.'

Mr Rathbone looked at her. 'Sir,' he said and waited.

'Sir,' said Nancy.

'Say all of it.'

She didn't want to, but she had no choice. 'You took advantage of him all those years ago, sir.' She didn't say 'I think' this time, because she knew. She *knew*.

'As a matter of fact, I did him a great service.' Mr Rathbone sat back in his chair. He rested his elbows on the arms and clasped his hands. 'Less than an hour after he had replaced the stolen money – using, of course, the money I had provided – the company accountant checked all the funds on the premises – in the safe, the petty cash, everything. Had I not provided the money for your father to put back what he had taken, the theft would have been revealed immediately and you would have grown up without a daddy, because Daddy would have been doing hard labour. He didn't tell you that part, did he?'

Nancy's fingers curled over palms that were suddenly clammy. It didn't bear thinking about. Imagine if Pa… And what would have become of Mam? If Pa had been sent to prison for a long time, maybe the twins would never have been born.

'I asked you a question,' said Mr Rathbone. 'He didn't tell you that, did he?'

'No…sir,' she whispered, remembering to add the crucial word, even though uttering it hurt her throat.

'Are you a clever girl, Nancy Pike? Clever enough to be taken on by the Miss Heskeths' school, at any rate. The question is, are you cleverer than your father? Well, are you?'

'I don't know, sir.'

'I hope for your sake that you are – for all your family's sake. I sent Pike to do a job for me and he failed. Even though success would have released him from my service, nevertheless he failed. Such a dud, your father. So meek and mild, no backbone. Have you got backbone, Nancy? Have you got what it takes to rescue your family? Pike owes me a great debt. I will release him from it and will return his signed confession in return for…your cooperation. You live in that house. It shouldn't be difficult for you to lay hands on the page-cutter.'

'It's locked away, sir.'

'How interesting – how pleasing. Your instant response isn't "I shan't steal it." It's "I can't, because the page-cutter is under lock and key." It's good to see you have inherited your father's sticky fingers.'

'Pa hasn't got sticky fingers – and neither have I. He made one mistake – just one – when he was young and desperate.'

'And now you're the one who is young and desperate. Are you desperate, Nancy? Desperate to save your family? It lies within your power to do so.'

'I can't do it,' said Nancy.

Mr Rathbone eyed her shrewdly. 'Can't or won't?'

'Can't…sir. I wouldn't be able to get the key to the inner cellar. It's in Miss Hesketh's dressing-table drawer.'

'Don't be ridiculous. Of course you can get it.'

'I can't risk it. I'm never alone in the house, sir.'

'Never?' There was a sneering note in his voice. 'You expect me to believe that?'

'It's true. I think the only occasion I've been on my own for any length of time was when Pa came round and wanted to go in the cellar. Even if I could pinch the key from the dressing-table, I couldn't go down the cellar. Before you suggest it,

I couldn't sneak down while the ladies are busy teaching, because one of them uses the dining room and I'd have to go through that to reach the kitchen.'

'I wasn't going to suggest any such thing.'

Could he really see how impossible it was? Tears of relief welled up behind Nancy's eyelids. Mr Rathbone made no move. He simply sat and watched her, his eyes dark in his long, narrow face.

'I had thought you cleverer than your father, but now I'm not so sure. You shan't have to hang onto the cellar key, you foolish girl. A matter of seconds with it is all you require. After that, you must choose your moment to go down to the cellar. While lessons are in progress sounds ideal.'

'But—'

'Leave quietly via the front door and enter by the kitchen door. Go down to the cellar, then return the same way, and no one will be any the wiser.'

Nancy's heart thumped. She couldn't bear to let down the Miss Heskeths or Gabriel and Belinda. But the alternative was to let her family down dreadfully.

She clung to the last hope of reprieve. 'But it would be such a risk to take the key.'

'Weren't you listening? A moment is all you need. You won't even have to remove it from the room, just take it from the drawer and put it back again.'

Nancy was curious in spite of herself. Mr Rathbone opened his desk drawer and laid a large metal key on his blotter.

'I imagine this is the sort of key,' he said. 'This is the key to my back door.' He held out his hand. In his palm was a lump of putty. He broke off a small piece. 'Flatten it in your hand, like so.' He picked up the key. 'Then firmly press the blade of the key into it.' He held out the putty for her to see. It bore a clear imprint of the key-blade. 'You do it.'

A feeling of dread weighed her down. She really was going to be forced to commit this theft. But she was fascinated an' all. She picked up the putty and tore off a piece. Taking the key, she pressed it in, then removed it.

Mr Rathbone examined her effort. 'That won't do. You need to exert equal pressure along the blade. Do it again. No, don't squash that one. I want you to do several and I expect each one to be better than the last.'

Should she mess them up on purpose? But it was such a simple task. Mr Rathbone would never believe her incapable of it. She did another, then another and another.

'Look at them,' Mr Rathbone ordered. 'Tell me what's right and wrong about them.'

Nancy scrutinised them. 'This one's uneven. This one's better.'

'But still not perfect. Try again.' He produced more putty.

Nancy carried on. Soon she had produced several good impressions in a row.

'Good,' said Mr Rathbone. 'You've got the hang of it. These are your instructions. Find an opportunity to make a putty-impression of the cellar key. Take it to a locksmith and ask him to make a key for you. You will find sufficient money here.' He placed coins on the blotter. 'You will then retrieve the page-cutter from the cellar. If you are contemplating getting caught accidentally on purpose and throwing yourself on the Miss Heskeths' mercy, I would remind you I have your father's letter – his signed confession, I might say – in my possession. You have a fortnight in which to complete this task. Two weeks today, you shall bring the page-cutter here. Make sure you come after four-thirty. The house will be empty that afternoon, but I'll make sure I'm back by then. If you do this to my satisfaction, I'll return Pike's confession to him.'

'And leave him alone for evermore,' Nancy added. Never mind the theft. Never mind her conscience. Think of Pa being free at last from Mr Rathbone. Think of the family having more money. Think of Mam's health.

'There's one final thing,' said Mr Rathbone. 'I have to be certain you'll bring me the correct item. I remember how many boxes of bric-a-brac there were in the bookshop that time, and I expect there were more than I saw. It's possible that there could be more than one page-cutter among the Tyrell junk, so I'll show you the letter-opener I have in my possession, then you'll have no difficulty in recognising the companion piece. Stand in the hall while I get out the letter-opener.'

Nancy left the study.

'Close the door properly, girl,' snapped Mr Rathbone.

She clicked it shut. So he kept the letter-opener hidden away, did he? It was hardly surprising after the way he had hung onto it when he should have given it back. After a minute, the door opened and Mr Rathbone returned to his chair as she followed him inside. She looked round, but nothing seemed disturbed or out of place.

Mr Rathbone wafted a hand at the blotter, on which lay a slender silver knife, its handle engraved with fancy carving.

'There's this as well.' Mr Rathbone held up a flimsy piece of paper, covered in handwriting. 'Your father's letter. I will return this to him after you bring me the page-cutter. Do you understand what is required of you?'

She nodded.

'Take the money for the locksmith and the pieces of putty you've already used. That gives you more than enough.'

Nancy scooped up the pieces of putty with their various key-impressions and slipped them into her pocket. What had she got herself into?

Chapter Twenty-Eight

PRUDENCE BROUGHT VIVIENNE downstairs, pausing outside the hotel lounge to squeeze her hand. Vivienne gave her a grateful glance. The door was open. Without speaking, Prudence nodded across the room to the alcove, wanting Vivienne to see her uncle before he knew they were there. Vivienne pressed her lips together, her bosom rising and falling. Maybe Niall sensed her scrutiny, because he looked round and saw the pair of them – or maybe he saw only Vivienne. He came to his feet, taking a step towards them, then stopped.

Prudence and Vivienne crossed the room.

'You look like my mother and my aunt.' Niall's gaze was fixed on Vivienne's face. His eyes filled and he shook his head, half-laughing, half-wondering. 'I'd know you anywhere.'

Prudence sought refuge in formality. 'Vivienne, this is Mr Niall Henderson. Mr Henderson, may I introduce Vivienne Atwood. Your niece.'

'My dear girl,' said Niall. 'My dear girl.'

'Are we supposed to shake hands?' Vivienne sounded breathless.

'That'll do for a start,' said Prudence.

Self-consciousness created a pause, then Vivienne offered her hand, which Niall took. Instead of shaking it, he held it in both hands before raising it to his lips and then pressing it to his cheek.

Vivienne pulled away. 'I'm sorry,' she said at once. 'I just wasn't expecting that.'

'Let's sit down, shall we?' said Prudence. 'Unless you two would prefer to be alone?' That hadn't occurred to her until this moment.

'No. Stay,' said Vivienne.

'I think that's best.' Niall waited for them to sit before he resumed his seat. 'You're Mrs Atwood?'

Vivienne clasped her hands loosely in her lap. 'I'm a war widow.'

'I'm sorry to hear that.'

'I've spent the past few years working.' She sketched an outline of her career to date. 'It keeps me busy.'

'I mean no disrespect to your late husband,' said Niall, 'but I hope you'll eventually meet someone else. I wouldn't like to think of you being alone for ever.'

'Why shouldn't women work and find satisfaction that way?' Vivienne replied.

'I meant no disrespect to your capabilities either,' said Niall. He turned to Prudence. 'May I suggest that we dispense with formalities? This is by way of being a family reunion, so please address me as Niall. And may I call you Prudence?'

Prudence inclined her head. 'What about you?' she asked him. 'You've heard a little about Vivienne. It's time to reciprocate.'

'You know I worked in a legal practice and I've now retired, though I'm young to do so. I want to make the most of being with my family.'

'Your family?' Vivienne prompted.

'I am the proud father of five daughters.'

'Five!' Prudence exclaimed, unable to help herself. 'You didn't hang about pining, then.'

'It wasn't a question of pining. I had to get on with my life. I met – and I should point out that this was several years after I knew you and Patience – I met a widow, a delightful, warm-hearted lady, who had two young daughters.'

'So two of your daughters are stepdaughters,' said Prudence.

'That's right. Not that the step-relationship is of any moment to me. Vicky and Leonora are as much mine as are the others. There have been occasions over the years when someone has asked me which two are my stepdaughters and my answer is always the same: I don't remember. My daughters are my daughters and I love them all.' Niall gazed at Vivienne. 'And now I have a niece as well.'

'You say that so easily,' said Vivienne. 'It's not altogether easy for me. My dad – my adoptive father – is still alive. I want you to know that.'

Niall bowed his head. 'I take nothing for granted.'

Vivienne sounded as if she was choosing her words with care. 'I don't wish to give offence. Miss Prudence has told me how you offered to help her after – after your brother abandoned her and so I know you're a good person. But my dad might not be so understanding. He's protective of me. You know what dads are like.'

A smiled touched Niall's lips. 'I do indeed. I have nothing but respect for your adoptive father's position as your father. You are to him all that my daughters are to me.'

'I apologise if I appear edgy,' said Vivienne, though in that moment she seemed more relaxed. 'This is an emotional moment, but I'm truly pleased to meet you.'

'Thank you,' Niall replied.

Prudence had the oddest feeling that she was being granted a glimpse of the life that might have been – herself with her daughter and her brother-in-law. The feeling swirled around her, sharp and tender at the same time.

'I'm sorry if this makes things difficult for you,' Vivienne told Niall, 'but I'd prefer it if you didn't tell your brother about meeting me. To tell you the truth, I don't think he deserves to know.'

Niall released a breath. Raising one hand, he scrubbed it across his chin, then he turned to Prudence.

'Forgive me. I should probably have told you before you brought Vivienne downstairs, but I was so eager to see her.'

Prudence stiffened. 'Told me what?'

'About Jonty.'

'I don't want to know,' said Prudence. 'Whatever he did with his life, I don't want to hear it.'

'Please let me tell you,' said Niall. 'Believe me, I fully understand why you hold such a poor opinion of him—'

'Oh, you do, do you?' The words burst from Vivienne's lips before Prudence could speak. 'You understand? Well, that's very generous of you, not to say more than a little patronising. Jonty Henderson is a rat of the first water, who took advantage of Miss Prudence's feelings for him, and if you try to speak on his behalf, I – I shall think badly of you.'

Prudence was touched beyond words that her daughter should take her part with such fierce protectiveness. She looked at Niall. Was he about to sink in her estimation? Had coming here been a terrible mistake?

Niall looked down at his hands – playing for time? Deep in thought? When he looked at the pair of them, he astonished Prudence by smiling.

'You're both looking at me so accusingly. When I first saw you, Vivienne, the resemblance between you and my mother took my breath away, but now I can see Prudence in you as well.'

Prudence lifted an eyebrow. 'In an accusing look? I'm not sure how flattering that is.'

'I understand your reluctance to hear about Jonty and I wouldn't ask you to listen to what I have to say unless I had a good reason for sharing it. Please trust me for a few minutes.'

'Trust you?' said Vivienne. 'I don't know you.'

'You don't know me personally, but you have heard enough to share Prudence's good opinion of me. Can we please take that as our starting point?' Niall looked straight at Prudence. 'I'm ashamed of the way you were treated all those years ago, but you don't know the whole story. Won't you let me tell it?'

The temptation to refuse was strong, but, in spite of herself, Prudence was curious. She nodded.

'Jonty and I were both young men in the family law practice. When he – when he came home from Scotland, he told our father what had happened. My father had social aspirations and—'

'And they didn't include a hotel receptionist who was in an interesting condition,' Prudence said tartly.

'Quite. He quickly arranged for Jonty to go on another business trip, this time to the Transvaal.'

'Goodness,' said Prudence. 'He really was determined to get Jonty out of the picture.' She pressed her lips together. It wasn't like her to interrupt, but she was unexpectedly nervous. 'Please continue,' she said.

'Before he left, Jonty told me why he was going. You see, I was the one who had been meant to go. My father would never have told me why he'd changed his mind and sent Jonty instead, but Jonty wanted me to know. I was appalled by their behaviour – both of them – and I looked into the possibility of giving you financial assistance. It got back to my father that I'd been making enquiries and he was outraged. He – well, I'm sure you can imagine his attitude.'

'Tell us,' Vivienne said quietly.

'He said that providing money was the last thing one should do in this sort of situation. He refused point-blank to have what he termed an illegitimate brat as his first grandchild. Nevertheless, I went to Loch Lomond and met you, Prudence, but you turned down my offer of help. And that wasn't the only thing that happened there. I also met Patience – without knowing at first that she was your sister – and I fell in love with her. *We* fell in love.'

A sharp pain took up residence in the back of Prudence's throat. 'And I sent you packing. End of story. I'm not sure what Vivienne and I are supposed to have gained by hearing about your father's hard-hearted views.'

'It isn't the end of the story,' said Niall. 'Do you think I went away simply because you told me to?'

'Didn't you?'

'Your father came to see me.'

'Pa did? *Pa?*'

'Graham Thornton let slip something of what had happened, and Mr Hesketh insisted upon being told the rest.'

'About – about my pregnancy?' Prudence's heartbeat raced at full tilt before slowing almost to nothing. Pa had known. *Pa.*

'Your father was outraged by what had happened to you,' said Niall, 'and now his younger daughter was involved with the brother of the man… He wouldn't countenance it. He was the one who banished me, not you.'

For once in her life, Prudence was lost for words. Pa had known about the baby. He had never said a word, never once given the slightest indication. *Pa.* She had always rather scorned him, because he had given up work to live the life of a scholarly gentleman even though he didn't have the money to do so, a decision that for his daughters had been the start of the slide into genteel poverty. All Pa had cared about was his books and his learned papers. It had been Patience's job to run the house and take care of him and Prudence's to keep the wolf from the door. And, all along, he had *known*.

'I had no idea,' she whispered, shaking her head. She couldn't meet their eyes.

'There's more,' said Niall, 'if you can bear to hear it. I think you ought to – both of you.'

Vivienne looked at Prudence and Prudence gave the tiniest nod of her head.

'Go on,' Vivienne told Niall.

'You may need to prepare yourselves for a shock. I had hardly got home from Loch Lomond before word came that Jonty had been killed in a train crash as he crossed France.'

Vivienne pressed the flat of her hand to her bosom. 'Whatever I thought you might say, I wasn't expecting that.'

Niall sat forwards. 'The train wasn't heading south. It was coming north. Do you see what that means? If he'd been going south, he'd have been on his way to the Transvaal, but he was heading north. He was on his way home. He was coming back to marry you, Prudence.'

'You can't possibly know that,' Prudence retorted. 'You've got no business saying it.'

'But I do know it – I swear. I can't prove it, because I burned the letter a long time ago, but some weeks after his death, a letter arrived that Jonty had written to me when he was in France, in which he said he had decided to stand by you after all. He was ashamed of abandoning you and he wanted to make amends.'

Prudence stared. 'Is this true?'

'On my honour. I wish now I'd hung onto the letter, but it seemed safest not to in case my mother came across it. She knew nothing of what had happened in Scotland and it would have broken her heart all over again. She was a dear woman.'

'I don't know what to say – I don't know what to think.'

Jonty had been on his way back to her – but would she have wanted him after what he had done? Would she ever have trusted him again? Had she even still loved him by that time? When he had left her, she had been desperately shocked. That feeling had eventually been replaced by anger. He had let her down in the worst possible way, leaving her with no choice but to get on with her life in the best way she could muster. She hadn't had either the time or the inclination to weep and wail over Jonty Henderson. He hadn't deserved it.

Did he deserve it now that she knew he had changed his mind?

Vivienne squeezed her hand and Prudence smiled. She had her daughter in her life and that was what mattered.

'I went back to Loch Lomond to tell you,' said Niall. 'I thought you deserved to know, but you had already left.'

'You could have told my parents,' said Vivienne. 'They would have passed on a message.'

'I didn't know they were part of Prudence's arrangements. I knew they were aware of the pregnancy, because Graham Thornton was the one who inadvertently told Mr Hesketh, but, for all I knew, they had waved Prudence goodbye and been relieved to see the back of her. At any rate, I didn't approach them and I had no means of finding Prudence.' Niall looked at Vivienne, his eyes soft. 'Maybe Jonty wasn't such a complete rat after all.'

A pause. Then 'Maybe,' Vivienne conceded. It was obviously something she needed to absorb before she made any decisions – not unlike Prudence.

'Well, this has been most...illuminating,' Prudence said, using the dry, steady voice she used when she wanted to conceal her thoughts. 'I thought I was the one bringing you a surprise by introducing your niece.'

Niall smiled at her. 'That was certainly unexpected. The best surprise I have had in a long time. When I came here to meet you, I could only imagine you were here about Patience.' Forestalling her, he added, 'I want you to know that I've been on my own for some years.'

'On your own?' Vivienne flashed a look at Prudence. 'You mean, you're a widower?'

'Yes. My oldest grandchild is ten and she is the only grandchild my Jennie saw. It has been a deep and lasting sorrow to me that she didn't live to see her other grandchildren. She'd have adored them.' He trained his attention on Vivienne. 'When I said I wondered if this meeting would be about Patience, that doesn't mean I'm in any degree disappointed to meet you. I couldn't be happier about it. I hope you'll allow me to keep in touch with you to whatever degree you feel comfortable with. I don't wish to upset Mr Thornton, but I would be honoured to occupy a corner of your life.'

'I think I'd like that,' said Vivienne, 'but it's too soon to commit myself to anything. I have a lot to think about.'

Niall nodded. 'I understand.' To Prudence, he said, 'I've never stopped feeling bad about abandoning Patience.'

'You didn't abandon her,' Prudence pointed out. 'There was no choice, under the circumstances.'

'When I walked away from her, I never expected to find another girl. Then along came Jennie and I dared to love again. I vowed that my wife and children would be the most dearly cherished family ever, because I was so grateful to have a second chance. But I never forgot Patience. I never forgot how badly I hurt her.'

'We both hurt her,' said Prudence, 'did she but know it.'

'Do you think she might like to see me again?' asked Niall.

Chapter Twenty-Nine

PRUDENCE AND VIVIENNE arrived home on Sunday afternoon, opening the front door onto the fruity, spicy aroma that declared this to be Stir-Up Sunday, the first Sunday in advent, the day when, according to tradition, the Christmas pudding was prepared. Patience loved traditions and special occasions. Prudence experienced a pang of regret for the various times over the years when she had stubbornly refrained from making a fuss over an occasion that Patience had attempted to turn into a little fête. What a difference it would have made if her observation of 'You've gone to a lot of trouble. Thank you' had been accompanied by a warm smile and a hug. What a bigger difference it would have made if she had participated in the preparations.

But she never had. Responsibility for the household maintenance and finances had been thrust upon her when she was a young girl after Mother's early death. Pa had left her to it and she had been proud to assume the duty, though she had been angry with Pa, too, for abdicating his own responsibility. Had that anger, together with her natural inclination towards seriousness, made her hold herself aloof from domestic pleasures? Later, after the emotional devastation of giving up her child, she had drawn her duties and responsibilities around her like a cloak. Over the years, her naturally quick brain had veered more and more towards criticism, judgement and intolerance.

Well, not any more.

Putting down her carpetbag in the hall, she didn't pause to remove her coat and hat before heading straight towards Patience, who had come through to the hall to welcome them home.

Prudence gave her a brief hug. 'Are we in time to stir the pudding? It smells delicious, as always.'

A look of surprise appeared on Patience's face, but there was pleasure as well. Disappointment, or possibly shame, caused a dipping sensation inside Prudence. Had she really been so mean with her praise all these years?

'Take your things off first and unpack while I put the kettle on,' said Patience. 'I expect you could both do with a cup of tea. How was your journey?'

Dear, guileless Patience hadn't questioned their going away together for a couple of nights. She had assumed it was an opportunity for them to get to know one another. Prudence felt a twist of anxiety at the thought of what she had to tell her sister later on.

She and Vivienne unpacked, enjoyed a cup of tea, then stirred the pud, as tradition dictated.

'Where's Nancy?' asked Vivienne. 'She should stir it too.'

'She's at the orphanage,' said Patience. 'She had the idea of getting all the children to stir the puddings. I'm surprised no one thought of it before.'

Prudence and Vivienne glanced at one another.

'Maybe I'll toddle along and lend a hand organising the children,' said Vivienne. 'I imagine they'll be jolly excited.'

When she had set off, Prudence said to her sister, 'Come and sit down. I have something important to tell you.'

Patience followed her into the sitting room. 'That sounds ominous.'

Prudence didn't waste time trying to allay her sister's

fears. When they were both seated, she clasped her hands and began.

'I want to talk to you about what took place all those years ago in Scotland and why I came to live at home again.'

'Oh.' A note of surprise – immediately followed by kindness. 'I shan't pretend never to have wondered, but I knew you wouldn't thank me for intruding. You'd have told me if you'd wanted me to know.'

'The thing is – the thing is, I don't just want to talk about what happened to me, but also what happened to you.'

'To me?' A flush invaded Patience's face. She shook her head. 'Whatever for? It was a very long time ago.'

'You came up to Loch Lomond to spend a holiday in the hotel where I was working,' Prudence said gently, 'and while you were there, you met a man. Niall Henderson.' She waited in case Patience took up the tale, but Patience said nothing. 'The two of you quickly fell in love, but he broke it off.'

Prudence felt a twist of hurt on her sister's behalf. Oh, the damage that had been done.

'There's a lot more to the story than you are aware of,' said Prudence, 'and I want to tell you everything. I'm not doing it to hurt you by dredging up unhappy memories. I have a good reason. I want you to understand that before I start.'

'You're talking in riddles.'

'Before you came to Scotland, I too fell in love. It made me behave in a way that was totally out of character and, as you are aware, Vivienne was the result.'

'I'm so happy that you've been reunited. There must be so many unmarried mothers who never see their babies again. They must spend their whole lives wondering.'

'There's no easy way to say the next bit. Vivienne's father was Niall Henderson's brother.'

Patience went utterly still, only the draining of colour from her face showing her shock.

'I'm sorry, Patience.'

Patience stirred herself. 'Niall is Vivienne's uncle? *Niall?* All these years, I never understood why he left me. Was it because of what his brother did to you?'

'I'll be honest. I told Niall to go – I'm so sorry for hurting you, but I couldn't bear to see you being involved with a member of that family. And – and Pa told him to leave you as well. That was the real reason he left – because Pa told him to.'

'Pa? Why would he do such a thing?' Patience gave a small gasp. 'Surely not to keep me here as his housekeeper?'

'It wasn't that. Pa knew about the baby. You may well look shocked. Believe me, I still feel shocked myself. I found out just yesterday.'

Patience looked at her. 'How?'

'Because the reason Vivienne and I went away was to meet Niall.'

Patience uttered a small cry and covered her mouth.

'Please hear me out. He's a widower and a prosperous man. He's never forgotten you and he hopes – oh, Patience, he hopes you'll wish to see him again.' A band of anxiety tightened in Prudence's chest. 'Might you wish to see him again?'

Patience didn't move. There was no sign of what was going on in her mind. At last she met Prudence's waiting gaze and Prudence caught her breath at the sight of the bleakness in Patience's pale blue eyes.

'See him again?' Patience whispered. 'I'm not sure I could bear it.'

Vivienne and Nancy left St Anthony's, cheerful and smiling. Stir-Up Sunday had been a great success and Nancy was full of it. It was good to see her looking happy. She had had rather a pinched look recently, now Vivienne came to think of it.

'How are things generally?' she asked. 'You've seemed a bit downcast.' She was sorry she'd asked when the pretty smile dropped from Nancy's face.

'Everything's fine,' said Nancy. 'I admit I'm wondering what will happen to me after Christmas. I'm sure the clerical post will be offered to Ginny. She's a natural.'

'The Heskeths won't abandon you, if that's what you're worried about.'

'Molly said the same thing, oh, ages ago, when I first came here.'

'Even if you aren't considered suitable for St Anthony's,' said Vivienne, 'you're gaining useful experience.'

'I know.' Nancy hoisted her smile back into place, but it wasn't the shining smile that Stir-Up Sunday had brought forth. 'Anyroad, I'm keeping myself busy with all the Christmas activities.'

'The children are loving every minute.'

'Do you think so?'

'I know so. I saw it for myself this afternoon and one or two little birds have mentioned it to me as well.'

Nancy gave a sigh of pleasure. She was probably dying to know who had spoken well of her, but she was too modest to ask. Vivienne considered telling her, but it wouldn't be professional. After all, if she and Nancy didn't live under the same roof, they wouldn't be having this conversation.

When they got home, Miss Patience was busy in the kitchen.

'Leave her to get on with it,' Miss Prudence murmured.

There was no chance for more just then, but, later, Vivienne snatched a moment. There was no need for her to ask.

'She's rather shaken, as you can appreciate,' Miss Prudence told her. 'I said Niall wants to see her, but—'

'Give her time.'

Vivienne sounded more confident than she felt. Poor Miss Patience. Would she be too rattled to meet up with her old love? They had stirred up her past with the best, most hopeful intentions, but had it been a presumptuous mistake?

Vivienne was still feeling unsettled herself. It was wonderful to have met her uncle, who was an upright man in every sense, a pillar of the community and a gentleman of integrity. He was an uncle to be proud of. She was still in the process of making her mind up about her father. Yes, Jonty Henderson might have wanted to do the decent thing in the end, but, before that, he had been a coward and a cad. Turning up trumps in the end didn't wipe out the damage he had done. During the war, Vivienne had met more than one girl who had been left in the lurch by a soldier and it galled her to think that men could take their pleasure and then walk away, leaving the girls to face the consequences. It was shameful to know that her father had been like that. But he wanted to do the right thing in the end and that was important too. She had a lot more thinking to do before she could come to terms with it.

The last thing Niall had said to her had been, 'I want you to know that I'm proud to have such a clever and beautiful young woman as my niece. I was deeply ashamed of my brother when he left your mother. But now I know that he wasn't just a bounder. He was a fool as well – an utter fool. He could have had you as his daughter.' He shook his head wonderingly. 'If you wish there to be a friendship between us, I'd be honoured and delighted, but it's up to you to decide what you wish the connection to be – or, indeed, if you even wish there to be one.' He pressed his card into her hand. 'Please take this. Think things over and I hope you'll write to me. If it ever feels right to you, I'll be proud to tell your cousins about you. Never doubt that.'

But what would Dad think? It was important not to get swept up in the emotion of the reunion. She must visit Dad and tell him in person. Besides, she felt the need to spend time with the darling man who had brought her up and helped her become the woman she was today. Dad was the best chap in the whole wide world. Any daughter would feel the same.

Prudence watched Patience with concern. All those years ago, things had gone so badly wrong for Patience through no fault of her own and without her knowing the reason why. Prudence longed to discuss it, though at the same time she wanted to give Patience enough time to think it through. After a couple of days, just when she was wondering if it was too soon to raise the subject, Patience was the one who brought it up.

'I've thought of nothing else,' said Patience. 'When you revealed that Vivienne was your daughter, it came as a huge shock. I never imagined there would be another shock to follow.'

'When Vivienne and I went to meet Niall, it was so that she could meet her uncle. At that point, we had reason to believe he was married. Had he still been married, or had he been a recent widower, I would have left things as they were and not told you about him. But he's been on his own for some years.' She could see that Patience wanted to ask, but was withholding the question. 'He said his wife had lived to see their oldest grandchild, but not the subsequent ones. The oldest grandchild is now ten.'

'And as he's been alone all that time, you think he might be in the market for another wife,' Patience said with unusual crispness, immediately followed by, 'I'm sorry. That was uncalled for.'

'On the contrary, I consider it extremely called for.' Feeling her way carefully, Prudence asked, 'Aren't you curious to see him again?'

'Curious? Of course I am. Is he – that is, I imagine he has aged well.'

'He's very distinguished.'

Brightness appeared in Patience's eyes – a sheen of tears.

'But what about me?' she whispered. 'I wasn't exactly a creature of beauty in my youth. Look at me now, old and faded.'

'You aren't,' Prudence began.

'I am, Prudence. I've spent my entire life admiring pretty girls and handsome women and trying not to envy them their looks. So would you have, if you'd ever bothered about such things.'

'Do I really need to tell you that it's what's inside that counts?'

'I know I'm shallow to care about my appearance, but I do and that's all there is to it. And then there's the fact that I've not done anything with my life.'

'That's not true,' Prudence exclaimed. 'You've always run this home beautifully.'

'Don't forget the flower-arranging and the charitable works. Oh yes, such a full life!'

'But that's how it's always been. I go out to work and you keep house.'

'It's such an empty thing to do if you aren't doing it for a husband and children. I've always known that and now it seems even more obvious. Remember what you told me about Niall's late wife? She married and had two daughters, then went through the anguish of widowhood before marrying again and having three more daughters.'

'It isn't a competition between the two of you,' said Prudence, refraining from adding, 'Besides, she's dead.'

'My point is, she led a full life whereas I've never done anything with my life and what if Niall were to find that disappointing?'

Prudence went to sit beside her and took her hands. 'Patience, listen. When he knew I wanted to see him, do you know what his first thought was? You. He's never forgotten you. Yes, he met another lady and married her and had a family, but he has never forgotten you. Now you may not be a dazzling beauty and you might not have crossed the Sahara on a camel, but when Niall Henderson heard from me, the first thing he thought of was you. Doesn't that count for something?'

Chapter Thirty

THE HORROR OF the theft Mr Rathbone had demanded of her hung heavily over Nancy. She had thrown the pieces of putty and the money into the drawer in her little dressing-table and slammed it shut, telling herself that she had two whole weeks so she needn't worry about it quite yet. Needn't worry? Just thinking of it made her feel queasy.

Was it her desperate need of a distraction that made the idea of a nativity play pop into her head? A nativity play: what could be more Christmassy?

First of all, she asked Mrs Rostron.

'That would be a considerable commitment,' said the superintendent.

That immediately made Nancy question her own ability. Nevertheless she lifted her chin. 'I won't let you down. I'll work hard at it and it will all be in my own time.'

'I hope you're putting as much effort into your clerical position,' remarked Mrs Rostron. 'I'd be most displeased if I thought you regarded your work here as an opening to lark around with the children.'

Nancy felt as if she had been slapped, but she knew Mrs Rostron was right. Even though she was certain she was going to lose her clerical post come Christmas, it was important to do her best, not simply as a matter of personal pride but also because she would need a good reference to help her find another job.

Another job. Her heart sank. Another clerical post – and what were the chances of its involving children? None.

That made it essential to enjoy being with the orphanage children now. The nativity play would be the jewel in the crown of all the festive things she was organising.

She asked the Miss Heskeths' friend Miss Kirby if she would write a script.

'I've never been asked to do that before,' said Miss Kirby, 'but over the years I've been involved in more nativity plays than you can shake a stick at, so I'm sure I can produce something. Let's discuss the parts.'

Nancy recalled her own experience of being in the nativity play at school – or rather, her lack of experience. There had been Mary and Joseph, the three kings, a couple of shepherds and the Angel Gabriel – oh yes, and an innkeeper – and the teacher had chosen the cleverest children for the speaking parts and the prettiest girl to be Mary. Being neither academic nor beautiful, Nancy had never stood a chance. She didn't want any of her orphans – her orphans? Just when had they become hers? But that was how they felt to her by now. Anyroad, she didn't want them to remember this nativity play for the way they had been left out.

'I want every child to have a part,' she told Miss Kirby. 'We can have lots of innkeepers and shepherds and a whole host of heavenly angels. I don't mean everyone has to have a speaking part, but everybody should go on the stage.'

'That's ambitious,' Miss Kirby murmured.

'And the three kings can have page-boys – and page-girls an' all.'

'I'm not sure there is such a thing.'

'And they can bring their three queens with them.'

Miss Kirby burst out laughing. 'Very well. You've convinced me. The shepherds can all sing "While Shepherds Watched" and the innkeepers can sing "O, Little Town of Bethlehem". That would work well.'

'And we can have shepherdesses,' added Nancy, 'and lady innkeepers.'

'Of course, not absolutely every child can have a part,' said Miss Kirby. 'The babies can't.'

'But I bet the smalls could. They can be sheep and we can teach them to go "Ba-a-a." They could do that.'

'If all the children are to appear in the play,' said Miss Kirby, 'who is to be the audience?'

'Oh.' Something inside Nancy deflated.

'It's not as though you can invite all the parents, like you can at school,' Miss Kirby said gently and with a finality that brought Nancy close to tears.

But she refused to give up. She wanted to talk it over with Miss Hesketh and Miss Patience, especially Miss Patience, who had been so kind and helpful with the Christmas stockings, but both ladies appeared preoccupied at the moment, as did Vivienne. She could try asking Mam, but that would mean waiting until Saturday and she couldn't afford to lose a single precious day.

She set off to walk home from St Anthony's and as she turned the corner into Beech Road, she collided with someone – Zachary. They danced apart. He touched his hat to her, uttered a quick apology and made to continue on his way.

Nancy's heart practically jumped out of her chest in an effort to follow him. 'Zachary – I mean, Mr Milner,' she called. As he turned back, she said, 'I'm sorry. I didn't see you coming.'

'You looked quite fierce,' said Zachary.

'Just deep in thought.'

'A problem?' Zachary asked.

He sounded as if he was really interested and Nancy melted. It was daft, because he was indifferent to her, but she couldn't help it. She found herself pouring out her dilemma.

'If you haven't automatically got an audience,' said Zachary, 'you need to go out and find one.'

'You mean knock on doors and ask folk to come?'

'No, that would take too long. What if you offered your nativity play to an existing audience? The orphanage children go to St Clement's Church, don't they? Ask the vicar if you can do your play in the church. The congregation will be your audience.'

'But I'd imagined doing it in the dining hall.'

'Sometimes you need to look at things differently.'

Was he right? 'You're very clever.'

'Not really. It can help to have an outsider's point of view. There's such a thing as being too close to a problem. There have been times when I could have done with having my brother there to talk things over with. It makes a difference.'

'You must miss him dreadfully,' Nancy ventured.

'I do. Not all the time, not any more, not like it used to be. But there are times when something happens or something is said – and it can be just the tiniest thing – and...' Zachary shook his head. 'You don't want to hear about that.'

But she did, oh, she did. She would give anything to ease his sorrow.

'How is the nativity play coming along?' Zachary asked. 'Aside from the lack of an audience, I mean.'

'The children are loving every single moment. I'm very proud of them. And everyone is so kind about helping. A lady who used to be a teacher wrote the script, and all the nurse-maids are joining in, and Mr and Mrs Abrams have been real bricks. I feel lucky to be surrounded by good people who care about the children.'

'I was chatting to Mr Abrams a day or two ago – we're near neighbours, you know,' said Zachary. 'He said you used the fire blanket to extinguish a fire in the orphanage kitchen.'

'I only did what anyone would have done.'

'Ah, but did you? According to Abrams, you were the only one who remembered the fire blanket and how to use it correctly. Congratulations. You shouldn't be so modest about it. You prevented a sticky situation from becoming a great deal worse.'

'Thank you.' To be praised by Zachary left her almost breathless with joy. 'It's kind of you to say so.'

Zachary laughed. 'Not to mention that you've provided Milner's Fire Safety Services with a superb advertisement.'

Nancy laughed an' all. 'Idiot,' she said, then gasped. Had she really been so informal – so crass? Where were her manners? But Zachary was so easy to talk to. It was one of the first things she had noticed about him. She was sure it helped to make him good at his job. And now she had made a twit of herself by speaking out of turn. What must he think? 'I – I'd better get home. It was nice to see you again.'

Nice? *Nice?* It was exciting and heart-warming and utterly thrilling at the same time as being desperate and disappointing because nothing could ever come of it. It was many things, but nice wasn't one of them.

She left Zachary standing there as she hurried away. Every instinct shrieked at her to turn and look at him, but she refused to let herself down in such a way. Imagine if he saw. It would underline how crass she was. It would make her look like one of those flighty girls who were always available for a spot of flirting. And she wasn't like that, she wasn't – even though Zachary Milner made her heart beat faster. She wished she hadn't bumped into him. But if she hadn't, he wouldn't have had the idea about performing the nativity play in St Clement's.

The more Nancy thought about it, the more appealing the idea became, but she didn't have the authority to make such an arrangement. Once again she must go to Mrs Rostron.

'And you intend that every child will at some point be on the altar steps, performing?' The superintendent raised her eyebrows. Was she about to refuse? 'We'll have to see what the vicar says.'

Happiness radiated through Nancy and she was happier still when the vicar gave his consent.

'Now the real work starts,' said Miss Kirby.

The children were excited and the nursemaids liked the idea an' all. Everyone seemed ready to muck in. A variety of animal ears was made from papier mâché and some old holey sheets were offered up for costumes. Mrs Rostron even said that the pretty dresses the dancers had worn on May Day could be used.

'You've got your work cut out, getting everything organised, Miss Nancy,' said Nurse Carmel.

Everyone seemed pleased with her idea. What would they think if they knew that the girl who was planning this nativity play was also plotting to steal a precious page-cutter from under her landladies' noses?

'Molly and Vivienne are going to do our teaching for us this evening,' Prudence told Patience, 'just as they did on the evening when Lawrence and Evelyn came round to discuss Lucy.'

'Dear Lucy,' said Patience, apparently choosing to focus on their niece rather than on the reason for asking Vivienne and Molly to step in. 'I'm glad everything worked out so well for her.'

Prudence would have liked to say that she hoped everything would work out equally well for Patience, but she held her tongue. Hard though it was, she had to accept that, much as she wanted this for Patience, that didn't mean it was what Patience would, in the end, want for herself. When she saw Niall again, would she want him by her side?

'Would you help me to get ready, Vivienne dear?' Patience asked Vivienne.

'It would be a pleasure,' said Vivienne and whisked her straight upstairs.

When Patience reappeared, she was wearing her Sunday dress with a dove-grey silk scarf that belonged to Vivienne prettily arranged around the neckline. Did that soft colour make her eyes look bluer or was that Prudence's imagination? Vivienne had even done her hair differently. For years, Patience had worn her bun low on the back of her head, but Vivienne had lifted it higher, which had the effect of highlighting Patience's cheekbones.

'You look very nice, dear,' Prudence said.

When the doorbell rang, Prudence for once got up to answer it.

'Don't leave me on my own with him,' said Patience.

'He's here to see you, not me.'

'Stay to start with, at any rate. We'll see how it goes.'

Leaving Patience all a-flutter with nerves in the sitting room, Prudence went to the front door. She admitted Niall and hung up his dark-grey wool overcoat in the little cloakroom opposite the foot of the stairs. His three-piece suit sat well on him, showing the breadth of his shoulders and the length of his legs. He wore a silk handkerchief in his top pocket, but affected no other adornment: Prudence recognised that about him. Jonty had had a soft spot for tie-pins and flashy cuff-links, but Niall didn't.

'Good evening, Niall. Patience is in the sitting room.'

Niall's broad forehead and strong jawline had always given

him an appearance of confidence, but there was an ediginess about him this evening, a mixture of excitement and uncertainty in his dark eyes. Prudence opened the door, though she couldn't bring herself to watch the moment when these two people, this couple that had been torn apart, saw one another again after so many years. Years which Niall had filled with work and a flourishing family life. For Patience, years of quiet domesticity, which had always lacked the fulfilment she craved, the fulfilment that had been snatched from her by cruel circumstances.

'Won't you sit down?' Prudence offered. 'It's a chilly evening. Would you care to sit by the fire?' Goodness, it wasn't like her to babble. The others' nerves must be getting to her. Turning to Patience, she said bluntly, 'Are you sure you wish me to stay?'

'Yes,' said Patience at once.

'Yes – if you don't mind,' said Niall, which made them both look at him. 'I don't wish to blunder in and say the wrong thing, or to appear to make certain assumptions, but there is something I must say at some point and I'd like both of you to hear it.' He glanced from one to the other. His eyes were dark and there was a twist of anxiety about his mouth. 'When I met you on the banks of Loch Lomond, Patience, I truly loved you, but your father made it clear he would never let me marry you. You were under twenty-one and he wouldn't have let you have a say in the matter. As hard as it was to give you up, I thought it would be worse for you if you knew your father was against us. After all, you had to return home with him and live under his roof. Imagine doing that, knowing he had torn you from a loving relationship.'

Patience was silent, her face still and thoughtful, then a new light started to awaken in her light-blue eyes. 'All my life, I've viewed myself as the lesser sister, the weaker one. I used to be grateful that I was the younger one, because how would I ever have managed to do all the things that you did, Prudence, after Mother passed away? As a girl, I used to thank God on my knees every night for letting me be the younger one, without all the responsibility, though I felt guilty as well, as if I was being weak and feeble for leaving it to Prudence to be strong and capable. I've never quite stopped feeling that I have lived my life in your shadow, Prudence. When I first knew you, Niall, you made me feel special and worthwhile. For the first time in my life, I felt as if I mattered. I could feel myself growing into a better person.'

'Oh, Patience,' Prudence whispered.

'Then you left me and I went back to being the lesser sister, only it was worse because I'd glimpsed the person I might have been...the person I thought I was supposed to be.'

It was Niall who broke in to say, 'I wish you could see yourself through my eyes, Patience. To me, your softness, gentleness and compassion are your beauty and your strength. When I first met you, I felt as if I had been waiting for you all my life. And much as I loved my Jennie, the mother of my daughters, I can say with no sense of injustice or disrespect to her that I feel the same way now. I have been waiting for you, Patience. I didn't know I was waiting, but I was.'

Prudence expected Patience to glance away, embarrassed, but she didn't. She and Niall gazed at one another.

Prudence stood up. 'I'll leave you to talk.'

Chapter Thirty-One

SATURDAY. IN ONE week's time, Nancy would have to take the page-cutter to Mr Rathbone's house. She still hadn't done owt about it. She had ignored it for a whole week, but she couldn't keep on ignoring it. It wouldn't miraculously go away. She ought to get the key cut. That wasn't theft. Oh, who was she trying to kid? It might not be theft, but it was one step closer towards committing theft.

It was strange to think how determined she had been to set aside her principles when Pa had talked to her about the family's dire situation – and, yes, of course she wanted to help them, to make life better for them – but even the thought of stealing made her stomach feel as if a handful of worms was squirming away inside her. Then she would remember the letter Pa had written – his confession, Mr Rathbone had dubbed it – and Mam's poor health. It was in her power to assist her whole family and lift them into a better life. How could she turn her back on that? She couldn't.

In her bedroom, Nancy opened her dressing-table drawer and took out the pieces of putty she had brought from Mr Rathbone's house. She lined them up in order from the wonky first attempt to the final two or three, which were steady and fit for the purpose Mr Rathbone dictated. She wasn't alone in the house, but the Miss Heskeths and Vivienne were all downstairs. Should she? Shouldn't she? She didn't want to, oh, she didn't want to, but if she swiped the cellar key for just one moment to make the necessary impression, might that help her to cast the whole wretched business out of her mind for now? This could be her one and only chance to get at the key. Suppose she didn't bother and then another chance didn't present itself. That would mean she wouldn't be able to steal the page-cutter – but it would also have consequences for her family. She had to put her family first, she had to. Any decent daughter would.

She drew a deep breath, but, instead of filling her with resolve, it left her feeling shaky. Refusing to think further, she scooped up the pieces of putty with the two or three earliest attempts and squished them together between her palms. On the landing, she paused. She could hear voices downstairs. She stood outside Miss Hesketh's door, her heart beating hard. She knocked, just in case, even though she was sure the room was empty.

There was no reply. In she went, not bothering to look round, just heading straight for the dressing-table, on top of which lay a matching brush and comb and a glass dish with a few hairpins, and that was all. No scent bottle, no powder. Underneath was a single shallow drawer. It opened smoothly – and there was the key. Nancy's mouth was dry as dust as she firmly pressed the blade of the key into the putty, then lifted it neatly away so as not to smudge the impression.

Back went the key; she shut the drawer and left the room, her hand trembling as she closed the door behind her. In her own room once more, she placed the putty in her drawer at the other end from the other putty pieces and shut the drawer fast enough to make the dressing-table rock.

But she couldn't shut away her worries. She blinked back tears as she brushed her hair and got ready to go out. She was to meet Miss Kirby at St Anthony's for a rehearsal, after which all the children would be taken along to St Clement's, where they were to have their first rehearsal inside the church.

The Miss Heskeths and Vivienne were all going out this afternoon with a gentleman called Mr Henderson, who was an old family friend. It seemed a bit odd that Vivienne was included, but it showed how fond the Miss Heskeths were of her.

'I'll be out all afternoon an' all – I mean, as well,' said Nancy, hoping no one would notice the heat that had flooded her face. Had she been left here alone, Mr Rathbone would undoubtedly consider this the perfect opportunity to search the cellar's inner room.

At the orphanage, Nancy and the nursemaids had their work cut out keeping the children quiet and as calm as possible while Miss Kirby took the various groups through their parts. Miss Kirby was a godsend, her years of experience in the classroom making her the ideal person to run the rehearsals. Nancy was sure she could never have done it herseslf. She wouldn't have had the authority, especially today, when the kids were as high as kites at the prospect of rehearsing inside the church later on.

Molly arrived with two sacks, which she dumped in a corner. She approached Nancy.

'I've had an idea for the angels. Come and see.'

Molly opened one of the sacks and took out a piece of bamboo about a foot in length, attached to one end of which was a circle of wire.

'It's a halo.' Molly opened the other sack. 'Tinsel. Wind the tinsel round the wire and, hey presto, you have a twinkly halo.' The child holds the bamboo like an umbrella.

'It's perfect and so simple. Thank you.'

'Send the angels to me and they can do their own.'

When it was time to walk the short distance to the church, Nanny Duffy had a firm word with the children.

'We're extremely fortunate to be permitted to use St Clement's. While we are there, please don't forget that it is a church and our behaviour must reflect that. I shall be watching to ensure everyone behaves properly.'

Then it was Miss Kirby's turn.

'This is very exciting, but don't forget we have an important job to do and must work hard this afternoon, as well as remembering that the church is a special place where we must behave nicely. Have a look round at the nursemaids and Miss Virginia and Miss Nancy. When we come back from our rehearsal, I hope their faces will be shining with pride. Who thinks I can rely on them to be on their very best behaviour?'

A forest of hands shot up.

Everyone was sent to put on their hats and coats and outdoor shoes. Presently a long crocodile of pairs walked hand in hand along High Lane to St Clement's, where the children were settled into the side-pews.

'While you aren't performing, you will be part of the audience,' said Miss Kirby. 'We may have to move you all around a bit until we work out the right place for everyone to sit. You'll have to be careful to leave the pews silently when it's time for your part in the play.'

'It'd be best to sort out where to put the smalls right away,' said Nurse Eva.

'They won't be able to creep out silently,' added Nurse Philomena.

'Why not put them over there with some nursemaids?' Nancy pointed. 'They can sit on the floor instead of in the pews. They'll be at the front but over to the side and they needn't move at all during the performance.'

The smalls were duly settled in position.

'And what do you say every time someone says "sheep"?' asked Miss Kirby.

'Ba-a-a,' bleated the smalls and everyone laughed.

The rehearsal began. There was a lot of stopping and starting as they got used to their new surroundings and the children practised creeping out of their pews in plenty of time before they needed to be in position to perform.

They reached the part where Mary and Joseph were to be turned away from a succession of inns. A line of innkeepers stretched across one side of the area designated as the stage, with another line on the other side. Mary and Joseph went to the boy at the head of the line on the left, who bellowed, 'No room here,' and then slipped away as Mary and Joseph headed to the opposite line, where the girl at the front called out, 'No room at my inn,' and so on.

It went well, but Nancy's brows tugged into a frown. She went to Miss Kirby.

'What if we dotted the innkeepers around the church, including in the choir-loft? They could call out their lines from all over and the audience wouldn't know where the next voice was coming from.'

They tried it, taking a while to position each innkeeper.

'You won't have Mary and Joseph walking up to you as a prompt to say your line,' warned Miss Kirby, 'so you have to pay attention and remember when it's your turn. Take your time. When it's your go, count to three in your head, then say your line as loudly as you can without shouting.'

It took a couple of goes to get it right, but it was most effective.

'It'll send shivers down the audience's spines,' Nurse Carmel said to Nancy. 'Not in a scary way, but in an exciting way. Where did you get the idea?'

'It just came to me. Someone told me recently that sometimes you need to look at things in a different way.'

Nurse Carmel gave her a look that suggested this was

the daftest thing she had ever heard, but Nancy didn't care. The reminder of Zachary's advice had sparked another idea. Could she? Dare she? There was no time to dwell on it now, but she stored it up for later.

That evening, she stood in front of her dressing-table and opened the drawer. At one end was the putty-impression of the key to the cellar's inner room, at the other the putty-impressions of Mr Rathbone's back-door key.

Could she? Dare she?

Prudence silently applauded Niall's sensitivity. Instead of expecting gentle Patience to spend time with him alone, he took her, Prudence and Vivienne to a matinee performance at the theatre, followed by a delicious meal at the Claremont Hotel in the famous dining room that overlooked the ball-room, then he brought them home by taxi.

'Wait for me, please,' he instructed the driver as he helped them from the vehicle and escorted them up the garden path to their front door, where he shook hands with Patience and Vivienne, dropping a kiss on Vivienne's cheek. Then he took Patience's hand, covering it with his free hand as he smiled with obvious tenderness.

'May I see you tomorrow?' he murmured.

'I have my domestic duties to see to,' Patience began, whereupon Vivienne, who was behind her, popped her head over Patience's shoulder.

'Yes, please,' said Vivienne. 'She'd love to.'

'Vivienne!' Patience cried, blushing.

'I'll pick you up at ten,' said Niall. Letting go of Patience's hand, he raised his hat. 'Good evening, ladies. Sleep well.'

They went inside, hung up their things and went into the sitting room.

Vivienne kicked off her shoes and wiggled her toes. 'What a perfectly spiffing afternoon. He was generous to take all of us out. He even offered to bring Nancy along.'

'He's a generous man,' Patience said quietly, pausing before she went on, 'It was something I noticed in him years ago.'

A well-heeled man, and generous to boot. If Patience married him – and Prudence didn't want to take anything for granted – but if Patience were to marry him, as she had wanted to all those years ago, she would live in comfort such as she had never known before, which was such a satisfying thought. Patience was a dear, always putting others first and never thinking ill of anyone. If anyone deserved a life in which money was no longer a worry, that person was Patience, after all the years she had spent stretching the housekeeping and darning on top of darns.

Prudence came home from the office on Monday to find Patience humming to herself as she used the leftover lamb from Sunday to make shepherd's fritters.

'There was no need for you to come back from your day out to make tea for the rest of us,' said Prudence.

'Yes there was,' replied Patience, seasoning the mashed potato and adding a little milk to bind everything together.

'Are you seeing him again tomorrow?'

'He's taking me to an afternoon showing of a Charlie Chaplin film.'

'What a treat.'

'I'm looking forward to it.' Patience turned to face Prudence. 'But mainly I'm looking forward to being in Niall's company.'

'I'm pleased for you.'

'I'm still struggling to comprehend how my life has changed in a matter of days. Once I get over the shock, I'll thank you for reuniting us.'

Prudence's heart swelled. There had never been open affection between her and Patience, which was entirely because of herself, she knew. Patience would have thrived within such a relationship.

The front door opened and Nancy called, 'I'm home,' which put an end to the conversation, but that night, while Prudence was preparing for bed, there was a gentle tap on her bedroom door and she opened it to find Patience standing there in her dressing-gown and hair-net.

'Are you ill?' Prudence asked.

'Of course not. May I come in?'

Prudence stood aside, then closed the door behind her.

'I've been thinking about what I said earlier,' said Patience, 'about your having reunited Niall and me.'

'What of it?'

Patience ran the tip of her tongue nervously over her lips. 'Do you mind? Does it hurt? After what his brother did, seeing Niall must be a reminder to you of everything you lost.'

Prudence waved a hand, inviting her sister to sit on the bed while she pulled out the stool from beneath the dressing-table to sit on for once in her life. Normally it stayed tucked away out of sight.

'No, it doesn't hurt, but bless you for your concern. Since Vivienne revealed her identity to me in the summer, having her here and getting to know her has brought me such joy and satisfaction that I can promise you there is no room for old regrets. My daughter has been restored to me, which is something I never imagined could happen; and if you and Niall—'

Patience gave a little gasp. 'Prudence—'

'No, let me say it. You deserve your own happy ending. You of all people deserve it. It has always grieved me that you have had to live the life of a spinster. If you and Niall decide to marry, no one will be happier for you than I, I promise you that. Niall deserves a good wife and I daresay his daughters deserve a good stepmother; and if he and they get you, they'll be jolly lucky.'

Patience's laugh was self-conscious, but there was a delight in it too.

'Thank you, Prudence. You've made me feel so much better. I was actually considering writing to the *Vera's Voice* problem page.'

'You weren't!' Prudence exclaimed.

'I wanted to ask about a spinster on the way to fifty rekindling her one and only romance from the days when she wasn't much more than a girl. I wondered if I dare admit to feeling like a girl again – until I look in the mirror, that is. I was going to sign it Worried Lady.'

Not long ago, Prudence would have scoffed at the very idea of such a letter, but now she went to sit on the bed beside Patience and took her hand.

'Dear Worried Lady,' she said. 'Circumstances denied you this opportunity when you were young. Now you have a second chance. Embrace it with all your heart.'

'Do you really think so?' Patience's eyes shone with tears.

'What matters is what *you* think. You have to do what is right for you.' Prudence smiled. In recent weeks, her inclination to smile seemed to have grown. 'I think we both know what that is.'

'He hasn't asked me yet.'

Prudence remembered that moment in the hotel in Annerby. She recalled Niall's words. 'I could only imagine you were here about Patience.' And, a little later, his question: 'Do you think she would like to see me again?' And she remembered the look in his eyes.

He will. But it wasn't her place to say so.

'Tomorrow will be our last day together,' said Patience. 'He's returning home on Wednesday. That'll allow us both some thinking time.'

But it turned out that Niall had already done his thinking.

While Prudence was at work on Tuesday, she glanced at the clock now and again, imagining Patience and Niall going for a walk, having a bite to eat, going to the pictures. How strange her own life would be if they married. Aside from her months in Scotland, Prudence had lived under the same roof as Patience from the day of Patience's birth. Life without her would require some adjusting to.

That evening, when Prudence arrived home from the office, Patience was already there. She might be falling in love for the first time all over again, but she still came home to put tea on the table and do her share of the evening's teaching.

After tea, Nancy excused herself to return to the orphanage to help make crowns and other headdresses.

'You two go and put your feet up for a while before lessons,' said Vivienne, 'and I'll bring you a cup of tea.'

She was just bringing in the tray when the doorbell rang.

'I'll go.' Vivienne put down the tray. 'It's too early for pupils.'

'Maybe it's carol singers,' suggested Patience.

'I should hope not,' said Prudence disapprovingly. 'They ought to have sung at least two verses before ringing the bell.'

Vivienne disappeared. Prudence sipped her tea, aware of voices in the hall – and was that chuckling? A moment later, an alto and a baritone started singing 'The First Nowell' outside the sitting room. A few lines in, the door opened and Vivienne and Niall entered. They tried to keep up the singing, but laughter got the better of them.

'Have you come to say your goodbyes?' Prudence asked Niall. 'I know you're leaving tomorrow.'

'I'll get the dining room ready for lessons,' said Vivienne, 'so you three can have a chat.'

Niall's gaze was on Vivienne as she left the room, a thoughtful smile showing his delight in his long-lost niece.

He turned to Prudence and Patience. 'Actually, I've come to say more than goodbye.' The warmth in his eyes as he looked at Patience left no room for doubt as to what the question would be.

Prudence started to rise. 'I'll give Vivienne a hand.'

'No,' said Niall. 'I think you should be here. May I sit beside you, Patience?' He did so, taking her hand. 'The three of us are bound together in a way that is unconventional, to say the least. Two sisters, one of whom has given me a niece whom I hope to get to know, and the other who is the love of my life.'

'Oh,' emerged from Patience's lips on a soft breath.

'I want you to be my wife, Patience. I wanted it all those years ago, but it wasn't to be. After that, my life followed a different path – and a happy one. I had a wife I loved and five daughters whom I adore. So far they have given me eight grandchildren and I hope for more. Now circumstances have brought me back to you and I know that, as devoted as I am to my family, I need you to make my life complete. I am a family man through and through and I want you to be part of my family. Will you? Please?'

Prudence sat utterly still. Niall might have started by including her, but this moment was for him and Patience. Dearest Patience. It had always hurt her to be plain and thin, but just now happiness lent her a glow that drew out the beauty of her gentle, loving nature.

'Nothing could make me happier than to marry you,' Patience whispered.

Niall kissed her hand. 'You've made me the happiest man on earth. Let's start by telling our niece, shall we?'

Vivienne took her time setting up the lessons. There wasn't much to do. She placed the table-felt neatly on the table and positioned the typewriters on top, then got out the boxes of mocked-up invoices and delivery lists.

The door opened behind her and Miss Prudence looked in. 'Could you come through to the sitting room, please?'

Assuming that her uncle wished to say goodbye, Vivienne followed Miss Prudence. When they walked in, Niall and Miss Patience were seated together, openly holding hands. Niall politely rose, though he kept hold of Miss Patience's hand. Vivienne smiled. She knew what was coming – well, she very much hoped she did. As soon as the other two were seated, Niall resumed his place.

'Vivienne,' said Niall, 'I know lessons will start presently, so you'll forgive me if I come straight to the point. I have asked Patience to be my wife and she has done me the honour of accepting.'

Vivienne laughed as elation raced through her. 'Oh, that's wonderful.'

'You don't mind?' asked Miss Patience.

'Why would I mind? I think it's splendid and I hope you'll be very happy together. In fact, I know you shall.'

Niall and Miss Patience stood up and she hugged them.

'This calls for a celebration,' said Miss Prudence, 'though I fear the most we run to in this house is sherry. Fetch the best glasses, if you please, Vivienne.'

They toasted the happy couple, but when they all sat down again, Vivienne, prompted by an odd feeling of protectiveness, perched on the arm of Miss Prudence's chair.

Miss Patience looked across at Vivienne. 'You'll be my niece twice over – by blood and by marriage.'

Vivienne sat up straighter. She knew now precisely what she wanted from her relationship with her uncle.

'That must be a secret between the four of us. No one else must ever know.' She looked at Niall. 'You said you'd be happy to tell my cousins about me and I appreciate your willingness to acknowledge me. If you were to share with your daughters what happened in Scotland, no doubt it would help them to understand how special Miss Patience is to you, but it would also make them view Miss Prudence in a certain way and that wouldn't be right. Miss Prudence is entitled to her privacy and her good name.'

'Of course she is.' Miss Patience looked stricken.

Miss Prudence said nothing, but Vivienne felt a gentle pressure against her arm.

'You're correct, of course,' said Niall, 'but I hope this doesn't mean you have decided against a relationship with me.'

'We'll feel our way,' said Vivienne. 'There's my dad to consider as well, remember, and nothing in the world would make me upset him. I am the ladies' friend as well as their lodger and the world will be pleased to see me on good terms with the husband of one and the brother-in-law of the other. I know you wanted more than this, but we have to consider appearances.'

Niall nodded. 'You're right. Maybe I wasn't being realistic. I was just so happy at the prospect of welcoming you into my family.' His expression was rueful. 'You're more sensible than I am.'

'I am the daughter of two eminently sensible mothers.'

'Don't worry, ladies,' said Niall. 'As Vivienne says, the truth will be a secret for the four of us to keep. You need have no fear of what will be said when I go home and talk to my girls.'

'When you prepare them for the shock,' Miss Patience murmured.

'When I tell them about the sweetest lady in the world.'

Nancy ran through their words with a few of the children and Nurse Philomena played the piano so they could practise their carols. The nativity play was to end with everyone, including the audience, singing 'O Come, All Ye Faithful' and Nurse Philomena was teaching those girls who had suitable voices to sing the descant in the final verse. When they weren't needed, a lot of the children, especially the youngest, stood gazing at the pictures of apples, oranges and holly that Nancy had pinned to the walls when the dining room was empty.

'Miss Nancy says if we keep looking at them, magic will happen,' Nancy heard a child say to Nurse Carmel and she had to turn away to hide her smiles.

A few minutes later, Carmel appeared by her side. 'The kids would stare at them morning, noon and night if they could, waiting for the magic. What is going to happen?'

Aware of little ears all around them, Nancy merely smiled. 'I've no idea. It's Christmas magic.'

Gradually, during the evening, the numbers reduced as each age group was sent to bed. A couple of the younger ones gave Nancy a goodnight hug and then their friends wanted to do the same. She was thrilled. She hugged each one and kissed the tops of their heads.

'Don't let the nannies see you doing that,' Carmel cautioned her, 'especially Nanny Duffy.'

Nancy was startled. 'Why not?'

'You're not allowed to play favourites. It's the rules.'

'I wasn't playing favourites. It was the children who came to me.'

'You have to treat them all the same. That means no displays of affection.'

'Oh, the poor children,' said Nancy. Imagine not being able to have a cuddle!

'Don't give me that injured look,' said Carmel. 'I didn't make the rules.'

Layton One approached. He was Belinda's brother, Michael. Nancy knew he was called Mikey by his family and friends, but she had to call him Layton One.

'Come and see the shepherds' crooks Mr Abrams made for us, Miss Nancy,' he said and she went with him. 'Thanks for organising the play for us, miss.'

'Lots of folk are organising it. Miss Kirby, the nursemaids—'

'But you started it.' Layton One was a good-looking boy, dark-haired and blue-eyed like his sister. 'It was your idea. Everyone knows that. We all wish you were a nursemaid instead of one of Miss Allan's clerks, then we'd have loads of fun.'

Oh, if only, but she was only here to see if she was any good as a clerk. As for nursemaids' jobs, they were hard to come by, because once a girl got a nursemaid post here, she stayed until she left to get wed.

There were no two ways about it. Come Christmas, Nancy would have to leave. She didn't want to, she really didn't. She looked at her pictures of fruit and holly. Her little piece of Christmas magic would very likely be the last thing she would ever do for the orphans.

The sweetest lady in the world. That was what Niall had called her. How wonderful it was to be loved. Alone in her bedroom, preparing for bed, Patience drew in a deep breath, savouring the moment, savouring life itself – savouring *her* life, which had turned into a magical place, where Niall loved her and wanted her to be his wife and where Prudence was not hurt by this, because she was satisfied with her new-found relationship with Vivienne.

Patience felt a tingle of anticipation. She couldn't wait to meet the girls – well, young women, really – who were going to be her stepdaughters. She had heard all about them from their doting father. Imagine – Niall wanted to share all his daughters and grandchildren with her. She would be surrounded by a large family, which was what she had longed for ever since she was a little girl. Would his daughters take to her? Oh, but she didn't think she could bear it if they didn't.

Imagine not living here any more – imagine not living with Prudence. They had lived together all their lives – here, in this house. They had never lived anywhere else, except for Prudence's months in Scotland. Patience had looked after this house since the day she left school. It had been her life's work. She had tried to find fulfilment in it while knowing that, for her, true fulfilment could only come from having her own family.

What would it be like for Prudence to live here on her own? Well, she wouldn't be on her own, strictly speaking, because she would have Vivienne and any other pupil-lodgers, but might it be hard for her to be the one left behind while Patience went off to her wonderful new life with her new family? She hated the thought that maybe Prudence would have to pay the price for her happiness. There were practical considerations too. It wasn't just a question of whether Prudence would miss her. Who would look after Prudence?

Patience sat at her small dressing-table. She perched on the stool every night and morning, making a little ritual out of her toilette – unlike Prudence, who pulled out her dressing-table stool once a year to stand on it to get her bedroom curtains down for washing and left it stuffed underneath for the rest of the year. Patience unscrewed the top off her face cream, releasing a faint whiff of sweetness, but, instead of dipping in her fingers and applying the cream to her face and neck, she leaned forward and gazed at herself in the looking-glass.

Her face had been young and smooth when she met Niall first time round. Now she was older, hanging onto her forties by her fingertips. She had never had good looks to recommend her and now she was middle-aged to boot. All she could do was slather on the creams and lotions as usual – no, not quite as usual. Niall had called her the sweetest lady in the world. Did that account for a new glow?

Prudence had advised her to embrace her new life with all her heart. And she would. Oh, she would.

Chapter Thirty-Two

Nancy opened the drawer in her dressing-table and removed the key the locksmith had made for her. Her heart had beat like mad when she handed over the putty-impression to him. Surely only a person harbouring sinister intentions would have a putty-impression and what if he asked her questions she couldn't answer? But he hadn't appeared to think owt of it. Perhaps folk did this all the time. Anyroad, he had made the new key and taken her money and she had left the shop, almost wobbly with relief.

Lord, if she had been that nervy about getting the key cut, how would she manage what needed to be done today? The answer to that was simple, wasn't it? She couldn't afford to be feeble about this. She would get one chance, and one chance only, to do this. Right first time: it was the only way.

She weighed the key in her hand, keeping her fingers wrapped around it as she ran downstairs and pulled her shawl around her shoulders. She put on her hat, still with the key clamped inside her fist. Only when she put on her gloves did she slide it into her skirt pocket. She blew out a breath. Time to go.

She left the house and set off for Mr Rathbone's house in Seymour Grove.

'Sometimes you need to look at things differently,' Zachary had said and that was what she had done. Mr Rathbone wanted her to look at the situation his way. He wanted her to steal the page-cutter from the box in the cellar, thereby freeing Pa from the hold Mr Rathbone had over him. Mr Rathbone probably didn't imagine there was any other way of looking at the matter.

But there was.

Yes, Nancy had had a key cut, but it wasn't the putty-impression of the inner-cellar door she had handed over the counter in the locksmith's. It was the best of the impressions of Mr Rathbone's back door key.

Now she was on her way to his house to put things right once and for all.

As she walked along Whalley Road and drew near to Mr Rathbone's house, every nerve-end and instinct she possessed urged Nancy to creep along, hugging the garden walls, but that would make her look guilty. She must hold up her head and walk along as normal, going in through the Rathbones' garden gate as if she had every right to do so. Her biggest worry was that the household's plans might have changed. Mr Rathbone had said that the house would be empty this afternoon until he returned home. As long as all that still held good, she should be all right. Mr Rathbone had instructed her to bring him the page-cutter after half past four, so she needed to be gone well before then.

She made her way up the side-path to the back door. Between here and the next house was a four-foot wall with some shrubs on the other side, so no one from next door could see her at the back door. She stopped and listened, but even if there had been someone in the kitchen, she wouldn't have heard through a thick door like that. She took the key from her pocket, slipped it into the lock and turned it. It moved smoothly. There was a tiny click as the mechanism unlocked. Gently, Nancy turned the door-knob, easing the door open a crack. She listened again – nowt. The maid must indeed be out.

She opened the door a bit further and slid into the kitchen, automatically raising herself on tiptoe on the tiled floor. Once more she strained to hear, but her ears were crammed with the hammering of her heartbeats, as loud as a band of marching drummers. Crossing the kitchen, she opened the door and peered into a short corridor, beyond the end of which was a tall parlour palm and a hall-stand of dark wood.

She crept to the hall and stood for some moments, sensing rather than hearing the quietness of the empty house, before she went to Mr Rathbone's study. Please don't let him have locked it. That would scupper her plan on the spot. But no, the door opened, sending tingles skittering across her skin.

The room was just as it had been two weeks ago. She put her shawl on top of the cabinet in the corner near the door. She had had plenty of time to think about this. Last time, Mr Rathbone had sent her out of the room while he retrieved the letter-opener and Pa's letter to show her, so they must be hidden in here somewhere.

She started by checking all the desk drawers. There were two pillars of drawers, one each side of the knee-hole, as well as a long shallow drawer across the top of that space. Although every drawer had a key-hole, none was locked. Each one slid open smoothly and she sorted through its contents, lifting items gently and settling them back into position. The drawers in the pillars contained writing paper and envelopes, a bottle of Quink for topping up the ink-well set in the desktop, cheque books, books of financial records and a money-box. Each of the bottom drawers was deeper than those above. One contained a bottle of Scotch. The long central drawer had various small items such as a drawing compass and a box of tacks and, tucked in a corner, a small blue glass dish with two keys in it; presumably one of them opened the money-box. But there was no sign of the letter-opener or the letter.

Where next? She tried the cabinet in the corner, but it held bottles, decanters and glasses. Crikey, he liked his booze, didn't he? She felt around at the back, but to no avail. She stood and looked round the room, searching for another possible hiding place. Would it be mad to force her hand down the backs of the armchairs' upholstered seats? Yes, it would. The only thing madder than that would be if Mr Rathbone had shoved his booty down there.

Where, then? She opened the glass doors of the book-cases and ran her hand over the tops of the books, but found nothing. Neither had any of the books been pulled forwards to conceal summat behind them. She opened a few of the books and flicked through the pages, seeking Pa's letter, but it wasn't in any of the books she tried and, anyroad, she didn't have nearly enough time to check every single book. Besides, surely he would keep the letter-opener and the letter together. That would make sense – wouldn't it?

She started to panic. She had to find them, she had to. Everything depended on it. She thought back to her previous visit. Wherever the things were, it had taken Mr Rathbone only a moment or two to remove them, which not only meant they couldn't be anywhere that was difficult to get at, but also reinforced the idea of their being together. Were they hidden close to the desk? Maybe the desk had a secret compartment. Some desks did – well, they did in the mystery stories she borrowed from the library, anyroad.

Nancy returned to the desk. Starting with one of the pillars, she opened each drawer and felt around at the back, but nothing gave way beneath her fingers. When she opened the centre drawer to try the same thing, her glance fell on the blue glass dish containing the two keys. One for the money-box and one for...what?

First, she needed to check if one really did fit the money-box. Yes, right first time. She replaced the box quickly, frightened of being caught red-handed. Now she must find what the other key was for. Something near or nearish to the desk.

Standing still, she looked all round. The key was small. Was she looking for a smallish box, like the money-box? There was nowt of the sort on the mantelpiece or the shelves behind the desk. She started to walk round the desk, catching her toe on the edge of the rug. She stared down. A second later, she was on her knees, rolling back the rug. Could there be a hidey-hole set in the floorboards? No, there wasn't, but instead of feeling disheartened, she suddenly felt alert.

Zachary's words appeared once more in her head. 'Sometimes you need to look at things differently.' Had she been more on the right lines when she looked under the rug than when she tried the desk and the bookcase? She had tried the obvious places. Now she had to look at things differently – look at the room differently.

She was sure the hiding place must be near the desk. If not under the floorboards beside it, then where? If Mr Rathbone was at his desk and he stood up, where would be within reach?

The paintings of the galleons in full sail.

Standing beneath the pictures, Nancy reached up and lifted the lower edge of one of the frames. The painting wobbled slowly as she moved it away from the wall. Beneath it was nowt but wallpaper. She tried the other one – and her heart crashed against her ribs at the sight of a door, about eight inches square, set into the wall.

She grabbed the chair behind the desk, only to find it was on castors, so she scurried round the desk to where there was a wooden chair on the other side. Positioning it beneath the painting, she climbed up. Lifting the painting from the picture-hook dangling from the rail, she stepped down and leaned the picture against the side of the desk before climbing back up and inserting the key in the lock. It was the correct size. She turned it – and the lock clicked open.

The door opened to reveal a small cupboard with two shelves. There were some long envelopes, plump; presumably with papers. A couple of shallow boxes were labelled with dates. And on the top shelf, slotted in at one side, was the letter-opener, lying on top of – please, let it be – yes – Pa's letter.

Relief and gratitude swept through her as she removed them. Stepping down, she placed them on the blotter in the middle of the desk, then climbed back up to close and lock the cupboard.

And that was when she heard the front door open.

'I missed your company last week,' said Mrs Rostron and Vivienne tried not to show her surprise. It was unlike the superintendent to say anything remotely personal. Molly and Vivienne had been known to speculate about her private life. 'Mrs' was a courtesy title, so she had no husband to go home to – well, had there been a Mr Rostron, she wouldn't have had the superintendent post at all, because the orphanage, in common with most employers, required a woman to resign upon marriage.

'The only thing we can be sure of,' Molly had said, 'is that she lives rather better than Miss Kirby.'

Mrs Rostron, unlike Miss Kirby, must earn a reasonable salary, albeit a lower one than a man in a similar post would have earned. But at the end of each day, did she return to an empty home?

Vivienne, Molly and Mrs Rostron were in the orphanage's sitting room, having their weekly tea with home-made biscuits after Molly's teaching session with some of the fourteen-girls.

'Mrs Abrams said last week that you had gone away for the weekend,' Mrs Rostron said to Vivienne. 'Did you have a pleasant time?'

'Yes, thank you. I went up to a town called Annerby. Have you heard of it?'

She described Annerby and answered a few questions.

'Were you visiting friends?' asked Mrs Rostron.

Vivienne pretended to laugh. 'With parents in the hotel trade, I moved from one place to another every few years. I know people all over England. Talking of moving, how is Hannah settling in?'

Hannah was a fairly recent orphan, who had originally been placed in a much larger orphanage, where she had retreated right into her shell and been very unhappy. It had been Vivienne's suggestion that she might benefit from a move to a smaller orphanage and Mrs Rostron had been able to accept her at St Anthony's.

'It's only been a few days,' said the superintendent, 'but let's hope for the best. Apparently she told Nanny Mitchell that this orphanage sounds friendlier because it has a person's name. She was previously at Gasworks Street Orphanage.'

Molly laughed. 'I can see how St Anthony's sounds more appealing than that.'

'I must admit I've always had a small reservation about naming an orphanage after St Anthony,' Vivienne remarked.

Mrs Rostron raised her eyebrows. 'What's wrong with St Anthony?'

'Nothing, but I think it's unfortunate that he's the patron saint of lost things.'

'How so?' said Mrs Rostron.

'Lost *things*. Lost children would be more appropriate.'

Molly smiled. 'I remember you saying that the first time I met you. You've got a bee in your bonnet, haven't you?'

Vivienne was startled. Was that how it seemed? It didn't feel like that. To her, it seemed a relevant opinion, nothing more.

'There isn't a patron saint for lost children, as far as I know,' said Mrs Rostron. 'Perhaps one day whoever it is who decides these things will rectify the omission.'

'Maybe,' said Vivienne, 'but it still seems a shame to name an orphanage after the patron saint of lost things.'

Mrs Rostron frowned, then she smiled her customary half-smile. 'It may sound odd to you, but I am very territorial about St Anthony's and I don't like to hear it being criticised.'

'I can understand that,' said Vivienne, 'and I certainly don't intend any disrespect. It's just that St Nicholas's would be the perfect name for an orphanage, because he is the patron saint of children.'

That drew a proper smile from Mrs Rostron. 'Yes, I see that. Unfortunately, the naming of such institutions isn't given to imaginative people like you.'

Molly laughed. 'The person who named Gasworks Street Orphanage certainly didn't have any imagination. I'll tell you who does, though: Ellen. She said that while the cleverest girl-fourteens are getting office tuition, what about some others having cooking lessons so that they learn more than the basic things they do at school.'

'That's a good idea,' said Vivienne. Perhaps it could lead to jobs as kitchen girls with the promise of being trained to be cooks, but it wasn't her place to say so, not right now. If Mrs Rostron said something similar, she could support it, but to leap in with her own ideas might be taken amiss.

Mrs Rostron nodded. 'Ellen was a sound choice for head

girl.' She smiled wryly. 'But with Christmas coming, I'm sure this wouldn't be the right moment to mention it to Mrs Wilkes. She has enough on her plate – no pun intended. How are your office girls coming along, Mrs Abrams? Does Abigail Hunter show signs of putting accuracy before speed yet?'

'I mentioned that Miss Hesketh herself will be coming to see a lesson and check everyone's progress. I didn't actually say she would decide who was worth keeping on and who wasn't, but I overheard the girls whispering it to one another. If that doesn't make Abigail pull her socks up, nothing will. Miss Hesketh has a reputation for being fierce.'

'Let's hope that does the trick,' said Mrs Rostron. 'Abigail is a capable girl. It would be a shame if she wasted this opportunity.'

'These girls are so young,' said Molly, 'yet we expect them to make grown-up choices.'

'It's not long since the school leaving age was thirteen,' Mrs Rostron reminded her. 'A few years ago, Abigail Hunter and the rest would already be out at work. They are privileged to have an extra year of education. Please don't be soft on them. That wouldn't do them any favours. Life is hard and it will be harder for them, because they haven't got families to support and guide them.'

'Not to mention needing jobs that involve bed and board,' Vivienne added.

'Precisely,' said Mrs Rostron.

'What we really need is a hostel for our leavers to stay in,' said Molly.

Mrs Rostron smiled at her. 'With ideas like that, Mrs Abrams, you might find yourself on the Orphanage Committee.'

That made Molly laugh. 'I don't think the Committee would welcome the wife of the orphanage caretaker.'

Why not? Why was it only 'worthy' ladies and gentlemen who sat on such bodies? There was more than one way of being worthy. Take Mrs Wardle. She might have a finger in many a charitable pie, but where was her compassion? Molly, on the other hand, was brimming over with that quality. Vivienne couldn't help picturing herself on the Orphanage Committee. She loved St Anthony's and was always happy to come here; she loved feeling involved. It was her favourite aspect of her job. Might she, the daughter of a successful – and frankly, rather well-off – hotelier, and the widow of a man who had died for his country, be considered suitable to serve on the Orphanage Committee, should a place become available? Would her position at the Board of Health be regarded as an asset – or a conflict of interest? Mrs Wardle worked at the Board of Health, of course, but what she did was unpaid, which made it acceptably 'worthy'. Yet wouldn't the Committee – wouldn't the committees and boards of all such institutions – benefit from being opened up to people who worked for a living instead of just the wealthy? People sometimes said that the world had changed since the end of the war – but it hadn't changed that much.

What a shame. She would so love to be more involved with St Anthony's.

Nancy froze. Someone had entered the house – far earlier than she had expected, so maybe it wasn't Mr Rathbone. Not the servant – she would have gone round the back. The front door closed. There were no voices. If this was Mrs Rathbone on her own, surely she would have no reason to come into her husband's study. If it was Mr Rathbone, he wouldn't necessarily come in here either. You would be more likely to go into the sitting room, wouldn't you, after you had taken off your coat?

Except that – oh heck – she had left the study door open. Whoever was in the hall, please don't let them notice. Heart thudding, she shut the cupboard, fingers fumbling as she locked it. She still had to re-hang the painting. Was there time? She stepped down onto the floor, returned the key to the little blue dish and shut the drawer; but as she reached for the painting, there came the sound of footsteps crossing the hall.

Nancy ducked down, crouching in the desk's knee-space. There was no modesty panel and she saw the door open further, then Mr Rathbone's legs appeared. He stood for a moment, then his feet shifted as if he was looking round. Wondering why the door had been left open? Trying to recall if he had shut it? Oh – if he spotted the wooden chair out of place... But he left the room, closing the door behind him.

Wobbly with fear, Nancy rose to her feet. She must hang up the painting, then she could climb out of the window. But, even as she reached for it, the study door crashed open and she swung around to face Mr Rathbone.

'You!' Mr Rathbone's nostrils flared. His eyes were dark with fury. 'I knew there was something not quite right when I looked in before. The painting – and my chair. It's you, the Pike girl.'

His gaze landed on the letter-opener and letter lying on the blotter and his mouth opened as if about to release an almighty roar. Nancy grabbed the things off the blotter, fastening them tightly within the fingers of her left hand. Instinct made her bend her knees a fraction and lift her heels, preparing her for flight.

When Mr Rathbone started across the room, she seized the glass paperweight from the desk and hurled it at him, achieving no more than a glancing blow, but it was enough to make him stumble as he threw up his hands for protection.

'You little bitch!'

He lunged at her, but she sprang round the other side of the desk and made a dash for the door. A hand landed heavily on her shoulder, but she wrenched herself away, though the force of her action almost saw her measuring her length on the hall floor. A few staggering steps kept her upright as she hurled herself towards the front door, but there was that hand on her shoulder again and this time it heaved her away from the door and practically sent her spinning.

Breathing heavily, Mr Rathbone advanced upon her. Thin he might be, but there was nowt puny or weak about him. Nancy's skin turned clammy.

'You bloody menace,' growled Mr Rathbone. 'Coming here, stealing from me. I'll show you.'

He made a grab. Nancy scooted backwards and banged into summat. There was a smash – china or glass – as an item fell to the floor. Mr Rathbone's lips twisted into a sneering smile. She was cornered and they both knew it. He reached out and, before she knew what she was doing, the letter-opener was in her right hand and she jabbed upwards, catching his cheek.

With a yell, he clutched at the side of his face, but it must be shock more than anything else, because she certainly hadn't managed to incapacitate him. Taking advantage of his momentary lapse, she rammed the letter and the letter-opener into her pocket as she dodged round him and raced for the door, tugging it open and jumping down the steps, her feet sinking into the gravel as she landed on the path.

She didn't look back. She didn't need to.

'Stop! Thief!'

He was coming after her. Running on gravel was like running through soft sand. She focused on the gate and didn't look anywhere else. She made it to the gate and dashed through it onto the pavement, just avoiding running into a couple walking arm in arm and then having to dance round a lady with a baby-carriage. There were exclamations and startled glances. Could she appeal for help?

But Mr Rathbone was on her heels.

'Stop that girl!' he yelled in a voice of authority. 'She's a thief!'

The startled expressions changed, hardened. A man some ten yards away hurried towards her and another man ran across the road to help.

Nancy ran for her life.

Chapter Thirty-Three

'STOP! THIEF!'

Zachary looked round, startled. He had borrowed the laundry's cart for the afternoon to deliver fire safety goods to Oak Lodge, the old soldiers' home in Seymour Grove, where the decorating was now finished and Mr Peters was ready for Zachary to install both extinguishers and fire blankets. Jerry the laundry pony was trotting along at an easy pace through the chilly, grey afternoon. The shout from close by had Zachary sitting up straight on the bench-seat. He couldn't have Jerry being frightened.

'Stop her! Don't let her get away!'

Zachary's attention homed in on a tall, thin gentleman with rage in his dark eyes, who had run out of a garden gate. The houses along Whalley Road were good-looking places for the well-to-do, the kind of houses he associated with doctors, bank managers and businessmen. This gentleman's three-piece suit and the glint of gold at his collar fitted in with that. Who was he yelling after? Who was the thief? Zachary was more interested in keeping Jerry happy. Jerry was a placid creature, but Zachary had never had to handle him in a fraught situation and didn't want a panicked animal on his hands.

There were several passers-by, who were looking round and stepping closer to the fuss. Two men took to their heels, apparently eager to join the chase, and Zachary felt a stab of concern for the woman, whoever she was. To have three grown men belting after her seemed harsh. On the other hand, if someone, anyone, stole something he valued, such as his fire extinguishers, he would be glad to have a crowd helping him.

Anyway, with those two men assisting, the man in the suit didn't require Zachary's help. With a light flick on the reins and an encouraging word, he urged Jerry to pick up the pace. They only had to get as far as the corner and drive through Oak Lodge's gates. Jerry clopped along the road, showing with a toss of his head and a twitch of his ears that he wasn't impressed by the raised voices and the commotion.

The cart drew alongside Oak Lodge, where long curving stems of winter jasmine speckled with tiny yellow blooms waved over the wall. Zachary glanced at the large house. He was glad to be here again. He had arranged to come at a time that would allow him, after he had fixed all the extinguishers in position, to have time for a chinwag with the old soldiers who had captured his heart the first time he came here. He had been back several times since and intended to be a regular visitor in the future.

He slowed Jerry, turning the cart to go through the wide gateway. It was a good job he was on time, because Mr Peters had already opened the gates and was standing behind one of them, ready to shut them again. As the cart entered the premises, Zachary brushed aside a stem or two of winter jasmine that was being over-friendly. Ahead of him, much of the front garden was winter-bare. Tall spirals of clipped yew provided shape and a vast clump of yard-high grasses with tufty, feathery tops added a ghostly note.

As soon as the cart was through and Mr Peters began to close the first gate, Zachary reined in Jerry and jumped down to close the other one. At the same moment, there was a yell from along the road.

'She's dodged round. She's heading up that way. Stop her! She's a thief!'

'What the devil—' said Mr Peters.

Zachary looked down the street and his eyes all but popped out of his head as Nancy – Nancy! – raced towards him, her face flushed with exertion, blue eyes wide with panic. Thundering along the pavement in her wake came the gentleman, followed by two other men. Why on earth was this gentleman after Nancy?

As the gentleman flung himself forwards, arm outstretched, his hand about to clamp onto Nancy's shoulder, Zachary stopped thinking and wondering. The only thing he knew in that moment was that the girl he loved – yes, loved – was in danger. Reaching into the cart and flinging aside the tarpaulin, he grabbed a fire extinguisher and, leaping from the gateway in front of the stranger, he 'extinguished' him.

The gentleman staggered to a halt. The men behind him stopped as well, one of them bending over, hands on knees as he caught his breath.

'Nancy! Nancy!' Zachary shouted after her.

She glanced over her shoulder, then slowed and stopped, though she didn't return.

'How dare you!' spluttered the gentleman, wiping his face with his hands and blinking energetically. 'You idiot – you oaf! What was that in aid of? I'll see you in court for this. You, sir!' He pointed at Mr Peters, who was open-mouthed with shock. 'You saw what he did – as did these gentlemen here.' He swung round to include his fellow pursuers.

'Mr Rathbone, are you all right?' asked Mr Peters, aghast. He turned on Zachary. 'What possessed you? Mr Rathbone is a respectable gentleman, well-known in this neighbourhood. What did you think you were about?'

'Aiding and abetting a thief,' exclaimed the gentleman – Mr Rathbone. 'That's what he was doing. Aiding and abetting a thief, I say.'

'This young lady isn't a thief,' Zachary retorted. 'She's a decent girl and I can vouch for her. She would never steal anything. I promise you that, sir,' he added, addressing Mr Peters.

'You would say that,' sneered Mr Rathbone. 'You're her accomplice.'

That made Mr Peters and the other two men stare at him in astonishment. Zachary knew how they felt. The accusation stunned him.

'Ha!' exclaimed Mr Rathbone. 'That's taken the wind out of your sails, hasn't it? She ran back this way deliberately to enable you to incapacitate me at the vital moment.'

That brought Nancy marching back.

'Leave Mr Milner out of this,' she flared. 'He's innocent and he's not my accomplice.'

'Ah – then you admit your own guilt,' said Mr Rathbone. 'Unfortunately for the pair of you, Miss Pike lacked the wit to make good her escape. She's as dim-witted as her father before her.'

Zachary's forehead puckered in consternation. What the heck was going on – and what did Nancy's father have to do with it? There was only one thing he knew for certain and that was that Nancy Pike had never stolen anything in her life. As he looked at her, his heart swelled with emotion. He didn't know what was happening here, but he didn't need to know. He trusted Nancy. He believed in her. It was as simple as that. Nancy Pike was a good person. He would stake his life on it.

Zachary threw back his shoulders and lifted his chin. 'I think we should send for the police. This situation is for them to sort out.'

'I agree,' said Mr Peters.

'Now wait a minute,' said Mr Rathbone. 'There's no call for that.' He looked at Nancy through narrowed eyes. 'I just need Miss Pike to return to me the items she took.'

'She hasn't taken anything,' Zachary said stoutly.

'Oh, but she has and I want my property returned to me.'

Mr Peters looked directly at Nancy. 'Have you taken things belonging to Mr Rathbone?'

Nancy's lips twisted nervously as she shifted from one foot to the other. Zachary's confidence dipped, but only for a second.

'Well, girl?' Mr Peters demanded. He was a genial man by and large, but he was clearly inclined to side with Mr Rathbone and his tone as he addressed Nancy was sharp.

'Her silence speaks for itself,' Mr Rathbone declared. 'I think we should take this matter indoors.'

'Indeed, sir, you are welcome to make use of one of Oak Lodge's rooms,' offered Mr Peters.

'I think not, thank you.' Mr Rathbone held out his arms and looked down at himself. 'I should return home and get changed before I catch my death.' He curled his lip as he looked at Zachary. 'Thanks to the soaking this...fellow saw fit to give me.'

Mr Rathbone and Mr Peters now both looked at Zachary, who knew himself to be at a grave disadvantage. In spite of the hearty soaking, Mr Rathbone's expensive suit showed up Zachary's clothes for what they were – decent enough but nothing special. Even bareheaded, having quitted his house in a steaming hurry, Mr Rathbone looked the complete gentleman while Zachary's bowler for once didn't seem to confer any dignity. He was nowhere near as tall as Mr Rathbone either and the man literally looked down on him. Mr Rathbone didn't think much of Nancy Pike's protector. That was obvious.

But it hadn't escaped Zachary's notice that Mr Rathbone hadn't wanted to send for the police. Why not, if he believed himself to be in the right? There was something going on here above and beyond the accusation of theft, but could he, a lowly fellow who slept under the counter, get the better of a grand gentleman like Mr Rathbone?

'You,' said Mr Rathbone, pinning Nancy down with the power of his gaze, 'come with me. Or would you prefer that I send for your father?' Now he turned to the two men who had assisted in Nancy's pursuit. 'My thanks to you both.' He inclined his head. 'Perhaps you will kindly do me one more service and escort this girl to my house, just to ensure she doesn't attempt to give me the slip.'

'Fine,' said Zachary. 'I'll come too, if I may.'

'You may not,' began Mr Rathbone.

'To see Miss Pike being marched off by three men, and not one of them a *police*man, isn't something I can permit, sir,' said Zachary. Nancy flung him a look of anguish at the mention of the coppers, but he didn't send her so much as a reassuring glance. 'I'm her friend and her former employer. Zachary Milner of Milner's Fire Safety Services.'

The veiled threat of involving the police seemed to do the trick.

'Very well.' Mr Rathbone heaved a dramatic sigh. 'If you must – though I'm not convinced Miss Pike would wish a friend to witness her shame.'

'I'm coming and that's that,' said Zachary. 'I'm sorry, sir,' he added to Mr Peters. 'I don't know how long this will take.'

'This is highly irregular,' said Mr Peters.

'I'll join you at Oak Lodge as soon as I can.' Zachary hesitated before adding, 'I appreciate your forbearance.'

'Not to worry,' said Mr Rathbone. 'I'm sure that not much forbearance will be required. I intend to deal with this matter swiftly and decisively. Would you care to lead the way down the road, Mr...Milner, did you say? Or do you need a minute to see to your donkey first?' He paused, but Zachary didn't rise to the bait. 'I'll follow you with Miss Pike; and if these two gentlemen would kindly bring up the rear? Just in case she decides to make a break for it.'

The two men nodded, though they were looking disgruntled by this time, the excitement of the chase having subsided into a wordy argument.

'Go on with you,' Mr Peters said to Zachary. 'I'll see to the pony.'

Zachary glanced at Nancy. She looked pale and scared. Confused, too. She must be wondering what the heck he intended. Determined to waste no time, Zachary set off down Whalley Road. He wasn't happy about not being able to walk with Nancy, but what option was there? The sooner they reached Mr Rathbone's house, the sooner this could be sorted out.

He slowed his pace as he went further down the road, unsure from which gateway Mr Rathbone had erupted. He glanced behind, seeking guidance, only to find that Mr Rathbone had stopped several houses back. The long, thin fingers of one hand were clamped over Nancy's mouth while those of the other dug into her shoulder as he propelled her wriggling form onto his property. Zachary darted back, bowling the two self-appointed guards aside. He belted after Mr Rathbone and wrenched Nancy free. He wanted to pull her to him and hold her close, but had to be satisfied with freeing her from Mr Rathbone's grip.

There were slashes of colour on Mr Rathbone's narrow cheeks and he was breathing heavily, but his manner was as cool as you please when he said, 'She was trying to escape, just as you'd expect of a thief. I said she would. I was merely holding on.'

Tempting as it was to urge Nancy to run for it while he tackled Mr Rathbone, Zachary knew they both had to see this through to its conclusion.

'I suggest we all go indoors,' he said, aiming for a dignified voice.

'Very well,' said Mr Rathbone. He delved inside an inner pocket and produced his wallet, startling Zachary: was the man about to try to buy him off? But Mr Rathbone offered a reward to each of his two helpers. 'Many thanks for your assistance, gentlemen. It's reassuring to know that there are law-abiding men around.' The sneer he aimed at Zachary suggested that Zachary wasn't one of them.

Mr Rathbone waved a hand toward his front door. In spite of her exertions, Nancy's face was now ashen. She went up the steps and through the half-open door. Zachary followed quickly in case Mr Rathbone intended to dart inside and slam the door in his face.

Was he finally going to find out what was going on?

Chapter Thirty-Four

WHEN MR RATHBONE banged the door behind the three of them, it sounded to Nancy like the crash of doom. She didn't know whether to be grateful for Zachary's support or to die of shame on the spot. Was he going to find out the terrible thing that Pa had done? What would he think of her then? It would give him the worst possible impression of her family. He would think them a bunch of ne'er-do-wells and he would look back at her incompetence when working for him and conclude that it stemmed from an inherited tendency to get away with whatever she could.

Mr Rathbone kept them standing in the hall, towering over the pair of them as if they were naughty children.

'Turn out your pockets,' he ordered Nancy.

She didn't move. She couldn't. She couldn't let Zachary see that she was indeed a thief. Oh, and she had thought herself so clever, getting the key to Mr Rathbone's back door and sneaking inside. Had she really imagined it would be that simple? Mr Rathbone would take it out on Pa a hundredfold.

'What is Miss Pike meant to have taken?' asked Zachary.

'Ask her.' Mr Rathbone seemed to be growing taller by the minute. He laughed. 'There's no point asking her. She's been struck dumb.'

Zachary took a step forward. 'If something is missing from your house, what proof have you that Miss Pike took it?'

'Don't be idiotic, man. You saw her run from my house, or if not from the house itself, then out of the gate.'

'No I didn't. I was unaware of anything until I heard you shouting. Nancy— Miss Pike could have appeared from anywhere.'

'Could she indeed?' Mr Rathbone flashed a cold smile. 'Firstly, in that case, why did she run away? And secondly—' He strode to the study doorway, where the door stood open. He didn't go inside but simply reached in and when he withdrew his arm, he was holding her shawl. 'If she wasn't in my house, what is this shawl doing here? I hope you aren't about to suggest that my wife would wear such a shoddy article.'

He tossed her shawl onto the floor at her feet. Nancy was too proud to pick it up even though she knew she would have to at some point. To her surprise, Zachary bent down and took it, making a point of brushing it down with his other hand. Oh, what a kind man he was – and not afraid to show it either, even in these circumstances, in front of this hateful man. Nancy expected him to give it to her, but instead he kept it and that said summat about him an' all. Another man would have thrust it straight into her hands, but not Zachary. It might sound barmy, but she took it as a sign of his support for her.

That was the moment when she changed her mind. It was such an extraordinary thing to happen that she almost laughed. Changing your mind was meant to happen gradually, wasn't it? While you were unaware of it? But not this time. This time she *knew*. She went from shame and secrecy to trust and openness in an instant – and all because Zachary Milner had had the good manners to pick up her discarded shawl.

She looked squarely at Zachary and it didn't matter that her voice shook as she said, 'Mr Rathbone is correct. I did take things from him – two things.' She almost took them out of her pocket, then didn't, not because she didn't want to show Zachary, but because of the danger of Mr Rathbone leaping across the hall and grabbing them.

'Ha! She admits it,' crowed Mr Rathbone. 'What d'you say to that, Milner? Not so keen to be her champion now, I expect.' Holding out his hand towards her, he snapped his fingers rapidly three or four times as if she were a hapless waitress and he a rude customer. 'Give, give, give.'

Nancy kept her eyes on his face for a moment until she gauged he wasn't about to stride across and pull her about. Then she turned her gaze on Zachary.

'But the things I took are things he should never have had in the first place,' she declared.

'What's that you say?' demanded Mr Rathbone. 'There! You've admitted the theft. Now return my possessions.'

'Wait,' said Zachary. 'I want to hear this.'

'Don't be a fool, man. I granted you admittance to my house so you could see I meant the chit no harm.'

'You didn't intend to let me in at all if you could help it,' said Zachary. 'All you wanted from me was that I didn't involve the police – and...' his hazel eyes narrowed as he glanced from Mr Rathbone to Nancy and back again 'and for my presence to shame Nancy into complying with your demands.'

'Exactly,' Nancy exclaimed. 'But I refuse to be ashamed – because if I'm ashamed, then you've got power over me, Mr Rathbone, just like you've had power over my pa all these years. That's the truth of it,' she said to Zachary. Oh, please let him understand.

'Most touching,' said Mr Rathbone. 'My heart bleeds.'

Addressing Zachary, he went on, 'There, you see. She's a thief from a family of thieves.'

'What's this power you have over them?' asked Zachary.

'Her father's signed confession.'

Nancy trembled inwardly as Zachary turned disbelieving eyes on her.

'Then why didn't you want the police involved?' he asked Mr Rathbone.

'Because I knew Pike when he and I were young fellows working in the same warehouse. Out of the generosity of my heart, I have protected his good name for years.'

'Protected him?' Nancy cried. 'Used him, you mean; forced him to do your bidding. You're a brute. Not in the fisticuffs sense – you've no need for that – but in a bullying, controlling way.' She swung round to look at Zachary, the urgency of the situation making her torso lean towards him and her chin jut out. 'Yes, Pa was a thief – once and once only, out of desperation, because my mam was sick. He thought Mr Rathbone was his friend and he foolishly wrote him a letter in which he admitted to the theft. Mr Rathbone has held this over his head ever since and used it to make him do jobs for him, and Pa has to take time off work to do so, which means his wages get docked. We've been on our uppers for as long as I can remember – and that's the reason. It's because Pa is under Mr Rathbone's thumb. And I know how wrong he was to steal the money, but he didn't do it because he was bad at heart. He did it because he was at the end of his tether and it affected his judgement.'

A deep stillness descended on the hall. Then the silence was broken when Mr Rathbone slowly clapped his hands together, once, twice, three times.

'A most affecting performance, Miss Pike, but all you've done is show up your father as the fool and the thief that he is. You've already admitted that being light-fingered runs in the family. Now it's time to hand back my possessions. Come, girl, do as you're bidden and I'll say no more about it.'

Before she could stop herself, Nancy's hand went to cover her pocket. Mr Rathbone's eyes flickered and Nancy bit the inside of her cheek.

Zachary spoke up. 'So your wish not to bring in the police stems from not wanting to bring trouble to Mr Pike's door?'

'Precisely. I'm glad you see it my way, Milner. I'm a reasonable man. Let Miss Pike retain the letter and I'll end my association with her father. He's a miserable sap, anyway. All I require is the return of my letter-opener.' Mr Rathbone stared into Nancy's eyes. 'It's the letter you want, not the letter-opener. Don't you want your father to be freed from running my little errands?'

She did, oh, she did, but—

'Don't give it to him, Nancy,' Zachary said quietly.

'What?' exclaimed Mr Rathbone.

'I don't understand the significance of the letter-opener,' said Zachary, 'but I do know this much. Mr Rathbone has spent years blackmailing your father—'

'Blackmail is an ugly word,' said Mr Rathbone, 'and I've already said Miss Pike can keep the letter.'

'Blackmail is against the law,' Zachary continued. 'You've got the letter, Nancy, and it's proof—'

'– of Pike's guilt,' Mr Rathbone said loudly.

'And also of your guilt, Mr Rathbone. I'm sure you wouldn't wish that to become public knowledge.'

Mr Rathbone seemed to rear up. His head went back, his chin jerked. 'The theft and the blackmail cancel one another out. You can't expose me without exposing Pike. Keep the letter, Miss Pike. You're welcome to it. I have no fear of what you'll do with it. You'll burn it if you have any sense.'

He seemed about to move, about to take a step closer. Nancy's body swayed, ready to leap backwards, but Mr Rathbone stayed put.

'Just give me my letter-opener and you're free to go,' Mr Rathbone said softly.

'No.' She shook her head, looking at Zachary as she added, 'He calls it his, but it isn't.'

'Is it your father's?' Zachary frowned. 'Or what he stole?'

'It's nowt to do with all that.'

'Precisely,' said Mr Rathbone. 'Nothing to do with that and nothing to do with you. I'm allowing you to keep the letter. You owe me something in return.' Again there was the suggestion of imminent movement, but once more he didn't budge from the spot.

'No, she doesn't.' Zachary shifted his weight. His shoulders moved and up came his head. He turned his face slightly to look at Nancy, so that she alone saw him mouth the word *Ready?* 'The letter isn't a bargaining chip, Mr Rathbone, so kindly stop making out that it is. As for the letter-opener, if Nancy says it isn't yours, then—'

Everything seemed to happen at once. Mr Rathbone darted forward and Zachary threw the spread shawl at him. For half a moment, Mr Rathbone was tangled in it as if he had run into a wet sheet on a washing-line. Nancy scurried backwards to the door, which Zachary threw open. He grabbed her hand and they ran down the steps together.

In the gateway, still holding hands, they turned to look back at the open doorway where Mr Rathbone was shouting after them and waving his fist. Then they glanced at one another and a feeling of light-heartedness burst free inside Nancy before they ran down the road together.

*

Nancy and Zachary were still hand in hand when they came to the gates of Oak Lodge, where they slowed to a halt. Nancy looked back, but there was no sign of Mr Rathbone. Before she could feel astonishment or relief or owt else that he wasn't following them, Nancy realised that her turning back to look had put a strain on their linked hands, making the intimacy feel suddenly too obvious – making it inappropriate. Her gaze met Zachary's and their hands fell away from one another's. Warmth crept across her cheeks and she glanced away.

Zachary cleared his throat. 'He won't come after us – or he won't come after you, I should say. He can't. He's lost his control over your family and he knows it. He can't denounce your father as a thief because your father can tell the world about the years of blackmail.'

Nancy frowned. 'D'you mean that throughout all those years, Pa could have stood up to Mr Rathbone at any moment and refused to give in to him any more? But he couldn't do that, could he?' she went on, answering her own question as she thought it through. 'He had too much to lose.'

'And Mr Rathbone had proof of the theft,' said Zachary, 'but it would have been his word against your father's about the blackmail.'

'And the world would have found Mr Rathbone much easier to believe.' Nancy pictured the two men, one every inch the well-to-do man of business who could now call himself a gentleman, the other a meek, nervous fellow from lower down the social ladder, who had for years struggled to make ends meet. 'As far as Pa was concerned, he was trapped for ever.'

'It's over now,' Zachary said quietly.

Nancy felt an odd sense of being disoriented. After all the turmoil she had been through, it was over; but what she had gone through was nowt compared to what poor Pa had been forced to endure over the years. Darling Pa. He would think all his Christmases had come at once. She couldn't wait to tell him.

'Thank you from the bottom of my heart.' Her hands seemed to reach out of their own accord towards Zachary. She pulled them back.

'I'm glad I was here.'

'I was never more amazed in my life than when you turned the extinguisher on him.'

Zachary grinned. 'I can't think where that idea came from – can you? Seriously, I just knew I had to – to save you.'

'Really?' She longed to ask why, but didn't dare.

'Those things I said about you being a good person: I meant every word. I just knew you wouldn't have done anything wrong.'

She smiled ruefully. 'Though I really did steal summat.'

Zachary shook his head. 'For the best and most honourable of reasons. You've saved your father from being under Mr Rathbone's thumb.'

'I couldn't have done it without you. I dread to think what might have happened if you hadn't stood up for me and then come with me to his house.'

She looked at Zachary, trying not to let her gaze linger. He had called her honourable, but he was the honourable one, helping a lady in distress.

'Mr Milner.'

Nancy looked round, dragged out of the warm moment by the sound of another voice.

'Mr Peters,' said Zachary, stepping away from her. 'I'm on my way inside now. I'm sorry to have kept you waiting.'

'Everything sorted out now, is it?' Even though Mr Peters was looking at Nancy, it was Zachary he was speaking to.

'Yes, it is, thank you.' Zachary looked at Nancy. 'Wait a minute. You can't go home like that. You must be freezing.'

Nancy realised she had no shawl, but as for being freezing, the blood was coursing through her veins and she was too happy and grateful to care about the temperature.

'Take my jacket,' Zachary offered.

'No, thank you.' What, make a holy show of herself walking through the streets wearing a man's clothes? Arrive in Wilton Close dressed like that? 'I'll be fine.' She glanced at Mr Peters, who had cast his gaze up to the heavens. 'I'll get along now. Goodbye.'

It was a wrench to leave Zachary when what she wanted more than anything was to talk over everything that had happened, but he had a job to do. The day was drawing in and it wouldn't be long before the lamp-lighter came round. Nancy started off along the road. The urge to go straight to Bailiff's Row was so strong as to be almost overpowering, but Pa wouldn't be there for ages yet. At the warehouse, the other men worked long days Monday to Friday and then half the day on Saturday; but Pa had always worked all day Saturday, spending the afternoon and early evening sweeping up and washing the windows. Nancy understood now that this was a way of earning a bit extra to try to make up for the wages he missed out on whenever he had to run an errand for Mr Rathbone. Well, not any more. With Zachary's help, she had saved Pa from that hateful man – and not just Pa, but the whole family. Mam and the twins would never know what had happened, but they would all reap the benefits – well, they would if the benefits weren't swallowed up by Pa having to support her when she lost her job at St Anthony's.

Nancy headed for Wilton Close. In spite of having been too excited earlier to notice the cold, the sharp nip in the air was getting to her now, as were the equally sharp looks of disapproval from shawled women, who no doubt considered her only half-dressed without a shawl around her. She put on a spurt.

When she opened the front door, she was surprised to hear laughter and voices raised in pleasure. She felt as if she had burst in upon a party, but her intention of creeping upstairs was scuppered when Vivienne appeared in the hall.

'I thought I heard the door. Come and hear the news.'

As Nancy entered the sitting room, Miss Patience rose from the sofa where she had been sitting with Mr Henderson and drew Nancy to the fireplace.

'You poor child, you look chilled to the bone. Sit on the hearthrug. Get as close as you can to the fire and I'll make you a hot drink.'

'No, you won't, Miss Patience,' said Vivienne. 'I'll put the kettle on.'

Nancy wasn't at all sure about doing summat as informal as sitting on the rug in the presence of Miss Hesketh, but that lady nodded at her, so she did.

'You stay here and tell Nancy your news,' Vivienne said to Miss Patience.

'Oh – oh, yes.' Miss Patience looked flustered but happy an' all. She smiled at Mr Henderson, who stood up and put his arm around her.

'I'm proud to tell you,' said Mr Henderson, 'that this lovely lady has consented to be my wife.'

But you're so old was Nancy's first thought, instantly followed by the certainty of how happy they looked. Miss Patience's thin face was no longer plain but had a radiant glow and Mr Henderson's dark eyes were filled with tenderness. A lump formed in Nancy's throat. Love was love at any age.

She got to her feet and kissed Miss Patience's cheek. 'What a surprise – but a very happy one.'

'Thank you, Nancy dear. Now back to the fireside with you. Your hands are frozen.'

333

Vivienne reappeared. 'Have you told her? Isn't it wonderful, Nancy?'

'Yes,' she said, and she meant it.

Miss Patience and Mr Henderson resumed their seats.

'We knew one another many years ago when I was about the age you are now, Nancy dear,' said Miss Patience. 'Circumstances separated us, but now we have met up again.'

'And you're getting married,' breathed Nancy. Oh, to think of young lovers being forced apart, then meeting again when they were old. It was bittersweet. Imagine if she and Zachary— she caught herself up sharply. They weren't a couple. Just because he had put himself out to help her this afternoon didn't mean owt. Well, it did. It meant he was a decent young man who wouldn't stand by while someone was in trouble, but that was all it meant.

It all rushed back: how she and Zachary had got the better of Mr Rathbone; how Pa was going to earn a proper, regular wage and life was going to be better for the Pike family. A flush invaded Nancy's face and she just hoped the others would think she was sitting too close to the fire.

She couldn't wait to tell Pa. Emotion swelled inside her. Oh, she couldn't wait to tell Pa.

Chapter Thirty-Five

O N SUNDAY MORNING Nancy walked down Bailiff's
Row, her pace brisk not just because she was excited
about giving Pa the good news but also because there was a
penetrating chill in the air and Miss Patience's jacket with
her own summer shawl on top weren't sufficient to see off the
cold. She would have to buy herself a new winter shawl, but
she couldn't do that until she found herself a new job after
Christmas. In spite of being happy for Pa, she experienced a
dipping sensation in her tummy. The closer Christmas came,
the more wretched she felt at leaving the orphans behind.

By, but Bailiff's Row was a shabby road. She had always
known it, but her weeks in Wilton Close had heightened
her awareness of it. The once-red bricks were coated in
soot and the shops were narrow and mean-looking, their
windows in dire need of a good wash. After every so many
buildings were covered alleys giving access to the rear. Each
alleyway stank of cabbages, stale beer and cat pee and in
more than one huddled a bundle of rags that denoted a
homeless wretch.

Nancy's gaze sought out the upper storeys, some of which
raised her spirits with their half-decent curtains with, here
and there, an aspidistra on display, but other windows had
filthy nets or a broken pane stuffed with newspaper. Oh, it

was hard to call yourselves respectable when you lived in Bailiff's Row.

She had never understood how bad it was until she moved away. Well, she needed to get used to it again pretty quickly, because it wasn't only her job that was at stake. As soon as she finished her course at the Miss Heskeths' school, she would be expected to move out to make way for the next pupil-lodger. And what if she couldn't find another clerical post? Would she end up back in the pie shop? At least she had been good at that – or would the Turners not want her back because she had made herself too good for shop work now?

She let herself in and ran up the stairs to the flat, calling, 'It's only me.' She had attended the early service that morning so as to have time to visit her family before returning to Wilton Close for Sunday dinner, and this afternoon she hoped to see Belinda.

The flat was empty, but while it was disappointing not to be greeted and made a fuss of, it was good an' all, because it meant Mam had felt up to going to church this morning. Nancy went downstairs to the kitchen to put the kettle on so that Mam could arrive home to a hot drink. Humming, she brought a tray up and fetched the tea-cosy from the drawer.

'Take the stairs slowly, Marjorie,' came Pa's voice from the staircase a minute or two later. 'I tried to warn you against going out in this weather.'

'Don't make a fuss,' said Mam.

Then there was silence, the four on the stairs evidently standing still, waiting for Mam to gather her strength. Nancy held her breath, willing Mam to tackle the rest of the stairs. If she could have handed over some of her own energy, she would have done it willingly.

The sounds started again and then Mam appeared.

'There, I said I could manage, Percy. Oh, look – our Nancy's here. I didn't expect you, love. That's better than any tonic, that is.'

Nancy helped her off with her things, though Mam declined the arm Nancy offered to help her to her chair. That was typical of Mam. She would screw all her strength together to go out; then, when she got home, she would refuse the support she now needed, because she wanted to look as if the expedition hadn't drained her, even though they all knew it had.

When everyone was settled and Nancy had poured the tea, the family wanted to hear all about the ongoing preparations for Christmas at the orphanage.

'Has anyone guessed yet about the pictures of the apples and oranges?' Lottie asked.

'No,' smiled Nancy, 'and you shan't trick me into telling you what's going to happen.'

'The twins will be starting work in the new year,' said Pa. 'They've got half-time jobs because of turning twelve after Christmas.'

'Doing what?' Nancy asked.

'Shop work,' said Emily. 'I'll be at the dry-cleaner's and Lottie's got a job downstairs.'

Nancy's heart sank. Lottie would stink to high heaven of tobacco. Would she end up with yellow fingertips?

'There's no need to look like that,' said Lottie.

'I wasn't aware I looked like anything.'

But it took more than that to squash Lottie. 'We can't all be office clerks like you.'

Nancy had to glance away. If – when she lost her job at St Anthony's, she very likely wouldn't be a clerk ever again.

'We won't know ourselves with the extra bit of money coming in from the twins,' said Mam. 'The Pikes are on the up at last.'

'I'm that proud of my lasses,' said Pa, but even though his lips formed a smile, there was shame in his eyes.

When it was time for Nancy to leave, she asked Pa to walk her to the bus stop and he rose to his feet with such alacrity that she knew he had spent her visit fretting over the Mr Rathbone situation.

As soon as they were outside, Nancy took the letter from her pocket. 'Here, Pa, this is for you.'

He took it with a hand that quivered. His other hand, inside its knitted glove, dashed away a tear. 'Thank you. Thank you, Nancy.' Pa's gaunt cheeks seemed to fill out, as if joy and relief were plumping up his skin. 'I'm so sorry you were put through this. I've been worried sick that Mr Rathbone would make you do what he wanted and then refuse to give you the letter.'

'It wasn't like that. I didn't steal the page-cutter.' She explained about getting hold of the letter and the penknife. 'I'm going to return the penknife to Mr Gabriel Linkworth. It's his by rights.'

'But how will you explain getting it from Mr Rathbone? You won't – you won't tell Mr Linkworth about me, will you? About what I did?'

'I'll say Mr Rathbone changed his mind about keeping it, but couldn't return it because of Mr Linkworth not having the bookshop any more, so then you offered to return it through me giving it to Miss Layton.'

Pa nodded. 'Good. That should work. It's bad enough you having to know without others being in on it an' all.'

Nancy stopped walking. Tugging on his threadbare sleeve, she turned him to her. 'You're wrong, Pa. It's isn't bad that I know. It's good, because I was able to help you. And – and I should tell you that I'm not the only one that knows. I haven't told you everything that happened at Mr Rathbone's house.

I didn't just let myself in and take the things. He came back and caught me.'

'He what? Oh, Nancy.'

'Don't fret, Pa. I got away and Mr Milner was there – Mr Zachary Milner: do you remember? I worked at his shop. He sells fire extinguishers. He helped me; he stood up for me.'

The flesh on Pa's face deflated into the old familiar thinness. 'D'you mean you told him?'

'I had to. I needed him to understand. What you did was wrong, but the way Mr Rathbone has controlled you all these years is wrong an' all. And Zachary – I mean, Mr Milner knowing about it puts you in a stronger position because he's taken your side. You should be grateful for that. I know I am. Mr Rathbone can't do anything to you ever again. You've got the letter back. And Mr Rathbone can't do owt about losing the letter-opener because he should never have had it in the first place. You're free, Pa. You won't have to do Mr Rathbone's bidding; you won't have to lose any more wages. You're free.'

Pa raised a shaking hand to his forehead. 'Oh, Nancy,' he whispered. His chest caved in and tears trickled down his face.

Nancy put her arms around him and they clung together.

'You can be a good provider from now on, Pa,' Nancy said into his ear. 'You can be the husband and father you always wanted to be.'

Nancy arrived at the end of a tatty-looking lane that she hoped was Grave Pit Lane. Miss Patience had warned her that there was no board with a road name; and Miss Hesketh had lent her a pair of galoshes, 'because it's the filthiest lane imaginable. It has no cobbles, just a cinder path and even that peters out halfway down and turns into a dirt track; and you'll need to go right to the far end.'

Fancy living in a woebegone place like this. There was a straggly line of cottages with poky windows.

Before Nancy could start down the lane, Belinda came into sight, accompanied by another girl. Seeing Nancy, Belinda waved and put on a spurt. Nancy set off down the lane to meet her.

'This is a nice surprise,' said Belinda. 'Were you on your way to see me? This is my sister, Sarah. Sarah, this is the friend I told you about: Nancy Pike, who goes to the business school.'

'You're lucky,' Sarah said to Nancy with a dramatic sigh. 'You're not only at the business school but they found you a job.'

'A temporary one,' said Nancy.

'You'll make yourself indispensable, though,' said Sarah. 'That's what I'd do.'

'I'm on my way to meet Gabriel,' said Belinda, 'and Sarah has to go into town because she's got a shift at the hotel where she works.'

'Speaking of which,' said Sarah, 'I'd better get a move on.'

Nancy and Belinda kept pace with Sarah as she hurried to the top of Grave Pit Lane, where she said her goodbyes and set off in a different direction while Belinda linked Nancy's arm and headed along the road back towards Chorlton.

'Where are you meeting him?' asked Nancy.

'He's meant to be collecting me from End Cottage, but we haven't seen one another for a few days, so I thought I'd meet him halfway.'

'You couldn't wait any longer,' said Nancy with a smile. That was exactly how she would be if she was Zachary Milner's girl. 'Listen, I've got summat for you – well, it's for Gabriel, really. It's a letter-opener.' She drew it from her pocket. 'A gentleman called Mr Rathbone has had it in his possession since some time earlier this year.'

Belinda took it. 'I remember. He was meant to give it back. He was reimbursed for everything he'd bought, but he hung onto this. How did you come by it?'

'My dad used to do jobs for him sometimes.' Oh, the joy of that *used to*! 'Mr Rathbone changed his mind about keeping it, but the bookshop had closed down and he didn't know how to find Gabriel.'

'All he had to do was contact Gabriel's solicitors. He knew who they were.'

'I don't know owt about that,' Nancy said quickly, hoping that Belinda wouldn't give it another thought. 'Anyroad, when I told Pa I'd met you and you're Gabriel's fiancée, he told Mr Rathbone I could give it back.'

'Thank you. I suppose Gabriel will add it to one of the boxes of bric-a-brac in the cellar.'

Nancy hesitated. It was important to say this right. 'Actually, I think perhaps you ought to get it valued. Pa says there's a matching page-cutter. Mr Rathbone told him they might be worth summat as a set.'

Belinda was silent for a moment before saying, 'That makes sense. I remember Mr Rathbone wanting to buy both items, but I'd put them in separate boxes and he only got this letter-opener.' Nancy expected her to say summat like, 'I'm glad we've got it back,' but what she said was, 'I wonder what made him hand it back now.'

'I wouldn't worry about that,' Nancy said. 'Here comes Gabriel. Why don't you run ahead and tell him?'

As Vivienne walked to Soapsuds House on Sunday afternoon, with her tasselled woollen scarf wrapped round her neck against the cold, she felt so happy that she could have done hopscotch along the pavement like a child. She turned the corner into Soapsuds Lane and, just as she had every time since Mr Milner had run to fetch the doctor to attend Lucy, she looked past Soapsuds House to where his shop stood further along. He was a likeable young man and she hoped his business would flourish.

Her attention was drawn back to Soapsuds House as the door opened and Aaron and Danny emerged, clad in coats and caps. Danny wore a man's cap that was much too big for him. It had belonged to his late father and Vivienne suspected he would wear it until it fell to pieces and even then he would expect Molly to darn it back together for him. And she would.

Molly appeared, standing on the doorstep, arms wrapped across the front of her blue dress and woolly cardie to keep herself warm as she saw her menfolk off. Danny spotted Vivienne and waved, which made his parents look round. Vivienne picked up her pace.

'Where are you off to?' she asked Danny.

His blue eyes were bright in his narrow, oval face. He had looked worried and wary all the time when he was sent to St Anthony's earlier this year when his father was in a sanatorium near Southport, hanging onto life by a thread, but now his features looked cheerful and relaxed, just as they were meant to.

'Uncle Tom is meeting us at the corner of Church Road and we're collecting some of the lads from St Anthony's to go onto the meadows for races and French cricket,' said Danny. 'It isn't the cricket season, but Uncle Tom says it's all right to play French cricket because it's not real cricket,' he explained.

'I'm pleased to hear it,' said Vivienne, matching the boy's serious tone. 'Trust Uncle Tom to know these things.'

Aaron kissed Molly's cheek. 'Get back in the warm, love.' He stepped aside to let Vivienne into the house. 'C'mon, son.'

Aaron and Danny set off. Molly shut the door and smiled at Vivienne.

'It does my heart good to see them together,' said Molly. 'They adore one another. Danny loves Tom too – well, he loves all my family, but Tom in particular. Tom loves having a nephew after all those nieces. Give me your coat and go through. We can hog the fire and warm our toes.'

It wasn't long before they were settled with cups of tea beside them in Molly's cosy parlour.

'You look pleased about something,' said Molly.

Vivienne put down her cup and saucer and leaned towards her friend. 'I'm more than pleased. I'm delighted and the best bit is that Miss Patience has given me permission to tell you.'

'Tell me what?' There was already a smile on Molly's lips, as if Vivienne's happiness was catching.

'She's engaged.'

'She's *what*?'

'Engaged to be married.'

'I know what engaged means,' said Molly. 'I don't know what to say…I never imagined… Oh, how mean that sounds – as if love is just for the young.'

'It's the loveliest story,' said Vivienne. 'She and Mr Niall Henderson met many years ago and they liked one another very much, but – but it happened when Miss Patience was on holiday in Scotland.'

'A holiday romance,' said Molly. 'Is this Mr Henderson a Scot?'

'No, he's from somewhere in the north of Lancashire.'

'So they had their holiday romance and then both went back to their normal lives.'

'I suppose so.' Vivienne didn't like glossing over the truth when talking to such a dear friend, but it was imperative she kept the secret. 'Niall Henderson ended up marrying someone else and he has five daughters and some grandchildren. He and Miss Patience were reunited recently and…' She spread her hands, laughing.

'And they've fallen in love for the first time all over again. Oh, I think it's perfect. I assume you've met him. What's he like? By which I mean, does he deserve our utterly adorable Miss Patience?'

'Do you know, I think he does. He's intelligent and charming and every inch the family man.'

'Five daughters!' said Molly. 'Miss Patience will love being part of a big family. I hope the daughters take to her.'

'Why wouldn't they? She's such a love. I'm not sure how long their mother has been gone, but it's some years. And let's face it, it's not as though their father intends to present them with a giddy young thing their own age as their stepmother. I know that sounds as if I'm making a joke out of it, but I'm not really. Just wait until you see them together. They were made for each other.'

'I'm very happy for her. I always suspected that she views the pupil-lodgers as the daughters she never had – and now she's going to have real daughters.'

'And grandchildren,' Vivienne added.

'Talk about happy endings,' said Molly with a sigh. 'And before you ask, that was a sigh of pleasure for Miss Patience, not of regret for my own situation.'

'How are you feeling?'

'Stronger,' said Molly. 'Adopting Lucy's baby wasn't to be and I've accepted that. It was a wonderful dream while it lasted. Aaron and I knew we mustn't take anything for granted, because it was no secret how opposed Mr Hesketh was to the thought of our having the child, but we never imagined that it would be Lucy who would break up the plan. Of course, she was perfectly entitled to change her mind. Even when I was at my most distressed, part of me was glad she had.'

'You were remembering giving up your own baby,' murmured Vivienne, resisting the instinctive urge to pull Molly against her shoulder and hug her.

'It was the hardest thing I ever had to do,' said Molly, her greeny-hazel eyes awash with sorrow. 'I wouldn't have wished that on Lucy, no matter how much she thought it was what she wanted – then, in the end, she didn't want it. She wanted to keep Charlie and marry Dickie and probably go on to have more babies. I understand that.'

'It doesn't make it any less painful for you, though.'

'No, it doesn't. Adoption means so much to Aaron and me. Well, look who I'm saying this to – you know better than anyone how much it matters and what a difference it can make to a child's life.'

'I couldn't have been luckier in my adoptive parents.'

'I hope that's what happened to my baby, my son. I hope he is growing up in a loving, stable family and I hope his parents love him to bits. I hope they're giving him all the love and attention I can never give him. And it isn't just because of him. It's Danny as well. It's such a privilege to see the strong bond between him and Aaron. Neither of us can imagine our lives without him now. So when Lucy asked if we would consider adopting her child, it felt completely right and natural. I'd got to know her quite well when I lived in Wilton Close and I went with her to Maskell House on that frightful day when Miss Hesketh and I were supposed to leave her there. Aaron and I never questioned for one moment whether we should or shouldn't agree to adopt her baby. We both want Soapsuds House to be full of children and we're happy for our family to be a mixture of our own children and adopted children. Adoption *matters*.'

'That reminds me of something Niall Henderson said. Two of his daughters are actually his stepdaughters, but apparently if anyone asks which are which, he says he can't remember.'

Molly nodded approvingly. 'Now I know I'm going to like him,' she said with a smile. 'He's a man after my husband's heart.'

'I'm glad to know you've come to terms with not having Lucy's baby,' said Vivienne. 'I know he would have been born any day now if he hadn't come early. I'm sure that's been in your mind.'

'It has,' Molly agreed, 'but so has something else. This is a secret at the moment. We haven't told anybody yet, but I want you to know, because you understand how much I was looking forward to being the mother of a Christmas baby.' Her lips twitched under the pressure of an irrepressible smile. She laid a hand on her stomach. 'I'm going to have a summer baby instead.'

Chapter Thirty-Six

WALKING TO THE orphanage on Monday morning, Nancy felt she was being torn in half. It was wonderful to picture Pa going to work today knowing he would never again be forced to use his work hours to run errands for Mr Rathbone; wonderful an' all to think that at the end of this week, on Christmas Eve, the children were to perform their nativity play. She was so proud of them for all their hard work. But Christmas Eve would also be the day when Mrs Rostron made her announcement about Ginny and Nancy, and Nancy was in no doubt as to what that announcement would be. This coming Sunday, Christmas Eve, was to be her very last day in the place she had come to love; and on Monday next week, she would be obliged to confess to her family that she had lost her job. What a Christmas present for them.

But she must set aside her own worries and make her final week at St Anthony's as good as she possibly could. She owed that to the children she cared for so much. She owed it to herself an' all. It was important to make the best of things, no matter what.

That afternoon, when the children came in from school, they were in high spirits because tomorrow was the last day of term and they couldn't wait for the holidays to start. Nancy was staying for tea this evening so she could run another rehearsal and help put the final touches to the costumes.

But the rehearsal didn't go well at all.

'They're as high as kites because of school finishing tomorrow,' said Nanny Duffy. 'I advise against a rehearsal tomorrow evening.'

Although she was disappointed with today's rehearsal, not to mention panic-stricken at the thought that the nativity play might turn into a shambles, Nancy wasn't sorry to agree, because it meant she could go and see Zachary in his shop tomorrow after work. She hadn't seen him since Saturday and, even though she had thanked him then, the least she could do was call in and say thank you again. Or was that just a made-up reason because she wanted to see him once more and any pretext would do?

When she arrived back at Wilton Close, lessons were under way. She slipped upstairs to her room. Vivienne's door was open and, as Nancy reached the landing, Vivienne appeared in the doorway.

'How was the rehearsal?'

'Pretty bad. It's end-of-term excitement, Nanny Duffy says.'

'I'm sure she's right. It's a pity you weren't here earlier. Miss Layton and Mr Linkworth came round. They're a nice couple, aren't they?'

'Yes, I like them. Did they come to fetch something from the cellar?'

'Yes. How did you know?'

'Lucky guess.'

So now Gabriel and Belinda had the page-cutter as well as the letter-opener. Was Mr Rathbone correct about the two pieces together forming a valuable set? Oh, Nancy hoped so. It could make all the difference in the world to her friends.

It seemed to be a time for good things to be happening – to

Belinda and Gabriel, to dear Miss Patience and to her own family an' all. But what about herself? It was all very well things looking up for the Pikes, but what about when she lost her job and dragged them down again?

On Wednesday evening, Nancy hurried out of St Anthony's. It was a shame to leave when there was such an air of excitement because of term having finished that day, but she had to see Zachary.

'Are you going home, Miss Nancy?' Hannah asked, looking disappointed. She was part of a group and the other faces fell an' all.

'I have to visit somebody,' said Nancy.

'We thought you might play games with us,' said Hannah, 'to celebrate the school holidays.'

For a moment, Nancy wavered. Having the children seek her company felt special, but she longed to see Zachary. 'I'm sorry, Hannah. I've got to go. Bye, love.'

She borrowed a spare coat from the cupboard under the stairs, hoping she wouldn't get into hot water if she hung onto it all week. She would receive her final wages on Friday and she really ought to buy a thick shawl or a second-hand coat on Saturday, but she couldn't justify that if she was going to lose her job on Sunday.

She set off through the darkness for Zachary's shop. The evening was dry but there was a knife-sharp edge to the cold. Pools of pale-golden light fell from the street-lamps, guiding her way. As she turned the corner into Soapsuds Lane, she heard children's voices singing a carol. A group of children clustered round the front door of Soapsuds House. They finished singing the second verse of 'Away in a Manger' and then one of them knocked on the door and they started on 'Once in Royal David's City.' The door opened and Molly, Aaron and Danny stood listening. As Nancy passed by on the other side of the road, Aaron dropped some coins into the cap the biggest child held out and the children hurried away, chattering in delight at the Abramses' generosity.

Outside Zachary's shop, Nancy came to a standstill. The blind had been pulled down over the big window, but the glass pane in the door was still uncovered and she could see Zachary behind the counter, leaning on it as he bent over some papers. He looked like he was ticking things off on a list. He wore gloves without fingertips and he had a scarf wound round his neck.

Nancy tried the door and found it locked, but the sound made Zachary look up and he came to unlock it, allowing her to slip inside. If it was warmer in here than it was outside, it didn't show. Zachary shut the door but didn't lock it.

Nancy cleared her throat. 'I came to see how you are after what happened on Saturday.'

'I'm fine, thanks. The question is, how are you – and your family? I imagine your father must be relieved.'

'Yes, he is. This will make such a difference to him – to all of us. I'm grateful to you for standing by me. That's the real reason I came: to say thank you.'

'I was glad to help. I'd have done the same for anyone.'

'Oh.' Well, that put her in her place.

Zachary frowned. 'That didn't come out quite the way I intended. What I meant to say—'

'It's quite all right,' Nancy put in quickly. Why on earth had she imagined it would be a good idea to come here? She ought to leave, but she couldn't do that without adding something to the conversation first or it would look like she was marching off in a huff. 'I hope you didn't get into trouble with the gentleman from Oak Lodge.'

Zachary glanced away. He walked over to the counter and took his place behind it. 'I did, as a matter of fact.'

Nancy caught her breath. 'And all because of coming to my assistance.'

Zachary shrugged. 'It couldn't be helped. Nobody would have left a girl to face that situation alone.'

'Did you get a roasting?'

'Just a bit.' Zachary smiled at her, but it was only a half-smile. 'It wasn't your fault.'

'What did he say?'

'The first time I went to Oak Lodge, Mr Peters and I got on – I was going to say like a house on fire, but I suppose I should avoid expressions like that.' Zachary smiled ruefully. 'Anyway, he was impressed with the service I offered and said that, all being well, he would recommend me. That meant a lot. He's involved in the local community and he knows shop-keepers and guest-house owners and businesses with offices.'

'Oh, Zachary – I mean, Mr Milner,' breathed Nancy.

'When I went into Oak Lodge after saying goodbye to you, I set up the extinguishers and positioned the fire blankets and we put dates in the diary for training. Mr Peters said he was pleased with what I'd done, but he'd changed his mind about recommending me as, in his words, I'd given priority to a fracas in the street instead of to my customer.'

'Didn't you tell him about Pa and the blackmail?'

'Of course not. That's your family's private business. I wouldn't dream of spreading it around.'

'I'm sorry things turned out that way.'

'It's a pity,' said Zachary, 'but, as I said, it's not your fault.'

Nancy felt as if it was, though, as she trailed home. Zachary had acted as a gentleman, not just by helping her but also by keeping Pa's grubby secret, and now his business would suffer because of it – because of her, and not for the first time.

She was still thinking about it when she returned to the orphanage next morning, where the atmosphere was one of building excitement.

'That's partly thanks to you,' Nurse Carmel told her in the nursemaids' common room. 'We always do special things at Christmas, but we've never had so many special things happen as we have this year.'

'I think some of the children will likely explode,' said Nurse Philomena, throwing herself into an old armchair as if she was exhausted.

Nancy had never been sorrier to be a clerk. While she did her best to concentrate on filing, the nursemaids helped the children put up decorations. They had made enough paper-chains for the dining room and the common rooms. The tree was erected and decorated, and Nanny Mitchell took some of the children to the garden of one of the orphanage's local supporters to cut holly. All the Christmas stocking decorations were attached to long lengths of string that were fastened along the dining room walls at the children's eye-level so they could all enjoy them before Mr Lowe, Mrs Granger, Mrs Wardle and Colonel Lavender from the Orphanage Committee came to judge them and hand out prizes for the best ones. All this went on in an atmosphere of happy anticipation laced with the scents of gingerbread, spiced yule loaf and jellied pork brawn.

Miss Kirby held rehearsals in the church during the afternoons. Nancy screwed up her courage to ask permission to attend, but, when she started to speak, Miss Allan raised her eyebrows and Nancy didn't finish, just returned to her work. At the end of the day, the children clustered round her, full of how well their play was going. Delighted as she was to hear it, it made her wish all the more that she could have been there.

Friday was her last working day, which nobody seemed to realise. She would be here anyroad on Saturday in her own time for the dress rehearsal in the church and again on Sunday, Christmas Eve, for the play itself, after which everyone would come back to the orphanage and Mrs Rostron would make her announcement about which of the two temporary clerks was to stay on in a permanent capacity.

Nancy couldn't bear to think about it. Besides, there was an important job she needed to do before then. Zachary might not feel about her the way she felt about him, but that wouldn't stop her.

On Saturday morning, she returned to Whalley Road, feeling self-conscious as she passed by Mr Rathbone's house. When she came to Oak Lodge, she marched to the front door and boldly rang the bell. Her heart beat hard as she waited.

The door was opened by a maid in a black dress and white apron with a frilled edge.

'I need to see Mr Peters, if you please,' said Nancy. 'It's important.'

Chapter Thirty-Seven

ZACHARY PUSHED A skewer through the large potato and packed it expertly in the cinders in the bottom of the fire to bake. Wrapping his bacon in linen, he laid it in the bottom of his iron pot, placing over the top of it a thin wooden board with holes in it, on top of which went a peeled onion, again wrapped in linen. Later, he would pour hot water into the pot and hang it over the fire; and a little later still, he would add a linen bag of carrots and beans. He was adept at open-hearth cooking these days. On one side of his fireplace stood the fire-irons and coal-scuttle that you'd find in any house; and on the other were his tongs, ladle, spoon and slice, all long-handled. As well as his kettle and cooking pot, he had invested in an old-fashioned cistern, a large lidded pot with a tap near the bottom, which held twice as much water as his cooking pot. As long as it hung over the fire, he had constant hot water.

He stood up, wiping his hands on the cloth that hung on a nail. He would enjoy a good meal in an hour or so. At the other end of the room, he had put up a curtain pole that stretched all the way across – not that that was very far – and he had purchased a pair of second-hand curtains of heavy velvet, which, when drawn, covered not merely the small window but the entire wall, providing a modicum of insulation. These curtains he now drew before he entered the shop, shutting the door behind him to keep the warm in, to unfold his bed and put on the sheet and blankets, with his overcoat laid over the top. Then he filled his stone hot-water bottle and popped it under the bedding. He would refresh the bottle just before he went to bed.

He had just returned to his storeroom-cum-living quarters, appreciating the warmth that greeted him as he opened the door, when there was a series of knocks on the shop door. Who could that be? He hadn't heard any carol-singing. The knocks came again. Zachary smiled wryly: someone was desperate for fire extinguishers, apparently.

He glanced down at himself. He had removed his suit and was in a pullover with a tweed jacket over the top for warmth, but there was no time to change and, anyway, it couldn't possibly be a customer at this time.

He went to the door and lifted the edge of the blind.

'Mr Peters!' He couldn't get the door open fast enough. 'Is everything all right?' Zachary's heart sank. Surely there couldn't be a problem with his fire extinguishers.

Mr Peters marched in, slapping his hands together and making 'brrr' movements with his shoulders.

'So here's your shop, Milner. It took me a devil of a time to find it.'

'The address is on all my paperwork,' said Zachary.

'That's all well and good, but the locals don't appear to be aware that this is Crossland Road. They call it – what was it? Soapsuds Road?'

'Soapsuds Lane.'

Zachary closed the door, uncomfortably aware that he ought to offer his visitor a hot drink and a seat by his fire, but he couldn't possibly let Mr Peters see the humble way in which he lived. It would do his professional appearance no good at all.

But Mr Peters didn't seem to care about hospitality. 'I apologise for barging in on you. I didn't even know if you lived on the premises, but I couldn't let Christmas go by without at least trying to bring my own version of good cheer. The last time I saw you, I said I wouldn't recommend you to other businesses. Well, I had an unexpected visitor at Oak Lodge earlier on, a Miss Nancy Pike.' Mr Peters smiled and his eyes crinkled. 'She said you didn't know and the look on your face proves it.'

'She went to Oak Lodge?'

'She did indeed, and she told me what happened last Saturday. She told me about her father and admitted the terrible mistake he made years ago. She said Mr Rathbone had helped her father by repaying the money he stole; and when, last week, Mr Rathbone accused her of theft, it was because he was tainting her with the same brush as her father. She said that the way you stood up for her made all the difference and that – well, that you didn't deserve to get into hot water with me because you'd done a good turn for her.' Mr Peters slapped Zachary on the shoulder. 'All credit to you for keeping Mr Pike's unfortunate past to yourself, lad. That was jolly decent of you, all the more so when I was hauling you over the coals for letting me down.'

Zachary was scrambling to keep pace with this version of the truth that Nancy had told.

'I did you a disservice,' Mr Peters went on. 'I said you didn't deserve to be recommended, but I've changed my mind. You helped a young lady in distress and you showed you can keep a secret, even if it's at your own expense. I'll be glad to recommend you. If you let me have some business cards, I'll start tomorrow. We have a tradition at Oak Lodge of inviting friends and neighbours for sherry and mince-pies and some of the neighbours run guest-houses, so that's where I'll start.'

Zachary shook his hand warmly. 'That's most generous of you, sir.'

'Not at all.' Mr Peters stopped smiling and looked serious. 'It wasn't easy for Miss Pike, you know, washing her father's dirty linen in public like that. She looked utterly miserable, but determined as well, determined to do right by you. She's the one you should be thanking, not me.'

Zachary went early to St Clement's on Christmas Eve to get a good seat for the St Anthony's nativity, which was due to start at six o'clock. The organist was playing softly in the background and there was a quiet hum of conversation as people in the pews murmured to one another. It was a good turn-out, considering that these children were orphans with few relatives between them. Maybe the locals were here because this was such a novel idea. And not just a novel idea, but Nancy's idea. Zachary drew a deep breath that was filled with pride, except that he had no business feeling proud, did he? She wasn't his girl.

The buzz of voices grew louder and Zachary looked round. Except for a few side-pews with 'Reserved' notices, the church was full and some people were standing. Zachary got up to offer his place to a woman who was on her feet. Now that he was standing, he had an uninterrupted view of the simple stage that had been constructed in front of the altar, and also across the audience. He saw a few faces he recognised, including the two Miss Heskeths.

Presently Mrs Rostron walked up the aisle and stood in the centre of the stage.

'Thank you all for coming to see the St Anthony's nativity. The children have all walked here in their costumes and are taking off their coats and hats in the back of the church.

After that, we'll get them into position. I hope you enjoy their performance.'

She stepped down. There were some loud whispers, then the children trooped up the aisle. Little ones were grouped to one side of the stage. They were dressed in white, with headbands with white ears attached, some of which were already wonky. Zachary heard a nursemaid whisper to them, 'What do we say when someone says "sheep"?' and the children all said 'Baa-a-a', which sent laughter running round the church and people sat up straighter.

The reserved pews filled with children in various costumes and headdresses. It looked like every child was dressed up ready to take part. From what Zachary remembered of school plays, it was only the chosen few who got parts. Good for Nancy.

The play opened with Mary being visited by the Angel Gabriel, a lad in cricket whites accompanied by a host of angels with tinsel halos bobbing about on wire over their heads. When Mary and Joseph set off for Bethlehem, they walked down the aisle towards the back of the church. Meanwhile, some children got up from the side-pews and came towards the stage. They wore dressing-gowns with tea-towels as headdresses. A boy-innkeeper stood to one side of the stage, a girl-innkeeper to the other. In twos, threes and fours, the others climbed onto the stage and approached one of the innkeepers.

'May we stay at your inn?'

'Yes, you may,' said the innkeeper, standing aside to let them pass, at which point they climbed off the side of the stage and returned to their seats.

At last, it was Mary and Joseph's turn. They walked up the aisle and onto the stage, only to be turned away by the two innkeepers.

'No room at the inn.'

'No room at the inn.'

Then, from somewhere down the side of the church, another voice piped up, calling, 'No room at the inn.'

And from the far side of the font, 'No room at the inn.'

And then – crikey, was that from the choir loft? 'No room at the inn.' Everyone tilted back their heads to look.

'No room at the inn,' called another voice.

'No room at the inn.'

It was electrifying. Zachary felt the hairs stand up on his arms.

A new innkeeper stood in the middle of the stage. 'You can sleep in my stable with the donkeys and the sheep.'

'Baa-a-a,' said all the sheep and everyone laughed.

As the play continued, the atmosphere was attentive and genial, with a dose of childish excitement mixed in. The baby Jesus received visits from a mass of shepherds and shepherd-esses, who sang beautifully, and a football team's worth of kings, accompanied by queens, pages and dancers; and if the dancers performed a Scottish reel, well, why not?

The play ended with most of the children back in the side-pews and the heavenly host filling the stage, apart from the corner occupied by the sheep, and all the children singing 'Silent Night'. There was a moment's deep silence and then the applause began. It wasn't just polite applause, but warm, mean-ingful applause, with the audience holding their hands up to chin-level as they clapped. Zachary clapped as hard as anybody. Some of the women had tears running down their faces. Were they relatives of the orphans or just soft-hearted locals?

When Mrs Rostron appeared once more on the stage in front of the beaming heavenly host, the applause subsided. The superintendent made a short speech, thanking everyone for coming and thanking the staff and friends of the orphan-age who had helped in various ways.

'Two people in particular have worked hard to produce this play: Miss Kirby, who is a retired teacher, and our own Miss Pike, one of our clerks.'

A loud whisper could be heard saying, 'She means Miss Nancy,' and at that a cheer went up from the children and they all clapped like mad until a single raised eyebrow from Mrs Rostron quelled their enthusiasm.

'Thank you, children. It is good to know you appreciate the work that has been done on your behalf.' Mrs Rostron smiled at the audience. 'The biggest thank you of all that I have to say is to the children themselves for working so hard and putting on an excellent performance this evening. Give yourself a big clap.' When that died down, she said, 'It's my pleasure to ask our audience to join in with the final carol, "O Come, All Ye Faithful". When it comes to each chorus, please let the children sing the first "O Come", then the children and all the ladies will sing the second one and finally everybody will sing the third one. Will you all please stand up to sing.'

The rousing carol rang out joyfully, filling the church with good cheer. To his surprise, Zachary had to stop singing because his throat was choked with tears. All at once he missed Nate dreadfully. He hadn't had much to do with church or praying since his brother died, but, having had his heart warmed by the children's nativity play and now being surrounded by folk belting out this most popular of carols, he felt that, here, now, he was in the right place.

At the end of the carol, everyone sat down and Mrs Rostron asked the audience to remain seated while the orphans left the church, which Zachary knew would take a while because they all had to get their coats and hats before they could set off.

'And if any relatives of the children or friends of the orphanage would like to return to St Anthony's with us,' said Mrs Rostron, 'there will be cocoa and gingerbread.'

As soon as the stage was empty, Mr Abrams knelt down beside one end of it and fiddled about underneath. Zachary went over.

'Need a hand?'

'Thanks. The stage has to be removed this evening.' Abrams grinned. 'They won't be wanting it at midnight service. I've got permission to stack the pieces in the church hall for now.'

As they began to dismantle it, some men came forward from the pews to help and the work was soon done. The other men returned to their wives and Abrams slapped Zachary on the back.

'Come to St Anthony's for a hot drink.'

There was nothing Zachary wanted more. He wanted to see Nancy and thank her for what she had done for him in going to see Mr Peters.

At the orphanage, it was strangely quiet.

'The children are all upstairs,' said a nursemaid. 'They'll be brought downstairs together and they've been told to be as quiet as mice.'

'Why?' asked Zachary.

The nursemaid smiled. 'Come and see.'

She led him and Mr Abrams into the dining room, at one end of which stood the Christmas tree. Mrs Abrams and another nursemaid were busy lighting the clip-on candles.

'If you've got a stepladder,' said Zachary, 'I'll light the top ones.'

When the tree was finished, the gas-lights on the walls and those hanging from the ceiling were extinguished, so that the only light in the room came from the magical glow of the candlelight. Mrs Rostron opened the door and the children came creeping down the couple of steps into the room in single file, the smallest ones in their nightclothes and dressing-gowns. Zachary caught many a soft gasp and his heart filled with emotion at the wonder in the children's faces. The older ones obviously knew what to expect, but they were still delighted. Where was Nancy? Ah, here she came, with some of the very oldest children – the fourteens, that was what they were called, wasn't it?

Zachary caught her eye and she came over to him.

'Isn't it all perfect?' she asked.

Zachary looked round. It was a dining room, that was all, with whitewashed walls, a wooden floor and long tables and benches. At one end was a large serving hatch. It was the last word in ordinary. But with the children gazing at the tree, its candles providing the only light in the room, and with the delicious aroma of ginger in the air, yes, it was special. Zachary looked at Nancy. Her expression was soft with happiness. Yes, it was perfect.

He cleared his throat and shifted his gaze. The pictures of apples and oranges, which he had seen when he came to install the fire extinguishers, caught his eye. There were pictures of holly now too.

'You have to tell me,' he said to Nancy. 'Why are they there?'

'I've no idea.' Nancy laughed. 'It's part of the Christmas magic.' She put a finger to her lips. 'Not in front of the children,' she whispered.

The children seemed to Zachary to be enthralled by the tree and unlikely to overhear, but he changed the subject. 'Mr Peters came to see me yesterday. He said you went to Oak Lodge.'

Nancy nodded, looking shy. 'I wanted to help.'

'You did that all right. Mr Peters is going to recommend me after all.'

'That's good news.'

'It's the best Christmas present I could have had.'

'I'm sure Mr Peters realises that,' said Nancy.

'I'm trying to thank *you* for it, not him. You're the one who made it happen. I'm very grateful.'

'It didn't seem right, you missing out because of helping me.'

'I know how difficult it must have been for you, talking about what your father did.'

'Shhh!' Nancy glanced round. 'Keep your voice down.'

'I'm sorry.' Zachary could have kicked himself. He withdrew a few steps and when Nancy followed, he said quietly, 'You didn't tell Mr Peters about the blackmail.'

'Heavens, no.' She looked shocked. 'The last thing my family needs is to get into more trouble.'

'I know it must have hurt you to put all the blame on your father, yet you did it to help me.' Zachary drew a breath. This was the moment to say that he didn't just appreciate it for the sake of his business, but on a personal level as well, because – because he thought the world of her and—

'If it helps your business, it'll be worth it,' said Nancy. 'It was the least I could do after the mess I made when I worked there.'

'You weren't that bad.'

'Oh yes I was. You were right to get rid of me. I'm about to be sacked from here an' all – and in front of my family. They came to see the nativity. I didn't know they were coming. It were meant as a surprise.'

Nancy's voice wavered and was that a sheen of tears in her eyes? Zachary desperately wanted to comfort her, but she looked away.

Mrs Rostron clapped her hands. 'Attention, everybody. Children, wherever you are, please sit down, on a bench if you're beside one or on the floor if you aren't. I have something important to announce.'

The children sat down. Some of the adults sat on the benches, others remained standing. There was a series of soft *pops* along the length of the room as the nursemaids switched on the gas-lamps. Mrs Rostron signalled to Mrs Atwood to join her.

'As you all know,' said Mrs Rostron, 'I have to make an important announcement. In fact, there will be two announcements. I will make the first because it was my idea and Mrs Atwood will make the second because it started off as hers. Afterwards Mrs Wilkes and her kitchen staff will bring trays of cocoa and gingerbread through as a special treat.' The superintendent looked round, making sure all eyes were on her. 'Please will Miss Virginia and Miss Nancy join me over here.'

It was all Zachary could do not to grasp Nancy's hand and pull her into his arms to protect her from publicly losing her job. The two girls threaded their way towards Mrs Rostron. Nancy managed a wobbly smile, but at the last moment pressed her lips together and dipped her chin. Zachary wanted to bound across the room and proclaim to the world how wonderful she was.

'All you children know Miss Virginia because she grew up here,' said Mrs Rostron, 'and Miss Nancy has made her mark by joining in with your games and working so hard on preparing for Christmas. What you children don't know is that there's only one clerical job. Miss Virginia and Miss Nancy have both been trying out for it and today is the day I have to announce who will be given the position on a permanent basis. I am delighted to tell you that Miss Allan's new junior clerk will be Miss Virginia.'

The children clapped and Virginia covered her mouth with her hands, but Zachary focused on Nancy, his chest filling with pride and sorrow as she gave Virginia a kiss on the cheek.

Mrs Rostron held up her hand for silence.

'I haven't finished my announcement. I'm sure all the children will agree with me that Miss Nancy has done a great deal for them, especially in relation to the nativity play. The Orphanage Committee has agreed to make the funds available so we can offer her the post of nursemaid – wait, I haven't finished yet – with particular responsibility for children's activities.'

The hall erupted into applause. Nancy looked stunned.

When the clapping died down, Mrs Rostron said, 'I hope your applause isn't premature. Miss Nancy hasn't accepted the position yet.'

Tears rolled down Nancy's cheeks. 'Oh, yes,' she said. 'Yes, please.'

'Congratulations, *Nurse* Nancy,' said Mrs Rostron and there was more clapping, this time accompanied by cheers. 'Now it's time for Mrs Atwood's announcement – but first, a word from the chairman of the Orphanage Committee, Mr Lowe.'

Mr Lowe stepped forward. 'All of you children are familiar with Mrs Atwood, who has become a regular visitor here in recent months through the course of her work. Recently, Mrs Rostron told the Orphanage Committee about an idea Mrs Atwood had had. I thought it was a very good idea and my colleagues on the Committee agreed. I now call upon Mrs Atwood to tell you about it.'

All eyes turned to Mrs Atwood. She was a good-looking lady, though not a patch on Nancy Pike, as far as Zachary was concerned.

'My idea is simple, but I think it's very special. The orphanage is named after St Anthony. Does anyone know what he's the patron saint of?'

Some hands went up and she chose a child.

'He's the one you pray to when you lose something.'

'That's right. He is the patron saint of lost things. I can see why the orphanage's founders chose him, because in a sense orphans might be said to be lost; or at least they have lost their families. But St Anthony is the patron saint of lost *things*, not lost children, so while he does a lot of good work, I don't think he's quite the right saint for this orphanage. There isn't a saint for lost children, but there is a saint for all children and that is St Nicholas. So we're going to change the name of your orphanage to St Nicholas's.'

A hand shot up. 'St Nicholas is Father Christmas, isn't he?'

'He is.'

'Then we'll be the Christmas Orphanage.'

There were gasps of delight all round the room and 'The Christmas Orphanage' was passed from child to child, first in whispers, then in louder voices.

'We're going to be the Christmas Orphanage!'

Chapter Thirty-Eight

NANCY WAS LAUGHING and crying at the same time. She had spent weeks trying to prepare for the moment when she would inevitably lose her job, knowing that it was going to break her heart to leave the children behind – and now she wasn't leaving after all. In fact, she had been handed the job of her dreams. It was almost too wonderful to take in. But something she knew with crystal clarity was that this would mean she wasn't going to be a drain on her family's resources and she closed her eyes in gratitude as a heavy weight was lifted from her shoulders.

Best of all, she had gone from dreading her family witnessing her downfall to having them here to share her unexpected success. She hadn't known they were coming to the nativity. At the end of it, when she was busy stuffing little arms into coat-sleeves and doing up buttons in double-quick time, Lottie and Emily had bobbed up in front of her and kind-hearted Nanny Mitchell had said that of course the whole family must come back to St Anthony's for cocoa and to see the tree. Now Mam sat on one of the benches, trying to look as if she wasn't leaning against the table. Her face was pinched and drained, but her eyes were bright with joy. She held out her arms and Nancy, joining her on the bench, slid into them.

'My clever lass,' Mam said into her hair.

'Ginny's the clever one,' said Nancy.

'There's more than one kind of cleverness,' said Mam.

Nancy got up for Pa and the twins to hug her, then she was swamped by children and staff alike, all calling her Nurse Nancy.

'What with Nurse Nancy and the Christmas Orphanage, I don't think I've ever seen the children so excited,' said Nanny Mitchell.

Mrs Rostron clapped her hands for attention. 'If you're a fourteen-girl, stay standing. All the other children, sit down where you are, please.'

The kitchen staff and the fourteen-girls came round with trays of cocoa and gingerbread. After this treat, it was time to take the littlest ones up to bed.

'Are you going to help with the children?' asked Pa. 'We'll say goodbye now.'

Nancy looked at Mam, feeling a tug of concern inside her chest. It was high time that she went home. Nancy just hoped the journey wouldn't be too much for her. She gave Mam another hug.

'Thank you for coming.'

'I wouldn't have missed it for the world, chick.'

Nancy followed the line of children upstairs, where they cleaned their teeth and said their prayers before climbing into bed. Excitement fizzed inside Nancy at the knowledge that this would be a part of her daily life from now on.

She returned downstairs, eager to help supervise the next lot of children, but Zachary started walking across the room towards her and her heart bumped against her ribs.

'Nancy, there you are.' It was Belinda, accompanied by Gabriel. 'Congratulations on your new job. My brothers are chuffed to bits. They really like you.'

'And congratulations on the nativity,' Gabriel added. 'Belinda's mum cried when Jacob said his lines on stage.'

'He used to be a tearaway,' said Belinda, 'but being here has turned him round.'

'He worked hard not just at his part but helping with props,' said Nancy. 'So did your other brother.'

'Mum's bursting with pride and so are Sarah and I.'

'I'm glad you enjoyed the play,' said Nancy.

'We're here to say thank you as well,' said Belinda. 'The letter-opener you returned to us – I can't tell you what a difference it has made.' She had to stop to blink away tears.

'The page-cutter and the letter-opener as a matching pair are worth a considerable sum,' said Gabriel. 'We don't know precisely how much yet, because they're going to be put into an auction next year. We've been advised to let Foster and Wainwright's in Chester handle the sale.'

Nancy had never heard of the company, but if the pieces were being sent all the way to Chester, that made them sound very grand and valuable.

'We can hardly believe it.' Belinda's unshed tears made her blue eyes look like they were sparkling with joy. 'Gabriel will be able to leave his job and have his bookshop with a flat above it. We'll be able to get married. We thought we'd have to wait ages for this and now it's really happening.' She kissed Nancy's cheek. 'And it's thanks to you bringing the letter-opener back to us and telling us about its value.'

'All I did was fetch it to you. It was Mr Rathbone who sent it and who knew about the two pieces being valuable.'

'Oh, him!' said Belinda in a huffy voice. 'I remember him coming into the shop. Such a rude man. I'd much rather give you the credit.'

Belinda didn't know how right she was – and she never would know. There were still secrets and always would be. No matter how richly he deserved it, Nancy could never speak out against Mr Rathbone, because he would tell everyone about Pa being a thief. It was best all round to let things lie.

'You've given us the best Christmas present possible,' said Belinda.

Nancy was called away to help escort more children to bed. When she came back, the visitors had departed. Belinda, Gabriel, Mrs Layton and Sarah had left, as had the smartly dressed members of the Orphanage Committee and their spouses. The children's relatives, a mixture of folk in their humble Sunday best, had gone an' all. Something inside Nancy slumped. She had so hoped for another word with Zachary, but that was daft, because he had already spoken to her this evening and it wasn't as though he was interested in her, not in the way she longed for. As far as he was concerned, she would always be the dopey girl who had made expensive mistakes in his shop.

Aaron, Molly and Danny were still here and so were Miss Hesketh, Miss Patience and Vivienne. They were all talking with Mrs Rostron. Catching sight of Nancy, Vivienne beckoned her over.

'I see you've already started your new job,' said Mrs Rostron, making Nancy blush.

'Many congratulations, Nancy dear,' said Miss Patience. 'I'm delighted for you.' With a twinkle in her pale-blue eyes, she added, 'When you had your business school interview, my sister said she saw something in you.'

'I did,' said Miss Hesketh, 'though I was wrong to think you had the makings of a clerk. What you have, Nurse Nancy, is imagination and initiative.'

These words from anyone would have made Nancy proud, but hearing them from Miss Hesketh meant more than she could say.

Mrs Rostron raised her voice to address the remaining children. 'Will you please all go to your common rooms until bedtime.'

Shepherded by nursemaids, the children dispersed.

'We ought to be getting home,' said Molly, ruffling her son's hair. 'This one needs to settle down before bed.'

'We should go too,' said Miss Hesketh.

'That means you as well,' Mrs Rostron said to Nancy. 'You'll have plenty of weekend and night duties once you officially start. Go home and make the most of Christmas Eve.'

'There's something I have to do before I go.' Nancy glanced up at the drawings of apples, oranges and holly pinned up around the walls.

'I think it's time you explained your Christmas magic,' said Mrs Rostron.

Nancy dared to say, 'I'm sorry, but you'll have to wait and see,' and then wondered if she'd gone too far.

But Mrs Rostron smiled in her usual restrained way, though there was kindness in her eyes. 'Very well.' She turned to the others. 'I'll see you out and then I'll check on the children.'

'I need a stepladder,' Nancy said to Aaron.

'You ladies go and get your coats.'

'*Dad*,' hissed Danny.

'I beg your pardon – ladies and young gentleman,' said Aaron, making Danny groan. 'I'll catch up with you in a minute.'

With Danny politely holding the door, Mrs Rostron, the Miss Heskeths, Molly and Vivienne all trooped out. Aaron went to the door at the far end of the dining room, beside the serving hatch. When Aaron reappeared, he wasn't carrying the stepladder. He walked down the room with a big smile on his face.

'The stepladder will be here in a minute. I just asked somebody to lend a hand.'

'Who?'

'Someone who's been killing time carrying trays to the kitchen and putting away the washed and dried crockery, anything so as to have an excuse to stay in the hope of seeing you, Nurse Nancy.'

'Who?' Nancy asked again, but Aaron just smiled and went to find his family and friends.

The door next to the serving hatch opened and Zachary appeared with the stepladder.

He stopped. 'Abrams said he needed this.'

'It's for me,' said Nancy.

Zachary carried it along the room. Nancy couldn't take her eyes off him. Had he really hung around to see her? It wasn't possible. Aaron must be mistaken.

'I have a job to do,' she said.

'Can I help?'

'There's no need, thank you.' Oh, what had made her say that? She should have snatched at his offer. No, she shouldn't. She would only make a fool of herself.

'It's no trouble,' said Zachary. 'I'd like to help.'

'I need to fetch summat from the cold store.'

'Before you do,' Zachary said quickly, 'I have something to say.'

'Yes?'

'I haven't congratulated you yet on your new job. It's impressive.'

'I'm very happy with it, but don't make it out to be more than it is. I'm only a nursemaid.'

'A nursemaid who's had a post created specially for her in recognition of her talents.'

'Talent? Me?' Nancy laughed.

'Yes, you.' Zachary's hazel eyes were warm. 'I know you've been told off plenty of times for the mistakes you made as a clerk.' He spread out his hands. 'I'm one of the people who did the telling off. But I think you're so used to hearing what you've done wrong that you don't realise what you've got to offer. St Anthony's – or St Nicholas's, I should say – is lucky to have you. You're going to make a real difference to the children's lives.'

'D'you think so?'

'I know so.'

'Thank you.'

They looked at one another.

'I'd best get on,' said Nancy.

She moved to go round Zachary, but he moved an' all and they ended up doing that funny little side-stepping thing.

'You stop. I'll go round,' said Nancy, but Zachary put his hand on her arm, sending tingles all the way up to her neck and down to her fingertips.

'Congratulating you isn't really what I wanted to say. What I wanted to tell you, what I've wanted to tell you for a long time, is that I like you. I like you a lot. I've never liked any girl the way I like you. Do you think you could like me too?'

Nancy felt almost light-headed. He liked her. Zachary Milner liked her. It might not be the adoration she felt for him, but, even so, her heart was pounding.

'Do you think you could?' he whispered.

She nodded. 'I already do.'

Zachary half-laughed. 'That's good, because when I say I like you...' he came closer, gazing into her eyes, though he made no move to touch her, 'what I really mean is that I'm in love with you, Nancy Pike.'

Nancy caught her breath. She closed her eyes and her lashes settled on her cheeks.

'I – I hope I haven't been too forward,' said Zachary.

For answer, she opened her eyes, reached up and cupped his face in her hands. 'You weren't being forward,' she whispered. 'This is being forward.'

She brushed her lips against his. There was a moment of stillness, then he slipped his arms round her and kissed her. Nancy's heartbeat raced and her thoughts scattered to the winds.

When the kiss ended, Zachary rested his forehead against hers. 'I've wanted to do that for ages. Shall we try it again? Just to make sure?'

At the end of their second kiss, Nancy snuggled against him. 'I had no idea you cared about me. This has turned into the best evening of my life. The children's nativity, my new job – and now you – us.'

'Good things are meant to happen in threes,' Zachary murmured.

Nancy gently pushed herself free. 'Today, they happen in fours. I have my special job to do.'

'What is it?'

She indicated the pictures. 'They're going to turn into real apples, oranges and holly.'

Zachary frowned and smiled at the same time and her heart did a little flip.

'You'll see,' she said.

She took Zachary to the cold store, where she had hidden her shopping bag, which Zachary carried back into the dining room. Nancy emptied it onto a table, putting the rosy-red apples, oranges and sprigs of holly into groups. Last, she took out a pair of scissors.

'We need to take down the pictures one by one and cut out the drawings so there's a hole in the middle of each piece of paper. Then we hang each one up again with a piece of fruit or holly hanging up to look as if it's where the hole is – where the drawing was.'

'And the children will think the drawings have come to life.'

'I wish I could have got something more special than fruit,' said Nancy, 'but I couldn't afford it.'

'We'll save that for next Christmas,' said Zachary. 'We'll get penny-whistles and peg-dolls and tin soldiers and hair ribbons. We'll get enough for all the children to have one each.'

'Next Christmas?'

'You don't mind, do you? I don't mean to make it sound as if this year's idea isn't special.'

'I mean – next Christmas. You think we'll still be a couple?'

'I know we shall,' said Zachary, 'and for many Christmases to come, if I have anything to do with it.' He hesitated. 'And when I say "many Christmases", I mean until death do us part.'

The breath caught in Nancy's throat. Did he mean—

Zachary sank to one knee, taking her hand in both his. 'Lovely Nancy, will you marry me? We'll have to wait a while because I have to get my business going properly and save up, but I promise I'll look after you as well as I can – always – and not just you, but our children.'

'Our children?'

'I'm a twin and your sisters are twins. We're bound to have a set of our own, don't you think?' Zachary gazed up into her face. 'Please say you'll marry me.'

'Oh yes,' Nancy exclaimed. 'Yes, yes, yes.'

She pulled him to his feet for a kiss, surrendering happily to the warmth of his embrace. When the kiss ended, they snuggled close together and Nancy knew this was where she wanted to be now and always.

Zachary smiled at her. 'Come on. Let's get this job done.'

It took a long time because it was so fiddly, but at last all the fruit and holly was hanging up. Nancy made sure that all the cut-out drawings went into her bag. She couldn't have the children coming across them.

When it was all finished, ready for the children to boggle at in the morning, Nancy gazed round and sighed contentedly.

'Christmas magic,' she whispered.

'No, *this* is Christmas magic,' said Zachary and kissed her.

Acknowledgements

I am grateful to the whole team at Corvus, especially Carmen Balit who designs the beautiful covers for this series.

Also to Catherine Boardman, Julie Cordiner, Beverley Hopper, Vikkie Wakeham, Zoe Morton, Lynne Folliott and Deborah Smith for their support of the Surplus Girls series; and Kevin, who came up with the brilliant idea of teaching the orphans to tie knots.

Huge thanks to three friends who helped when I was up to my neck in edits – Jen Gilroy; Jane Cable, who magicked up a blog out of thin air; and Christina Banach, who sent chocolate.